A Faithful Departing . . .

Some commotion began at the front of the church. There were shouts, screaming. And then gunfire. Lloyd sat frozen on his bench. What in the name of God was going on? Pilgrims were scattering from behind the altar and then a ladder was lifted; more gunfire sounded, and, incredibly, the image disappeared. Guards had arrived and there was more gunfire. Some terrible desecration was in progress. Lloyd rose to his feet and ran toward the front of the church. Whatever was happening had to be stopped.

He was almost to the altar when a gunman with something pulled over his face emerged, followed by others like himself carrying something. The first man came running toward Lloyd and he planted himself in the aisle. The masked man turned his weapon on him.

The first shot missed him, and there was a scream at the back of the church. The second shot ripped into his chest. He was shot again as he fell, and then shot once more. But he was beyond feeling by then.

RELIC OF TIME

❖ The Rosary Chronicles ❖

RALPH McINERNY

JOVE BOOKS, NEW YORK

THE BERKLEY PUBLISHING GROUP
Published by the Penguin Group
Penguin Group (USA) Inc.
375 Hudson Street, New York, New York 10014, USA
Penguin Group (Canada), 90 Eglinton Avenue East, Suite 700, Toronto, Ontario M4P 2Y3, Canada
(a division of Pearson Penguin Canada Inc.)
Penguin Books Ltd., 80 Strand, London WC2R 0RL, England
Penguin Group Ireland, 25 St. Stephen's Green, Dublin 2, Ireland (a division of Penguin Books Ltd.)
Penguin Group (Australia), 250 Camberwell Road, Camberwell, Victoria 3124, Australia
(a division of Pearson Australia Group Pty. Ltd.)
Penguin Books India Pvt. Ltd., 11 Community Centre, Panchsheel Park, New Delhi—110 017, India
Penguin Group (NZ), 67 Apollo Drive, Rosedale, North Shore 0632, New Zealand
(a division of Pearson New Zealand Ltd.)
Penguin Books (South Africa) (Pty.) Ltd., 24 Sturdee Avenue, Rosebank, Johannesburg 2196,
South Africa

Penguin Books Ltd., Registered Offices: 80 Strand, London WC2R 0RL, England

This is a work of fiction. Names, characters, places, and incidents either are the product of the author's imagination or are used fictitiously, and any resemblance to actual persons, living or dead, business establishments, events, or locales is entirely coincidental. The publisher does not have any control over and does not assume any responsibility for author or third-party websites or their content.

RELIC OF TIME

A Jove Book / published by arrangement with Tekno Books

PRINTING HISTORY
Jove mass-market edition / November 2009

Copyright © 2009 by Tekno Books.
Cover image of "Vintage Grunge Background with Floral Pattern" copyright © Ebtikar / Shutterstock; image of "Man" copyright © Philip and Karen Smith / Iconica / Getty Images; image of "St. Peter's Basilica" copyright © Charles Krebs / Getty Images.
Cover design by Diana Kolsky.
Text design by Laura K. Corless.

ISBN: 978-0-515-14704-9

JOVE®
Jove Books are published by The Berkley Publishing Group,
a division of Penguin Group (USA) Inc.,
375 Hudson Street, New York, New York 10014.
JOVE® is a registered trademark of Penguin Group (USA) Inc.
The "J" design is a trademark of Penguin Group (USA) Inc.

PRINTED IN THE UNITED STATES OF AMERICA

10 9 8 7 6 5 4 3 2 1

For Michael Baxter

Septem dierum cursibus
nunc tempus omne ducitur;
octavus ille ultimus
dies erit iudicii.

—LITURGIA HORARUM

Prologue

❖ I ❖

He was fifty-six years old and nervous as a boy.

It was the three days in Chicago with Catherine that decided him to make a pilgrimage to the shrine of Our Lady of Guadalupe in Mexico.

In a corner of the lobby, to the left of the desk where the concierge sat importantly, Japanese tourists had stacked their luggage and, having checked out, were milling around the small area, awaiting their transportation to O'Hare. Lloyd had gone into a far room off the lobby, which few guests ever discovered, and stood at the window, anxiously awaiting the arrival of Catherine's taxi. Each time one swooped to the curb, he moved nearer the window, expecting her to step out. Her plane from Minneapolis had landed an hour earlier and she had called him from the baggage area.

"I'm here."

"I should have met you there."

"Don't be silly."

"I booked your room."

A small silence, but it was a big announcement. They would have separate rooms. It seemed a denial of what they both understood this reunion meant.

"Good."

Ever since her call, he had been on the lookout for her cab. Stupid, of course. It was a long ride from the airport and with any traffic at all . . .

He was fifty-six years old and nervous as a boy. Catherine had heard of Monica's death a year after the event and written him, expressing her sympathy. She hadn't known Monica. Lloyd hadn't seen or heard from Catherine since they were kids. His own grief had become familiar by the time her note arrived and he was ready for the more pleasant memories it brought. It had been months before he could bring himself to take Monica's clothes to Saint Vincent de Paul. He enrolled her in several perpetual Mass societies, and he prayed for her every day. How perfect their marriage seemed now that she was gone, the long illness over; the house, so full in the days before her funeral, now empty, just himself and his memories. He felt almost unfaithful to Monica when he answered Catherine's letter. And then she telephoned, the start of a habit. Once a week at first, then several times a week, they had lengthy telephone conversations.

"I have the advantage of you, Lloyd. I know what you look like now."

The photograph on the dust jacket of his most recent book.

"That picture is ten years old."

"And have you changed so much since it was taken?"

Changed? He wanted to tell her of the agony of Monica's illness, of the long hours nursing her, keeping her at home, as she had wanted, of his feeling of being an amputee when at last she died.

"Send me a picture," he said.

"If I can find one ten years old."

When the photograph arrived, just a snapshot, tucked into a greeting card—how had she known it was his birthday?—he put the photograph on the refrigerator door, in among those of Monica and himself, their kids, the grandchild. When they talked on the phone, he would wander into the kitchen and address Catherine's photograph.

"You're still beautiful."

"Ha."

✤ II ✤

"Want to mess around?"

They had lived in south Minneapolis, her family's house just across Minnehaha Creek from the Kaisers'. Lloyd's mother had cleared her throat and looked suspicious when Catherine would go by with her cocker spaniel, Amos. No leash was needed; they were inseparable. Lloyd had liked the deliberate pigeon-toed way she walked and the tomboy look of her.

"There she goes again," his mother would say.

"She's on her way to visit Peggy Lindsey."

"Uh-huh."

What did his mother have against Catherine? Lloyd never understood her disapproval, but it effectively chilled any interest he might have had in Catherine. But then, at first by accident, they would meet near the creek in the evening and follow it toward Lake Hiawatha where there was a bench on a hill overlooking the lake. During the walk, Amos loping along beside them, they never held hands; their conversation was about anything but the fact that they were walking together. But when they got to the bench, she sat very close to him and when she looked up at him, her expression inviting, he had leaned toward her and felt her lips on his. His arms went around her and she held him tightly. They might have been auditioning for Rodin.

Afterward, she would lay her head on his shoulder and they'd look at the lake. From time to time, she would lift her head and look up at him and again he kissed her. That was all. He could feel her breasts against him, but he would never have dared touch them. Then one night she asked him to come home with her when they returned from sitting by the lake. As soon as they were inside, it was clear there was no one else at home. She led him to the couch as if it were their bench. Their kisses grew passionate; he fondled her; he moved his hand beneath her skirt. She groaned and then abruptly pulled away, jumping to her feet.

"No, no, no," she said, as if talking to herself.

He agreed. He was frightened by what he had done. He had never touched a girl before as he had Catherine. The memory of her empty house and what they had nearly done on the couch seemed to confirm all of his mother's suspicions. It helped to think that it was Catherine who had led him on.

He stopped going down to the creek in the evening, unless his father was practicing seven-iron shots on the great stretch of grass that ran along the northern bank. One night Catherine was there with Amos and came over to talk. Lloyd's father obviously liked her. He liked her dog, Amos, too. She asked what club he was using.

"Want to try it?"

She did. She addressed the ball his father tossed her. She stood over it, very still, and then with great deliberation drew back the club. Her follow-through was perfect. The ball lifted in an arc and came to ground a hundred and fifty yards away. Lloyd joined in when his father applauded. But Catherine was looking at the club head. It was an old Wright & Ditson with the desired yardage engraved on it.

"That wasn't one seventy-five," she said. Did she consider her perfect shot a failure? His father wisely chose not to hit any more balls and soon they were on their way home, and Catherine and Amos were crossing the bridge, going in the opposite direction.

"Do you think it was a lucky shot?" his father asked.

"You should have asked her to hit another."

He thought about it, then shook his head. "She probably would have gotten a hundred seventy-five with the second shot." Smiling, he shook his head. "Not bad looking either."

Lloyd mumbled something.

"Are you friends?"

"Oh, I wouldn't say that."

"Just don't take her out golfing."

A lifetime had gone by since that summer interlude with Catherine. But it had apparently always been there, in his memory, and her letter brought it all vividly back. The snapshot she had sent was of someone still identifiable as the girl she had been, hair still worn short, the same sardonic smile. But what would she look like in the flesh?

✤

In the Whitehall Hotel, Lloyd was distracted by the efforts of the concierge to sell some tickets to a pair of reluctant tourists. He had just turned again to the window when someone spoke beside him.

"Lloyd?"

He was startled and that helped, all his rehearsing gone for naught; here they were facing one another. She lifted her cheek for his kiss.

"I hope it's a smoking room," she said when he took her to the receptionist.

It wasn't. There were no more smoking rooms available. "I must have got the last one," Lloyd said.

"Then that's all right. One's enough."

He waited in the lobby when she went upstairs to unpack. Catherine was still lithe and agile, a slightly older girl, a woman. A woman who had flown to Chicago to spend a few days with him, a reunion after all these years. How natural it had been to kiss her cheek.

When she came down, they went into the bar and had a glass of wine, and then another. Afterward they went out and strolled along the Miracle Mile. He told her they would go to Navy Pier tomorrow. They ate in the hotel restaurant and then settled down again in the bar, where smoking was still permitted. More wine and pointless, pleasant chatter. Of course they did not talk of Monica. Not directly.

"You're still wearing your wedding ring."

He looked at his hand as if surprised to see the golden band that Monica had slipped on his finger so many years ago.

Catherine said, "I got rid of mine before I got rid of him."

"What happened?"

"He was a son of a bitch. Of course, I compared him and every other man with you."

"Come on."

She looked at him steadily. "It's true."

What she had said couldn't possibly be true, but it was pleasant to think she meant it. It was after eleven when they went up. Their rooms were on the same floor.

"That's convenient," she said. "I can come over for a smoke."

She opened the door of her room and he looked it over, as if to make sure it was worthy of her. This time when she lifted her face he kissed her on the lips. Then she pushed him away.

"I'll come by later. For a cigarette."

When she came she was in pajamas but with the robe the hotel supplied over it. Lighting a cigarette, his hands were unsteady. She looked up at him, took his hand, and brought the flame to her cigarette.

"Two on a match," she murmured.

Within ten minutes they were two on a bed. They had talked about their walks along the creek; he remembered kissing her; he remembered the evening when they sat on the couch in her parents' living room.

"Want to mess around?" he asked.

The words emerged as if with a will of their own. They had always been his overture to Monica.

"I thought you'd never ask." She went to the bed, got out of the robe, and then, incredibly, took off her pajamas as well. His eyes were on her as he stripped off his clothes. She had sat at the end of the bed and now fell backward onto it.

They spent most of their three days together in bed, going out seldom; the swift visit to Navy Pier seemed a little penance to justify fleeing back to the hotel. They alternated rooms; they lay together spent and content.

"I've always loved you, Lloyd."

He did not know what to say. "Me, too."

"Narcissus."

"You know what I mean."

"Say it."

He said it. But even as he said it, he knew he did not mean it, that he could never mean it. Her very availability, the things she did when they were in bed together, overwhelmed him, and, when he was alone, his conscience started up.

⚜

"What medal is that?" Catherine asked. She was straddling him at the time and she lifted the medal from his chest.

"My mother gave it to me."

"Awww."

"It's a miraculous medal."

"It sure is," she said, tweaking him.

She had let whatever faith she had slip away long ago.

"You still believe it all?" she asked.

"Yes." He didn't want to talk religion with her. Not like this. Not ever. He wished she hadn't noticed the medal. His mother *had* given it to him, when he made his First Communion, at the age of ten. He had worn it ever since, taking it off only on the rarest of occasions; for example, when he had a chest X-ray. He should have taken it off before he got into bed with Catherine, but there had never been time.

"All of it?"

She meant Catholicism. He nodded.

"Including that it's a sin for us to be in bed together?"

"Maybe that's why it feels so good."

Ho ho, big joke, but it wasn't any joke for Lloyd. For several days he had managed to avoid reflective thought, but Catherine's teasing about his medal and what they were doing made the voice of conscience roar within him. He enjoyed every minute of their time together and yet longed to put her in a cab for the airport. As soon as she was gone, he would go over to Saint Peter's on Madison Avenue, where confessions were heard from morning to night, so the priests must be used to hearing every variety of sin.

Her plane left at 11:30 so they had a leisurely breakfast in the hotel. Catherine leaned toward him. "Every couple here looks illicit."

"How can you tell?"

"They look as innocent as we do."

"I'll take you to the airport, Catherine."

"You will not. But you can help me pack."

But when they got to her room it was obvious she had already packed. She came into his arms and then her hand was on him.

"There isn't time," he said gruffly.

"There is for this."

❧

On the way down in the elevator, he decided he hated her. He couldn't wait to put her in a cab and hurry to Saint Peter's and confess her out of his system. For a woman who had been divorced nearly twenty years she seemed a very practiced lover. And he didn't like it. Oh, he had enjoyed it, but he didn't like it.

After her cab had pulled away, her hand fluttering good-bye from a back window, Lloyd started immediately up the street. Saint Peter's was blocks away, miles, on Madison, but he would walk. He crossed the river and strode on; not taking a cab seemed already a kind of penance for what he had done. He was ashamed of himself. He drove out thoughts of Monica. It was remorse rather than shame that he should feel. He had offended God, he had gone to bed with a woman not his wife, and they had done things he had never done with Monica. Catherine had acted like a courtesan. No, he mustn't blame her. *He* had sinned; that was the point.

There was a huge Carrara marble crucifix over the main altar of Saint Peter's. A Mass was being said, and scattered through the pews were secretaries, bank clerks, bag ladies, the homeless. Along the sides were confessionals, and over one a small light glowed. Red. Someone inside. He went immediately there and waited. No need to examine his conscience. His sins were on the tip of his tongue.

The door of the confessional opened and an old woman emerged. Lloyd waited for her to let the door close and then, pulling it open, stepped in and was alone in the dark. He knelt before the grille and was aware of voices, a penitent on the opposite side. He waited. On the long walk over, he had rehearsed, seeking ways to express the sins he had committed. The grille slid open.

"Bless me, Father, for I have sinned."

He stopped. He felt a sudden panic. The priest was waiting. Lloyd leaned forward, his head against the grille. "I don't know how to begin."

"We'll start with the capital sins then."

"It was a woman, Father."

He began to babble, trying to say it all at once; the priest—he could make out his profile through the grille—was old. He nodded through the recital. A moment of silence.

"Will you see her again?"

"No!"

A pause. "Make an act of contrition."

The familiar words came trippingly to his tongue. The priest began the formula of absolution. Lloyd felt that he was standing under a shower of grace and forgiveness.

"Take this, son." A little slip of paper appeared beneath the grille. "For your penance, pray that psalm. And ask Our Blessed Lady to help you."

⁂

Outside the confessional, he went to a pew and looked at the sheet the priest had given him. Psalm 51. "Have mercy on me, God, in your kindness. In your compassion, blot out my offense. O wash me more and more from my guilt and cleanse me from my sin."

He hurried through the psalm, feeling lighter than air. When he was done, elation left him. It had all been too easy. Three days with Catherine and after a few humbling minutes, it was all wiped away. Now that he had confessed, he longed to make up for what he had done in some dramatic way, a more demanding way. Once, penitents had been sent on long pilgrimages, to shrines. . . . He thought of Lourdes, he thought of Fatima. And then an image over a side altar decided him. Our Lady of Guadalupe.

⁂ III ⁂

Penitents sat on benches.

Mexico City lay in a blanket of smog, looking unreal. Lloyd went to his hotel, to his room, and then immediately back to the lobby, where he asked the clerk for directions to the shrine of Our Lady of Guadalupe. She handed him a brochure; obviously his request was a familiar one. In minutes he was in a cab and on his way, hurtling through the city, taking no notice of it.

In the square outside the church, he stood staring at the facade. It was a great round church, somewhat reminiscent of the stadium of the New Orleans Saints. Just an observation. He had not come here as a critic. There was a large bronze statue of Pope John Paul II off to the right, commemorating his visits here. Lloyd crossed the square and entered the church. His eye was drawn immediately to the image of Our Lady, behind and above the altar. That was the point of the circular design; from no matter what part of the church, the eye was drawn to the miraculous picture of Mary. Lloyd hurried toward it.

Centuries ago, Juan Diego had encountered a beautiful lady who instructed him to speak to the bishop. The bishop's reaction to the illiterate peasant was doubtless understandable. He wanted proof. Again the lady appeared to Juan Diego and asked him to fill his cape with beautiful roses, which, despite the season, were there in abundance. The roses were to be the proof the bishop asked for, but when Juan opened his cape and the roses spilled out, there on the cape was the image of the lady he had seen. That image was what Lloyd and other pilgrims had come to venerate. The Lady of Guadalupe.

There was a moving belt beneath the image, so pilgrims would not cluster beneath it. Many were sighing, a man was weeping. Lloyd got in line, his eyes lifted to the image that had been miraculously imprinted on the cape of Juan Diego. The moving belt took him all too swiftly past the image. He went back and got into line again. Three times he moved beneath the image, prayers forming on his lips—no need to conceal his gratitude here—and then went to the back of the basilica. There were confessionals there and lines of penitents waiting. Lloyd joined them. He wanted to confess again here. Tell God once again that he was sorry, that he would never again offend Him. He could not have formed a clear image of Catherine if he tried.

Penitents sat on benches, sliding along toward their turn in the confessional. Lloyd sat and closed his eyes, wanting to be just another pilgrim, another sinner, one of the vast army of believers who throughout the ages had lifted their hearts in joy and sorrow to the one who created them from nothing.

Some commotion began at the front of the church. There were shouts, screaming. And then gunfire. Lloyd sat frozen on his bench. What in the name of God was going on? Pilgrims were scattering from behind the altar and then a ladder was lifted, more gunfire sounded, and, incredibly, the image disappeared. Guards had arrived and there was more gunfire. Some terrible desecration was in progress. Lloyd rose to his feet and ran toward the front of the church. Whatever was happening had to be stopped.

He was almost to the altar when a gunman with something pulled over his face emerged, followed by others like himself carrying something. The first man came running toward Lloyd and he planted himself in the aisle. The masked man turned his weapon on him.

The first shot missed him, and there was a scream at the back of the church. The second shot ripped into his chest. He was shot again as he fell, and then once more. But he was beyond feeling by then.

❖ PART I ❖

Holy Heist

CHAPTER ONE

❖ I ❖

"And this is war, ladies and gentlemen."

Latin Americans, believers and nonbelievers alike, were stunned by the news that the image of Our Lady of Guadalupe had been stolen from its shrine in Mexico City. The borders between their various countries hark back to colonial times, but the Spanish and Portuguese had long since intermarried with the native Indian population. In the wake of the sacrilegious theft, the whole of Latin America experienced an almost mystic sense of solidarity. The Virgin who had appeared to Juan Diego was *theirs*. Her image appeared in haciendas and in hovels. The Mother of God figured in the furtive devotions even of unbelievers; everyone rendered fearful by natural disaster or turbulence at high altitudes, if only in his heart, prayed the familiar words: *Santa Maria, Madre de Dios, ruega por nosostros pecadores, ahora y en la hora de nuestra morte.* The outrage in Mexico City made it seem that their most powerful advocate with Her Son had been taken from them. Who in the name of God was responsible for such a sacrilege?

In the days following the theft—and the incidental deaths of some half dozen pilgrims caught between the small band of thieves and the ineffectual basilica guards pursuing them— there came a series of denials of responsibility from various groups that might reasonably have fallen under suspicion.

A political explanation seemed ruled out. Members of every party went to the shrine and advanced across the plaza on their knees, many clutching unfamiliar rosaries in their manicured hands.

The nativist groups that sought to reassert the claims of lost Mayan and Incan civilizations? They issued emotional denials and vowed to sacrifice the perpetrators in the ancient way when they were apprehended.

In the silence of those first days, the question in everyone's mind was, why? Why would anyone commit such a sacrilege?

Missionaries from the north who had been evangelizing zealously to wean the people from their superstitious religion (and meeting with surprising success, not least because they tried to fuse evangelical Protestantism with the simple devotions of the natives—many chapels were named after saints, and not a few bore the name of Nuestra Madre de Guadalupe) became the object of dark suspicions. These were somewhat allayed when evangelical missionaries and their flocks joined the great processions that wound through the cities of the south, led by a bishop in towns where there was a bishop, the monstrance containing the Eucharist carried aloft, banners with the image of Our Lady of Guadalupe fluttering overhead while bands played music that was not even remotely liturgical. All this in public reparation to the Virgin for the terrible deed that had been done.

Not many years before, in Mexico, priests had been hunted down and killed in a political effort to expunge the faith of the people and replace it with Marxism. Even after the persecutions ceased, it remained illegal for priests to appear in clerical garb. Now, in this hour of crisis, clad in glorious vestments, they led the procession through the streets as if the whole of Mexico City had become a cathedral.

❖

On the fourth day the terrible, infuriating revelation came, and offended piety gave way to rage. The Rough Riders, a militant group that had joined the Minutemen and others who had gathered on the southern border of the United States to do what the Border Patrol was either unwilling or unable to do—stop the flow of illegal immigration from the south—announced that the sacred image was in its possession.

Theophilus Grady, head of the Rough Riders, called a press conference in El Paso to make his announcement. In jodhpurs, shiny knee-high boots, and a Sam Brown belt, with pistols on his hips, a black tie under the brown collar of his shirt, and a huge mustache beneath his meaty nose, Grady stared out at the assembled journalists through his steel-rimmed glasses.

"Four days ago a brave band of Rough Riders took custody of the image of Our Lady of Guadalupe in the shrine in Mexico City."

This was the first sentence on the sheet of paper he held. Before he could go on, pandemonium broke out, and questions were hurled at him. Grady waited calmly, then raised his hand. When something like silence was restored, he resumed his statement.

"The United States has been under invasion along our southern border for years. The people have repeatedly expressed their desire that our politicians fulfill their constitutional obligation and put an end to this. All they have received in reply are words, empty words. There has been official collusion with this influx of illegals. They are accorded the benefits and privileges of citizens even though their illegal status is acknowledged. It is acknowledged and dismissed. Giant corporations and industrial farmers, small businesses, too, and the wealthy who employ and exploit them clearly favor this constant and unauthorized flow of cheap labor across our border. We Rough Riders and others have done what we could to put spine into the Border Patrol. No wonder they are demoralized. Two members of that patrol have been tried and sent to prison for doing their job. The time has come for decisive action. We will hold the image we have taken hostage until the Mexican government, and other governments, especially our own, put a stop to this invasion."

Throughout the tumultuous question period, Grady alone retained his calm, treating the members of the media as children, hostile children.

He told them that the image was in a secure place, that no harm or damage would come to it. But it would be retained until . . .

He was unruffled when he was told that by taking responsibility for what had happened in Mexico City, he was taking responsibility for those who had been killed during the theft of the image. He dismissed this as the collateral damage inevitable in war.

"And this is war, ladies and gentlemen. A country that is invaded is *eo ipso* at war with the invader."

His calmness infuriated his audience. Who, he was asked, had appointed him protector of the border?

"Who appointed the Minutemen? I use the phrase historically, not for our companions on the border."

❖

When Grady left the press conference he was whisked away in a car to a waiting helicopter and disappeared to no one knew where. The camps of the Rough Riders along the border were gone. There remained only the Minutemen and others to confront the rage that boiled up from the south. Immigrants had always approached the border stealthily and stolen across to economic opportunity unobserved. Now armed bands approached the border and gunfire was exchanged. Paul Pulaski, head of one branch of the Minutemen, said that he and his followers would hold the border against these now armed invaders until federal troops arrived.

But would federal troops be sent?

From the White House came yet another condemnation of vigilante groups. An apology was sent to the Mexican government. It was returned. Only the restoration of the image of Our Lady of Guadalupe to her shrine could pave the way for diplomacy.

Senators vied with one another in expressing at great length their condemnation of what had happened. In the well of the House it was suggested that if troops were sent to the border it should be to round up the vigilantes.

The cardinal archbishop of Washington spoke to a disinterested group at the National Press Club about the Church's teaching on just war. He did everything but apply the teaching clearly to what was happening on the southern border of the country.

✦

A day after Theophilus Grady's press conference, things took a turn for the worse. The volunteers along the border found that they were under fire from the rear as well as from across the border. Miguel Arroyo, founder of Justicia y Paz, announced that he had authorized volunteer formations to come to the aid of their erstwhile countrymen who were pinned down by rifle and mortar fire along the border. Soon something very much like civil war raged. Men streamed to the scene of action, either to support the beleaguered Minutemen or to attack them from the rear. A dozen Border Patrol posts were taken over by vigilantes without resistance, perhaps with something of relief.

Neither Mexican nor American troops were involved in the border war, both governments issuing promises of non-involvement.

It occurred to cynics that the governments, by professing neutrality in the war that raged on their common border, assumed that the combatants would take care of the problem by wiping one another out. And the casualties grew. Medics and nurses were soon among the vigilantes, tending to the wounded. What the bloody skirmishes were for became problematical. The vigilantes were doing what they had long vowed to do, protect the border with force, but the bands from the south had no clear objective until Latinos already in the States came to their support. Talk began of a Republic of California. Arroyo piously promised to show leniency toward the illegal aliens currently firing on those who were once again his countrymen.

Meanwhile the mass of Latin Americans wanted only the return of the image of Our Lady of Guadalupe to her shrine.

✦ II ✦

"I'll find him."

"Get it!"

The president had listened impatiently to their reports,

asked what could be done, and then interrupted with that curt command.

"Get it and get it back to them." He hurried, bandy-legged, from the room, his right arm out from his body and slightly bent, as if he were about to draw.

Vincent Traeger rose with the others and they left silently. Down by the gate in the media encampment, among cameras, bleachers, and umbrellas, reporters huddled in the rain. Traeger and the others went down the walk and through the gate and some minutes later were in the car and on their way.

"Get it," someone repeated.

Traeger could see that his companions had no idea how they were to carry out that barked order from the commander in chief. Through the car's tinted glass, Washington in the rain seemed to be melting as they sped through it. What the hell am I doing here? Traeger wondered. But he already knew. He had put essentially the same question to himself when he had been summoned by his old boss, Dortmund, to his new address.

"A retirement home?"

"Don't call it that."

"What do you call it?"

"Third base. Maybe, stealing home." With the plastic tubes feeding oxygen into his nostrils, Dortmund looked almost grotesque when he smiled. Good God, were they still relying on him?

The topic, of course, was the unpleasantness along the southern border. Traeger stirred in his chair. All this he could get from the media. Already he had the uneasy certitude as to why he had been summoned.

"Grady," Dortmund said. It might have been a groan.

"Grady," Traeger repeated.

Theophilus Grady. What a cowboy. Traeger had watched the El Paso press conference on television and the sight of the maverick who had been drummed out of the agency made all the commotion seem a farce. Did Grady really have the stolen image?

"He could just be taking advantage of the situation," Traeger had told Dortmund.

"Someone has that image."

Traeger nodded. If Grady was bluffing—and when wasn't

he?—the real thieves would not be happy to have their thunder stolen. Dortmund was shaking his head, and the plastic tubes caught the sunlight. They were in a little patio reached through sliding doors from the living room of his condo in what he refused to acknowledge was a retirement village. Dortmund continued to shake his head.

"Not even Grady. I told them you were the man to track him down."

Traeger lit a cigarette and Dortmund watched him enviously. Even with emphysema, he looked as if he were about to ask for one. It had been thoughtless to light up before the old man.

⁂

Now, across the river in a windowless room, the three who had accompanied him from the White House sat in silence. Who was in charge?

Boswell, the man in the glen plaid suit and polka-dot tie, his silvery hair falling across his forehead, looked at Traeger.

"You know this fellow Grady?"

"I knew him."

Silence.

"Can you find him?"

It might have been a job interview. Why the hell, with all the resources at their command, weren't they already in search of Grady?

"I'll find him."

"Get it," the one with a paunch said. The others smiled at the quotation.

After a moment, Traeger nodded.

For the next several hours, he was taken from office to office and readied for his mission. The reason for using someone no longer connected with the Company became clear. The official view was that the little war raging on the southern border was just a minor dustup, no need to make a federal case of it. Better to have a trained freelancer remove the cause of the skirmishes.

"We'll get it back where it belongs when you recover it."

Traeger remembered a rooftop in Rome when his old colleagues had become the enemy. He wondered if he could trust them now.

When he left, he was armed, briefed, provided with a variety of IDs. He was driven to Reagan by Boswell.

"How is Dortmund?"

"Old."

Boswell nodded as if age was something that happened to others. "He's a legend."

"That's what he tells me."

"He praised you to the skies."

No need to comment on that.

At the airport, he got out, having shaken Boswell's hand. He hurried into the terminal, past the baggage area, and into a men's room. Ten minutes later, he emerged and crossed the street and climbed the stairs to the Metro station. He was on his own and he would start now.

Back in the city, he went to Amtrak and bought a ticket to Chicago, a roomette for the overnight journey. There were several hours before his train would leave. He went outside, where, from a bench, he called Dortmund.

On the phone, the old man sounded vigorous and almost young. Traeger told him about his day.

"Thanks for recommending me."

"What else do you have to do?"

Did Dortmund think that he, too, spent his days sitting in the sun on a patio?

"Watch your back" was Dortmund's final word of advice.

❖

Traeger had dinner before boarding the train and once he was on, locked himself in his roomette. He let down the table and opened the laptop he had been issued. His own was in his briefcase. Before the train pulled out of the station, he was reading what the agency had on Theophilus Grady. The old stuff he already knew, but it was clear that Grady had been under surveillance ever since he organized the Rough Riders.

Grady was a throwback. He would have flourished under Wild Bill Donovan, but had rubbed the bureaucracy that had grown up over the years the wrong way. Grady had wanted war when the policy of the Company was truce. His last assignment had been in Albania, where he had led a band of rebels who descended from their mountain redoubts to raise hell and havoc. That an American was involved in those incidents had infuriated the State Department. Grady had failed to respond to orders to get the hell out of Albania and come home. In the end, they'd had to go for him, Traeger and others. He was metaphorically stripped of his epaulets and fired from the Company. Predictably, he had called a news conference to protest the lily-livered policies that were leading the country into ruin. After his five minutes of fame, he disappeared from public view. But not from surveillance.

"We have a man in his outfit," Traeger had been told.

He waited.

"No need to know his name."

"What has he said about the stolen image?"

There was a long silence. "We think he may have gone over."

In his roomette, Traeger smiled. He realized he had more respect for Grady than for the well-groomed men who had briefed him. But what in hell was the guy doing stealing religious images? What he said, no doubt. Diplomacy and threats had not stemmed the tide of illegal immigration. It seemed doubtful whether the will to stem it existed. Sacrilege aside, Grady had hit upon a sure way to catch the attention of our neighbors across the border. Even if he wasn't behind the theft, he had turned it to his advantage.

Somewhere in western Pennsylvania, Traeger let down his bunk and lay on it fully clothed. With the lights off, the window no longer mirrored the roomette and he lay on his side and watched the country slide by, clusters of lights from time to time, the dim silhouette of farm buildings, and trees, trees, trees. Well, the state was Penn's woods, after all.

Would he be able to find the tree he sought in the woods he was about to enter?

❖ III ❖

"The man's an atheist!"

Her father had been astounded when Clare Ibanez told him that she had taken a job as secretary to their new neighbor, Jason Phelps.

"The man's an atheist!"

"It's not catching."

"What kind of work would you do?"

"He is trying to put order into his papers, his publications, a lifetime accumulation."

"He would be wiser to burn it all."

Jason Phelps had taught at Berkeley for most of his academic life. His renown as an anthropologist was all but eclipsed by the personal crusade he had undertaken a decade or so ago. It was one thing to encounter superstition in backward tribes and civilizations, but the fact that mad beliefs had survived into the late twentieth century and now into the third millennium stirred him to zealous debunking. His little book on the liquefaction of the blood of Saint Januarius in Naples was scathingly dismissive. He had tried, without success, to obtain some small portion of whatever liquid was in the reliquary.

"Of course my request was refused," he wrote. "It would be like a magician permitting you to see how he accomplishes his deception."

So, too, at Nevers in France, he had sought permission to examine the incorrupt body of Saint Bernadette, the seer of Lourdes. He was given accounts of the several exhumations that had preceded putting the body in its glass case, on view to the faithful. The fact that he was given the accounts made him skeptical of them.

But it was Lourdes itself that had drawn his particular fury. There, scientists with undeniable credentials subjected supposed cures to just the kind of painstaking examination that Phelps himself advocated. And time and again they concluded that there was no natural explanation for the fact that a person suffering from a terminal illness had come to Lourdes, prayed to Our Lady in the grotto in which she had appeared, drank the water, and came away cured. Certified by scientists! It was too much to bear. To give the patina of objective truth to such preposterous claims! Of course there must be a psychological explanation, some psychophysical power that science had yet to identify, something perfectly natural, triggered perhaps by the visit to Lourdes, but scarcely the result of sending up a few prayers to a simpering statue. What could not happen had not happened; it was as simple as that.

Two years before, Phelps, a retired widower, had bought property in the Napa Valley, just a few acres from the vast estate of Don Ibanez, no great loss to the vineyards, and on it he had built the comfortable two-story house in which he intended to spend his last years, years after which he was positive that nothing but nothingness awaited him.

Clare's father paid a courtesy call on their new neighbor in his role as hidalgo of the locality. The Ibanez family had settled in California five hundred years earlier, the first arriving with the conquistadores, others attached to the Jesuit and Franciscan missions. It was early in the eighteenth century that the Ibanez family had come to the Napa Valley. Their real estate had embraced fifty square miles, much of it vineyards that produced the grapes from which their wines were made. Don Ibanez, as he styled himself, presented a dozen bottles of wine to Jason Phelps and welcomed him to the neighborhood.

Some days later, Phelps returned the courtesy, presenting Clare's father with signed copies of several of his books, all anthropology. Don Ibanez still had no inkling that Phelps was a crusading debunker of things religious. Nor did this come out when he took Phelps to the chapel some fifty yards from the house. It was a replica of the basilica in Mexico City, and within, as in the original, there was the image of Our Lady of Guadalupe high above the altar.

"No need for a moving walkway here, of course."

"Moving walkway?" Phelps asked.

Clare's father was happy to explain.

"Why go to Mexico when they could come here?" Phelps had asked.

Don Ibanez laughed. "But this is merely a reproduction. The actual cape with the image on it is in the shrine in Mexico City."

"Interesting."

Thus civility and reticence got the two men through what might have been a testing encounter. It was not until a week later that Frater Leone, a Benedictine who lived in the hacienda and said Mass in the little basilica, identified their neighbor for her father.

"The man who wrote the book about the shroud of Turin,"

the priest explained. The two men spoke Spanish when they were together.

"But he was obviously impressed by the chapel here!"

"That surprises me. He is a belligerent atheist."

"Atheist!"

His book on the shroud of Turin was written to refute any suggestion that the tests that had been made, careful scientific tests, supported the legend that had made the shroud an object of veneration as the cloth in which the body of Jesus was buried and on which was found, like a photographic negative, an image of the body it had enclosed.

"But they found the shroud to be authentic," Don Ibanez said.

"Most drew that conclusion. But there were members of the scientific team who drew a negative conclusion."

"And Phelps is among the deniers?"

"That puts it rather mildly."

If her father had known this when Phelps was buying his land, he would have had the sale canceled, something he could easily have done. Now, he had half a mile up the road a skeptic, an atheist, an enemy.

Clare shared her father's religious beliefs and his devotion to Our Lady of Guadalupe but not his weakness for unusual religious phenomena and his tendency to make Marian apparitions the center of his creed.

It was on her morning jog that she had first encountered Phelps, puffing along on his bicycle, keeping mortality at bay. She stopped to talk to him.

"I want to stay hearty enough to finish my work," he said, breathing heavily.

"Your work?"

He explained.

"But can't you get someone to do that for you?"

"Oh, I could never entrust it to anyone else. A helper, yes. A helper I could use. But in this remote region . . ."

He looked at her through unkempt eyebrows.

"What do you do all day?" he asked.

She laughed. "This and that." She would not mention the novel she was writing. It had seemed a kind of therapy to begin it after she had broken up with George. "Come home," her father had said. "What you want is peace and quiet."

Was it? In any case, she came home, not intending to stay, but doing so, for nearly half a year. What an indolent life it seemed, how luxurious and carefree, after working in the Catholic Worker house that George ran in Palo Alto. How she admired him. He seemed a saint, otherworldly, totally disinterested in money or prestige or any of the things that drove others their age. When she praised him, he looked at her with his deep, deep eyes.

"Come and help."

She was a student at Stanford, as he had been. She stopped going to class. She spent much of her day there, helping George and the others with the "guests," drunks and addicts and derelicts who had reached bottom without any hope of rising again. So the point was simply to be of help to them as they were, without expecting some great transformation. "Sufficient for the day is the soup thereof" was one of George's maxims. And he wasn't being cynical.

Clare had kept her apartment and that led to George's suggestion that she live in the women's residence. Besides the building in which the guests were received and fed and clothed, there were two houses, one for men, the other for women. George lived in the first, and he suggested that she take a room in the second. He showed her through the place. He was very proud of it. In the kitchen was a woman with a baby on her hip and a neckline that was not daring but serviceable, facilitating breast-feeding the child she held. The boy seemed to have some sort of rash.

"Infantigo," the mother explained.

George took the baby and the woman showed Clare the upstairs. It was all she could do not to shudder. Here was poverty indeed. There was nothing romantic about it. It was squalid and unclean and . . . But why go on?

"So what do you think?" George asked when she came down.

"Nice."

"Did Sandy show you your room?"

"I think I saw them all."

She went to the door and outside, where George joined her. "You don't like it."

"George . . ." She searched his face for understanding. But how could you explain to Saint Francis that you just couldn't live his way?

"It takes getting used to."

She could believe that, but why should one get used to squalor and dirt? It was the beginning of the end of what had promised to be something very serious between her and George. Eventually she fled to her father and the haven of the Napa Valley.

On their second morning encounter, Professor Phelps formally asked her to come help him with his accumulated papers. She agreed.

"The man's an atheist!" her father cried.

No doubt. But he was also considerate, fastidious, grateful, and witty. And it gave Clare something to do now that she had despaired of her novel. Dorothy Day had written a novel, before her conversion; that seemed to be the genesis of the idea. Working with Professor Phelps on his papers was less demanding.

❖ IV ❖

She put her hand on his.

The bishops of the United States had earned Neal Admirari's grudging approval by the way in which they defended illegal immigrants. The hierarchy had been notably timid and tepid on most moral and social issues, with exceptions of course, but the exceptions were not Neal's cup of tea.

"You think Catholic politicians who are cheerleaders for abortion and all the rest should be given communion?"

This from the recently widowed Lulu van Ackeren, once the love of his life and now returned to journalism as a contributor to *Commonweal*.

"Let's not politicize the Eucharist," Neal said unctuously.

Opposing Lulu's views was something he did as much to stir her into anger as to express his own thoughts. When she was angry, the years seemed to wash away and she was once more the girl she had been. Her hair was still blondish, doubtless due more to art than to nature now, and the great blue eyes still sparkled with youthful fire. It had always been argument that had lit the fire of love between them. Ever since her return, Neal had been wondering whether their grand passion would know a second act. Patience was the watchword now, because of his indecision and the fact that she was, after all, still in mourning of a sort. Besides, if it came to that, he would be husband number three.

"Read the Catechism," she urged.

"First chance I get. How about Catholic politicians who support an unjust war?"

"There are two schools of thought on that, and you know it."

"There are two schools of thought on everything."

They were in the bar of the hotel in El Paso where the media had gathered, but their table was off in a corner, a small table, which made it difficult not to keep knocking her knees with his. Their argument now was a diversion, just getting into practice again. They were on the same side so far as immigration went. And Benedict XVI, bless his former Holy Office—formerly the Inquisition—heart, was clearly on the side of the poor who defied the law and swarmed across the border. The pope had made the telling point that the way to stop immigration was to make things more tolerable in the immigrants' native lands.

"Two more, kiddo," Neal called to a passing waitress.

"I don't want another," Lulu said.

"These are for me."

Of course she'd have another drink. It was a professional obligation to have a snootful if one were to protect the public's right to know.

"I had forgotten what rowdies the media are."

"One does one's best."

"You." She dropped her chin and gave him the benefit of an approving look. They had met that morning at an early Mass, and that set them apart from their colleagues. Most of them had no idea who Our Lady of Guadalupe was.

"Patroness of the Americas," Neal had said authoritatively when the question arose.

"North and South both?"

"You got it."

Background stories on Theophilus Grady and his Rough

Riders had appeared in most of the media represented here, cobbled together by researchers in New York and Washington. Neal had needed to do little research for the two pieces he had written for his syndicated column. Was Lulu impressed by the heights he had reached? A syndicated column was the dream of every member of the print media. Several websites had tried to lure Neal away but he still couldn't bring himself to believe that that was where the future lay.

"The print media is dead," Nicholas Pendant had assured Neal.

"Are."

"Is that right?"

"You got fact-checkers?"

"Of course we've got fact-checkers. Papers are dying all over the country, Neal. And it's not just the general illiteracy. It's far easier and quicker to log on to Mercury to get the news."

Mercury was the up-and-coming website and Pendant could prove it.

"You have links to my column now."

"See? You log in yourself."

For the nonce, Neal settled for being wooed by Pendant.

"You all use the same arguments, Nick."

"Who you been talking to?"

"I never kiss and tell."

"I'll top any offer, Neal. I mean it."

"I'll remember."

"Don't sign with anyone without talking to me."

"I promise."

Lulu was unimpressed by the possibility. "The web? Come on."

"It may be the future, Lulu."

She was as baffled by talk of podcasts, YouTube, and all the rest as he was. Once journalism had been simply a matter of putting words on paper and shooting them off to the printer. Now news was immediate and sent out in ways that only kids seemed to understand. For all that, Neal used a laptop now and could zing his column off as an e-mail attachment to the syndicate and that was that. But in the end, his stuff appeared in print, as it always had. If newsprint was evanescent, what could be said of what appeared on a computer screen?

"I'd rather be a dinosaur," Lulu said.

"Your skin's too smooth."

She snatched her hand away when he covered it with his own. A good sign, if a good sign was what he wanted. A pliant Lulu was an oxymoron. Two more drinks arrived and Lulu took one, poured what was left of her previous drink in it, and lifted the glass in a toast.

"To the pope," Neal said.

"To the pope." She drank deeply. "I haven't had this much to drink in I don't know how long."

"It's only a venial sin."

"Drinking?"

"Not drinking."

She put her hand on his. Her left hand. The rings were gone. Were they really back to square one again?

"I just did a piece on the rosary crusade," Lulu said.

The crusade, announced on EWTN, was the idea of Miriam Dickinson, an ageless Catholic apologist, alleged descendant of the poet.

"How can you be a descendant of the Maid of Amherst?"

"Obliquely."

"Indeed."

The crusade had caught on; several bishops had blessed the idea. Storm heaven with prayer so that the image of Our Lady of Guadalupe would be restored unharmed to its shrine.

"Neal, what if it is never recovered?"

"Say your rosary."

"I do."

He believed her. Lulu was the most delicate arrangement of appetite and piety. Her hand still lay on his. He pushed his knees against hers, and she turned sideways in her chair.

"Watch your knees."

"I'd have to bend over. Did I tell you of my replacement?"

"Really?"

"No."

She made a face, a cute face. Her knees came back into contact with his.

On the various television sets around the bar a large man with a florid face appeared.

"Halvorson," Lulu groaned.

There were cries of "Turn it up" from bar stools and tables. Something like a hush fell and the fruity tones of Halvorson, a minister, but one of the guardians of the separation of church and state, filled the bar.

"We have no dog in this fight," Halvorson intoned. "The might of the United States of America cannot be engaged in a religious quarrel of no interest to the mass of Americans. I know that some of our fellow citizens share the beliefs of those who do homage to this picture, and that is their right and I will fight for it to the death. But it is a private right, not a public matter."

Halvorson had been galvanized by a bipartisan group in Congress demanding that the president send troops to the border. The governor of Louisiana had called up the National Guard, merely a gesture; there was no border of that state that was plagued with immigrants. But the idea that federal troops would be involved in what was now happening on our southern border filled Halvorson with righteous rage.

The argument of the bipartisan group was that armed foreigners were threatening to invade. So far, the Minutemen had kept them pinned down, but they did not have enough forces to both defend the border and handle the rear-guard action mounted by those stirred up by Miguel Arroyo.

The image of Halvorson faded; the television sets were muted; serious drinking resumed.

Neal said, "Prayer is fine, but Ignatius Hannan has the right idea."

❖ V ❖

What does it all mean?

Those who come out of modest backgrounds and then find themselves wealthy beyond the dreams of avarice react in various ways. One is to mimic the life of a late Roman emperor or former president, cater to the flesh, make an ass out of oneself, pile up possessions—houses, cars, horses—and marry or at least mate regularly. Professional athletes, the affluent gladiators of the age, are often drawn to this path. But if money and earthly goods cannot fully satisfy the heart, the flesh does little better. Drugs and the oblivion they offer are only a desperate last resort.

Another path is political, advocating government policies and bankrolling the politicians who promise to enact them, policies that are often aimed at the economic status of the donor; hence the huge number of zillionaire liberals. "Soak the rich" is a slogan that exercises an almost mystic attraction on the affluent. Accountants with an eye for loopholes and shrewd financial advisers can of course cushion the blow.

A third path is less frequently traveled. Once unlimited wealth has revealed its limitations, thoughts turn to the questions posed to rich and poor alike. What does it all mean? What is the purpose of life? Or, more relevantly, "What does it profit a man if he gains the whole world and suffers the loss of his own soul?" Out of this questioning religious conversion can come, with the added blessing that one is able to contribute to all kinds of worthy causes. Huge unpublicized benefactions soothe the soul and one returns enthusiastically to the religious practices of his youth. The last was the path that Ignatius Hannan had taken.

Even as a boy he had found the computer no more mystifying than an abacus. In his early teens, he was already a tester of beta programs, and he was soon hired by an electronics company at a salary that dazzled his parents. But he remained immune to money as money. For some years, the sheer fun of devising new programs was sufficient for him; eventually, in his twenties, he founded Empedocles, and before he was thirty he was listed among the twenty-five richest men in the country. When his head touched the ceiling of the Crystal Palace of wealth, something happened. One sleepless night, surfing the channels of distraction, he came upon EWTN, where Mother Angelica seemed to be speaking directly to him with the simplicity of his sainted mother. He was overwhelmed. He flew to Birmingham, where he confessed his sins, the minor sins of an overly busy man, and vowed to change his life.

He did. He found again the devotion to the Blessed Virgin

that he had learned at his mother's knee. He resolved to put his wealth at the service of the Catholic Church. On the grounds of Empedocles he had an exact replica of the grotto at Lourdes erected. And he had remained single, a species of eunuch for the kingdom of heaven's sake. Ignatius Hannan was stunned by the outrage perpetrated in Mexico City.

"They'll find it," Ray Whipple, his right-hand man, insisted.

"Of course they will," said Laura. Her status would have required him to have two right hands.

"There's no of course about it. What is being done?"

"We won't know until it's over."

Hannan seemed not to have heard. "Get hold of that fellow Traeger."

"Nate, he's retired."

"I'll bring him out of retirement. I like that man."

Traeger had been the key to the recovery of the third secret of Fatima and in the process had been betrayed by his old associates in the intelligence community.

Laura promised to get hold of Traeger and summon him to New Hampshire.

This proved to be a promise impossible to keep. There was no answer at the phone numbers Laura had for Traeger. Then she remembered Dortmund and succeeded in putting through a call to him.

"He's on assignment," the old voice said.

"Mr. Hannan wants to hire him to recover the stolen image of Our Lady of Guadalupe."

A long pause. "Tell Mr. Hannan that things are under way."

"I don't believe it," Hannan said when Laura reported to him. "That's government double-talk. If the administration was serious they would . . ."

He wasn't sure what he expected them to do. But then he was neither a politician nor an operative like Traeger. He believed in relying on people who knew things he did not.

"If not Traeger, someone like him."

Ray Whipple said he would see what he could do.

And that was how Will Crosby came to Empedocles, flown in from the Boston airport on a company helicopter, and coming crouched under the still whirling blades toward a waiting Ignatius Hannan.

Crosby had turned his background into a successful investigation agency. He had come on the assumption that Hannan had some problem with competitors, the sort of problem Crosby had built a reputation on handling. His eyes rounded when he learned what was expected of him.

"That's not in my usual line."

"It's not in anyone's usual line. I've heard good things of you."

"Your grotto reminds me of Lourdes."

"It ought to. It's an exact replica. Have you been to Lourdes?"

"I took my mother there in her last illness."

"And?"

"She died in peace."

Crosby's mention of his mother reminded Hannan of his own. It seemed to form a bond between them. And when they got down to the theft of the miraculous image of Our Lady of Guadalupe, it was clear that Crosby and Hannan were kindred spirits indeed. Crosby wanted time to think. He went out to the grotto and sat there telling his beads. When he came back, he said, "I'll do my best."

It was then that Ignatius Hannan revealed that he planned a two-pronged attack. The efforts of Crosby would of course be kept from the public. What everyone would know was that Ignatius Hannan was offering one million dollars for the safe return of the sacred image.

"Anyone who would steal that picture will give it up for money."

"You may be right," Crosby said.

"Within a week, I will double the amount."

"I wouldn't do that."

"Why not?"

"They'll wait to see what you'll offer the following week."

❖

Will Crosby was a large man, over six feet tall, his face an arrangement of planes that did not reveal his mind. He was in excellent physical shape, and he had a wife and grown children, one at Notre Dame; one at Christendom College in Front

Royal, Virginia; and a daughter at Thomas Aquinas College in Santa Paula, California. Ray Whipple had listed the man's feats in the CIA, any one of which recommended him for the task Hannan now hired him to undertake. After starting his own agency, he single-handedly rescued a senator's daughter, still intact, from kidnappers who were negotiating with a Saudi sheik for her purchase; that alone would have recommended him to Hannan. The rescued girl had subsequently written a book about her ordeal, one that was banned by various libraries around the country for its alleged Islamophobia.

"You'll start immediately?"

"I have associates who can take care of lesser matters."

The two men shook hands; the helicopter lifted, dipped once, seemingly toward the grotto, and then rose gracefully and disappeared over a tree-covered hill. Hannan turned to Laura.

"Prepare a statement about the reward."

❖ VI ❖

When I was hungry, you fed me.

George Worth was appalled by Miguel Arroyo's call to arms. Pacifism was a central tenet of the Catholic Worker movement and in recent years the plight of immigrant workers had become a dominant concern. No wonder. The center in Palo Alto, and others across the Southwest, all the way to Houston, provided refuge and aid to the Latinos who had learned that the utopia they had sought gave them at best an equivocal welcome. Their labor was welcomed but now, with the federal crackdown, many were being rounded up as they emerged from work. Employers were first warned, then fined. The party, it seemed, was over.

George missed Clare. At first he had considered his attraction to her to be a weakness. She was beautiful, but Dorothy Day had been beautiful at Clare's age. She was a child of privilege, but who was not? George's family lived in affluence in Winnetka. When he admitted this to Clare, it was meant to indicate that they were more alike than different. He understood her reaction to the poverty in which he and the guests lived. It had taken him a long time to overcome it himself. Now that he was more or less used to it, he almost missed the aversion he had felt at first. But his conversations with Clare had seldom alluded to what he was sure explained her going.

"George, if this country is as bad as you think, why should you want to protect the illegals coming into it?"

"Don't call them illegals."

"What should I call them?"

"Brothers. Sisters." He smiled. "Jesus." How many guests bore the name Jesú?

"They're exploited here, you say so yourself."

"They will have an effect on the injustices they suffer."

Dorothy Day had spoken of the plight of nonunionized workers, the sweatshops, the bullying bosses, but all that now seemed a bygone world. American workers were now members of the bourgeoisie, comfortable, well paid, materialistic.

"What changes?"

"They'll keep jobs in the country."

The fact was that the big unions now backed globalization, even at the manifest expense of their members, with jobs outsourced from Pennsylvania, Michigan, Ohio, everywhere, and whole industries packing up and resettling in Taiwan, Latin America, wherever they were able to lower their wages and increase their profits.

Once immigrants had been farmworkers for the most part, harvesting the crops of the country, glad for the grueling labor that enabled them to send money home, or return with it when the season was over. In college, George had been a volunteer, spurred on by Campus Ministry to devote his summers to the cause of the farm workers. The poverty they lived in rivaled that from which they had fled, although some farmers provided decent housing. George had never thought of this as political action. Radicalizing immigrant farm workers had always seemed to him a misunderstanding. Oh, he had lifted his voice in protest against the plague of industrial farming, with whole counties, it seemed, under the thumb of the giants in the food industry. Of course that kind of farming was more efficient, but it could be done with a few men on machines. His second summer, he had joined the workers in the field.

Agriculture exercises a mystic attraction on the city boy, particularly one from the affluent suburbs. To nurture and eventually harvest the fruits of the earth seemed a religious experience. The caprices of nature—frosts, flood, and drought—contributed to the sense that farming could only succeed with the help of God. Moving through the rows of ripe tomatoes, filling his basket like the others, George felt the endless sweaty, exhausting task seemed a form of prayer. But he learned not to voice such lofty thoughts to his companions when they gathered in the evenings. The local bishop appointed a priest to the immigrants and they were grateful for the Mass he said for them each Sunday, but their religion was one of practice, not discussion. On a wall in every shack was the image of Our Lady of Guadalupe with, at night, a candle burning before it.

In senior year, he read the autobiography of Dorothy Day; he subscribed to the Houston *Catholic Worker*; he found his destiny.

"A soup kitchen?" his father had asked, trying to keep calm. The summers spent with the farmworkers had seemed a harmless romantic notion next to this. At least George hadn't gone to Cuba to cut sugarcane for Fidel.

"We will provide food, of course. And lodging."

"Do you know how many of these people have gotten into the country?"

George knew.

"So tell me how one soup kitchen can help them all."

"I will help those I can."

Of course his father opposed government programs to help the poor. His contempt for the "nanny state" was total. Universal health care, ever-rising minimum wages, regulation after regulation—all that interfered with the fundamental law of economics. Supply and demand and a firm eye on the bottom line. A rising tide lifts all boats. His father knew that all a man had to do was lift himself by his own bootstraps. He had done it himself.

"I don't believe in political solutions, Dad."

"Good!"

His father thought he had won an argument. Mother Teresa of Calcutta was once interviewed by Malcolm Muggeridge, who had marveled at her efforts to collect and comfort the dying. It was, perhaps, the beginning of his conversion. But at the time he had asked the old nun why she didn't agitate for a social, a political, remedy for such poverty.

"And let others do it?"

It was watching that interview over and over that had converted George to the religion he already professed. To living it. Blessed are the poor. And the companion of that was, the poor you will always have with you. There was no "solution" to poverty any more than there was a solution to original sin. This was a vale of tears, even in Winnetka. One on one, person to person. The Good Samaritan hadn't troubled himself with the fact that he could not simultaneously help every wretch beside the road. He was here; this wretch was here; he did what he did. That was the answer.

"A drop in the bucket," his father said.

"Not if everyone did the same."

"But not everyone will."

"That doesn't take away my obligation."

They had agreed to disagree. His father had listened impatiently when George told him how the fathers of the modern economy, and later Marxists, had opposed alleviating the plight of the poor. The former had thought that, eventually, all would benefit from industrialization; the latter had counted on a revolutionary uprising to bring down the system.

"I am not a Marxist, George."

"Of course not."

John Paul II, in *Centesimus Annus*, had eloquently restated the Church's position on unbridled capitalism, but his words had been twisted into a defense of the reigning political economy. Well, the pope had seemed to waffle a bit on government solutions. George preferred Dorothy Day's and Mother Teresa's positions. Do what you can for the poor and beaten. Don't try to shuffle it off on others, on sweeping solutions that worsened the problem. One day at a time. A bowl of soup. When I was hungry, you fed me. His father had begrudgingly put up the money for the house in Palo Alto. George had taken only half of what he offered.

❖

If his father was unable to see the point of the Catholic Worker movement, Miguel Arroyo was in his way worse.

When George had shown Miguel around during his first visit to Palo Alto, Arroyo's reaction was like that of Clare Ibanez later.

"I can send some people to help clean up this place," he said when they were settled in George's office.

"It always gets dirty again."

"This is all fine and good, George. But the problem is bigger than this sort of thing can handle."

Miguel had been ecstatic when he had led through the streets of Los Angeles an army of illegal immigrants demanding . . . Demanding what? Their rights. And rights were what others owed oneself. That, too, was a shifting of the burden. They should begin by helping one another.

Of course, Miguel had a problem analogous to his own. Latinos whose presence in the country went back generations, legal immigrants, many of whom were as hostile to the influx of illegal immigrants as any Anglo.

"German and Russian Jews," Lowry murmured. It wasn't just the pipe in his mouth that made his words obscure. Lowry ran the kitchen. He was in his sixties, a repentant communist, returned to the faith of his fathers so long as it took the form of the Catholic Worker house in Palo Alto. He explained.

The Jews who had come to America early and had prospered and assimilated were put off by the hordes that poured through Ellis Island from Eastern Europe. These were low class and politically radical. Zionists. The established Jews wanted nothing to do with them, save perhaps as cheap labor in the Garment District. Zionism? Were they supposed to consider themselves as displaced desert dwellers from the Middle East? Give me a break. They were Americans! Zionism did not conquer American Jews until after World War II. Not that many chose to relocate to Israel.

The Los Angeles demonstration had been theater, a one-time event, a media event, however Miguel crowed about its success. Now he was advocating an armed uprising; he wanted California to secede from the Union, unite with the Baja, and eventually . . . Eventually all those states with their Spanish names, Nevada, Arizona, Texas, Montana, would, like California, be recovered.

"Under the Spanish crown?"

Miguel of course had dismissed the suggestion. Did he even have a clear notion of what he wanted?

George drove down to Los Angeles to find that Miguel was not there.

There were huge posters of Che and Fidel and Chavez in the outer office.

"When do you expect him back?"

A shrug. "He's up north."

"Napa?"

Another shrug.

Miguel had met Clare on a later visit to Palo Alto and George had watched with mixed emotions as Miguel, with his dancing eyes and pearly teeth under the dramatic mustache, had played the Latin lover to an indifferent Clare. When he learned that she was the daughter of Don Ibanez his smile froze. Clare's father was the spokesmen for those Latinos with generations of prosperity behind them. They disdained such agitators as Miguel.

"A great man," he said.

"Thank you." But he went on in rapid Spanish. Clare pretended that she did not understand. *"No habla?"*

Clare's only answer was a smile.

"Why didn't you speak to him?" George asked her later.

"He talks like a commercial on a Spanish radio station."

Immediately, she was sorry for what she had said, a snobbish condescension doubtless learned from her father.

❖ VII ❖

"Can I buy you a cup of coffee?"

Traeger rented a car in Chicago. Flying was too quick and he wanted the thought-inducing monotony of a long drive. Besides, he had to figure out where he was headed. In St. Louis, he phoned Dortmund and learned that Ignatius Hannan had hired Crosby.

"What for? He's offering a reward."

"Covering his bets?"

"Does Crosby know I'm on this?"

"Who would tell him?"

Well, who would tell Dortmund that Crosby had been hired by Hannan? That fragile old man, sunning himself on his retirement patio, oxygen feeding into his nostrils through plastic tubing, seemed to be as much in touch as director emeritus as he had been during his active years. Traeger reminded himself that it was Dortmund who had recommended him to his current successor. How many directors had there been since Dortmund? A series of pygmies.

He felt at once annoyed and reassured at the thought of Crosby on the same mission as he was. Cooperation of the public and private sectors? But he remembered, too, Dortmund's parting admonition. Watch your back. How many were after the same objective? He also remembered that the Company claimed to have a mole in the Rough Riders. The more he thought of it, the more he wished he were on his own.

Obviously, Theo Grady had not returned to Rough Rider headquarters in Santa Barbara. If he had, his arrest would have become public by the time Traeger arrived in Chicago. Hence the rental car and his south-southwest itinerary. The Rough Rider camps along the border had been struck, leaving the mess to the Minutemen, who were apparently defending the border effectively. It was what they had wanted to do for a long time. So where should he go?

California, here I come? But why? He would not be the only one to wonder if the call to arms from Justicia y Paz had been a reaction to the theft of the sacred picture or part of a coordinated effort. Traeger had requested, and received, what the Company had on Miguel Arroyo, an e-mail now snug in the computer he had been issued. He had read it in a truck stop just after crossing the Mississippi. An alliance between Arroyo and Grady was improbable enough to be possible. One the fiery exponent of the history of the Southwest and California, the whipper-upper of frenzy among illegal immigrants, now claiming the territory for its original settlers in a delayed victory for the conquistadores; the other the chauvinist Grady, who seemed to have forgotten that his family was only a couple generations out of County Mayo. One thing they had in common was pride in a supposed purity of blood. Arroyo claimed descent from sixteenth-century Spaniards who had settled in

California, arriving from Mexico City shortly after 1529. That was the year of the Virgin's apparition to Juan Diego, as Arroyo boasted. Grady, on the other hand, was proud of being, as he put it, pure Irish, which probably meant a mixture of Celt and Dane and French and who knew what else. When Traeger thought of it, the great globe itself seemed always to have been the theater of constant migration, emigration, and immigration, making the idea of pure blood dubious. But why would Grady ally himself with someone whose aims seemed diametrically opposed to his own: open versus closed borders? He might have recognized in Arroyo what he could not recognize in himself—an impractical romantic.

There was only one passenger in the car that had been on his tail since St. Louis, a dark blue Pontiac with tinted windows, although of course the windshield was clear. Traeger had slowed to make sure that there was only one man besides the driver. The Pontiac slowed, too, ignoring the chance to pass. Traeger sped up. Watch your back, Dortmund had said. Approaching an oasis that arched over the freeway, he turned in at the last moment, not flicking on his turning signal. The Pontiac did the same.

Inside were fast-food places, restrooms, large windows through which travelers could look down on the road that had carried them here from the west and east. Backpack slung over one shoulder, Traeger went to the men's room at the far end and, looking for feet beneath the closed stall doors, felt like that senator in the Minneapolis airport. He stepped into a stall next to the one where dropped trousers all but hid the shoes of a man seeking comfort. There was a set of car keys on the floor next to the dropped trousers. Traeger listened for the sound of flushing, then snatched the keys and got out of his stall.

Out the north door then, he hurried toward the parking lot, punching the door opener on the ignition key he held. Lights began to blink and he headed for them. All he had taken with him was the backpack that held the two computers. He pulled open the door of the car, threw in his backpack, and a minute later was headed down the ramp and barreling eastward. There was no sign of anyone following him now.

The next oasis was forty miles away but that wasn't his destination. By the time he got back to his rental car, the driver of the Pontiac should have given up, realizing that he had been flummoxed. Normally, doubling back over miles he had already covered would have been an annoyance. But not now. In any case, the miles flew by as Traeger tried not to think how clever he had been. Nearly an hour passed before he had found an exit leading to a bridge over the freeway and was driving westward again to the oasis where he had left his car. He went slowly through the parking lot, looking for the Pontiac and not finding it. He parked, left the keys on the seat, and walked back to his rental. Once behind the wheel, he relaxed and lit a cigarette.

There was a metallic tap on the window beside him and he looked up into the smiling face of Will Crosby. Traeger rolled down the window.

"Can I buy you a cup of coffee?" Crosby asked.

"Where's the Pontiac?" Traeger asked when he had gotten out of the car and shook hands with Crosby.

"What Pontiac?"

"What are you driving?"

"A Toyota."

"I think we've got company."

Before they went inside, they checked out the parking lot again, making sure the Pontiac with the tinted windows was not there. Crosby insisted that he had not noticed the Pontiac.

"I was too busy keeping an eye on you."

They ordered coffee and sat in silence, consulting their own thoughts. Traeger said, "So you talked with Dortmund."

"Everybody talks to Dortmund."

There was no point in brooding over the Pontiac. Neither of them had an explanation that wasn't wild guessing. But Traeger was certain that his employers had put a monitor on him. All the precautions of the Amtrak ride and the rental car now seemed foolish. Apparently alerted by Dortmund, Crosby had seen him while he was cooling his heels waiting for the train's departure for Chicago. He had flown from Boston to Dulles and, having hit on the Amtrak idea, too, was on the train with Traeger.

"I thought we might talk in the club car."

"I had a roomette."

"So I learned. I wish I had thought of that. Where are we headed?"

"First, we get off this freeway."

Crosby nodded. "And then?"

"How long since you've been in El Paso?"

"That question occurs to me every time I'm there."

"What was your idea?"

"Following you."

"And before you accidentally saw me in the Amtrak station?"

"I was still pondering possibilities. We'll do better pooling resources."

Outside, Traeger told Crosby that he would follow him. Crosby shook his head.

"No, I'll follow you. You have seniority."

"How much is Hannan paying you?"

"I'll split it with you."

"That's fair enough."

Crosby was driving a Toyota. Well, he was too young to remember Pearl Harbor. First chance he got, Traeger turned off the freeway and headed south on a good state road. The problem he now faced was how to get rid of Crosby.

The solution proved to be the human bladder: Crosby's. Traeger pulled off at Crosby's signal and accompanied him inside the oasis. They exchanged ignition keys as a precaution. As soon as Crosby was comfortable in a stall, Traeger left, transferred his things, let the air out of two tires of the car he was leaving for Crosby, and was on his way.

✤ VIII ✤

"I need your advice."

"You won't remember me," the caller said to Clare. "My name is Miguel Arroyo and we met—"

"Of course I remember you."

"George Worth introduced us. Are you on leave or what?"

"What do you mean?"

"I thought you were his assistant. George's."

"No."

"Just a volunteer?"

"Why are you calling?"

There was no accusation in Miguel's voice, but, reminded of what she now considered her desertion of George, Clare felt riddled with guilt. She had tried to tell herself that it was only her attraction to George, but of course that was not all of it. How was it possible to agree so completely with the principles that drove George's life and then, in effect, reject them? There was no way she could have lived the life he lived, in those conditions, with those people. How shallow that made her feel.

"Could we get together?"

"Where are you?"

"Not ten miles away."

"How did you know I was here?"

"I didn't. I called your cell phone number."

"Where did you get that?"

A pause. "George."

"So how would you know where I answered my cell phone?"

He laughed, and she remembered his face, his eyes, his teeth. He seemed summed up by his accidents. No, that wasn't fair. In his way, Miguel was as much a zealot as George. She couldn't believe that George would give him her number. She had seen his reaction to Miguel's performance when the founder of Justicia y Paz came on to her at the house. She told Miguel so.

"I couldn't lie to you."

"Good."

"Lowry gave me your number."

Lowry! How had he gotten hold of it? Clare was certain she had never given it to the cook at the Catholic Worker house in Palo Alto. She could hardly accuse Arroyo of lying. But he had already admitted to lying once. Someone, obviously Lowry, must have told him that she was no longer working with George.

"Why should we get together?"

"I need your advice."

Who can resist such a claim? His statement put her on a

pedestal of authority, someone who could give sage advice, someone he needed. And so she agreed to meet him in Pinata.

"I could come there."

"I'll meet you."

Imagine inviting Miguel Arroyo into her father's home. Don Ibanez looked with utter contempt on Justicia y Paz, considering it a mere instrument of Miguel Arroyo's ambition. What hurt the most was that Don Ibanez had known Miguel's grandfather.

"A saint, Clare," her father had whispered, "and I mean that. When he was in a room it was charged with his presence. He made a holy hour before the Blessed Sacrament every day. His charities were enormous. He swore the beneficiaries to silence, but, like those cured by Christ who were enjoined to keep their cure silent, they had to make it known."

Whenever Miguel and Justicia y Paz came up, her father lifted his eyes to heaven and wondered what the saintly grandfather would think of such nonsense.

❖

Miguel was waiting for her on the walk in front of a Mexican restaurant, surrounded by a half dozen admirers. They stepped back when Clare came up, recognizing her as her father's daughter. On their faces she could see the wonderment that Clare Ibanez was meeting with Miguel Arroyo. Miguel took her arm and led her down the walk.

"How can I meet with your father?"

She stopped and stared at him and got the thousand-watt smile in answer.

"No, not to ask for your hand."

How could she not laugh? Had George ever made her laugh? Had she ever seen George laugh? The smile was turned off.

"It's about Our Lady of Guadalupe. Let's go over there."

There was a park of sorts between the divided lanes of the street; palm trees curved from the ground, and the bench looked about to be overtaken by the lush growth around it. It was on that bench that she heard an astounding story.

She mustn't ask how he knew, he said, after telling her that what he was about to say was utterly confidential.

"I know who stole the sacred image from the shrine in

Mexico City." Having said that, he fell silent, letting the words work their effect on her.

"You must tell the police."

He shook his head. "Then those who have it would destroy it."

"Why?!"

"Anyone who would steal such a thing would not hesitate to destroy it. I have to tell this to your father. He will know what to do."

"He would tell you to tell the police."

"I don't think so." He paused. "But, if he does, that is what I will do."

Much of what he told her was lies, she knew, and they were ineffectual lies. Well, not entirely. She drove him home in her car, leaving his van in Pinata. She drove in silence, with Miguel beside her, his elbow out the open window. When she went through the gate, which opened at her signal, he took in his elbow and raised the window, as if to get a better look at the place. He hopped out and his eyes widened under raised brows as he looked beyond the house where the replica of the basilica was visible.

"My God," he said in a low voice. "I want to see it."

They crossed the lawn and then the simulated plaza and into the circular church. Miguel stopped, his eyes drawn to the picture of Our Lady of Guadalupe above the altar. Then he drifted forward as if mesmerized. He showed no surprise to find that her father had not installed a moving walkway beneath the picture, like the one in Mexico City. But everything else was just like Mexico City.

He whispered, "What is the scale?"

"Everything here is one-seventh the size of its original."

"And the picture?"

"Oh no, that's the exact size of the miraculous one."

He nodded. Then he crossed himself, kissed his knuckle, and bowed his head. He was still silently praying when her father came in.

Don Ibanez stopped, letting the door close behind him. Miguel, hearing the door, straightened and then Clare led him to her father.

"Father, this is Miguel Arroyo."

Her father seemed to recognize Miguel but he called on generations of aristocratic restraint. He bowed. Miguel began to put forth his hand, thought better of it, and returned her father's bow.

"Senor Arroyo wants to speak to you, Father," she whispered. "I'll leave you alone."

❖

Outside she walked slowly away, but the door of the little basilica did not open again behind her. Well, that was the perfect place for Miguel to give her father his astounding news.

The door of the basilica was still closed when she got to her car. She drove it around to the front; she would have to take Miguel back to Pinata when the discussion was over.

The hacienda, shaded by the many trees around it and thanks to its thick walls, was cool on even so hot a day as this. The windows in the rooms were pulled open and curtains moved slowly in a slight breeze. Ten minutes went by, and then another ten. What advice would her father give Miguel?

Half an hour later, Clare was surprised to see her father's car go down the drive. Her father was at the wheel, Miguel a passenger.

❖ IX ❖

" 'Tis a consummation devoutly to be wished."

"Why did you never marry?" Lulu asked.

"Word got out."

She laughed, making her breasts bounce. Neal Admirari was still trying to figure out where this was going. Wherever that was, neither of them seemed to be in any hurry to find out. They were now called the Devoted Duet by their colleagues.

"And I can't even sing."

They bounced then, too. Lulu and he were certainly devoted to sipping single-malt scotch, no ice, no water, and keeping apart from the others. The media moved like a nomadic band, taking their cue from the television crews, assuming that whoever sent them elsewhere knew what they were doing. Now they were in Phoenix, where the sound of rifle fire and mortars were audible. They were drinking too much. So Neal suggested they go to San Diego.

"What on earth for?"

"I want to show you where I went through boot camp."

"Neal, I can't afford it. I am not on an expense account."

"You paid your own way here?"

"Well, after all, I knew you'd be here."

Once, not many years ago, he had proposed marriage, and learned that there was the impediment of a husband. He had advised her to get an annulment, but a pall had descended upon them. They drifted apart. It was difficult to believe, when he was with her, that she had been married twice, the first finally annulled, the second ended by death, just months ago. Third time lucky? Lulu still looked virginal. He had never forgiven himself for taking her to bed where, afterward, he found out about that first husband. He had felt that he was corrupting her. They were both Catholic journalists then. "What is a Catholic journalist?" "A Roman reporter." She had even laughed at that. Well, it was good exercise for her breasts.

"I'll buy your ticket."

"You will not!"

"I don't mean buy. I'll use some of my miles. They keep accumulating."

"That's different."

"From what?"

"Being a kept woman."

Was she a keeper? They flew to San Diego, where he booked them into a hotel, separate rooms.

"Now I'll call a priest."

"What's wrong?"

"I thought I'd get a blessing on our love."

She looked at him in silence, trying to figure out what he meant.

"His name is Horvath. We were in the seminary together. He's in the chancery and will know how to fix it."

More silence. She drew her lower lip between her teeth. Her eyes left his, then came back.

"You're serious."

"I am. What do you say?"

Her smile grew gradually on her plush lips and then her teeth appeared. "I do."

And she did, some hours later, in a side chapel of the cathedral, Horvath presiding. The justification was that this was an emergency.

"What emergency?" Horvath was an older version of his youthful self, the spiky hair graying, the fat nose keeping his eyes apart.

"She is a proximate occasion of sin."

"Neal!"

Horvath seemed embarrassed. What did he think people got married for? But Neal was glad to see that his old classmate was an untroubled celibate.

Their honeymoon trip was a visit to the Marine Corps base, where he talked their way past the guard, and then led her out onto the mile-long parade ground. They looked back at the seemingly single building that formed a bracket around the parade ground.

"It was still camouflaged when I was here."

He waited for a tug of nostalgia, but it did not come. He had been just a kid when he went through, eight weeks of hell, but proud as punch when his platoon marched past the platform full of brass, a marine at last.

Back at the hotel, he canceled her room, and they moved into his but immediately decided to go downstairs and drink. Single malt.

"We should ask for married malt."

Not much of a bounce out of that one. Were they sipping Dutch courage? After an hour he suggested they go up.

"'Tis a consummation devoutly to be wished."

"If I had any breasts, they would bounce."

He explained it to her in the elevator. They were already pressing against one another. They undressed each other on the way to the bed and it was everything it should have been. Afterward, she lay naked in his arms and the silence was golden. When his arm started to go to sleep, he untangled.

"I think I'll douche."

She looked alarmed.

"It's French for shower."

"I've never had a French shower."

They had it together.

He called room service and ordered their dinner, which they ate wearing only the terry-cloth robes they found in the closet. They took turns glancing at the bed. After round two, he turned on the television, which was how they learned of the kidnapping of Don Ibanez.

CHAPTER TWO

❖ I ❖

"What are you knitting?"

Ignatius Hannan had made few friends among his fellow electronic billionaires, but then there only were a few who survived the almost daily revolutions that rendered yesterday's epic breakthrough obsolete early this morning. It was no industry for observers. The few at the top were at least as inventive and resilient as anyone they hired. Still, Hannan did not find his peers congenial, and doubtless vice versa. They were, after all, competitors, and they had all been personally narrowed by their abstract imaginations. When they turned to philanthropy other differences emerged. Bill Gates promoted contraception, Hannan the Catholic Church, the former with accompanying press releases, Hannan sub rosa, as he had learned to say. But Don Ibanez had become as close a friend as Hannan had.

When Ibanez heard of the replica of the grotto at Lourdes that Hannan had built on the grounds of Empedocles, he asked him to come out and see his own replica of the basilica in Mexico City. Hannan made a special flight to see it, bringing Laura and Ray along. And so Laura had met Clare and they became friends. Laura had been given accounts of the tragic progress of Clare's relations with George Worth, and she knew of her part-time employment with Jason Phelps, their agnostic neighbor. The terrible news of the kidnapping of Don Ibanez sent Laura rushing in to tell Nate.

"Have you talked to her?"

"I'd like to be with her."

A beat or two, then a nod of his head. He picked up the phone and gave the order. "They'll be ready whenever you are."

"Oh, Nate. Thank you."

"I may come out myself." It was as much question as statement. Laura kept his schedule.

"You have four days with appointments that could easily be postponed."

"Get a hold of Crosby. And keep me posted."

Posted! This venerable cliché evoked snail mail, and coming from one of the agents of the instantaneous communication and dispersal of information it seemed truly quaint. She had a fleeting image of the Pony Express from a book of her girlhood, the rider racing from post to post, the brim of his hat blown back, saddlebags filled with letters written on lightweight paper. Like World War II V-mail, Ray had said.

"How would I know?"

"How did you know about the Pony Express?"

❖

Now that she was married to Ray, Nate had mixed feelings about her continuing at Empedocles. A married woman should stay home, that was his conviction, held all the more firmly by a single man.

"What would I do at home?"

"Once you have a family, you're fired."

"Once I have a family, I'll quit."

But so far, they'd had no luck. Sometimes she had the superstitious fear that she and Ray were being punished for the affair that had preceded their marriage. The religious atmosphere of Empedocles would have made such thoughts inevitable, even if there hadn't been her brother, Father John Burke, now part of the bureaucracy of the Vatican. He had finished his dissertation and Nate had insisted that they all attend the defense. Nate had been impressed by the concerned cardinals in the audience.

John had written an expanded, annotated, and massive development of the rationale with which the then-cardinal Ratzinger had accompanied the publication of the third secret of Fatima. John's dissertation defense had been more a celebration than an ordeal, with all those dignitaries gathered in the Palazzo della Segnatura for the occasion. There had been a standing ovation after the unanimous vote of acceptance was announced. *Summa cum laude.* Nate had wanted to give John a huge dinner afterward, but that had to wait until the following day, as John was taken off by the cardinal who hoped the promising young priest would be named as his successor as acting prefect of the Vatican Library.

"What would be an appropriate gift?" Nate had asked.

"Why don't we ask John?"

The gift had been a magnificent chalice, which Laura helped him pick out in one of the church goods stores along the Via della Conciliazione. John had been reconciled to the extravagance by the thought that the vessel would be used at Mass, and thus was more an honor to Our Lord than to himself.

"Will you be here forever, John?"

She meant the Vatican.

"That's not up to me."

Several times, he had confided his hope that, his degree won, he could go home and teach in the diocesan seminary or, even better, be assigned to some obscure parish where he could do the work of a priest. Did he imagine becoming an assistant to someone like Father Krucek, the priest with whom he had stayed when he came home during the flap over the missing third secret of Fatima? Laura could imagine her brother made a bishop, then a cardinal, and then . . . But that was absurd.

All such thoughts were pushed away now in the aftermath of the outrage that had been committed at the basilica of Our Lady of Guadalupe.

⁂

On the flight out, Laura tried unsuccessfully to reach Crosby. Nate wanted him to direct his full attention to the missing Don Ibanez now. Laura was almost impressed by the fact that her boss ranked a missing person above the missing sacred portrait. Ray had commented on the seeming paradox of these two enormously wealthy men, Don Ibanez and Nate Hannan, striving for the simple piety of the peasant.

"Can you buy your way through the Needle's Eye?"

Laura knew the reference was to a gate into Jerusalem, but still the metaphor suggested the literal needle. Imagine that sewing had gone on way back then. She herself had taken up knitting, causing a surge of expectation in Ray.

"What are you knitting?" he asked, his eyes aglitter with potential fatherhood.

"Socks."

"For whom?"

"My husband."

"Oh."

They had stopped talking about her seeming inability to get pregnant. Nate had suggested a novena. That was all right with Ray. "But I want to become a father the old-fashioned way."

Below her the piebald Midwest was visible through fluffy clouds, a quilt of fertility, breadbasket of the nation, and more and more of the world, and it had other labels besides. Flyover country. How easily one became used to flitting about the world in a private plane, free of all the fuss of commercial travel, the security checks, the delays. And she could use her cell phone during the flight.

They had passed over the Rockies when Ray called and told her Crosby was on the line.

"I'm told you're on your way," Crosby said.

"You're in California?"

"I could meet you. You're coming in to Oakland?"

"Yes. I want to be with Clare Ibanez. Any news about her father?"

"Maybe. I'll tell you when you get here."

Jack Smiley, the pilot, gave her an ETA and she passed it on to Crosby.

❖

They went out over the Pacific before coming into the Oakland airport where, having landed, they taxied to the area reserved for private aviation. Crosby came out of the building as Laura crossed to it. On the drive up to the Napa Valley, he told her that Miguel Arroyo had been taken in for questioning.

"Miguel Arroyo!"

"He had been up there to see the daughter. Apparently they met in a Catholic Worker house in Palo Alto."

Laura knew all about the house in Palo Alto, and of Clare's unhappy love for George Worth. But Miguel Arroyo?

When they arrived, Laura was told that Senorita Ibanez was in the basilica. The reference was to the replica visible from the back of the huge hacienda.

"I'll talk to her first alone," she told Crosby and he gave her a little salute in reply.

The circular church was empty except for Clare, sitting immobile in a back pew, eyes closed, a rosary running through her fingers. Laura sat beside her. The girl turned, surprised, and then threw herself into Laura's arms and wept. What do you say to a girl whose father is missing? After ten minutes, they rose and went outside. There was a bench flanked by beds of lush flowers Laura could never have identified.

"What's this about Miguel Arroyo?"

"Laura, I had to tell them. He was here. He said he had to see my father. I left them alone and then I saw my father's car go down the drive."

"Was he alone?"

"Miguel was with him, I'm sure. Oh, how I hate tinted windows. But I had driven Miguel here after we met in town."

"Did he say why he wanted to see your father?"

"Laura, it must have been a ruse. Oh, what a fool I am. My father could not abide Miguel and his bellicose approach."

The search for Don Ibanez's car had been unsuccessful. And Miguel Arroyo had been found in the headquarters of Justicia y Paz in Los Angeles. He expressed angry surprise that he should be accused of such a thing. Yes, he had talked with the venerable Don Ibanez.

"What about?"

"I can't tell you that."

"Laura," Clare said, "he had no way to get to town. I drove him here."

"Did you tell the police that?"

"Yes."

Confronted with this, Arroyo said that Don Ibanez had taken him to Pinata where he had left his van.

Crosby came across the lawn to the bench and all this had to be told again.

At the end of the day, Clare had agreed with the greatest reluctance to go back to helping Jason Phelps, anything to distract herself.

"Can you stay, Laura?"

"I will if you want me to."

"Please."

The following morning they went together to Jason Phelps's place.

✣ II ✣

"Where can we meet?"

Theophilus Grady had commanded his Rough Riders from a two-story building just south of Santa Barbara, within earshot of the audible roar of Highway 101. The building, like the camps along the border, was abandoned now. Traeger sat in his parked car in the empty lot wondering what else he had expected. After the El Paso news conference, there had been nothing but silence from the man who had precipitated the crisis. Casualties along the border were mounting, and the caballeros who, aroused by Miguel Arroyo, had been harassing the Minutemen defending the border now found themselves under fire from bands of volunteers who had entered the fray. Where the hell it would all end was a good question.

Meanwhile the rosary crusade for the return of the sacred portrait gathered force and spread throughout the nation. The networks and cable news shows had covered this with surprising tolerance. Just for laughs, Traeger got out of the car and walked to the entrance of the building. The door was open and a little gray-haired lady peered at him over the reception desk.

"No one's here."

"Aren't you someone?"

She displayed the tips of her denture. "I'm just minding the store."

Her name was Gladys Stone, according to the plastic plate on the counter.

"I'd like to leave a message."

"I told you, no one is here." Another display of denture. "Other than myself."

"Tell them Traeger was here. Vincent Traeger."

"Tell who?"

"The people who aren't here. Grady will do. We're old friends."

"You're not so old."

Good Lord, she had become coquettish. Traeger would have had to be a lot older than he was to respond to Granny's come-on.

He wrote his name, handed her the slip, and headed for the door.

"How can he get in touch?" Gladys called after him.

Aha. He turned and went back to the desk. Would Marilyn Monroe look like Gladys if she had lived? He took the slip and wrote his cell phone number on it.

"I could give you mine, sweetie."

"You flatter me."

Flatten would have been more like it. Was it the weather or just California that made growing old so dreadful a prospect?

"Come on back. It's lonely here."

❖

As he drove away, he wondered if Hannan's offered reward for the return of the portrait was having any more luck than he was. And what was Crosby up to? He had started south, drawn by the Miguel Arroyo brouhaha, when his cell phone vibrated in his shirt pocket.

"Traeger?"

"Yo."

"I didn't know you spoke Spanish. This is Morgan."

My God, they should call an alumni meeting. Himself, Crosby, and now Morgan. They could gather on Dortmund's patio.

"You got my number from Gladys."

"Where can we meet?"

"Where are you?"

"Right behind you."

In the rearview mirror he saw the open convertible. The driver's hand rose in a wave.

"I'll pull off."

They sat at an outside table under an umbrella at a McDonald's, the building shielding them from the noise of traffic.

"They told me about you," Traeger said. "In Washington."

"What did they say?"

"Remember those laugh lines Dortmund used too often? 'On the other hand, I have four fingers, a thumb, and a wart.'"

"'And a mole on my father's side.'"

Morgan being identified as the Company's plant in the Rough Riders, they got down to business.

"Where is it?"

"You wouldn't believe me if I told you."

"Try me."

Morgan lit a cigarette. When he exhaled, the smoke drifted away on the hot breeze.

"Ignatius Hannan has offered a reward for it."

"Your pension isn't enough?"

"Hey, I'm still active."

"Tell it to Gladys."

Morgan laughed. "Isn't she something? Look, here's my plan."

Morgan wanted the million Hannan was offering, but could he deliver?

"Trust me."

Under the circumstances, that sounded like a joke. There had always been agents who, faced with oblivion, became double agents, working for the other side as well. Fear for one's life was, if not exculpating, an understandable motive for treachery.

"And there can't be any publicity, Traeger. My principals might not understand."

Oh, they would understand. "You would have more to fear from Grady."

"Grady's an ass. Remember Brando in *Viva Zapata*?"

"Will Crosby has been hired by Hannan. You should deal with him."

"Where is he?"

"Good question."

"I want to deal with you. Of course I'd cut you in, ten, fifteen percent."

Traeger felt like the Sanhedrin bickering with Judas Escariot. He said nothing.

"You work out the transfer, Traeger."

"How large is it?"

"Isn't it a million?"

"I meant the picture."

Morgan thought. "It would fit in the trunk of my car."

Two pairs of eyes drifted toward the convertible in which Morgan had followed him in to the drive-in.

"No," Morgan said.

"I didn't think so."

Traeger shook a cigarette free from the pack Morgan had tossed on the table. Morgan lit it for him, using an old-fashioned Zippo that flared up like a Bunsen burner at the flick of his thumb. Traeger was wondering how he could arrange to get the picture without Morgan getting the money. But then Morgan was probably thinking how to double-cross him as well.

"Give me a number to call."

"I'll call you."

A stupid precaution. After Traeger had avoided shaking hands with Morgan and was behind the wheel of his car, he checked his phone. Morgan's number was there. He punched it.

"Yes."

"You should say 'Yo.'"

After a pause, Morgan laughed. "Never kid a kidder."

❖ III ❖

"I'm a friend of Lloyd's."

When she returned from Chicago after those wonderful three days with Lloyd, Catherine Dolan had waited for him to call.

But several days went by and no call came. When she tried to reach him, there was no answer. She sat, sipping a martini and looking out at Lake Calhoun from the windows of her apartment in the high-rise just across the boulevard from the lake. Euclidean sails drifted across the rumpled water, going whither the wind whilst, and old problems in plane geometry distracted her. Why didn't he call?

The more she thought of those days in Chicago, the more her memories of them became unsettling. Lloyd had been ardent enough, God knows, but she had sensed that their meeting was an excursion out of character for him. She got down one of his books and stared at the photograph on the dust jacket. A popular account of Heloise and Abelard, which, she remembered, was surprisingly censorious. The usual thing was to romanticize the couple, but Lloyd had looked on the affair as Heloise did in her later letters to her maimed lover. Catherine had meant to kid Lloyd about that, but she hadn't. In the circumstances, it would not have been appropriate. Her own academic field, microbiology, was remote from his. She had taught for a time, then went to work for a private company and, unexpectedly, had made a pile from patented breakthroughs. So she had retired and, sitting in this very apartment, had daydreamed of the sweet long ago when she and Lloyd had walked along Minnehaha Creek in the summer evenings.

After days of silence and inability to reach him, she told herself that it was the way she had said good-bye to him, that final act of homage, that explained the silence. Every woman knows the transition from eager to sated lover, the act once done removing the allure that had drawn him to her. The eagerness would return, of course, and be succeeded by the same swift indifference. Finally, the eagerness, too, faded. Except in an animal like Richard, the son of a bitch she had married and then discarded in the interval between academe and commercial work. There had followed a string of affairs she did not like to remember. At the time, she had thought of herself as Edna St. Vincent Millay, or Dorothy Parker, promiscuous but what the hell, who's keeping score? Burning her candle at both ends, so to quote. She hadn't been successful in thinking of those men as mere toys, but then neither had Millay or Parker. Being a woman was hell. Men seemed able to take their pleasure and then forget. Look at Lloyd. The son of a bitch. Angry, she called again.

A woman answered. Okay. A little revenge.

"I'm a friend of Lloyd's."

"The wake is tomorrow."

"The wake?"

"The Mass is the following day."

"For Lloyd?"

A long pause. "Good Lord, hadn't you heard?"

"Tell me about it."

"Who are you?"

"Catherine Dolan. We grew up together in Minneapolis."

She realized she was speaking with one of Lloyd's daughters, Judith, who broke down as she told Catherine what had happened. Catherine, knowing certain facts Judith did not, listened in disbelief. Had he gone on pilgrimage in repentance for their three days in bed?

"Where will the wake be held?"

She jotted down the address in Indianapolis.

"Thank you," she said and hung up.

She sat stunned. Dead. Images of the two of them in that hotel bed in Chicago came to her, and she seemed in the grips of necrophilia. Then she began calling airlines. By God, she would go. There was a direct flight out of Hubert Humphrey and she booked a seat.

From the stack of newspapers in the back hall, waiting to go out with the trash, she took those that had covered the outrage in Mexico City and for half the night she tried to reconstruct what had happened to Lloyd. But it was what must have sent him off to that shrine that filled her with dread.

❖

The flight to Indianapolis was turbulent and she imagined the newspaper account of the crash. How would she be described? Who would care? She was in a proper mood for the wake, held in a dreadful funeral home on Meridian Avenue, on which governors and other notables once had dwelt. She parked her rental car and sat looking at the people going inside. Finally she had the courage to do the same.

An unctuous undertaker greeted her with brows raised in a question.

"Lloyd Kaiser," she said.

"Of course." He directed her to a viewing room, where chairs were set in rows. At the entrance was a book in which mourners entered their names. She wrote "Heloise Abelard," and went in among the chattering people, avoiding them all, seeking anonymity. She took a chair in the back row, but her eyes were drawn to the closed casket on which mourners converged, kneeling for a time, crossing themselves, and then going off. Catherine felt like an anthropologist studying a strange tribe. But they were her tribe, all Catholics as she herself once had been. As Lloyd had remained. She thought of the medal he had worn and her silly comments on it.

A tall young priest with a serious expression led the rosary and, listening to the once familiar prayer, repeated over and over, Catherine tried to remember what it had been like to believe all that, that God had become man and come to dwell among us, that by His stripes we are healed, that earthly life is the anteroom to eternity. But memories of her final sexual act with Lloyd disturbed her thoughts. Had he confessed and been absolved, once more all right with this world and the next? Irony and sarcasm were difficult in the room where his friends and children prayed for the repose of Lloyd's soul. She left before the general exodus and drove to her hotel.

The funeral Mass was at ten the following morning. It was easier to be anonymous in the church. She sat through it all, watching the priest at the altar, the same slim man who had led the rosary the night before. The Mass. She tried to remember the last time she had been to Mass. She and the son of a bitch had been married by a priest; she tried to remember why. There was incense and much blessing of the casket under a white covering in the central aisle. In the front pews were several young couples, his children, one youngster. It seemed an assumption of the occasion that any grief was concealed. It was all Catherine could do not to cry, for herself, for Lloyd perhaps, for the whole world of lost innocence the ceremony recalled.

The family followed the casket down the aisle, smiling almost cheerfully. Well, why not? Several had spoken after the Mass, maudlin commemorations of their dead father. At communion time, Catherine heard the words, "O Lord, I am not worthy to receive you." She could not have put it better herself. She remained seated in her pew while everyone else went forward. The body and blood of Christ. She had made her First Communion at the age of ten. Had Lloyd been among the group when for the first time they approached the communion rail at Saint Helena's?

When she left, she avoided the family and those pressing around them. She was behind the wheel of her car when a man came toward her.

"Going to the cemetery?"

She looked at him for a moment, then nodded. He attached a pennant to the front fender.

The procession through Indianapolis was under police escort. They drove through red lights, other motorists stopping in recognition of their supposed sorrow. Had anyone even wept? She remembered Judith, who had broken down on the telephone when Catherine called.

For years she had schooled herself to think, insofar as she let such questions form, that death is the end, that all the fuss over the decaying husk left when the run was over, funerals, mourning, monuments, all the rest, were carryovers from barbarism. Even cremation seemed overly dramatic. But at least it scattered the supposed remains and allowed the living to go on living. These were not convictions, just unexamined presuppositions, and she felt them assaulted by the graveside ceremony. Finally, there were tears, honest-to-God weeping, and she could have cheered. Lloyd deserved at least that from those whom he had left orphans, apparently well-provided-for orphans. Her own eyes blurred with tears as she looked on.

❖

She had hours in her hotel before her return flight was due. She told herself that it was perfectly understandable that she should have been moved by the events surrounding Lloyd's burial. The news of his death had come to her as a thunderclap after she had spoken in the hopes of shocking whoever had answered the phone. She had taken an envelope from the funeral parlor, and she now stuffed some money into it and wrote her name on it. And address. Then she flew back to Minneapolis.

❖ IV ❖

"Conquest of a conquistador."

Miguel Arroyo did not strike Neal as a man who was fomenting revolution, claiming vast territories allegedly stolen from his ancestors in the long ago, and now facing kidnapping charges. He swept into the visiting room with the ease of a dancer coming onstage. He had agreed to the interview because Lulu was with *Commonweal* and Neal was just part of the package. Arroyo's charm did not diminish when he learned Lulu was married.

"A working wife?" He expressed merry surprise. The guy could have been an actor. Maybe that was what he was.

"With a working husband." She nodded at Neal, who got a fraction of the smile, but then he concentrated on Lulu again.

"But you use your own name."

"Professionally."

"Ah." A slight alteration in the mustache, more teeth. You would have thought Lulu had told a dirty joke. Neal decided that he hated Miguel Arroyo. In the young man's presence he felt his age and was sure he looked it, and then some. Lulu was an affectionate woman and marriage was taking it out of him.

"I hope your lawyer agreed to this interview," Neal said.

"Oh, I'm my own lawyer." After graduation from San Diego University, the alleged Notre Dame of the West, he had studied law at Berkeley. But even so.

"A fool for a client?"

Lulu intervened. "What's all this about your kidnapping Don Ibanez?"

"A silly misunderstanding."

"His daughter said you drove away with him."

"In the passenger seat. He took me into town where I had left my car."

"And then?"

"I drove here. And was arrested."

"And what of Don Ibanez?"

He looked blank.

"Did he drive away? Which direction did he go?"

Arroyo was disappointed. "I went through all that with the police."

"Why were you there? To visit Don Ibanez, I mean."

"We have much in common."

He seemed serious. More than once, Don Ibanez had dissociated himself from the firebrand of Justicia y Paz. For the old man, the recovery of California was a romantic dream, all the more attractive for being unrealizable. He was under the spell of a lost cause. Neal wondered if the old man had forebears who fought with the Confederacy. He would look it up.

"You think of him as an ally?"

"I would not presume to speak for Don Ibanez."

"Has Senora Arroyo been in?" Neal asked.

"My mother has gone to God." He closed his eyes in commemoration.

"I meant your wife."

"Have you found her?"

"Is she lost?"

He leaned toward Lulu. "I have yet to meet the woman I am destined to marry."

"Is there anything between you and Clare Ibanez?"

"What did she say?"

"It has been speculated that you had gone there to see the daughter, not the father."

Arroyo sat back. "That would be George Worth. He meant to be helpful."

"Then there's nothing to it?"

"Would I tell you if there were?"

"Why would she accuse you of kidnapping her father?"

"I don't think she quite said that."

"Who is George Worth?" Neal asked.

He inhaled. "There are two kinds of revolutionary, the practical and the contemplative. George is a contemplative." He went on to describe the Catholic Worker house in Palo Alto. He urged them to go there. "Clare Ibanez worked there for a time."

"She did?"

"Imagine a girl with her background living in such poverty and squalor. Yet many others have done it. What do you know of Dorothy Day?"

He seemed disappointed that they already knew of the founder of the Catholic Worker movement. "A pacifist," he said. "But a saint."

"How's the war going?" Neal asked. This guy was getting on his nerves.

Miguel Arroyo frowned. "I have ordered hostilities to cease."

"And have they?"

"Communications are imperfect."

⚜

"He's a phony," Neal said when they left.

"He is not!"

"I think you made a conquest of a conquistador."

She looked at him and began to smile. "Jealous? Is Neal jealous?" She begin to tickle him, right there in public.

"He could be your . . ." Careful, careful. "Your little brother."

"He is cute."

"Cute!"

Before they left the building, they learned that Don Ibanez's car had been found in a parking lot at LAX. And that was where they went next.

⚜

By the time they got there, the police had already checked out the trunk of the car, doubtless influenced by *Prizzi's Honor* and a number of other movies. The trunk was empty. Lulu tugged Neal aside and they went inside the terminal.

"What for?"

"Why would you leave a car in an airport parking lot?"

"Tell me."

"Because you were going to catch a plane."

She was right. But it took time to establish it. Don Ibanez had flown out of Los Angeles on Mexicana. Destination, Mexico City.

❖ V ❖

"It would be worth dying for."

Ray called to tell Laura that they had a nibble on the reward that Ignatius Hannan had offered for the return of the stolen Lady of Guadalupe.

"Oh, good."

"Crosby is working with Traeger on it."

This good news, coupled with that of the discovery of Don Ibanez's car at the Los Angeles airport and learning that he had gone there to catch a flight, made it seem that it all would soon be over. Clare's father had not been kidnapped after all. When contacted in Mexico City, Don Ibanez had been astonished to learn that he had been the object of a police search. He called Clare immediately, and Laura listened to the young woman babble in Spanish to her father. After she hung up, she told Laura she had confessed to her father that it was all her fault.

"What else were you to think?" She wanted to ask why the old man had not told his daughter where he was going, but she sensed that criticism of Don Ibanez would not be welcome. "Is he on his way home?"

"Tomorrow."

She told Clare then of Ray's message. The young woman was overjoyed. "Oh, I wish I had known that when I was talking with my father."

Clare suggested that they go to the little basilica and say a prayer of thanksgiving. Laura knelt beside her and wished that she had the simple piety of Clare and her father, and of Nate Hannan, too. She and Ray seemed returned prodigal children, still with only one foot in the faith from which they had wandered.

After several minutes, Clare rose and walked toward the altar. She stood in front of it and stared at the softly illumined image of Our Lady of Guadalupe.

"Is anything wrong?" Laura asked when she joined her.

"No, of course not." But she had hesitated before answering.

❖

Back in the hacienda, they had lunch and then they settled down and Clare told her all about George Worth again. It was impossible not to feel Clare's anguish. This wasn't the impediment to love created by family feuds, the Montagues and the Capulets, the Whatchamacallits and the McCoys. The impediment wasn't external at all. It was Clare herself who was divided, not just reason against emotion, but a civil war of emotions. She wanted so much to share the ideal of George Worth, but she had been unable to overcome her aversion to the circumstances in which he lived that ideal.

"But couldn't the circumstances be changed, made less, well, whatever they are?"

"Of course they could. I could provide the money, or Father could, but George won't hear of it. The whole point of it is to be as poor as those he welcomes to the house. His life has to be precarious."

"Is he a Franciscan?"

"Worse." But she smiled when she said it. It occurred to Laura that the founder of the Franciscan nuns had been Saint Clare.

"I know!" Clare wailed.

❖

When Crosby arrived, Traeger was already there, looking completely unchanged from when he had been hired by Nate.

"First the secret of Fatima, now Our Lady of Guadalupe."

Traeger nodded. "I can't get out of church."

It seemed to dawn on Crosby that he had been Nate's second choice to recover the sacred image. But any negative thoughts he might have had about that seemed swept away by the thought of working with Traeger now. Neither man would give any details about what arrangements had been made to meet with the claimant of the reward.

"Nate wouldn't balk at that. His original idea was to add a million each week until the reward was claimed."

"Good Lord."

"I know. He saw that was foolish."

Clare offered to put the two men up in the hacienda, but they preferred staying in town. First they wanted to see the replica of the basilica. When they came back, Traeger asked if the picture there was an exact copy of the original.

Clare paused, then said, "Oh yes. Everything there is on a smaller scale, except that the picture has the exact dimensions of the original. He went to Mexico City when it was done. The artist worked in the basilica there at night, and my father and others were always with him. Afterward, he arranged to have it shipped here. The bishop came for the installation."

They went off to Pinata, saying they would be back the following day when Don Ibanez returned.

Her father arrived on an early flight and several hours later came up the drive. He took his daughter in his arms and thanked Laura for coming to be with Clare.

"Will you be going back now?"

Laura told him about Traeger and Crosby and the claim that had been made for the reward. The old man did not react as Laura had expected.

"A million dollars?"

"Surely it is worth that to get the image back. Mr. Hannan won't miss the money."

"Couldn't they just arrest the thief?"

"Such exchanges can be dangerous enough without trying that." Laura remembered the shoot-out on the roof of the North American College in Rome where the recovery of the third secret of Fatima was to take place.

The old man went out to his basilica, to make a visit, as he said. When he came back he was in good spirits. Traeger and Crosby arrived and Laura left the three men together, calling Ray so he could keep Nate posted, as he had asked.

"How will they make sure it is the original?"

"That is the first question they put to Don Ibanez. They're discussing the matter now."

The answer to the question, it emerged, was that Don Ibanez would accompany the former agents. He dismissed the warning that it could be dangerous.

"It would be worth dying for," he said solemnly.

❖ VI ❖

"Tell me about Jason Phelps."

When she approached the door of the Minneapolis Athletic Club, where she had a date for lunch, Catherine looked up at the skyway above. All the buildings in downtown Minneapolis were connected by such skyways, forming a vast network that enabled shoppers and workers to avoid the heat of summer and, more important, the arctic cold of winter. Then her eyes drifted to the right, to Saint Olaf's Church. The door of the club had been opened at her approach, and she hurried inside, as if to escape temptation.

Myrna Bittle, an anthropologist, and a colleague when Catherine had taught, was waiting in the lobby.

"You're a member here?" Myrna whispered. Her hair was cut unattractively short and she looked at her old friend through the round lenses of her heavily rimmed glasses. Of course a mere academic wouldn't dream of a membership in this club.

"I think you'll like it."

They were led through the dining room to their table. "White wine okay?" Catherine asked.

"White wine is okay."

Catherine was beginning to wish that they had met in the faculty club as Myrna had suggested. But she had wanted to treat her old friend, the better to enlist her help.

Ever since the funeral in Indianapolis Catherine had been assailed by temptation. She had tried to exorcise it by the remedy of drink, and she had actually called one of her old lovers, but that hadn't led anywhere. She couldn't imagine herself in bed with Mark. He seemed to be having the same trouble. So they parted with a quick kiss on the cheek and she fled into her building. All Catherine could think of were those days she had spent with Lloyd in Chicago. The fling after which he had gone off to Mexico City, apparently on pilgrimage, and been cut down during the theft of the image from the basilica. It seemed he had tried to stop the gunman who shot him.

A pilgrimage. Which meant that Lloyd thought of what

they had done as sinful, something of which he must repent. Catherine had a vivid image of his silver chain and the medal on it, which she had gently mocked. She had tried very hard to recall his reaction to that. Had she offended him? Did he honest to God still believe all that nonsense?

But was it nonsense? Of course it was. But after the shock of Lloyd's death, and the circumstances of it, after seeing his devout daughters at the wake and funeral and interment, the nonsense began to seem just something ordinary people believed. What she herself had once believed. It became almost attractive and she fought the temptation with all her might. Myrna represented another effort in that direction.

"So what's this all about?" Myrna asked, sipping her wine.

"How long has it been since we've gotten together?"

"God only knows."

"God?"

"A *façon de parler.*"

"For a moment, I thought you had got religion."

"Ha."

So she had been right to ask Myrna to lunch. Myrna was president of the local Hemlock Society, and she lectured often on the way so many societies had eased their elderly into what they thought was the next life. She had reviewed the books of Dawkins and Hawkins for the local paper, applauding their dismissal of Christianity, of theism, of superstition. She was especially enthused about Christopher Hitchens's *There Is No God.* Once she had gotten Myrna going on those books, all Catherine had to do was listen. It was like a purge listening to that bright, dismissive voice.

"I've been reading about that theft in Mexico," Catherine said tentatively.

"Our Lady of Guadalupe!"

"You know about it?"

"Catherine, I have files on shrines like that. Did you know there are books about supposedly incorrupt bodies, people dead for years, sometimes centuries, and there they are, all pink and pretty."

"Really?"

"Of course they're fakes."

"Can't that be proved?"

"It doesn't seem to matter. The poor fools keep showing up at the shrines."

"Were you raised atheist?"

Myrna's loopy earrings swayed as she laughed. "God, no. We were Episcopalians. That's sort of Catholic lite."

"I was raised Catholic," Catherine said.

"It's not your fault. Were you consulted?"

"Before my baptism?"

"That's just my point."

"How did you get over being an Episcopalian?"

"Could I have another glass of wine? This is going to take time."

The short answer to Catherine's question was: anthropology. The study of other cultures had enabled Myrna to get out of her own and see it with new eyes.

"Where did you get your doctorate?"

"Berkeley."

"In anthropology."

"Catherine, I studied under Jason Phelps! Let me rephrase that. Well, that, too. You've heard of him, of course."

"Myrna, my field was microbiology."

"Was?"

"I'm retired."

Myrna sat back. "Already? You must have made a pile."

"Enough."

Myrna looked around the dining room. "Enough for this?"

"And other things."

"Lucky you."

"Tell me about Jason Phelps."

Her mentor was a militant atheist, a renowned anthropologist, but more famous for his debunking books on Catholic superstitions. Myrna went on and on about his book on the shroud of Turin.

"What's that?"

"It's supposed to be the cloth in which Jesus was buried, and wouldn't you know, there is his image on the cloth. People actually believe this. Some scientists who were in the group that examined it believe it! Well, they refused to say their tests established that it's a fake. That is what really gets Jason's goat. The nitwit scientists who give aid and comfort to superstition. You must read his little book *Descartes and the House of Loreto.*"

"What is the house of Loreto?"

"Are you ready? It is the house in Nazareth in which Jesus was raised and which was miraculously transported to Loreto, Italy! The whole damned house flying through the air like a magic carpet. René Descartes, the father of modern philosophy, the inventor of methodic doubt, made a pilgrimage there in gratitude for his philosophical insights. Jason is marvelous on all that."

"Is he still alive?"

"He's retired now. He has a place in Napa Valley, where he is sorting out his papers. When he's done, he'll check out."

"Die?"

"Assisted suicide. I will never forget a lecture he once gave on Seneca. Those old Stoics had it right."

"He's your hero?"

"Jason? Call him that, I don't mind. If I could afford to, I would go out there and help him with his papers."

❖

The lunch had been everything Catherine had hoped for. The fresh breeze of pure reason blew through her soul. Her brain. Whatever. Myrna sent her copies of Jason Phelps's books. They helped even more than Myrna's lunch table account. Nonetheless, from time to time, when she least expected it, temptation struck. So she wrote to Jason Phelps, told him a little about herself, mentioned her friendship with his former student Myrna Bittle, and asked if she could come see him. She had mentioned Myrna's wish that she could help Phelps with his papers, and when he replied, he seemed to think Catherine was volunteering to do that. She decided not to correct him. She booked a seat on a flight to Oakland.

❖ VII ❖

"It still haunts me."

Jason Phelps received an e-mail from Myrna before the letter from Catherine Dolan came. He sat now at the outside table where he ate most of his meals and looked across the valley. How green everything was, all new and vital. The scenery provided a mocking contrast to his aging self.

Oh, he had aged well. The great hawk nose, his face lined and tanned, and the shock of white hair still impressed, he could see that, but it was his eyes under luxuriant brows that remained his great weapon. Weapon! He was still attractive to women—young women—but what did it matter? Memories of Myrna brought a wistful smile. It was all over, that sort of thing. So many things were all over now. Still, Catherine's letter had stirred his spirits and he invited her to come see him. After a single conversation, he accepted her offer to help put order into his papers. She was in the house now, under Clare's tutelage, learning the ropes.

Had he become a guru, the refuge of those plagued by superstition, eager to be relieved of their burden? It was inevitable, he supposed. Think of Seneca's *Letters from a Stoic*. Spiritual direction, that was what those letters were, in the same literary genre as *The Imitation of Christ*. How much stronger our convictions become when we see them mirrored in others.

"Catholic," Catherine had said the night before when the two of them were sitting on this very patio, getting acquainted.

"Good."

She was surprised. So he quoted Cardinal Newman. There is no point, in logic, between atheism and Catholicism.

"A pardonable exaggeration, which Newman had to explain over and over again. He meant that everyone is drifting toward the one extreme or the other. If he is not already there. And he was right. Only the extremes tempt us."

"Were you Catholic?"

"No, but I often wish I had been. My parents were Unitarians, believing there is at most one God, in the old joke. It's no religion at all, which makes it harder to lose. And of course every sort of Protestantism defines itself with reference to Catholicism."

"It still haunts me," Catherine said. She was a handsome woman, but troubled.

"Of course it does. No human state is entirely stable. There are times, sitting out here, looking at that magnificent valley, when I find myself praying."

"And what do you pray?"

"I disbelieve. Lord, help my disbelief."

She had a nice laugh. "You sound like a priest."

It was his turn to laugh. He thought of Frater Leone, who had come to visit shortly after he settled in here. The monk had acted as if he thought he had a new parishioner. Phelps had tried to shock the priest, but nothing worked. The man just nodded through the attacks on his absurd beliefs. Leone was not much younger than him and, like himself, was beyond surprise. That one session of confrontation had been enough. Since, they had become friends of a sort. He had learned to look forward to Frater Leone's pastoral visits. Know your enemy. That adage seemed to guide them both. It was from Leone that he had gotten a better understanding of his aristocratic neighbor, Don Ibanez.

"The fear of death," Jason had said, summing his neighbor up.

"That bourne from which no traveler returns."

"Because the traveler has ceased to exist."

"Perhaps."

"Perhaps! Do you have doubts?"

"A thousand difficulties do not make a doubt."

It was a quote from Cardinal Newman and it had taken Phelps back to the *Apologia*. Not that he had ever been far distant from it. If Newman's account of his conversion was the best there was, faith was built on sand, on a void, but it remained a fascinating exercise in self-deception. He must urge Catherine to get to know Frater Leone. There is no victory without an opponent.

"Don Ibanez showed me the basilica he had built," he told the priest.

"He has a great devotion to Our Lady of Guadalupe."

Phelps had been almost ashamed to think that the targets of his polemical books were all across the sea when only a few hundreds of miles to the south was the most influential superstition in the Americas. Frater Leone had brought him books and now Phelps was knowledgeable enough. The fable was both like and unlike so many others.

And then had come the outrage in Mexico City, the image stolen by a band of gunmen. Phelps had been as indignant as

Frater Leone. The theft was not an attack on all that image stood for; it was simply a ploy in some anti-immigration nonsense. Let the masses indulge in their superstitions. Jason Phelps had no expectation that such devotions would disappear. They had a role to play. His own writings had been aimed at the intelligentsia, those with a capacity to understand. Apparently Don Ibanez was not among them. So be it. He had no desire to bait his neighbor. Let the simple think that their incredible beliefs and practices were credible. That did little harm, and some social good. But it was essential that those with minds acknowledged, at least among themselves, that nonsense was nonsense. That was the only solid basis for tolerance. Phelps had been even more outraged by the disappearance of Don Ibanez. Oddly, Frater Leone, unlike Clare, had taken the kidnapping calmly.

"No harm will come to him."

"Because you are praying for him?" The old anger flared up.

"That, too."

Phelps decided that the priest was not a foe worthy of his steel. He told Frater Leone he was a Stoic. "In the immortal words of Doris Day, *que será, será.*"

"Providence is not fate."

"Indeed it isn't. Fatalism is rational."

He had followed events, on television and in the newspapers, the great deceivers. What an ass Theophilus Grady was, in his nineteenth-century getup, Teddy Roosevelt redivivus. The man made one long for the return of the death penalty. Even better, when the man was arrested they should deliver him up to the mercies of the Mexican mob.

And now Don Ibanez was back. One could almost believe that the old hidalgo had been rejuvenated by all these events, despite the anguish they must cost him. Imagine, popping off to Mexico on the spur of the moment. By contrast, Jason felt rooted in his retirement home.

❖

The second night, sipping wine, Catherine had told him of her most recent affair, mindless days in Chicago with a man she had known when they were young. There was no need for her to describe those days of wild passion, even if she had been inclined to do so. He could sense her carnal appetite, the eager despair of the would-be libertine.

"He was killed in Mexico City, Jason. He had gone to the shrine, no doubt out of remorse. It is awful to think of one-self as an occasion of sin, but I am sure that was his judgment of me."

"Nonsense."

Seneca had been right about sensual pleasure. After many years, Phelps had come to agree with the old Stoic. The pleasures of the flesh cannot satisfy and invariably they bring on unpleasant complications. Hilda had been a complacent wife but of course she must have suspected. But his affair with Myrna had been too much. In his passion, he had become care-less, almost taunting his wife, gone now to where betrayed wives go. And all of us, eventually. Seneca had recommended the pleasures of the mind. Moderate catering to the fire of the flesh, to be sure, but keep it cool, as students would say. Hav-ing Catherine in the house brought back wistful memories of the desires of the flesh.

✤ VIII ✤

"He wore a medal."

Clare regarded Catherine as her replacement and so the two women worked well together. One afternoon, Clare took her home to show her the hacienda and of course the basilica.

"Basilica!"

"It's the exact replica of a church in Mexico."

"Where the picture was stolen?"

"I'm praying so hard that it will be returned unharmed."

Catherine had fallen silent, her eyes fixed on the basilica.

"Would you like to see it?"

A nod.

Inside, Catherine drifted in a trance toward the altar and stopped. When Clare came up beside her, she found the older woman weeping. She would not have expected such religious devotion of her. Why? Because she had volunteered to help Professor Phelps? But she worked for him herself. Clare helped Catherine to a pew.

"My lover was killed here."

"Here!"

"In Mexico City. When the picture was stolen. He tried to stop them. . . ."

Of course people had been killed at the time; it seemed awful not to have remembered that. Now Clare did and she remembered as well reading of the American who had confronted the thieves and been shot down in consequence.

"He's a martyr," she declared.

"He's dead." Catherine looked toward the altar. "Is that a copy of the picture that was stolen?"

"Yes."

Catherine took a deep breath, as if to prevent herself from crying again. Clare said, "Let's go outside. But say a prayer for him first."

Catherine swung on her, angry. "I don't pray!"

Clare was stunned. They did go outside then, in silence, and Clare suggested going into the hacienda for tea. "Or a drink, if you want one."

"Yes, I do."

Clare led her to the sideboard, so she could make her own drink. But all Catherine did was fill a glass half full of rum and bring it to her lips. She looked at Clare over the rim of the glass. After tasting the drink, she said, "I'm sorry."

"Tell me about it."

"About what?" She was angry again.

"You said he was your lover."

"That's a fancy word for it, as fancy as calling what we had an affair."

Catherine drank more rum and then they went onto the veranda and sat.

"He was someone I knew when we were kids. He was a writer, so I became aware of him. His wife died and I wrote him. Then there were telephone calls. So we met in Chicago. Three days." She bit her lip, as if to stop herself from saying more. "Afterward, he went on pilgrimage to that shrine and was killed."

"Oh, Catherine, that's so sad."

"He believed all those things. He wore a medal. . . ."

Clare wanted to tell her again that the way he had died did make him a martyr, at least she thought it did. She would not have wanted to try to explain it to Catherine.

"You're not Catholic?"

"No!"

"But he was?"

She nodded. "I was, too, long ago."

There must be things to say in such a situation, but Clare could not think what they might be. To fill the silence she began to talk about George Worth. Whether in relief to have the subject changed or because she was interested, Catherine listened avidly. When Clare described the Catholic Worker house, Catherine said, "I don't blame you."

"I blame myself."

Before that afternoon, Clare had regarded Catherine as a self-possessed professional woman, poised, successful. Now they were two women, disappointed in love, sharing their stories.

"And so you came here to work with Professor Phelps. Had you known him before?"

Catherine told her about her friend Myrna, whose doctoral dissertation had been directed by Phelps. "He can help me more than I can help him."

"Help you?"

"It's a long story."

⚜

After she had taken Catherine back to Professor Phelps's house and returned home, Clare thought about the strange conversation they had had. The man she called her lover had been gunned down in the shrine of Our Lady of Guadalupe. He had been a Catholic, and Catherine said she had been one, too, long ago. Suddenly Clare was filled with dread at the kind of help Professor Phelps might be to Catherine.

I don't blame you, Catherine had said when she told her that she couldn't face life in a place like the Catholic Worker. No doubt she was just being kind or polite, but, remembered, the remark did not console. Catherine had also said that she didn't pray, that she had been Catholic once, and far from being ashamed of what she would not call her affair with the man who had been killed in the basilica in Mexico City, she clearly regretted that it had ended. It was even clearer what she thought of a man who, in remorse, had made his fateful pilgrimage to Our Lady of Guadalupe. All that made Catherine's sympathy feel like an accusation.

Her father's understanding of her return home was different. For him, people were called to different vocations and that was that. His own vocation consisted of wealth and ease and enormous holdings in Napa Valley, the deference of all. . . . She stopped. How many wealthy men were there who lived as her father did? He was proud of his property and had made it far more prosperous than how he had received it, but in a way George Worth probably could never understand, Don Ibanez was poor in spirit. Clare had no doubt that if tomorrow he lost everything, he would not lose the simple devotion that had led him to construct a replica of the basilica of Our Lady of Guadalupe on the grounds. If God's will had made him the heir of wealth, God's will could make him poor, and he would continue to say his prayers and show devotion to Mary. Her father, she realized, could very well reconcile himself to the kind of life George led.

Thus everything returned her to her sense of shame that she had turned away from the life the man she loved was resolved to lead.

❖ IX ❖

A version of Montezuma's revenge.

In Congress the usual cacophony went on, expressions of outrage, condemnation, demands that something be done, pleas for caution and prudence. Negotiations were urged. Negotiations with whom? The Mexican government disavowed any part in the skirmishes along the border as if it was simply a squabble among drug dealers. It was a further insult to suggest that there was any official sanction for what was going on. Senator Gunther from Maine and a half dozen apoplectic patriots demanded a lightning strike by the Marines to clear up the southern border once and for all. The White House insisted that progress was being made. Progress!

Theophilus Grady smiled. What a sorry bunch members of Congress were, and of course the administration continued being the administration, all its attention on the Middle East. The whole spectacle made Theophilus Grady even more pleased that he had taken the matter into his own hands.

Morgan said, "I'm glad we struck our camps."

We? Our? But Grady only said, "The Minutemen are doing all right."

They were installed in the mountain redoubt of one of Grady's financial supporters, Dougherty, a zealot from Pocatello who had three television sets on in the hope of getting news of the fighting. Dougherty had a huge battle map installed in the front room, next to the fireplace. But news from the various fronts was scattered. It was a harmless pastime. Grady's men among the Minutemen kept him informed. There was guerrilla warfare going on across much of the Southwest but casualties were low. Except at Gila Bend, Arizona, where a band of Latinos had emerged from the back of a semi and wiped out the Minutemen who had retreated to that city.

Grady wished now that they had stayed on the border. He did not like being above the fray, subjected to the enthusiasms of Dougherty and Morgan's assumption that he was in the inner circle. If chaos had been the purpose of the theft, the goal had been reached, but public outrage had yet to translate into the kind of action that would close the border definitively. Through network telephone he expressed his dissatisfaction with Gunther's efforts.

"Introduce a war resolution, Senator."

Silence. "How much do you know of the way the Senate works?"

"I am counting on you knowing."

"How are things really going?" the senator asked.

"On schedule."

"Meaning what?"

"Meaning that we have reached the point where the goddamn government has to get off its duff and defend the border."

"I'm working on the governors down there. They can call up the National Guard on their own authority."

Grady could see now that he should have gotten ironclad assurances from Gunther before the event. He had not expected this shilly-shallying; he had counted on a bipartisan reaction and swift retaliation, in the manner of the immediate aftermath of 9/11. That hadn't happened. He still held the ace of spades, the stolen picture, but where were the other players?

It was time to issue a statement.

❖

In the headquarters of Justicia y Paz in Los Angeles, the statement from the head of the Rough Riders had everybody jumping. Grady had announced that if the Mexican and American governments didn't move immediately to shut down the border he could no longer guarantee the safety of the picture of Our Lady of Guadalupe that had miraculously appeared on the cape of Juan Diego when he brought it filled with unseasonable roses as proof to the archbishop.

Miguel Arroyo tried to convince his staff that Grady's statement was just a psychological ploy. Suarez, who hadn't been inside a church in years, swore that he would track down Grady and kill the son of a bitch if it was the last thing he did.

Madelena assured him that Our Lady would strike Grady dead if he harmed her portrait.

"The way she did when he stole it?" Suarez asked.

Arroyo retreated to his office. Fiery as he was in his public statements, his calmness when the cameras were not on him had begun to annoy his companions in Justicia y Paz. Grady's statement had been an inspired stroke, no doubt of that. The question was, what effect would it have? Arroyo slipped away from the building and headed north. On an impulse, he stopped off at Palo Alto.

❖

George Worth's accusation was more in his expression than in his quietly spoken words.

"You have blood on your hands, Miguel. You must stop this."

Did George really think that he or anyone else was in con-

trol of the guerrilla bands who were harassing the Minutemen
and in turn being harassed by Anglo volunteers arriving
daily?

"I did not produce their outrage."

"You called them to arms."

In the Catholic Worker house, things went on as they always did. The defeated pushing their trays along the soup line,
come to be fed, come for a place to sleep. Food for now and a
bed for tonight. Beyond that their vacant eyes could not see.
How could George stand it, being around such losers? Miguel
took some satisfaction in the fact that most of the derelicts
were Anglos. No wonder Clare had fled the place. George was
someone you could admire from afar, but to work at his side
required the same devotion he had. Miguel had heard the
explanation. These derelicts were in effect Christ in disguise.
Well, God bless him, but Miguel felt the same way Clare had.
Let George do it.

"Has Clare come back?"

George looked at him, turned away, shook his head.

Miguel had asked the question in order to hurt George. Or
maybe just to see how much he missed the beautiful daughter
of Don Ibanez. He wished now he hadn't asked.

He continued north and on the way he thought of Clare
Ibanez. Don Ibanez regarded him as a rabble-rouser, Miguel
knew that. He understood it. It was obvious that the old man
considered the way he lived sufficient victory for the moment.
And of course his basilica meant more to him now than ever.
He did share Miguel's conviction that this state and many
others had been unjustly occupied for centuries by the foreign
government in far-off Washington, D.C. Latinos were treated
worse than blacks; they were treated as badly by blacks as by
Anglos. Worse, they were treated as invaders, illegal aliens.
But they or those whose blood ran in their veins had settled
these lands. They had far more right to them than the Jews who
insisted that the state of Israel had biblical warrant to their
land. Don Ibanez, it turned out, took the long view.

The old man had patiently laid out the forecasts of the
National Policy Institute and the polls of the Pew Research
Center.

"Young man, by midcentury, there will be 127 million of us

in this country. And the population of Mexico will reach 130 million. Sheer numbers will decide the issue. Anglos do not breed. They kill their unborn children. They have become sensualists. Justice will be done peacefully, no need to fire a shot."

"And we'll be dead by then."

"Not you."

What the old man suggested seemed like a version of Montezuma's revenge. Miguel didn't doubt those projections, but he didn't quite believe in them either. How often had such visions of the future been thwarted by unforeseen events? The present uproar would put the fear of God into Anglos, but then what? In public harangues, he suggested that what Don Ibanez thought would be settled by the silent swelling of the Latino population could be had now. He wished he believed that. But he had his own projections.

❖

Clare was still a wounded bird, ashamed of herself because she could not share the squalor of the Catholic Worker house with George Worth. That would pass, he was sure of it. Miguel had been all but overwhelmed by the peaceful affluence of the Ibanez hacienda, the grounds, the miles and miles of vineyards. That was a future Miguel could understand, not that he thought that everyone would end up in such a hacienda and with such extensive holdings. It was best not to think of the political corruption of Mexico extending over the Southwest. Had Don Ibanez given any thought to what Latino dominance might mean? A nearer and surer future had become Miguel's aim.

By marrying Clare he would immediately come into possession of all that the generations of the Ibanez family had acquired. What a headquarters for Justicia y Paz that vast estate in Napa Valley would be. Or he could turn the organization over to Suarez and cast blessings on the effort from an affluent distance. He had little doubt that he could, eventually, win the love of Clare Ibanez. But a first condition of that would have to be getting that picture back to the basilica in Mexico City. Until that happy day, he could not woo her. Nonetheless, the absence of the picture from its shrine had to continue. The one thing Miguel dreaded was that Theophilus Grady would disclose the secret alliance between the Rough Riders and Justicia y Paz. Between Grady and Miguel would be more accurate. None of their followers knew of it. Without Grady's help the movement of the picture from the basilica in Mexico City would not have been possible.

※

Lulu shook Neal Admirari awake, pointing at the television where the statement of Theophilus Grady was being read by a fatuous television reporter, seated on a stool, legs crossed, her skirt up to her hips, the golden hair a sprayed cloud about her empty head. She might have been reading of a wedding, a plane crash, the birth of quintuplets in Peru, anything, and the same manic smile would carry her through.

"Maybe it will work," Neal said, smacking his dry mouth and looking around for a glass of water.

"Do you know you do that in your sleep?"

"What?"

She tried to make the same sound, but she had been up for an hour, brushed her teeth, had a cup of coffee.

"How would I know, if I'm asleep?"

"Neal, what are we doing in California?"

"Making noises in the night."

But he took her point. The trouble with this story was that it was everywhere and nowhere. Grady spoke as if from a cloud, politicians from Washington, Miguel Arroyo from L.A. Grady was the story, but where in hell was he?

After a quick breakfast—he didn't want to spoil his appetite for lunch—Neal put through a call to Empedocles. No answer. He looked at his watch. No wonder. He would try again after lunch.

In the dining room Lulu had a glass of juice in her hand and sat frowning over it. "What doesn't make sense, Neal, is the claim of the ransom."

He nodded and went on eating.

"Once Grady lets go of the picture, he has no more leverage."

"Does he have it?"

Lulu thought about that. Grady didn't have to have the picture in order to use it for his own purposes, as he had. Did even

Grady have the guts to tell a lie like that? If he didn't have the picture, *someone* did. They would not like the swashbuckling head of the Rough Riders stealing their thunder.

"Maybe that's why he went into hiding."

"*Someone* contacted Hannan and wants the reward."

"That's what I want to check on with Ray Whipple."

But Ray Whipple was on his way west when Neal got through to Empedocles. Could he speak to Mr. Hannan? The answer, as he had expected, was no. No doubt the zillionaire was counting his money. Could he contact Whipple in the plane? Another refusal.

He finished breakfast and rose. "We're going to the airport."

"Los Angeles?" she wailed.

"No. Oakland."

❖

Ignatius Hannan was not counting his money. If he had, he would be a million short. Ray and Laura had taken that amount to California. As soon as the deal went through, they would call him and he would be with them within hours. He felt he was owed at least a look at what he was paying for before it was returned to Mexico City. Meanwhile, he went out to the grotto and said a rosary for the success of the mission Laura and Ray were on.

❖ X ❖

"Anything wrong?"

Morgan sounded offended when Traeger told him the money would be his as soon as they had authenticated that they were getting what they paid for.

"How are you going to do that? You don't get it until I get the money."

"We can do it on the spot."

"You're not bringing others with you!"

"Don Ibanez will know whether it's the real thing."

"Don Ibanez? Isn't he ancient?"

"Not as ancient as the picture you stole."

"Traeger, all this has to be very, very carefully managed. You realize I'm putting my life on the line."

"Just a public-spirited citizen."

"Within the next twenty-four hours, okay?"

Traeger told him maybe less. Don Ibanez wanted to know if he could trust the man. No need to tell the old man Morgan's background. What did he know of Traeger, after all?

When the call came from Ray Whipple, en route, Traeger called the altered cell phone number he had finally pried from Morgan.

"Is it worth a million dollars to you?"

Reluctantly, Morgan gave it to him. But now, when he called it, Traeger found himself talking with Gladys, the flirty sexagenarian at the abandoned Rough Riders headquarters.

"Is this Mr. Traeger?"

"Ah, you remember."

"Oh, I never forget a handsome face. You're calling about Mr. Morgan."

"Who's Mr. Morgan?"

"If you hold, I will connect you with his cell phone."

While he waited, he told himself that Morgan would be a fool not to take precautions. After all, he was double-crossing Grady. Odd that he would trust Gladys. And then Morgan came on.

"Do we have a deal?" he asked without preamble.

"The San Francisco airport."

"Not Oakland?"

"In long-term parking."

"Not private aviation?"

"Do you have it?"

"I'll be there."

"Within the hour." He hung up. Morgan sounded nervous. Traeger didn't blame him. Transfers were always tricky, and for everyone involved. Again, he thought of the rooftop of the North American College in Rome. And of Dortmund's reminder. *Watch your back.*

Crosby went on ahead in his rental car; he would play backup and witness to the exchange, from a distance. That was all right with Crosby.

Traeger went off in Don Ibanez's car, himself at the wheel.

He didn't want the old man's driver involved in this. Tomas didn't like it. Here he was all done up in his uniform and told he wasn't wanted. He could brood in his apartment over the garages. Beside him, Don Ibanez sat in silence, but his lips were moving. In prayer? They might need them.

✧

The Empedocles jet came in with Dodger Stadium in view below them, a game in progress. Ray tried to remember how long it had been since he had seen a baseball game live. He repeated that aloud.

"You could scarcely see one dead," Laura said.

Jack Smiley, the pilot, had suggested that he put the suitcase in the baggage compartment, but Ray did not want to let it out of his sight. And Laura kept her large shoulder bag with her. It seemed to Ray that a million dollars should have required a larger suitcase. It was strapped into the seat beside him; Laura sat ahead. If everything went according to Traeger's and Crosby's arrangements, their business would be done within the hour.

While Smiley taxied the plane toward the tower for private aircraft, Ray kept his eye on the parking lots they passed. Then he called out to the pilot.

"We're going to get out here, Smiley."

"I can't do that."

"Sure you can. Mr. Hannan's orders."

"He didn't give me any such orders."

"Do it," Laura said, politely, firmly.

The plane slowed to a stop. Brenda Steltz, the copilot, came back and opened the door and let down the steps. Ray went first, a good grip on the suitcase, and gave a hand to Laura. The pilot looked as if he would like to cry. As soon as they were on the concrete and Steltz had closed the door, the plane moved away.

As if they were getting out of a helicopter, they lowered their heads and hurried toward the parking area.

✧

At the entrance to long-term parking, Traeger lowered the window, punched a button, and took the ticket. He slipped it under the sun visor on his side of the car. And then he moved slowly

ahead, looking for some sign of Morgan. He saw the Empedocles plane come to a stop on the runway and two figures get
out. Laura and Ray, Ray with a suitcase. So far so good. He
stopped and waited for Hannan's two assistants, then got out
of the car and went toward them. The trouble was that there
was a steel fence between them.

Traeger said, "I'll put that in the trunk of Don Ibanez's car."

"No, that's okay."

Traeger held out his hand and waited. Laura said, "Give it
to him, Ray."

Whipple reluctantly hoisted the suitcase over the fence.

"Just follow the fence and you'll find the entrance."

He turned, punched the key he held, and popped the trunk.
In went the suitcase. He slammed the trunk door down and got
behind the wheel again.

"Those are Hannan's people," he told the old man.

"And that was the money you put in the trunk?"

Traeger nodded, and once more drove slowly forward. He
went up one aisle and down another but there was no sign of
Morgan. Then he noticed the car with the trunk lid up. A convertible with its roof in place. He went by it, went further down
the row, then pulled into an empty space.

"Wait here," he said to Don Ibanez.

For answer, the old man opened his door and stepped out.
Traeger didn't like it. Because he didn't like the look of that
open trunk of the car twenty-five yards away. He got out his
weapon and advanced on the car. When he got to it, he looked
into the empty trunk. He closed it and that was when he noticed the man behind the wheel.

He motioned to Don Ibanez to stay where he was, then
moved carefully along the side of the car. The man at the wheel
was Morgan. He was dead.

Where the hell was Crosby? Traeger went back to the old
man and then Laura and Ray Whipple came running up to him.

"Anything wrong?"

Traeger nodded at the man behind the wheel and Whipple
went forward and looked in. He actually tapped on the window. Laura had a look, too, but she seemed to know immediately the man was dead.

"Looks like you saved a million dollars," Traeger said.

He got no answer when he called Crosby. They could have left then, leaving Morgan to be discovered by some poor passenger when he came to get his car. Traeger called 911 and reported a dead man in a parked car in the long-term lot at the San Francisco airport. There was no point in not waiting for the police to come. Don Ibanez said he would wait in his car. He walked slowly off. Laura was trying not to look at the body behind the wheel. Ray was wondering if they should stick around. Don Ibanez rejoined them, looking disturbed.

No wonder. Someone had jimmied open the trunk of Don Ibanez's car. Traeger and Ray ran to it, then stood side by side looking into its empty depths. Ray looked at Traeger.

"Nice going, Traeger."

CHAPTER THREE

❖ I ❖

"Got another?"

Without Don Ibanez's patrician presence the next hour in long-term parking at the San Francisco airport would have been more difficult than it was. Laura and Ray Whipple got out of there—no need for them to stay—and off they went to wait for Ignatius Hannan across the field at private aviation. *Nice going, Traeger,* Whipple had muttered to him when, side by side, they looked into the empty trunk of Don Ibanez's car. Whipple could not think worse of Traeger than Traeger did himself. There were moments, after Laura and Ray left, when Traeger thought he and Don Ibanez should skedaddle, too. Imagine explaining what had happened. The dead man? I believe he's connected with the Rough Riders. Yes, the group that outraged Latin America and stirred up what has come to be called Desert War III. Of course the irreplaceable image of the Virgin of Guadalupe, recently stolen from its shrine in Mexico City, is also missing. And Ignatius Hannan had shelled out a million dollars in exchange for exactly nothing. Outside of that, Officer, have a nice day.

As it happened, none of these annoying details had to be gone into. Don Ibanez was at the complete and unhurried disposal of the homicide officers who arrived on the scene, while at the same time suggesting that he had much to do elsewhere. The two detectives, one with a crew cut fringe and a large natural tonsure, the other looking as if he could smell the body, were deferential to Don Ibanez. The first time the old man referred to Traeger as his driver had been irksome, but then he accepted the role and got lost in it. Let the old man explain how, having parked and started toward the shuttle bus station with his driver, on their way to the terminal, they had noticed the trunk door open and the man behind the wheel. What citizen would not have sounded the alarm? Well, the officers knew the rest.

"The trunk of the car was open?" The crew cut looked surprised, then thought better of it.

"It was." He turned to Traeger. "Was it not, Vincent?"

"Yes, sir."

"You closed it? Why?" the tonsured one asked.

"I asked Vincent to close it, yes. Sometimes people, in their anxiety to catch a plane, leave the motor of their car running."

Traeger could see the wheels turning in the investigators' heads. A gangland-type killing; whatever they were after—no doubt drugs—in the trunk. Things fall into categories, crimes into types.

As to what had happened to Don Ibanez's car, the jimmying of the trunk and the disappearance of a suitcase containing a million dollars in reasonably small bills—no need to complicate the investigation.

Don Ibanez gave them his card, indicating where he could be reached if for any reason he could be of further assistance.

"Your driver there, too?" the detective with the wrinkled nose asked.

"Of course."

A little salute. Don Ibanez bowed slightly. "Come, Vincent."

At the car, Traeger held open the back door while Don Ibanez got in. When he was behind the wheel the voice from the backseat asked, "Your name is Vincent, is it not?"

"Yes, sir."

"Now, now."

❖

When they got to the private aviation area, Ray told them—actually he addressed Don Ibanez—that Mr. Hannan was due in an hour. He and Laura of course would meet his plane. Don Ibanez said that he, too, would wait, apparently leaving Traeger with an option. He didn't take it. But where in hell was Crosby? Laura put the same question to him when she joined him where he had gone to make the call.

"Crosby doesn't answer his cell phone."

"Good Lord, I hope nothing has happened to him."

The thought had occurred to Traeger. With one dead body, a priceless religious object, and a suitcase with a million dollars in it, the setting was, as Dortmund might put it, fraught with danger. He did not encourage her fears, not least because Laura's expression was the one she had been wearing when he insisted that Ray Whipple hand the money to him over the fence. Laura went back to her husband. Traeger imagined what the two of them might very well think: he and Crosby had staged the whole thing and Crosby had gone off with the loot to their eventual rendezvous, where they would open the suitcase and run their hands through a cool million dollars. After all, who else knew about that money?

Anyone in the parking lot could have seen Whipple pass the suitcase over the fence to him and then put it into the trunk of Don Ibanez's car. Crosby, the one presumed witness; Crosby, who was to monitor the transaction and come swiftly to the scene if anything went wrong—had Crosby, like Morgan, decided to sell his soul? Traeger couldn't believe it. Morgan must have had his own Crosby on the scene. Maybe the treacherous Morgan had in turn been betrayed. Stewing in the little terminal of private aviation, Traeger wished that he had made another tour of that parking lot before leaving. Was Crosby, like Morgan, sitting dead at the wheel of his car, or crumpled on the blacktop awaiting discovery?

Ray Whipple avoided him. Well, Traeger wasn't anxious to talk to him either. *Nice going*. He might very well say more now that the loss of that money had really sunk in. Don Ibanez sat, eyes closed, the picture of a man without a worry in the world. But the old man had to feel a million times worse than Ray Whipple. What was a suitcase full of money compared with the miraculous image of the Virgin?

Traeger went outside for a cigarette. Smoking is dangerous to your health. What isn't? Think of all the nonsmokers he had known, men younger than himself, who were now dead. They might as well have lit up while they had the chance. Laura joined him.

"Got another?"

He passed the package to her, then lit her cigarette.

"Cigarettes always smell so nice when someone else is smoking them."

"How will Hannan take this?"

"Don't worry about it."

"Me, worry?" He tried unsuccessfully for an Alfred E. Neuman look. He did not want to think how he would explain this to Boswell. Or to Dortmund.

Laura pointed to Hannan's plane as it landed and then taxied to where they were waiting. Don Ibanez rose slowly and stood for a moment, as if composing himself.

"I will, of course, recompense Mr. Hannan for his loss."

Laura shook her head and laid a hand on his arm.

Hannan, in shirtsleeves, his suit jacket slung over his shoulder, moved swiftly toward the terminal and came inside in a rush of air.

"How'd it go?"

So they hadn't told him en route about the screwup. Ray Whipple, as if he had been rehearsing the tale, brought his employer up to date.

"You didn't get it?"

Don Ibanez came forward, and the two men shook hands. It was the failure to retrieve the sacred image that depressed Ignatius Hannan. Again, Don Ibanez said that he would replace the lost money.

"I just hope they wear Ray's size," Laura said.

The two men looked at her. Traeger, who had been keeping to the edge of the reunion, came forward. Laura hitched her shoulder bag higher and smiled at Hannan. Traeger, unable to stop himself, came up to her and pulled open the shoulder bag. It was full of money.

"You tricked them." He could not keep the admiration out of his voice. He felt only half as stupid as he had before.

"Not intentionally."

Their instructions had been to exchange the money for the image. At Traeger's insistence, Ray had handed his suitcase over the fence. But it turned out that he, too, thought it contained the ransom money.

"That was my idea, Ray," Hannan said. "Always divert the man with whom you are negotiating."

So Ignatius Hannan was not out a million dollars. Nor Don Ibanez either, if he would have insisted on recompensing Hannan's loss. But what Ignatius Hannan had wanted was the return of the miraculous image.

"We don't know where Crosby is."

Hannan's nose moved like a rabbit's. "You smell of smoke."

Traeger began to tell Hannan of the arrangements he had made with Crosby.

"Don't worry about Crosby," the zillionaire said. "I need something to eat."

"You must all be my guests," said Don Ibanez.

✣ II ✣

"Where exactly are you now?"

Crosby had arrived early, found a spot in long-term parking, lit a cigar, and waited. Planes landed at regular intervals, and others at less regular intervals took off. Being the backup man had its advantages, providing a few stolen moments of leisure. He and Traeger made an odd team, not that Traeger had wanted a team, but why should two men on the same assignment not pool their resources? Of course he had checked with Dortmund to make certain they were on the same assignment. You never knew with Traeger.

"Ignatius Hannan could not have made a better choice," Dortmund had purred over the phone.

"Traeger was his first choice."

"Only because Traeger had worked for him before."

In the course of the conversation, Dortmund had voiced his usual admonition. "Watch your back." They had kidded about such caution, calling him Rearview Dortmund, but it remained sound advice. Crosby smiled, remembering how Traeger, even though watching his back, had failed to notice Crosby on his tail as he whisked along the interstate. Of course he had his eye on another tail and Crosby had admired the way Traeger had shaken it. He himself just waited by Traeger's car, certain he would come back for it, and so he had. Crosby's smile faded. And then Traeger had given him the slip. Was Traeger still under surveillance by those who had called him back into action? Not that Traeger had been all that reluctant.

"You still in computers?" Crosby had asked. What had once been largely Traeger's cover had become his job after retirement from the Company.

"I sold the business," Traeger said.

That was all. But Dortmund had told him how Traeger had lost his secretary on his last assignment. How much violence all of them had stowed away in their memories.

A car pulled into an opening several rows over. No one got out. Crosby lifted his binoculars and Morgan leapt into view. The show was about to begin. Crosby rolled down the window and pitched his cigar.

Suddenly two men appeared, one on either side of Morgan's car. They were armed. Crosby sat forward, holding his breath. There was always the unexpected happening that changed all plans, and this was one of them. The back door of Morgan's car was pulled open and one of the men ducked in. Then the trunk popped. The second man, having checked it out, rapped on the roof of the car. *Pfft*. The sound of a gun with a silencer on it is distinctive, once heard never forgotten. Morgan fell forward. Busy with his glasses, Crosby imprinted the two men on his memory. Both of them were behind the car now, wrestling something out of it. They moved swiftly with the cumbersome object toward a vehicle down the row. A Hummer. Huge. Crosby, who had started his motor when he heard the *pfft* that had removed Morgan from this vale of tears, backed out of his space and followed.

As the Hummer cleared the airport and headed north, Crosby was about to notify Traeger what was going on. He decided to wait. What he had just witnessed might have been some part of the plan Traeger had not confided to him.

Up the coastal road and then a turn, taking them east, over the mountains and lesser hills and then into the wide-open spaces, eventually the desert. Fortunately, the Hummer used more gas than Crosby's rental and stopped several times to refill its tank. Crosby pulled in behind and kept a safe distance away.

The men took turns going to the john, and Crosby studied their magnified faces with his binoculars. He was sure he did not know them. Meaning, he was satisfied that they were not in the Company. He amended that. They had not been in it in his and Traeger's time. Back in the Hummer and off again, ever eastward. Where the hell were they going? Crosby was not only hungry but his bladder was sending him urgent signals. At the truck stops where the Hummer tanked up he had not wanted to risk going inside because one of the men would be in there and when he came out the Hummer would soon be on its way.

During the drive he had time to think. Morgan had been hooked up with Theophilus Grady and his Rough Riders. Grady had publicly claimed responsibility for the theft of the sacred image from the basilica in Mexico City. Morgan had tried to pull a double cross on Grady and market the picture for a cool million. It seemed obvious that those who had thwarted his plans were in the Rough Riders. And they were bringing the recovered treasure with them. So it looked as if Crosby would learn where Grady was holed up. He saw no reason now why he shouldn't check in with Traeger.

"Where were you when the shit hit the fan?" Traeger demanded.

"What are you talking about?"

"Someone got to Morgan before we did."

"I know. I saw it happen."

A pause. "You saw them empty the trunk? Morgan's trunk."

"I am on their tail right now. So what else happened?"

"The whole plan blew up when we found Morgan dead."

Traeger wanted details on what Crosby had witnessed. "Have you got the plate number of that Hummer?"

Crosby read it to him.

"Where exactly are you now?"

"We're going east on I-80. Reno is just ahead."

"Rough Riders?"

"That's my guess."

"If I knew where you were going I'd meet you there. They've got what we're after."

"I'm not going to try to get it back alone."

"Of course not. Once you're there, wherever *there* is, I'll join you."

"Good."

"And Crosby? Watch your back."

"Why, what's it doing?"

Crosby had been watching his back. There had been one false alarm, when he was certain a car was keeping with him, but it was too obvious, and soon the car pulled into an oasis and was seen no more. Crosby went back to admiring the country through which he was driving.

Once, years ago, he and Lucille had packed up the kids and just driven for two months, going all the way to the coast, the southern route on the way west, the northern going home. He remembered coming off the desert into Gila Bend with more than a sense of relief. The wasteland behind them was deserted; they almost never saw another car; the sun was merciless. It was a stretch of highway better driven at night, but once he had gotten under way, there seemed nothing to do but go on. And on he had gone. Lucille fell silent; even the kids in the back of the van settled down. The tension they had all been under became clear when they greeted their arrival at Gila Bend with a cheer.

It must have been a hundred in the shade, but a kid wearing just jeans was painting the overhang of the motel into which Crosby had pulled with his family. They were all into the pool five minutes after he registered, romping in the tepid water. What memories he had of that trip, and of so many other moments with his family. The kids were all grown now; there would be no more such family trips. He wished he could share these memories with Lucille. God, how he missed her. It occurred to Crosby that Traeger had no family. That was probably the best way, given the work they were in, but Crosby could not have borne the danger if he had not known that he would be returning to Lucille and the children.

Hours later, at Salt Lake City, the Hummer turned north

onto I-15. On the roadside signs the distance to Pocatello was given.

Ten miles out of Salt Lake he noticed the Hummer behind him, as huge as the one ahead. After another twenty miles, he was sure that second Hummer was following him. He put through a call to Traeger and told him what was happening.

"You're south of Pocatello?"

Crosby gave him the mileage.

"I'm on my way."

✣ III ✣

"Palo Alto, Palo Alto."

Emilio Sapienza, bishop of Santa Ana in Orange County, in moments of levity said that he was prelate of Disneyland and Busch Gardens; but usually he was serious, perhaps too serious. He disdained the insignia of office, wearing a red zucchetto only with reluctance, and then with a black cassock that looked as if he had had it from his seminary days. He preached the preferential option for the poor and, more surprisingly for a bishop, lived it. He was forever wandering around the farmers' markets in his diocese, haunting the barrios, speaking the Castilian that was almost unintelligible to Latinos. His one vanity was to think that, when his seventy-fifth birthday came in a few weeks, the Vatican would refuse his pro forma letter of resignation. He had miles to go before he slept, as the poet said, but which poet he, like Bertie Wooster, would not know, and he had no Jeeves to enlighten him. Whenever George Worth came to see him, Sapienza would shake his head and murmur, "Palo Alto, Palo Alto." He had wanted the Catholic Worker house located in his diocese and had never forgiven Worth for establishing it in Palo Alto.

"I began it when I was a student at Stanford."

"Start another here, George."

"One is more than I can handle."

Bishop Sapienza's unvoiced dream was that, if the Vatican did accept his resignation, he would found a Catholic Worker house in Santa Ana and live out his remaining years doing what George Worth did.

Like George, he had deep reservations about Miguel Arroyo. As far as Sapienza was concerned, hungering and thirsting for justice was a lifetime occupation, an objective attainable in the next world, not in this. Justicia y Paz seemed to think that justice was just around the corner and that it needed prompting by less than peaceful means. Not that Miguel himself had taken up arms against the Minutemen on the border. Already, Sapienza had officiated at several funerals of young men who had gone out to the desert to fight and come home in body bags. He blamed Miguel for that; Miguel who had sounded a call to arms and dramatically declared that California had seceded from the Union. The man was a romantic, a dangerous romantic.

"And all this over a stolen image."

George looked shocked. "It's hardly just another image."

Sapienza conceded this. But if one wanted instances of the desecration of the sacred, think of all the offenses against Our Lord in the Holy Eucharist.

"The people are so deeply devoted to Our Lady of Guadalupe."

"So am I, so am I. But I wouldn't go about shooting people for her sake."

"Neither would Miguel."

The two men commiserated with each other for an hour and then George headed for home.

"Palo Alto, Palo Alto," Sapienza called after him, a blessing, a curse, or just a joke told too often. But it could have been relief that George had left before the scheduled arrival of Neal Admirari. Lulu was with him, and it was the first Sapienza had heard of their marriage.

"Oh, we've been married in petto for years," Neal said breezily.

"I won't ask what that means."

Lulu said, "Never ask a wordsmith what he means."

"I will say you both look happy."

Somewhat to his surprise, Lulu dropped to her knees, tugging Neal down beside her, and asked for his blessing.

"You have been married, in the Church, haven't you?" he

asked in alarm. Sometimes people interpreted his lifestyle as a disdain for all the rules.

"No, in San Diego."

"That's close enough." And he raised his unringed hand in blessing over them. Lulu had to help Neal to his feet afterward. Sapienza could not have said why he liked these two, particularly Lulu. His dislike for journalists had been fed during his unhappy years in Washington, working in the Taj Mahal a block from the National Shrine of the Immaculate Conception. He hoped this wasn't because Lulu had written flattering portraits of him, especially since he had come to Santa Ana. Neal pretended to think that the town was named for a general.

"I think it was the other way around."

"You could rename it for General Arroyo."

Sapienza rolled his eyes. He had hoped that subject had left with George Worth, but after all these two were journalists and the theft from the basilica in Mexico City continued to be the central item in the news of the day, along with accounts of the guerrilla battles in the Southwest mountains and desert. But it was the mystifying presence of Don Ibanez in the long-term parking lot in San Francisco that the two had on their minds.

"It turns out that the man who was killed was a former CIA agent."

Lulu added, "It looks like a botched attempt to regain the image. Ignatius Hannan was there, too, with his staff."

"The dead agent was associated with Theophilus Grady."

"Hannan is offering a million dollars ransom for the image."

But it was the presence of Don Ibanez that intrigued Sapienza.

"And how does Don Ibanez explain his presence?"

"Who knows? He is incognito in his hacienda."

Sapienza had visited there; he had been given the grand tour; he had stood nonplussed in the replica of the basilica, trying not to think of what the money that had gone into it might have done for the poor in his diocese. Don Ibanez seemed to read his thoughts. Sapienza left with a sizeable check.

"And Vincent Traeger was there, too. Posing as Don Ibanez's chauffeur."

"Traeger?"

"Another former CIA agent. Hannan has hired him before."

"It sounds as if you have all kinds of leads to pursue." He might have been asking why they had come to him.

"We thought you could intervene for us with Don Ibanez."

"I scarcely know the man."

"He thinks the world of you."

Sometimes it was difficult not to take pleasure in such praise, culpable pleasure, he was sure. His great fear was that he was a showboat like Miguel Arroyo, drawing attention to himself by trying not to draw attention to himself. Several other bishops had followed his example and abandoned the episcopal regalia except on liturgical occasions. His first reaction had told him what others must think of him. Look, Ma, I'm simple.

"And how would I persuade him. If I tried?"

"Lowry, the cook at the Catholic Worker, suspects that Don Ibanez knows where the stolen portrait is."

George was lucky to have such a man in Palo Alto. Ah, the conversations he'd had with Lowry. Lowry, having returned to the faith of his youth after years as a communist, had seemingly lost forever the deference laity paid to the clergy, especially to bishops.

"Will you take up tent making, too?" Lowry screwed his vile pipe into the corner of his mouth.

"Only after I've survived a shipwreck or two."

But Lowry's remark had linked Sapienza to Saint Paul, to the first generation of bishops, the apostles, whom bishops down the ages descended from.

Now, in answer to the two reporters, Sapienza said he didn't have time or leisure to make a trip to Napa Valley.

"You could do it with a phone call."

As if to prove them wrong, Sapienza consulted a Rolodex and then rang the number of the hacienda. The daughter, Clare, answered. She had come to Sapienza when she had decided against staying on with George at the Catholic Worker. She would be better off in a convent. He agreed that such poverty was not for her. But even as he said it, he doubted that she would long take comfort from his endorsement of her decision. The real problem was her feeling for George Worth. So much for the convent.

"Oh, Bishop, he's not here just now. Is there anything I can do?"

"Just ask him to return my call. There's no rush."

Lulu and Neal hadn't liked that addendum, but still they thanked him. He watched them go out to their car, holding the slip of paper on which Lulu had written the number of her cell phone. He was to call them as soon as he heard from Don Ibanez.

Meanwhile, he drove to Palo Alto to have a talk with Lowry.

❖ IV ❖

"Where would you hide a book?"

Theophilus Grady stood at a picture window that provided a magnificent view he did not see, thumbs hooked in his holsters, pondering the news from San Francisco. Morgan, it was clear, was a traitor, but then Grady had known that for some time, thanks to Gladys Stone. He had yet to hear from the teams he had sent to shadow Morgan. He felt surrounded by people he could not trust, but distrust is the bane of the vigilante. Vigilantes by definition work outside the law, their sense of loyalty in escrow, so how could they be expected to be loyal to their leader? But finally word came. The two Hummers were on their way, and they were bracketing Crosby on the interstate as they came.

Crosby. He had zapped a photo of Crosby to Wortman in the second Hummer, and he made the identification. Grady tried to smile. At least it wasn't Traeger. The photo of Traeger had drawn a blank from Wortman. Traeger had led the squad that had spirited Grady out of Albania. Traeger was real trouble. But Crosby was not much less. It was clear from talking to Wortman in the second Hummer that Crosby had been a witness of what had happened at the San Francisco airport. He did not like to think what that meant for his old comrade. After some thought, he told the Hummer following Crosby to let him come on unmolested. Wortman expressed surprise and disappointment in the response.

"But keep him in view. I want to know exactly where he is once he gets here."

Wortman sounded like a man who did not intend to follow orders.

Some hours later, he was closeted with Ehman, the driver of the first Hummer, the one Crosby had tailed. He listened impatiently. Ehman had no idea how to report; most of it was jabber.

"Do you have it?"

Ehman looked blank.

"What you got from the trunk after you took care of Morgan?"

"That package? Sure, we have it."

"And the money?"

"Wortman has that."

Ehman and those with him seemed to know less about what had happened on the scene in long-term parking than he did. He had kept their tasks separate. He didn't want any of them pulling a Morgan on him. Well, now they knew what happened to traitors.

"We just got the hell out of there when the police arrived."

Did he want to be congratulated?

"Wortman picked up the car that must have followed me out of there."

"Where is he?"

"He should be here any minute."

Ehman knew nothing of the details of missing money that Hannan had put up for the picture. What in hell had Morgan thought he could palm off on them for a cool million? The cunning Arroyo had assured Grady that the image was safe.

"Where?"

"Where would you hide a book?"

Grady waited. Arroyo was a pain in the ass. Revolution makes strange bedfellows.

"In a library!"

Arroyo would say no more. The one thing they had for sure in common was the conviction that that portrait should not be returned to Mexico City, not for a cool million, not for anything. It was, after all, the casus belli. Grady had an informant on Pulaski's staff and knew at least something of what was going on out there. Maybe he should have stayed in place on the border, fought the good fight, as Pulaski and his Minutemen were. That would be a helluva lot better than being squirreled away here, dependent on reports. And relying on asses like Ehman. On the other hand, if they had not decamped, he would have been deprived of that triumphant news conference in El Paso.

So what the hell had happened in San Francisco? Of course he didn't believe a fraction of what he got from the media. He realized that he had been wiser than he knew to allow Crosby to come to where he was. Crosby could give him a better report on what had gone on in the long-term parking lot than Ehman or any of the others. And then, predictably, Mooney, Independent congressman from Arizona, was on the line.

"Congratulations!" cried the congressman.

What the hell did Mooney think had happened?

"It was a bloody mess, sir."

"But you recovered the thing! What if it had been returned? That would have ruined everything."

Despite his gringo name, Mooney was nine-tenths Latino, the darling of his Arizona constituents. He was Grady's vocal support in Washington and, more important, the main conduit through which essential government equipment flowed to the Rough Riders.

No need to enlighten Mooney, even if he could have. The congressman seemed to think that Grady had set the whole thing up, led Morgan into a trap, and got the picture back, as well as the money the zealot Hannan had put up. Not a bad day's work.

"I'd rather be down there with Pulaski."

"Hey, whose side are you on?"

The fact was that Grady could not have answered that question. As in Albania, he was satisfied with wreaking havoc in the unexamined hope that havoc would give rise to something good. Mooney had not liked Grady's press conference remarks in El Paso.

"We've been through that."

After El Paso, in answer to Mooney's objections, Grady had told the congressman that he was playing both ends against the middle. Keep them off balance, that was the thing.

Arroyo, on the other hand, had liked the way Grady took responsibility for what had happened in the basilica in Mexico City. Why wouldn't he? It took him off the hook, unless of course Grady changed his story.

❖

Wortman and those with him had not returned, and Grady was thinking of that bag of money. Crosby, he learned, had checked into a motel on the outskirts of Pocatello after following Ehman to where the road led up to his mountain cabin. Grady would have called it the Eagle's Nest, but he didn't like the connotations.

Having Crosby located gave him time to think of the next step. Sometimes he regretted not having Crosby brought to him right away. On the other hand, he doubted that Crosby would long remain a single threat, and it was important to learn who might join him.

Grady opened the package in the privacy of his bedroom and smiled. Morgan was a dead duck either way, betraying the Rough Riders and trying to palm off a copy of the missing image.

❖ V ❖

"Yo."

There was some comfort to be had from having been in communication with Traeger but Crosby had no illusions about his situation. He was on his own. He had long since driven out of range of immediate help. Traeger's reassuring *I'm on my way* was followed immediately by thoughts about how long that way was. With a Hummer ahead and a Hummer behind, Crosby had a problem, and he braced himself to make his move. But what would be theirs?

Crosby imagined the two huge vehicles forcing him off a bridge or off a mountain road. Or they could hem him in at a rest stop and do it the old-fashioned way. The one he was following had increased its speed. Where the hell were they headed anyway? They had gone through Reno and then Salt

Lake City and were now nearing Pocatello, Idaho. Pocatello. There were some funny names of cities when you came to think of it: Kalamazoo, Baraboo, Kokomo. Crosby's guess was that the Hummers were going to where Theophilus Grady was holed up.

The Hummer following him was closing the gap and Crosby picked up his weapon from the seat beside him, the hand on the wheel tensing. Here it comes. But the Hummer ahead speeded up and its rear lights went out of sight. Crosby let down the window beside him, and there was a roar of wind. The menacing grille of the Hummer came closer, increasing its speed. In the rearview mirror the damnably bright lights of the vehicle suddenly were no longer visible. They were coming alongside, the seemingly little windows high above the rental. Crosby brought his weapon to the open window and shot, first a front tire and then a rear, then stomped on the gas, but not before the Hummer began to lurch and career. His back window went as the Hummer returned fire, the shattering sound unnerving, and the rental was nicked by the Hummer's fender as Crosby shot by, but he kept control. Now in the rearview mirror he could see the vehicle careening, out of control, heading for the drop-off to the right of the road, so deep that the tops of trees seemed like roadside bushes. The driver must have slammed on his brakes because the Hummer went over sideways and, as the interstate curved gently eastward, Crosby saw the Hummer's lights seeming to grope the darkness wildly and then drop out of sight. He rolled up the window. He inhaled. The next breath you take may be your last. In that moment of maximum danger it was as if Lucille and the children had been with him in the car.

One danger past, he could call it off. Between the double lanes at intervals there were linking roads so that maintenance trucks could cross. He could get onto the southbound lanes and just get the hell out of there. Ninety percent of him wanted to do that, but the ten percent dominated. He had not come all this way just to save his own ass. The thought that the peril he was in had been cut in half drove away the fear he had felt when that Hummer pulled alongside him.

The Hummer ahead came into view again. It had begun slowing down as they neared a turnoff called Pueblo. Crosby slowed to a crawl and checked his mirror as if to make sure the other Hummer was truly gone. Watch your back. Letting up more on the gas, to keep the distance between the Hummer and himself, he was down to thirty miles an hour when the Hummer made its turn. Crosby was hardly moving when he made the turn himself, thinking ambush, but then he saw the back lights of the vehicle preceding him up the road. He cut his lights, using those red lights as guides as he closed the gap between them.

Another turn and then they were on a narrow mountain road, dark as a well, except for the three red rear lights ahead. Even the Hummer seemed to proceed cautiously. Crosby pulled over, let down the window beside him, and listened to the mountain wilderness. Through it he could hear the growl of the Hummer still. And then it stopped. Crosby eased onto the road and, headlights still cut, crept forward. He dipped in his shirt pocket for his cell phone and punched redial. Traeger's number.

"Yo."

"Traeger?"

"Where the hell are you?"

That voice bouncing off a satellite and into his ear, gruff, no-nonsense Traeger, made Crosby want to cheer.

"I am south of Pocatello, Idaho, a turnoff marked Pueblo."

"Okay. Why don't you hold everything until I get there?"

Crosby liked the suggestion that he would storm in on his own, invade Grady's hideout, if that was what this was, and round up all the Rough Riders single-handedly.

"How long will that be?" He tried to get reluctance into his voice but couldn't.

❖

Traeger was flying toward Salt Lake in one of the Empedocles planes, guest of the returning Ignatius Hannan, who had gone up front and taken the controls for a half hour before he joined Traeger in the cabin.

"Did you ever fly one of these things?" He was happy as a kid.

"I don't have a license."

"Neither do I." He frowned. "I've never had the time."

"That was lucky about the money."

"Lucky! What a boondoggle."

He glared at Traeger, then relaxed. "I'm not blaming you."

"Good."

"Or Crosby."

"Crosby's a good man."

Hannan accepted that. Maybe a good man was simply one Hannan had hired. But it was clear that the affluent little man took small comfort from having retained the million-dollar ransom. He was probably making that much in interest as they flew.

"We've got to get that image back."

Traeger nodded.

"You're a Catholic, if I remember."

"I would be even if you didn't remember."

Hannan liked the remark. Traeger didn't. Maybe if he was as rich as Hannan and had his own fleet of jets, he would get pious, too, and build a replica of the grotto at Lourdes in his backyard. Not that he doubted the man's sincerity. Once Ray Whipple had told him the theory he and Laura had developed. When Hannan hit fifty, he would divest himself of everything and head for the Trappists at Gethsemani in Kentucky.

"Come on," Traeger had said.

After a moment, Ray said, "You're right. He couldn't keep quiet."

"What's he like?"

"Sui generis."

Traeger waited.

"One of a kind."

"Smoke if you want to," Hannan said now. And then, "I like Don Ibanez."

"Quite a man."

"We let him down."

"He took it well."

And the old man *had* taken it well. The serenity of age? Maybe.

Hannan perked up when the call from Crosby came. Immediately, he went forward. When he came back, he said. "We can land in Pocatello."

They had to wait for a commercial jet before they could

land. Hannan had the pilot pull over to the regular terminal and came inside with Traeger to the rental car counter. Hannan slapped down a credit card. Not a million dollars, but Traeger liked the gesture.

"Be careful," Hannan said.

"I always am." Another remark that Hannan liked and Traeger regretted.

As he headed south, he called Crosby and told him where he was. Crosby mentioned an oasis he had passed just before the turnoff to Pueblo and they agreed to meet there.

⚓

There was a motel at the oasis, and Crosby checked in. The sight of the bed made him realize how tired he was. The stakeout in San Francisco, the long drive, the dangerous moment on the road when he put the Hummer out of commission and watched it plunge into darkness—a full day's work in any man's book. He decided he would just lie down and close his eyes.

He was brought out of a crazy dream in which a dozen Hummers drove across the roofs of cars parked at an airport, he heard again the shattering of the back window of his rental car, saw the menacing bulk of the Hummer loom beside him, both of them going like bats out of hell. The phone was ringing.

"Yes?"

"Traeger."

"You're here."

"There's a bar. Let's meet there."

It was a low-ceilinged place, with pecky cypress walls, beer signs flashing in the windows, tables, booths, two or three silent drinkers at the bar. They shook hands and headed for a back booth, where they reviewed the day.

"You saw who shot Morgan?"

"I had him in my binoculars. Both of them. Not that it matters."

Traeger waited.

"They've gone to God."

He described the incident on the interstate, and could feel Traeger's approval. What they couldn't figure out was what the hell had gone wrong in long-term parking. The image hadn't been recovered.

"They opened the trunk of Morgan's car."

"And removed something." Crosby paused. "Maybe it was in the Hummer that went off the road."

"Jeez."

They observed a moment's silence, thinking of that precious image consumed by flames when the Hummer finally rolled to a stop.

"You saw flames?"

"No."

They decided they would check out that Hummer in the morning. The waitress came and they ordered draft beer and hamburgers.

"French fries," Traeger added.

"They come with the burger. You want cole slaw, too?"

They wanted cole slaw, too. Crosby felt he could have eaten the table and a chair or two. How long had it been since he ate? Traeger seemed famished, too, and they ate in silence. Then Traeger put in a call to Dortmund. Crosby lit a cigarette and heard one side of the conversation. Mainly Traeger was reporting, telling him of the events of the day, at least as far as he understood them. There was silence then, while he listened. He listened for a long time before he turned off the cell phone.

"He says we should watch our backs."

❧

In the morning, they had a hearty breakfast and then drove into Pocatello to a sporting goods store and got rigged out for the task ahead. Back to the motel then, where they changed into hunters' gear and then set off in Traeger's rental.

"It gets breezy in mine with the back window shot out," Crosby said.

Traeger had examined the damage before they went into Pocatello.

"Jeez."

Now they went up the interstate again, keeping to the lower limit, while other cars shot past them. They found where the Hummer had left the road, crashing through a guardrail and clipping trees as it went. They kept going to the turnoff to

Pueblo and left Traeger's car there. The distance had seemed short in the car, but walking back was another thing.

The descent was precipitous, but it was easy to follow the path the Hummer had taken. Traeger went ahead, which was all right with Crosby. And then they saw it. It had come to rest on its roof. Doors of the vehicle were open. They approached carefully. Traeger, weapon drawn, took one side of the vehicle, Crosby the other. They might have been aiming at one another when they looked across the empty seats.

There was nothing in back either.

"Maybe they were thrown out," Crosby suggested.

But when they stepped back from the Hummer they saw a half dozen men surrounding them, rifles at the ready.

Traeger tried telling them they were just a couple of hunters, but their hand weapons told against that. Reluctantly they turned them over.

"Theophilus Grady is expecting you."

They went single file—Crosby, Traeger, their escorts—and it was not a walk in the park. There was nothing like a path, and the undergrowth between the trees was like the hedgerows in France. The exertion of the steep climbs and then steeper descents kept them silent. What was there to talk about anyway?

"How far is it?" Traeger called back over his shoulder.

"We're halfway there."

Halfway! It was like hearing that you'd gotten half the forty lashes you had coming. It was fifteen minutes later that they heard the roar overhead. An engine. A whir of blades. A helicopter. The column stopped and tried to see it through the tops of trees.

"That's not one of ours," someone said.

It sounded like a Chinook to Crosby. Traeger looked at him but said nothing. Twenty-five yards farther on, they could see the cabin through the trees. The helicopter had landed and there was the sound of gunfire. Their captors were looking at one another.

Traeger said, "Give us our weapons before you go. It looks like we're going to need them."

The handguns were hurled at them and then their escort melted into the trees. Going to help their besieged fellows? Not very likely.

Traeger and Crosby went to earth, lying still and watching the action. One of the black-clad warriors from the helicopter went down and that seemed to galvanize his fellows. There was an assault on the cabin, a bursting inside, more gunfire, then silence. While they watched, a Pontiac with tinted windows arrived.

Crosby and Traeger waited. It was ten minutes more before Theophilus Grady was hustled out the door, trying to retain his dignity as he was pushed toward the helicopter. His holsters were empty.

Twenty minutes later, after the helicopter had lifted off, there was only silence. The car with tinted windows stayed, the house doubtless being searched. Eventually, the driver came out carrying a package as big as he was. He stowed it carefully in the backseat, got behind the wheel, and the car slid away. Crosby looked at Traeger.

"Were they ours?"

"Maybe. The car with the tinted glass? That's the one that followed me out of St. Louis."

Then they went for their car, taking what they thought was a shortcut, which added considerably to the distance. They fell into the car finally, huffing and puffing after the long scramble through the woods, up and down, a helluva hike. Traeger got out his cell phone.

"Dortmund? Traeger."

He listened.

"Thanks a lot."

"He said he tried to warn us, but he had company."

"From the Company?"

"Who else?"

✢ PART II ✢

Holy Hoax

CHAPTER ONE

❖ I ❖

"What are your illusions?"

The arrest of Theophilus Grady was not announced immediately, doubtless so his captors could squeeze out of him where the missing sacred portrait was. If they were surprised at his answer, which he clung to throughout what must have been a pretty rough grueling, it was as nothing compared to the public reaction. No one believed that the head honcho of the Rough Riders did not have the missing portrait of the Virgin of Guadalupe.

"Waterboard the son of a bitch," urged Gunther. "The only thing that will quiet things down is the return of that picture."

Miriam Dickinson, who had inspired the rosary crusade to send up ceaseless prayers so that Our Lady's miraculous portrait would be returned to the shrine in Mexico City, where pilgrims could once more revere it, urged a redoubling of the effort.

From Washington came the announcement that a thorough search of Grady's Idaho hideout had not turned up the missing miraculous image.

As days passed, the awful thought occurred that Grady might be telling the truth. Garbled accounts of the events that had taken place in long-term parking at the San Francisco airport prompted some to think that, while Grady might have had the portrait, it had been seized by someone else. But who?

Working with Jason Phelps, Catherine had noticed the books that kept arriving from Amazon.com, all of them concerned with Juan Diego and his cape. When Juan Diego opened the cape to show the skeptical bishop the unseasonable roses he had gathered at the behest of the Virgin, her image on the cape drove away all doubts. It was that cape, that *tilma*, as it was called, revered for centuries, that had been forcibly taken from the basilica.

"Are you going to write about it?" Catherine asked Jason.

They were on the patio in the evening, sipping margaritas, the great valley spread out below them. Phelps passed a hand over his shock of white hair, sipped his drink, and smiled at her.

"There is no need. It's already been done."

Catherine did not understand. Most of the books that had arrived were devoted to authenticating the legend that had grown up around the miraculous portrait.

"Leoncio Garza-Valdés, a devout Catholic, a medical man, produced a book that went against the grain of his desires. He was like that fellow Weinstein, who set out to exonerate Alger Hiss and was forced to conclude that the man was guilty as charged. His former companions in championing Hiss never forgave him. And so it has been with Garza-Valdés."

"He thinks the portrait is a fake?"

"Oh, many have cast sufficient doubts on the received view of the portrait, and its dating. Garza-Valdés was driven to conclude that Juan Diego himself had never existed."

"And he convinced you?"

"He would convince anyone with an open mind. But an open mind is the last thing you can expect in such matters. I include myself, of course." Another smile, another sip of his margarita. "The supreme test for Garza-Valdés was the fact that John Paul II had canonized Juan Diego. Made a saint of a man who, as Garza-Valdés proved to his own satisfaction, never existed. And yet Garza-Valdés continues to be a Catholic and professes a great devotion to the Blessed Virgin.

But the whole story of the Virgin of Guadalupe is for him a fabrication."

"Then all this commotion over the theft . . ."

"Is ridiculous."

"That book should be translated."

"You think that would make a difference?"

Catherine could not have explained why she felt so elated by what the distinguished old skeptic was saying. It was as if one more safeguard against the temptation that had brought her to Jason Phelps had been removed. The seductive attraction of the faith that had sent Lloyd rushing off to Mexico to do penance for their torrid days in Chicago, the stirring of old memories of piety that she had felt at his funeral, seemed ridiculous indeed in light of what Jason was saying. She pulled her chair closer to his. Ever since they had become lovers, a transition that she regarded as part of her cure, she had come to revere this man. It was not fair to compare her visits to his bed with the passion she had known with Lloyd. With Jason, it was as if he were the beloved and she the lover. Actually, she preferred it that way. And he was tender in his slow and faltering lovemaking. She wouldn't have called it love, but she had gotten less satisfaction from far younger men.

"I wonder if Don Ibanez knows of Garza-Valdés's book."

"Oh, he must."

"Have you discussed it with him?"

"Certainly not. There is a manly simplicity in his devotion. Obviously, it gives him great consolation. None of us can live without illusions."

"What are your illusions?"

"That I am a young man again." He ran his hand over her head, down her arm, and clutched her elbow. She leaned forward and kissed him. How odd it was to feel more mustache than lips.

Catherine wished that Clare were still working on Jason Phelps's papers so that she could talk about all this with the younger woman. Jason might wish to leave Don Ibanez to his delusions, but Catherine would have felt strengthened in her own disbelief if she could reproduce it in Clare.

✤ II ✤

"It's a cozy little hotel."

They seemed like an old married couple when they flew back east, fed up with California and events they kept missing. Neal Admirari reminded himself that he was a columnist, not a reporter, and Lulu wrote for *Commonweal*, a magazine not exactly concerned with the breaking news of the day. Going to El Paso had seemed right at the time, but what difference did being there make to them?

"We should have stayed put."

"Then we wouldn't have married."

He looked at her, his nicely plump, pretty-faced, brand-new wife whose lips widened in a smile. Lulu was in the middle seat, Neal had the window, and the aisle seat was occupied by a kid who couldn't quite get comfortable—iPod plugs in his ears, a vacant look, but always squirming. Whenever he stretched one leg out in the aisle, he had to pull it back to let someone go by. Neal leaned toward Lulu and kissed her nose and the kid turned and stared. Neal smiled at him, invoking the old male camaraderie. The kid frowned and looked away, embarrassed.

"My place or yours?" Lulu asked.

Where they would settle had been their question for a week now. Neal had a loft in the Village. ("The Village!" Lulu was right; it seemed a desperate stab at his disappearing youth, like kissing Lulu on the nose with that kid looking on.) Lulu's apartment was in the Bronx, one he had never seen. She described it.

"We got it for a song."

"We?"

Neal's immediate predecessor. He didn't like the thought of being a replacement for whatshisname, a substitute sent in to play the third quarter.

"Neal, I don't want to live in a bachelor's pad."

"You make it sound more interesting than it is."

"I'll bet."

Neal let it go. If she wanted to think of him as Don Giovanni that was all right with him. It was the thought of all that moving and getting settled again that decided them to leave California and get at it. Neal had the summer place up in Connecticut and they would go there first.

"But I haven't a thing to wear."

"That'll be fine."

Again the smile. She whispered, "It's our anniversary."

She was right. Two weeks since the ceremony in San Diego. He would have kissed her again if it hadn't been for Ichabod with the iPod.

Lulu went back to her book. She was reading up on Our Lady of Guadalupe in search of an idea for an article. Neal settled back, put on his eyeshade, and consulted the darkness as recent events slid past his mind.

The Holy Heist, as the *New York Post* described it, had been the beginning, a handful of masked and armed men raising a ladder, wrenching the framed picture of Mary free, and then shooting their way out of the basilica, killing one American. He smiled. The old joke about the Catholic press. Earthquake in Tahiti, no Catholics killed. Kaiser. Lulu had googled the name. Lloyd Kaiser had been an Indiana author.

"What did he write?"

"History for young adults."

"Come on."

She read him some of the titles. One on Heloise and Abelard, a book on Patrick Henry, another on Henry Adams, yet another on the founding of Notre Dame. That one had hit the jackpot, selling like popcorn in the Notre Dame bookstore, and across the land as alumni bought it for their kids.

"Was Kaiser a graduate of Notre Dame?"

She shook her head. "Indiana. College of Dentistry."

"Come on."

He read the entry himself. Well, lots of people fled boring professions in order to write. Neal himself had once thought of writing a novel—who hadn't?—but it would have been a busman's holiday since he already wrote for a living.

"You should do a piece on him, Lulu."

"One American killed?"

"Hey, that's catchy."

Now he smiled into the darkness created by his eyeshade.

He might do a piece on Lloyd Kaiser himself. He began to compose it. There in the legendary basilica sat the author of popular history for young adults, on the mourning bench by the confessionals. A shot rang out and he leapt to his feet. . . . Neal drifted into sleep.

❖

They had to catch another plane in Chicago, and Neal had trouble getting fully awake. Lulu looked at him with almost maternal concern as they went through a waiting area, on the lookout for a list of departures and their next gate. Neal was yawning. His eyeshade still hung around his neck. He felt like putting it on again and letting Lulu lead him through the crowds.

"Neal, let's stop over. We're in no rush."

"We'll miss our connection."

"That's what I'm suggesting." She saw a passenger service desk for their airline and headed for it. Neal stood sleepily at her side while she arranged for them to fly out the next day, even succeeding in getting their luggage sent to baggage claim. While they waited for the bags to appear, Lulu said, "There's a Hilton over there."

"Uh-uh. Airport hotels are like sleeping in a plane."

So they took a cab downtown, Lulu giving the driver the address of the Whitehall on Delaware. A crowded little lobby, lots of Japanese and German tourists. Neal liked it.

"We always stayed here," Lulu said.

"Ask for the bridal suite." He'd be damned if he'd ask who "we" was this time.

As soon as they got to their room on the seventh floor Neal felt wide awake. The area around the hotel looked interesting.

"Navy Pier is within walking distance," Lulu said. "Or there's a little trolley."

"Were you here on one of your honeymoons?"

She put her arms around him. "I am now."

Later they ate in the restaurant on the street floor and had a drink afterward in the bar. In the lobby the concierge was sending tourists off to the theater. On his desk, in a tray, were newspaper clippings, and Neal was surprised to see that they were of the Holy Heist. He pointed this out to Lulu. When the man was free, Neal took the chair next to his desk and asked if the Cubs were in town. But neither Chicago team was playing in town. Neal had already known that. He picked up one of the clippings from the tray and the concierge looked sheepish.

"It's a little ghoulish, I know. The American who was killed there? He stayed here at the Whitehall just days before the event. He and his wife."

"I'm writing a piece on him." He showed the concierge his credentials.

"Then you already knew." The concierge looked relieved.

"Tell me about them."

The concierge had not really seen much of the couple. Most of his memories seemed to have been prompted by the events in Mexico City. But once they had bought tickets from the concierge.

"They might have been on their honeymoon."

Neal asked the concierge to tell him anything else he remembered, then they were led around to the manager's office. A little fellow with sandy hair and a Slavic face. His nameplate seemed to be missing some vowels.

"Splivic?"

The manager corrected Neal. He let it go, and told his story about doing a column on Lloyd Kaiser and his wife. On the way to the reception counter, Lulu had whispered, "He was a widower."

"Widower than what?"

She was right, yet the concierge had spoken of Kaiser's wife.

With some reluctance, the manager turned to his computer and sought the information Neal had asked for. Would he even be bothering about this if the concierge hadn't mentioned a wife?

Splivic found the records. Would he print them out? More reluctance, but he finally agreed. They sat listening to the printer behind the reception desk clatter away.

"Just Kaiser and his wife?"

The manager looked surprised. "Oh no, he was alone."

They took the printout of the guests registered on the days Kaiser had been in the hotel.

"I thought he was going to be my story," Lulu said.

"You can have the wife."

"Neal, he had no wife. The concierge must be confused."

"Just another guest he got friendly with?"

"It's a cozy little hotel."

On the little trolley taking them to Navy Pier, Neal figured out that Catherine Dolan had to have been Lloyd's companion. Hers was the only woman's name on the register of all the days Lloyd Kaiser had been here.

"Imagine her reaction when she learned he had been killed in the basilica."

"She was from Minneapolis."

Lulu put her arm through his and snuggled closer.

Neal said, "And there is his family."

"Oh, for heaven's sake. You aren't seriously considering writing about the man."

"Of course not."

But as they bumped along, he thought that maybe he would.

❖ III ❖

"Go see her."

The window showed the signs of hurried washing, sun lay on the dusty blades of the blind, a fly buzzed persistently about the room he called his office, and George Worth felt an animal content. Shelves made of bricks and boards contained the few books he had kept for his own, the rest going into the large room for the benefit of guests. The electric typewriter on his desk had once been the very latest marvel of its type, perhaps twenty or thirty years earlier. A Selectric, navy blue, that purred contentedly as his hands hovered over the keyboard. His fingers dropped to the keys and the globe on which the characters were molded danced across the page. Lines formed, no need for the carrier to move.

"A typewriter!" Clare had exclaimed.

He had thought at first she was chiding him for having taken possession of such a wonderful machine. It had been among donated items and from the moment George had seen it he wanted it. His mother had used such a typewriter. He had felt almost guilty as he bore it away to his office. But Clare was reacting to the quaintness of the Selectric. No one used typewriters anymore. His guilty possession was added to the list she seemed to be making of his self-deprivations. He stopped praising the machine when he saw her reaction. Saint George Worth in love with his poverty.

He missed her. He missed everything about her except her way of seeing his life as heroic. When he told her there were times when he, too, wanted to just walk away from it all, to live like everyone else, the way he had been raised, she clearly thought that he was making this up for her sake. Would she believe how rare such moments as this were, the sun on the window, a friendly fly for company, wanting to purr like the Selectric? But his office was his hideout as well as where he worked to keep the house afloat. The small income from the silly science fiction he wrote was often the difference between being able to go on another week or shutting the doors. Benefactors were more likely to bring old clothes and furniture, rarely something like the Selectric, which had replaced his manual typewriter. What asceticism would Clare have been able to imagine if she had seen that portable Underwood?

Of course he did not think his stories were silly when he wrote them. Could any writer disdain what he was actually writing? George doubted it. Hacks must have the same sense of exhilarated creativity as Tolstoy. The magazines that bought his stuff still billed themselves as science fiction publications, but there was no science in what George wrote. It was futurist fantasy, short on hardware, allegories of virtue and vice palatable because they were set in a far-off imaginary land. His favorite setting was the planet Aidos, a light-year or two from Mars, George Worth sole proprietor. The place was prelapsarian; there was an absence of religion except the universal unquestioned reverence for the Being who had brought Aidousians and their planet into existence. Aidos was more than a few light-years from the Catholic Worker house in Palo Alto where he wrote. His current effort, like several that had preceded it, was a veiled version of his love for Clare Ibanez.

He was interrupted by Lowry with news of what had happened outside Pocatello. George sometimes looked at the dated sports page of newspapers that lay around the common room, but that was it; so Lowry, who had retained an insatiable appetite for the trivial happenings of the day, was his main source of news of the world.

"Did they recover it?" The stolen portrait.

"Apparently not."

"Could I see the story?"

"Good Lord, it wasn't in the paper."

Vincent Traeger, the so-called former CIA agent, was Lowry's informant. Traeger had been the one to whom Lowry had made what he called his general confession when he had left behind his long involvement with those he could not bring himself to call terrorists. "No names," he had insisted, "just accounts of what had happened and what was planned. He already knew the names," he added, peering at George. Lowry seemed to see the way he lived now as a variation on the way he had lived before, only with a different end in view. He called the Catholic Worker house his private witness protection program.

"Why would he tell you?"

"Quid pro quo? He knows of my devotion to Our Lady of Guadalupe." That devotion had been behind Lowry's conversion. Before it, he had regarded the Virgin of Guadalupe as the patroness of terrorism. No wonder Lowry despised Miguel Arroyo.

"Tell me," George said, turning off the Selectric. Lowry nailed Brother Fly with a rolled-up magazine.

The story he narrated was soon supplemented by newspaper accounts, which concentrated on the arrest of Theophilus Grady, who had been holed up in Idaho while his theft of the sacred portrait was causing havoc on both sides of the border. Eventually such stories contained Grady's refusal to say where the stolen portrait was.

"Why?"

Lowry applied a match to his pipe. "I suppose he doesn't want the chaos he has caused to stop."

But then came the official announcement that the missing portrait had not been found in Pocatello.

For weeks the news that Lowry had been passing on to George stemmed from that awful event in the basilica in Mexico City: the storming of the border and the guerrilla war raging in the deserts and mountains, fanned by Miguel among others, although he had tried unsuccessfully to call it off. Repentance? He said that he now feared that violence would postpone the inevitable but peaceful accomplishment of his dreams of an altered California, a united Southwest. Only belatedly did George hear of what had happened in long-term parking at the San Francisco airport.

"Don Ibanez was there?!"

Concern for the old man could mask his love for Clare. Lowry had been witness to the whole sad thing, the mutual love and then the gathering depression when Clare realized that George was not doing what he did in Palo Alto only as a temporary thing. It was to be his life.

"You haven't taken vows," Lowry had said to him not long before.

If Clare couldn't join him, why didn't he join Clare? George was almost shocked to hear this from the man he regarded as his Peter Maurin. Did he think of himself as Dorothy Day? After the shock of the suggestion, it became his greatest temptation. Just walk away from all this and live like everybody else. Why not? Lowry was right. He had not made any solemn promise to God to go on like this forever. George plunged once more into the writings of Dorothy Day, looking for indications that she, too, had been tempted by the thought of just getting out, away from the drunks and addicts and woebegone losers, ladling out soup and clothes and trying not to preach to them. But the fact of the matter was that she had lived her long life without deserting. And she'd never married again. When George had told Clare that some houses were run by married couples she had not reacted as he had hoped.

"I couldn't live like this, George."

"One day at a time."

From her expression he might have been describing the way prisoners under a life sentence reconcile themselves to the endless time ahead.

"Go see her," Lowry said now, when George kept expressing concern for Don Ibanez. "Take a few days off. You'll be easier to live with."

❖ IV ❖

"I have a great devotion to Saint Juan Diego."

Catherine had insisted that she would like to visit one of the wineries but she really didn't pay much attention as the vintner gave them a royal tour befitting the daughter of Don Ibanez. Afterward, they sat outside in the shade sipping wine, the leaves rustling pleasantly in the slight breeze, the whole valley giving off a variety of perfumes.

"You've lived here all your life?"

Clare nodded. "I was born here. I mean, at home."

"And your mother?"

"I scarcely remember her. I was only three at the time she died."

"So you are your father's daughter."

"I suppose I am."

Catherine's remark had seemed to be a leading one, and so it proved to be. She wanted to talk about Jason Phelps. She wanted to tell Clare of the professor's attitude toward the Virgin of Guadalupe. Did Clare realize that the whole thing had been disproved?

"Of course he would think so."

"It's not just his opinion. He showed me a book, a book by a Catholic, who claims that Juan Diego never existed."

"Leoncio Garza-Valdés?"

"You know it?"

"Catherine, my father has every book ever written about the Virgin of Guadalupe."

"But have you read it?"

"Have you?"

"I don't read Spanish. Jason summarized it for me."

"It is a very serious book."

"But it doesn't convince you?"

"No. Oh, I can believe that not every bit of the image is miraculous. Others have touched it up. If nothing else, it is the eyes that would remove any doubt I might have."

"The eyes?"

Clare explained the images that had been found in the eyes of the Virgin, that they displayed optical laws unknown at the time of the vision or any later repainting. "One of the images is of Juan Diego, whom Garza-Valdés says never existed."

"And the pope canonized him!"

"That is a strong confirmation of the vision, isn't it?"

"But if he didn't even exist . . ."

"Not even Garza-Valdés goes quite that far. He says Juan Diego's existence is doubtful. So would be that of any ancestor of his of five or six hundred years ago."

"Would anything shake your belief in that vision?"

"Catherine, we don't have to believe such visions—none of them—Lourdes, Fatima, whatever. I would be perfectly free to ignore them all."

"But if the pope canonized someone who may not even have existed?"

"I have a great devotion to Saint Juan Diego. Would you like more wine?"

"I would."

Meaning she didn't want the conversation to stop. "Is Professor Phelps trying to undermine your faith?"

"My faith? Clare, I don't have any."

"Don't say that."

"It's true. You really don't know anything about me. The reason I came to Jason . . ."

Clare listened but what had caught her attention was the use of Professor Phelps's first name. And then out tumbled again the story of Lloyd Kaiser, with whom Catherine had been having an affair. When they parted he went off, apparently in remorse, to the shrine of Our Lady of Guadalupe. She seemed to think she was telling Clare this for the first time.

"He was the American who was shot there."

"The martyr."

And then Catherine remembered their previous conversation about this. She tossed her hand as if in apology.

"Obviously his pilgrimage has made a deep impression on you," Clare said.

Catherine put down her glass.

"I regard it as a temptation."

"A temptation?"

"You wouldn't know how seductive faith can seem after you have lost it."

Clare thought of George and his idealism, of the way she had longed to be like him, but just couldn't.

"Oh, I can imagine that."

But poor Catherine. Didn't she know that people even wrote books trying to prove that Jesus never existed? And God?

She dropped Catherine off at Jason Phelps's. Catherine scampered across the tiled porch and inside. Clare looked toward the house as she followed the circular drive to the road. Catherine seemed to have run into the house and into Jason Phelps's arms in one motion. At least she has that, Clare thought wistfully.

❖

She found her father behind the house, on a bench beneath a trio of palm trees. George Worth was with him! Clare stopped, remembering the way Catherine had run into Jason Phelps's arms. The two men rose as she approached.

"I will leave you two alone," her father said.

George seemed almost as uneasy with the remark as she was. On the way to the house, her father stopped to pick up some fallen leaves.

"Lowry insisted I get away," George said.

"And here you are."

She took her father's place on the bench and George, too, sat. An enormous silence formed, out of which, finally, he said, "How well you look."

The mad hope that he had come to her at last leapt in her breast, then died. She knew George too well for that. Catherine had her temptation, the threat of the faith, and Clare had hers. If she could not live as George did, perhaps he could . . .

"How is the house?"

"The point of getting away is to forget it."

She doubted that he would be able to do that.

"Your father seems very calm about all these recent events."

Clare realized that this was true. Others, whose devotion to the Virgin of Guadalupe was intermittent, certainly not the steady devotion of Don Ibanez, had reacted to the theft with rage and rallies and noise. And calls to arms. By contrast Don Ibanez seemed serene, confident that all would be well. Not even the thwarted exchange at the San Francisco airport seemed to have disturbed him greatly. Afterward, he had been the spokesman—calling Vincent Traeger his driver!—recounting the events as if he were not describing what amounted to a second theft of the sacred image.

"He has put everything in the Virgin's hands."

George nodded, his eyes going over the grounds, to the replica of the basilica, to the hills beyond.

"The house certainly can't compete with this," he said.

Was that how he saw her dilemma, the poverty in which he chose to live and this lovely tranquil place, she seemingly without a care in the world?

"Have you eaten?"

"I thought I'd take you out."

She turned to him, smiling. "A date?"

They had never had dates, the usual outings of young people in love. Side by side on the soup line was the best they could do.

"I saw a Mexican restaurant when I came through the town."

❖

They sat at an outside table, eating enchiladas and drinking Corona beer with slices of lime stuck in the necks of the bottles. The table was in a little courtyard behind the restaurant, on crushed rock, but the table didn't wobble. George put his hands on the edge to make sure it was set solidly. He looked at her. Their table in the common room at the house had wobbled. It was seated at that table that she had told him she could not stay.

"I miss you."

She nodded. The thought of going through all the anguish of denial again was more than she could take.

"I haven't taken vows," he said.

"What do you mean?"

"I'm not a monk. I could leave in a minute if I wanted."

"And come visit me?"

"Are you sorry I came?"

"Why did you come, George?"

"I love you."

"And I love you." She put her hand desperately on his. "But I can't love the house."

"I understand."

"You do not!"

"I wonder what else I could do."

Clare had the feeling a woman must have when a wavering priest finds her attractive and begins to talk about leaving. What power George was putting in her hands. He could work for her father, he could . . . But no!

"You could never leave it, George. Don't even think of it." She took away her hand. "I wouldn't let you."

She could not bear that responsibility. Imagine some great lady long ago having a conversation like this with Francis of Assisi.

"I'll come back with you, though. For a time. Like before."

A bird had come to peck at crumbs that dropped from the tables there in the courtyard, getting bolder as he neared them.

"And leave again."

She said nothing. She had never seen George like this, divided, anguished.

"How is Lowry?" she asked.

❖ V ❖

"Go to hell."

Paul Pulaski was wounded in an ambush and dragged to safety, and now he lay in a hospital in reoccupied Tucson, not quite believing the peace and quiet. Nurses, all starch and efficiency, came and went, bringing him endless cups of water he did not want and food that was tasteless, but it was the absence of danger that settled over him like another sheet.

His wound was not severe; the bullet had gone through the calf of his right leg, with lots of torn cartilage and bleeding, but it had missed the bone. He felt like you-know-who and his phony Purple Hearts when they whisked him away from his men. It was hard to believe, lying in a hospital bed, that out there in the desert and in the mountains, men were still shooting at one another. His wound could have been more serious. He could have been killed. Now he could let the thoughts come that he had been able to drive away while commanding his men.

What the hell were they doing anyway? Paul had joined the Minutemen in Indiana, a second-generation Pole who got fed up trying to explain the difference between legal and illegal immigrants. Of course he was all for legal immigrations. That was how his grandparents had come into the country. Now he was told that Poles were flying into New York without papers, working for a year or so, and taking the money back to Poland. Polish wetbacks. But who gave a damn about them or about the Latinos coming in by the truckload, day after day?

Once the shooting began, such thoughts had become luxuries. The objective was to seal the border and keep it that way. And that was what they had accomplished, at least for a stretch of a hundred miles or so. But how can you fence just part of a border and call it secure? Within a year he was commander of the unit. Not everyone could devote full time to the effort, but Paul could. He was twenty-eight, unmarried, and still lived with his parents when he wasn't in bivouac. His father thought he was nuts.

"Why do we have a National Guard? Why do we have an army, for God's sake?"

"You want me to join the army?"

"Hell no." That would mean the Middle East, where the contest kept producing heroes but was pretty hard to understand. Keeping illegal immigrants out of the country was a straightforward objective compared to that. As straightforward as his father's machine shop. A punch press knew its job and did it.

When that showboat Grady called a press conference in El Paso and claimed to have the stolen icon or whatever it was, Paul hadn't believed a word of it. He believed Grady even less when he learned that the Rough Riders had all decamped, disappearing who knew where. That press conference had intensified the fighting. Now they had found Grady and the son of a bitch admitted he didn't know where the supposed picture of Mary was. The whole damned thing was a game for him, strutting around like Teddy Roosevelt, or Patton. It was those silver revolvers on Grady's belt that convinced Paul the guy was a phony. The Minutemen had volunteered to protect the border and now they seemed involved in some kind of religious war.

"What if someone stole Our Lady of Czestochowa?" his mother had asked in horrified tones.

"Let God punish them," his father said.

But God seemed to be punishing the Minutemen. The National Guard had been put on alert in Arizona, but within twenty-four hours there was a stand-down. More than half the state was on the side of the invaders. And then they had enemies at the rear, but that pressure had been relieved when all kinds of ragtag bands arrived at the scene of action. The Minutemen were disciplined; they had been trained; they were a fighting unit. The newcomers deserved the name of vigilante.

There was a television in the room and Paul watched whenever a politician came on to rant and rave. Gunther wanted the army called out, but it was pretty clear his was a minority voice. The White House seemed determined to keep attention on the Middle East. Paul turned off the set.

On the second day, reporters came to interview him. It was obvious they considered him some kind of nut. Maybe he was. If he had been killed, if he couldn't have been identified, he would have ended up in the Tomb of the Unknown Nut.

"Didn't your family come from Poland?"

"My grandparents."

The point of the question seemed to be that he wanted to deny others the opportunities his family had had. It was pointless to try to explain the difference between illegal and legal immigrants. Then the priest came. Not the hospital chaplain—some guy from Seattle who wanted to straighten Paul out. Father Jim. Just call me Jim. He seemed to think they had a religious obligation to open the borders.

"You know the legend on the Statue of Liberty."

Father Jim seemed to think that boatloads of undocumented Polacks had slipped past the statue and landed on the shores of Manhattan.

"You're a Catholic, aren't you?"

"I've seen the chaplain."

"A good man." If Father Jim had talked to the chaplain he wouldn't have gotten much satisfaction from it. "Have you read what the pope said about immigration?"

"I've been busy."

"Trying to get killed keeping poor Mexicans out of the land of plenty."

"Father Jim?"

"Yes?" He moved closed to Paul's bed.

"Go to hell."

The chaplain got a laugh out of it when he heard what Paul had said. "No way to talk to a priest, Paul." But he was smiling when he said it. And then Gunther came.

He wore a seersucker suit and sailed his straw hat at the stand in the corner when he entered the room. He missed. He left the hat on the floor. He had the smile of a man who had just made a hole in one.

"A sense of the Congress resolution, Paul. I tacked it onto a bill that went through like shit through a goose."

It was the sense of Congress that Paul Pulaski was a hero. A wounded hero. Gunther smiled with triumphant slyness. The sense of Congress, hidden away where no one knew they were voting for it? That summed up what a screwed-up mess this was—skirmishes all over the place, oddballs shooting at other oddballs—no wonder the administration could consider the matter little more than an annoying distraction. But by God, the border was being protected.

"I want you to come to Washington. I want you to talk to the press. I want you to hit the circuit and explain things to your fellow Americans."

"No."

Gunther took this as the humility of a wounded hero. Paul had read *Sons of the Fathers*, about the Iwo Jima flag raisers who had been put on the circuit to sell war bonds and had lost their bearings in the process.

"You owe it to the country, Paul."

"The country doesn't seem to feel in our debt."

"There you're wrong. You are a certified hero, by act of Congress."

He let Gunther talk. He got rid of him only by saying that

he would think of it. No reason to go on about what he thought
of the crazy idea.

✣ VI ✣

"There are videos of the funeral."

Neal Admirari's agent hadn't thought much of the idea but
when several publishers expressed interest, Hacker got to work,
playing one publisher off against the other. Neal did a one-
pager, Hacker circulated it in an auction, and Mastadon Press
came in with the winning bid. Lulu had been dubious about the
idea of writing a book about the immigration wars that would
emerge from the story of Lloyd Kaiser, but the contract soft-
ened her skepticism.

"Want to be coauthor?"

"Just because you stole the idea you'd given me?"

"You want it back?"

"I'm no Indian giver."

They were in the place in Connecticut when Hacker phoned
with the good news.

"I told them six months at the outside, Neal," Hacker said.
"This is hot, but it could cool."

Neal accepted the deadline. He knew all about deadlines.
Besides, he might end up with nothing more than the hefty
advance. Hot projects do cool. He left Lulu at the summer
place and flew off to Indianapolis to talk with Judith, Lloyd
Kaiser's daughter.

✣

Judith Lynch lived with her family in Fishers, a little town just
north of Indianapolis, a commuter town. The house she lived
in was a slight variation on all the others in the development,
aluminum siding that rippled beneath Neal's fingers as he
stood at the door after pushing the bell. He could see the swing
set in the backyard, and there was a trike and wagon in the
driveway, which was why he had parked the rental at the curb.
The door opened and a woman looked at him through the mesh
of the screen door.

"Neal Admirari. I phoned."

"But I said I didn't want to see you."

"An understandable reaction. Something like this is hard to explain on the phone."

She had all but hung up on him when he called from Connecticut. She wanted her father to rest in peace. The screen door burst open and two kids emerged. Neal held the door while they exited and then went inside.

"I smell coffee."

She made a face and then suddenly she smiled. "My, you're persistent."

"With an idea like this it would be a mortal sin not to be persistent." He had seen the Madonna on a table and the sprig of palm behind one of the framed pictures. "Was that your parish church I passed?"

It was like the secret handclasp. Judith and her family were obviously good Catholics. That was the hook on which Neal hung the version of his project he outlined for Judith in the kitchen, at the table, sipping coffee.

"Tell me about your father."

She brought albums to the table and turned the pages slowly, a sad smile on her face.

"That your mother?"

"She preceded Father in death."

It sounded like a line from the obituary. Maybe it was.

"When was that?"

She thought. "Six years ago."

"And your dad never married again?"

"No!"

Neal was thinking of the woman Lloyd had apparently met at the Whitehall just before heading for Mexico City. Given Judith's reaction, he wasn't going to bring that up. Eventually they got around to her father's funeral. Judith put the visiting book from the mortuary on the table. She also had a list of those who had made memorial donations. He sat back when he saw Catherine Dolan's name on the list. He tapped it with his finger. Judith was smiling.

"Now that's a story," she said.

"How so?"

"We talked on the phone afterward."

This woman had been a childhood friend of her father's. They had started to correspond and then they agreed to meet in Chicago.

"She came to the funeral! Isn't that something?"

"It certainly is."

"The stories she told me of how they had talked and talked about when they were kids. She was devastated by what had happened to Daddy in Mexico City."

Neal was memorizing the address that Catherine had added to her name on the list.

"Think if they hadn't gotten together. That was what bothered Catherine, I think. How easily they might never have had the chance to talk about when they were kids."

Neal just shook his head at the mystery of life.

"I can't let you have these albums," Judith said.

"Of course not. Do you have negatives of some of these pictures of him?"

"There are videos of the funeral."

"I would like to see those."

She lowered the blinds in the living room and hooked the video up to the television set. Neal watched as one watches other people's home videos.

"That's her," Judith cried. "That's Catherine."

"Beautiful woman."

"Isn't she?"

❖

Catherine Dolan was a tangent, but one Neal found irresistible. Unless the concierge at the Whitehall was given to imaginings, Lloyd and Catherine had done a thing or two besides reminisce about their childhood. A flawed martyr, a penitential visit to Our Lady of Guadalupe after several days in the sack with Catherine? What poignancy that would add to the story. Judith would never forgive him, but it was the bane of his profession to create enemies while insuring the public's right to know. Even so, when he flew off to Minneapolis, he didn't let Lulu know where he was going. Her reaction would be the twin of Judith's.

Before going to the apartment in a building overlooking Lake Calhoun, Neal researched Catherine Dolan on the Internet, not expecting anything. That there were entries at all was a surprise, but the number was astounding, thousands upon thousands. When he went to call on Catherine he knew all about her academic career, the patents she held. Lloyd's childhood friend turned out to be a distinguished woman.

There was an elderly woman in the lobby of the building emptying a mailbox. She smiled vaguely at Neal when she opened the door to him.

"Do you know which apartment is Catherine Dolan's?"

This was going to be tricky. He had considered calling her before he came, but he just couldn't come up with a convincing lie, and the true reason for his calling did not sound like an open sesame. Let's talk about your fling at the Whitehall with Lloyd Kaiser. The woman had stepped back but she was still smiling.

"This is her mail. She wants the bills sent to her."

"Then she's moved?"

"She's away."

"Well, this is a disappointment. Where do you send her bills?"

The little woman became wary. "Why do you ask?"

Neal gave her an account of his visit to Indianapolis, of Judith's reaction to the appearance of her father's childhood friend at the funeral. He told her he was a writer who was considering a piece on Lloyd.

"He was killed in Mexico City, you know."

Her mouth opened in surprise. "No."

Neal nodded. "It's a very romantic story."

Before he left he had the address to which the little old lady sent Catherine's bills. Napa Valley! Care of Professor Jason Phelps. After he researched Phelps, Neal knew he was going to California.

❖ VII ❖

"Good bread."

George called Lowry, asking if it would be all right if he extended his vacation.

"Everything's under control. Relax, get some rest."

With George, that was like telling a model husband to go beat his wife. The kid was too intense. You can't last at anything if you're too intense. Lowry was getting a little R&R himself, a fifth of midway decent scotch, holed up in George's office lest any of the guests decided to fall off the wagon with him. The one thing Lowry understood about his refound relation with God was that God is mercy. Feeding and shooting the bull with the vacant-eyed drunks and addicts who sat around the common room, avoiding the television screen, just breathing in and breathing out, waiting for the next meal to be dished out to them, Lowry told himself that they were what he looked like to God, if so good. This life was a life of penance to him, and the problem was it was easy. At first he thought it would be a temptation to feel superior to the guests, but that passed quickly. How many of them had a bottle of scotch stashed away and waited for nightfall and a serious session of solitary drinking?

"How many guests do we have?" George asked.

Lowry counted those sitting around. "All I could see from where I stood were three long mountains and a wood. . . ." He murmured the lines to George.

"What's that?"

"Edna St. Vincent Millay."

"Don't know her."

"She never answers my letters."

Careful, careful. He never knew if George suspected that he dropped back into his old habits from time to time, just to remember where he had been. Millay. He had read her life; a real dingbat but an almost perfect poet. Like most people who couldn't stand themselves, she got into political agitation. Dorothy Parker was another. If you can't change yourself, change the world. Lowry knew the feeling. Most of his life had been a long vacation from himself and now, more or less reacquainted with the person he was and couldn't abide, he needed a little respite. The human race cannot stand very much reality. Sapienza understood that.

The bishop of Santa Ana had a decade on him, more or less, and liked to grumble about the fact that he had to write a letter of resignation when he hit seventy-five.

"When they accept it, I'm going to do what you do."

Well, maybe he would. The trouble was that Sapienza was a lot like George, a repressed optimist where good works were concerned. Both of them secretly believed that bums would seek a job, drunks dry out, and addicts go cold turkey and . . . And then what? Religion as the opium of nonaddicts? Lowry smiled and brought a match to his pipe. It gurgled like a water pipe. He should clean it out. But it would only get tarred up again. Besides, it tasted better this way.

He had an hour before he had to begin fixing the evening meal. After he put down the phone, he relaxed in George's desk chair. There was a pile of pages beside the typewriter. Lowry picked them up and began to read. He got halfway through a page and returned it to the pile. George was a romantic, no doubt about it.

Later, when he got the stew going, causing a ripple of interest in the common room as its fragrance drifted out there, Lowry almost liked the thought that he was in charge. The truth was that he was happy enough to be George's right arm or whatever, and he never felt that the fate of the house depended on him. Maybe that was what got to George. No, it was the girl, Clare Ibanez. Lowry could have told George that a girl like that would never settle into this kind of work. The trick was not to consider it a life sentence. George had been surprised when Lowry told him he hadn't taken solemn vows to live this life forever and ever. He had a done a lot already and maybe that was all he was meant to do. Lowry remembered that when he was George's age he was all afire for the coming revolution, enlisted for life, and look at him now.

From the kitchen he saw the car come into the lot, a new car, probably someone come to make a donation, look around as if in envy at this noble work, and then get the hell out of here. But the big guy who got out of the car and stretched was Traeger. Lowry watched him come to the door, still agile as ever, taking everything in. Traeger came through the door and Lowry came around the hot table, wiping his hands on his apron.

"Sorry, we're all full up."

"I know what you're full of."

They shook hands. "How long before you're free?"

"You want to talk? I can't leave here. I'm in charge."

Traeger looked around. "Here will be fine."

"You can have some stew. Stew and bread."

"Did you make it?"

"Of course I made it. I'm the chef."

After the guests went through the line, Lowry filled bowls for Traeger and himself and they sat at the end of one of the tables.

"Good bread."

"Day old. Maybe more. We get it for nothing."

Afterward Traeger helped with the dishes. KP. When the kitchen was spick-and-span, everything put away, and most of the guests had drifted off to the residences, they went into George's office and got comfortable.

"How far would I have to go for a drink?"

"How far can you reach?" He brought out the bottle.

They had several drinks before they got around to Traeger's reason for stopping by.

"I've been hired to do something and I don't know how to do it. I don't even know if it's still to be done."

Lowry waited. He could see how much that admission cost Traeger.

"That picture that was stolen from the church in Mexico City."

"There are a million reproductions of it. Turn in one of those."

"The original is on the back of a cape that is five or six hundred years old."

"Theophilus Grady didn't have it?"

"That's his story."

"Don't you believe him?"

Traeger thought about it. "Normally I wouldn't. But if the point was just to raise a little hell, he's done that. So why wouldn't he turn it over?" A pause while he sipped. "I think that maybe he did."

"Maybe he never had it."

Traeger sighted at him over the rim of his glass. They were drinking out of jelly jars. "You sound as if you know something."

"Arroyo."

Lowry felt the way he had years before when Traeger had

debriefed him about his radical days. Traeger considered the answer, filed it away, and they went back to drinking.

"This is pretty bad scotch."

"Day old. Like our bread."

There was maybe a drink left in the bottle when they called it a night. Traeger just looked at Lowry when he told him he could give him a bed in the men's residence. Lowry went outside into the parking lot with him. The lights of the rental blinked when Traeger pressed the key.

"You sure you should drive?"

"There's a motel a mile up the road." He pulled open the car door but before getting in, turned to Lowry.

"Thanks."

For the scotch? For suggesting he get on to Miguel Arroyo? Maybe both.

❖

It was in the motel up the road that Traeger received the summons to return to Washington.

❖ VIII ❖

"I'll make lunch."

The letter from Judith was forwarded from Minneapolis, which was something of a surprise since Catherine had asked only that her bills be sent on. When she left for California it had been late in the month, and she hated to have unpaid bills. It wasn't that she realized then how extended her absence would be. There were photographs of Lloyd in the envelope, several memorial cards, and a letter telling Catherine about the very nice author who was planning a book on her father. "It's where and how he died that fascinates him. He finds it symbolic or something. He can explain it to you when he talks with you."

Catherine threw down the letter angrily. When he talks with me?

"Bad news?" Jason asked, looking up from his desk.

"Not really. A letter from a woman in Indianapolis."

He shrugged and went back to his book. Well, why should

he be interested in a letter from Judith? Why should she? It dawned on her that the only address Judith could have given the author was that of her Minneapolis apartment where she had sent her letter. She picked up the envelope and half slid the photographs of Lloyd from it. She tried to stir up memories of the Whitehall, but all that seemed centuries ago now. The cure she had come for was all but complete.

But Judith's letter haunted her day. The memories of Chicago began to come back, as sweet and sad as ever. It was her parting from Lloyd that was even more vivid than their lovemaking. How tender he had been. And in his eyes she thought she read the promise that those few days together were only a beginning. She could almost believe that he had gone off to the shrine in Mexico City to thank Our Lady of Guadalupe for bringing back his youthful love. That was so much more welcome a thought than that he had fled there out of remorse and shame.

The kind of remorse and shame Catherine was beginning to feel about living with Jason. He was a very demanding person to work for, never commenting on what she did, certainly never thanking her or praising her. Of course he regarded it as an enormous privilege to work with so distinguished a scholar. No doubt that was why he showed so little curiosity about her career. Catherine had never read anthropology before, and if Jason was the best there was, she didn't consider it a very demanding field. All this fuss and bother about the customs of primitive tribes. Of course, that seemed largely an excuse for the hidden allegory beneath it all. We are all primitives. But are we? Catherine considered herself a sophisticated modern woman. She was not mirrored in the stupid eyes of all those bare-breasted females. What do old women have between their breasts that young women don't? A navel. She laughed aloud. How Lloyd had laughed. The joke had drawn from him an admiring comment about her own still firm, full breasts. Her hand rose dreamily, but she brought it to the beads she wore. If she closed her eyes she could feel Lloyd's hand on her breasts, recall his eagerness. Oh, God, those had been lovely days. She told herself that she would even have become a Catholic again for Lloyd if . . . if!

When she went back inside, she sat at the table in Jason's

study that she used to work on his papers, but the task had suddenly lost its savor. Across the room, those huge gnarled hands at the sides of his head, Jason sniffled as he read. It was a habit; he didn't have a cold. The sniffling was a kind of punctuation. How annoying it was. An old man reviewing the scholarly work of his lifetime. Would anyone else be as interested in it as he was? She stood.

"I'll make lunch."

She had to repeat it as she left the study. The old voice called after her, "It's not yet eleven thirty."

She ignored him. She just had to get out of the study and away from him. What in hell was she doing here? The great skeptic would cure her of the attraction she had felt at Lloyd's funeral, the liturgy measuring out her feelings, giving them direction, a direction she had been sure she had lost? That had been the reason behind her visit. And it had worked, more or less. She had slept with Jason out of gratitude. Now, in the kitchen, the thought of those great gnarled hands moving over her body as he sniffled in appreciation filled her with disgust. But it had seemed part of her cure.

After lunch, he started toward his room. "Time for my nap." He looked at her with those large, liquid eyes. He was asking her to join him, as she often did.

"I'm going to visit Clare," she lied.

"Couldn't it wait?"

His eyes were almost pleading. She followed him up the stairs like a wife.

❧

Later, she surprised Clare by asking if she could see the church out back again.

"Of course."

"It reminds me of him."

Clare nodded. "George is here."

"Oh, I'm keeping you from him."

"He's with my father."

But when they entered the replica of that great round church in Mexico City, the two men were there, in the front, looking up at the image of Our Lady of Guadalupe. Don Ibanez turned and beckoned them forward. He took Catherine's hand.

"And how is my atheist neighbor?"

"I'm fine."

He drew back. "I meant Jason Phelps."

"He's taking his nap."

"Wise man."

What if she had come to visit Don Ibanez rather than Jason and poured out her troubles to him? The two old men were much alike, despite the deep divide between faith and . . . whatever you could call Jason's outlook. When they left the church, Clare and George wandered away.

"You didn't mean that about being an atheist," Don Ibanez said. He had offered her his arm and they were walking toward the hacienda.

"Didn't I?"

He walked in silence. "That is between God and yourself."

Inside, he offered her a glass of his favorite red, and they were still sipping it when the young couple came in. Don Ibanez left them and Catherine felt suddenly like the uninvited guest she was. What would any of these three think if they knew she had been in bed with Jason Phelps not an hour earlier? She realized that she was sniffling. From a far room, the sound of a television set became audible. And then there came a great cry from Don Ibanez.

Clare ran to him and George and Catherine followed. No wonder Don Ibanez had cried out. There had been an assassination attempt on Miguel Arroyo.

CHAPTER TWO

❖ I ❖

"He didn't quite say that, did he?"

When Traeger was called back to Washington, he had a long flight on which to think of what was coming. It seemed best to make his mind a blank. Did retired bankers remember the bad loans they had made, and lawyers their lost cases? His own career seemed more like that of a surgeon who had watched platoons of patients go off to their eternal reward. In his case, most of the deaths had been by violence. For the bulk of his career, working under Dortmund, the long twilight struggle had seemed to make sense. The agency had always been too full of Ivy League types trying to act like their movie counterparts, but there had always been a solid core for whom the stakes were clear; right against wrong, freedom versus slavery. The globe itself had seemed divided between the two sides. And then the Berlin Wall had come down, and the Soviet Union collapsed; it had seemed the victory they had sought. Dortmund had sense enough to retire then. Ever since, the agency had seemed in search of a cause. When he could no longer admire his superiors, Traeger followed Dortmund into retirement. Since then, whenever he had been reactivated, it was in response to Dortmund's wish. And so it had been in the case of the theft of the image of the Virgin of Guadalupe and the turmoil that followed. Illegal immigration was not of itself enough to stir him, but wondering what others might be concealed among the poor devils sneaking across the border in search of a better deal gave him pause. And the floundering of Homeland Security, of course.

He took a cab from Reagan and soon was in the same room with Boswell, once of the glen plaid suit, now in a blazer and checked open shirt, but the same Wizard of Oz expression.

"Mission accomplished, Traeger."

"Weren't the instructions to get it?"

"This will please you."

He handed Traeger a letter from the White House, expressing the president's gratitude.

"I didn't do anything."

Boswell looked wise. "The main thing is that it was done."

"We have it?"

"The matter no longer seems urgent."

Superiors had always spoken with forked tongues, Dortmund excepted, but he, too, had often been enigmatic. It was difficult for an agent not to become duplicitous, an occupational hazard.

"Will Crosby and I were there when Theophilus Grady was taken."

"Crosby?"

"Perhaps you didn't know him."

"I knew him, of course. Did you enlist his help?"

"Our paths crossed."

If Boswell was suggesting that Grady's public denials were bullshit, Traeger figured he could be a little oblique himself. Didn't the man realize that if Traeger had been on the scene at Pocatello, he had seen that package carried from the house and put into the Pontiac with the tinted windows? Boswell rose and extended a manicured hand across his desk. Traeger took it, as if they were making a bet. He took his presidential letter, too, for what it was worth, and walked to the Metro stop. He hadn't been offered a ride.

He rode the Metro back to the airport, where he had checked his bag. When he had it, on impulse, he took a cab to the Marriott and checked in. Then, feeling like a tourist, he went for a walk. There were benches in Lafayette Park across from the White House and he sat there and fought the feeling that he had been discarded. And bamboozled. Mission accomplished. What the hell did that mean? The guerrilla war went on, Minutemen against enraged Mexicans, volunteers popping up here and there, vigilantes. It was a god-awful mess, and there was only one way to stop it. Get that picture back to where it belonged in the basilica in Mexico City. "Get it," the president had said. If the agency had it, why hadn't it been returned to its shrine? Traeger got out his phone and called Dortmund and told him he had been relieved.

"You don't sound relieved."

"I was asked to do something and I haven't done it."

"Can you come see me?"

"I was just going to suggest that."

"Great minds."

Traeger watched a pigeon strut by, seemingly pulled forward by the motion of its neck. "Tomorrow."

He had dinner in an Italian restaurant near his hotel, polishing off a bottle of Chianti along with a mountain of pasta. It was with a bit of a buzz on that he went back to his hotel. When he passed the bar in the lobby, his eye was caught by the large flat-screen television and he stopped. He went in and walked toward the set. He seemed to be the only one in the bar who was interested in the attempted assassination of Miguel Arroyo, the founder of Justicia y Paz. There was a shot of what remained of the convertible and then Arroyo, smiling into the camera, talking his head off.

❖

The next day, turning in to the retirement home, Traeger had a depressing thought about the future that lay ahead. He was in great shape, full of piss and vinegar, but so had Dortmund been within living memory. Traeger's. Age snuck up on one, that was clear. Traeger would rather go down in a plane crash or be swept away in a tornado than end up in such a pleasant, depressing place as this.

At the house, he went around to find his old mentor on his patio, with a huge book on his lap.

"Is that the phone directory?"

"*War and Peace*. A new translation. Of course you can read it in the original."

"I've read it in translation, too. Have you seen the Russian film version of it?"

"Tell me about it."

"I'll send you a copy." The movie had been made before the fall, but it was a faithful rendering of the story. Of course, the whole thing had been regarded as a prelude to the revolution.

Dortmund suggested that Traeger push his chair out onto the lawn. Under the high power lines. "I don't think we've had a secure conversation."

"I've been relieved of duty."

Dortmund nodded. "So you said." He looked away. "I was told."

"They don't have the portrait, do they?"

"I doubt it."

Traeger waited. Dortmund brought his lower lip between his teeth, looked up at the high power lines, and sighed.

"They like things the way they are."

The absent portrait continued to fuel the guerrilla war, and senators and congressmen were going crazy, demanding a sky-high fence along the border and that troops be sent to support the Minutemen and the Border Patrol. The demonstrations in Mexico City were no longer Eucharistic processions; the Church Militant was out and demanding blood. Two zealots had been arrested planting charges at the base of the Washington Monument. Graffiti defaced the Lincoln Memorial. All this was officially treated as the acts of terrorists, otherwise undescribed. No relation to what was going on in the Southwest was recognized.

Dortmund tried to explain the thinking of the men who had just sent Traeger on his way. Were they working for or against the administration?

"Probably both." Dortmund said.

"Boswell is the kind of man I never wanted to work with," Traeger said.

"He is much appreciated by congressional committees."

"I wonder whose side they are on."

"Have you read Feith's book on what led up to Iraq?"

"Yes."

"Perhaps they enjoy seeing the president unable to resolve this."

Traeger let it go. Under Dortmund, he had been trained to act for the sitting administration, whatever it was. Dortmund was suggesting that was no longer the case. The agency had assumed a political stance, and that meant a partisan one.

"How could they convince the White House they had recovered that picture if they haven't?"

"He didn't quite say that, did he?"

"He didn't quite say anything."

"Quite." The old man smiled. Once he had worked with a fop from MI-5. But he stopped himself from saying so. Garrulity was the vice of age. "What do you know of Miguel Arroyo?"

"Well, he escaped assassination. If that is what it was."

Dortmund's eyebrows lifted.

"Do you remember a man named Lowry?" Traeger asked.

"Ah, the repentant radical. What about him?"

"He is in a kind of homeless shelter in Palo Alto."

"The poor fellow."

"No, he works there. He's the cook."

"He's lucky to be alive." Dortmund paused. "But then we all are. Why did you mention him?"

"He had just advised me to check out Arroyo when I was called in. I don't like to leave a job undone."

"Don't."

Traeger looked at the old man. That one word spoke volumes. "What do you suggest?"

Again Dortmund munched on his lower lip. He looked at Traeger. "I would get in touch with Ignatius Hannan."

"He has Crosby."

"I think Crosby would like to get back to his family. We've talked."

"Have you talked with Hannan?"

"He'll be expecting you."

❖

There was something about New England that rubbed Traeger the wrong way. The terrain went against his Midwestern predilections, and he found the different ways of mangling English grating. Before heading for New Hampshire, he had checked out his office and when he set off it was in his own car, a non-descript Oldsmobile. He had tried a Toyota once, but thoughts of Pearl Harbor had made him trade it in for the Olds. The Toyota had been assembled in the States, but even so.

He went around Baltimore, skirted New York, and got into Connecticut. The interstate system was one thing Ike had done right while in the White House, but his reputation would depend on his military, not his political, career. His farewell address must have been written by some wacko on his staff. The military-industrial complex, as if a strong defense produced the menace it was designed to defend against. At Hartford, he turned north and headed for Manchester.

When he pulled into the driveway of Empedocles he was still asking himself why he hadn't stayed home when he got there. What was Hecuba to him or he to Hecuba? He had been honorably relieved; he still remembered what it was like to trust the judgment of his superiors—his conscience need not bother him if he just settled down to making money for a change. Maybe if he hadn't talked with Dortmund he could have done that, but the old man, frail and out of it as he seemed, had never retired in his heart. There was still the great battle to be fought, no matter if the longtime enemy had melted away into a hodgepodge of republics. The enemy was still out there, awaiting his chance, no matter what guise he assumed. The price of freedom was eternal vigilance. That might have been on Dortmund's coat of arms. It helped that they saw eye to eye on the caliber of those who had succeeded them. Dortmund had nodded knowingly when Traeger told him of the package that had been hustled from Grady's hideout into the Pontiac.

❖

"So your job is unfinished," Hannan said.

"I've been relieved."

"I wanted to hire you in the first place. Crosby is a good man. . . ."

"He is a very good man."

"It sounds to me as if all he did was follow you around."

"He would have done better on his own."

"I want to hire you."

"In Washington they told me that my mission had been accomplished."

"Talk to Don Ibanez."

Traeger looked around the office. Outside, the candles flickering in the grotto were visible. "All I want is expenses."

"You will have all my resources at your disposal. You can have a plane. I don't care what it costs."

✣ II ✣

"He was lying when he said he had it."

Laura's brother John was the youngest priest ever to be appointed prefect of the Vatican Library and Museums, an honor he disparaged by pointing out how his predecessors in the job had fared. Cardinal Maguire had been killed on the patio of his penthouse on the roof of the library and his assistant had been murdered right here on the grounds of Empedocles.

"That's hardly part of the job description, John."

John had been in the post a year now and had yet to move into the penthouse, saying he preferred his rooms in the Domus Sanctae Marthae, a residence within the Vatican walls for the priests and prelates who worked in the diminutive city. Country, actually. John had just given a lecture at Notre Dame and stopped off to see Laura before returning to Rome. Nate and Ray were inside, talking with Traeger. Brother and sister were seated on a bench facing the grotto that Nate Hannan had built, an exact replica of Lourdes. The impossibly rich founder of Empedocles had come back to the religion of his youth when thoughts about his wealth and the hectic life he led had brought large questions to his mind. What does it profit a man if he gains the whole world and suffers the loss of his own soul? Always a good question, even if you're not rich or likely to become so. Sometimes Laura was surprised Nate hadn't chucked it all and retired to a monastery.

"Retired?" John asked. "How old is he?"

"He and Ray were classmates at Boston College."

"So how old is Ray?"

"Don't you know? Let me put it this way. We were all class-mates."

"Making Hannan what? Twenty-nine?"

Laura squeezed his arm.

Nate's conversion had had its influence on Laura and Ray, too, but there was no need to go into that with John.

"There's a replica of Lourdes at Notre Dame, too, you know."

This prompted Laura to tell John of the actual basilica that Don Ibanez had constructed on his property in Napa Valley.

"A basilica?"

"In miniature. A replica of the shrine in Mexico City that's been so much in the news."

A pained expression came onto John's face. "Why would anyone steal a miraculous image?"

"The answer to that seems clear. Look at the chaos it has stirred up."

John turned toward her. "This isn't just a social call, Laura. The Vatican remembers the role that Mr. Hannan played in recovering the third secret of Fatima. Would he be willing to do something similar here?"

"John, he is way ahead of you."

She told him of the hiring of Crosby. "Remember Traeger? Nate wanted to hire him first, but he had already been activated by the CIA. They let him go and now he's back with us."

Boris, the chef, was delighted to have mouths to feed that might have some appreciation of his culinary skills. Nate Hannan ate like a bird and would have been happy with hot dogs. Boris, of course, affected the great starched hat of his profession and his girth suggested that the feasts he prepared did not go unappreciated by their creator. His great weakness was that he washed down his food in torrents of wine and, when thus elated, was likely to tell endless stories of the no-tables he had fed in his career. Taking this job at Empedocles made little professional sense, except, of course, for the king's ransom Nate had lured him with.

"I sometimes entertain," Nate had said, and the phrase became a mantra for Boris when he was in his cups. Laura and Ray had their lunch at Empedocles, providing a target of opportunity for Boris. In recompense, they were both on diets, diets impossible to keep to if they continued to lunch at Empedocles. They reconciled themselves to the rise and fall of their weights by saying it was only charitable to provide Boris with a raison d'être.

When they went inside, Nate was still in his office with Ray and Traeger. Laura peeked in and was immediately asked to join the discussion.

"John is here, Nate."

"John!" Hannan bounded from his chair and headed for Father Burke as if he meant to tackle him. But he came to a halt and reached out to pat him on the arms.

Once it was clear that Father John Burke was here as an informal emissary of the Vatican, seeking Hannan's help in restoring that sacred image to the basilica in Mexico City, Nate asked Traeger to bring John up to date.

Listening, Laura thought what an impossible task they had set Crosby, and it was no less impossible for Traeger. He spoke in a clipped manner, ticking off the things he had done— "all of them useless"—dwelling on the embarrassment of the events in long-term parking at the San Francisco airport and the fiasco near Pocatello when Grady had been hustled off before they could get to him.

"Then it's been recovered?"

Ray said, "Grady denies he ever had it."

"Maybe he's lying."

"He was lying when he said he had it."

The disposition of the Grady matter was mysterious. From coast to coast there were calls for an indictment for the murder of those poor pilgrims in the basilica in Mexico City. But no indictment had been brought.

"That makes his denial look plausible. If he wasn't behind the theft of the picture, he can't be held responsible for those deaths." Traeger sounded as if he were trying to convince himself.

Hannan got to his feet. "Come on. Boris will be awaiting us."

❖

There was turtle soup. There was Cornish game hen. There were haricots verts that seemed dropped from heaven rather than plucked from earth. There was a soufflé. White wine, red wine, a flute of champagne. Nate drank water, as usual. And, oh, the sauces. The salad followed the entree, of course, *à la mode française*. Lise, Boris's bitty but bossy wife, shooed him back to the kitchen whenever he appeared at the doorway, like a figure in a clock, anxious to watch his handiwork disappear. Laura drove thoughts of the spartan diet she was supposedly on from her mind. She smiled at Ray, deciding that she liked him better with a little weight on him. Before they left the table, Nate asked Lise to bring in Boris.

He came in and waved dismissively as they applauded him. His roseate complexion suggested that he had tried each of the wines, for approval, of course. Lise led him back to the kitchen.

✧

John and Traeger would spend the night in Nate's residence. On the way home, Ray said, "He hasn't a clue where that picture is."

"I'm not so sure."

He waited.

"You heard the remark he said Arroyo made when he visited Don Ibanez: 'Where would you hide a book? In a library.'"

"That picture is a helluva lot larger than a book."

"Well, there are large libraries."

✧ III ✧

"Come, there is something I want to show you."

Traeger would have liked to sit up next to the pilot, Jack Smiley, but that would have meant sitting on the lap of Brenda Steltz, the copilot, so he napped in the cabin for the first hour of the flight west, then had a beer, settled at the desk in Hannan's airborne office, and got out his computer. Being relieved had been a bit of a downer, but visiting Dortmund had had its usual effect and now, working again for Ignatius Hannan, Traeger felt his first enthusiasm for the project return. He let his fingers do the thinking as they moved over the keyboard of his laptop.

The premise of his recollections was that Boswell had both said the mission was accomplished, meaning that the image had been recovered, presumably in Pocatello, and yet allowed Grady to deny he had ever had the picture. The two of them, Boswell and Grady, could stand for the island in the liar's paradox, the island whose standard was "Here everybody is lying." But was that statement a lie, too? On the other hand, maybe the Pontiac had not belonged to the agency. But then who had sent in that Chinook?

It had now been three weeks since the theft of the Virgin of Guadalupe from the basilica in Mexico City. Traeger read what he had on the event, news reports, notes on conversations. He was determined to start from scratch and look for things he hadn't thought important before. Maybe they still weren't. But he found himself dwelling on the American who had been gunned down during the theft. Lloyd Kaiser. What had he been doing in the basilica? Why had he tried to stop the thieves? The answers seemed obvious. He had been a pilgrim and had been in the back of the basilica, waiting to go to confession, when all hell broke out. Wouldn't any pilgrim do what Lloyd Kaiser had done? Apparently not. He was the only one who had risen to the occasion.

Googling Lloyd Kaiser told him that the man had been the author of books for young adults. Citizen of Indianapolis, native of Minneapolis. It sounded like a Roger Miller song. He called up the website of the *Indianapolis Star* and found an obit that must have been written by one of the family. But there was also a news story on Kaiser, citing him as one of the many in the great pantheon of Hoosier authors. Traeger thought he recognized Booth Tarkington and Kurt Vonnegut, but the accomplishments of the others seemed as modest as Kaiser's.

After that blind alley, Traeger got back to relevant facts.

Theophilus Grady called a press conference in El Paso, claiming to have stolen the painting as a way to stop the invasion of the country by undocumented aliens. Grady was whisked away and soon it was learned that all the Rough Rider camps along the border were gone, leaving the subsequent uproar to Paul Pulaski and his Minutemen.

All the events in the guerrilla war aside, along with the fulminations of congressmen and senators and the odd silence from the White House, the next significant item was the emergence of Miguel Arroyo as spokesman for his fellow Latinos. The head of Justicia y Paz had issued a call to arms, but like Grady he seemed to shy away from any personal involvement.

Next was the deal with Morgan and the arrangements made for the exchange in the long-term parking lot of the San Francisco airport. What a fiasco. Morgan dead, whatever he had brought missing, and then Hannan's million-dollar ransom almost missing but for Laura's shrewdness. From cover, Traeger and Crosby had seen the package carried from the house to the Pontiac with tinted windows.

Meanwhile, Crosby had gone back to his own business. Traeger put through a call but Crosby was not available. Traeger left his number.

The one good thing that had come out of the fiasco in the parking lot had been Crosby's tailing of the Hummer. That had brought him, and eventually Traeger, to Grady's hideout near Pocatello, Idaho. And then the big Chinook landed and Grady was taken into custody by former colleagues of Traeger and Crosby. And then the package had been put into the Pontiac with tinted windows.

Apart from the recent assassination attempt on Miguel Arroyo, that seemed to be it. But Lowry had urged Traeger to go see Arroyo, as he would have done if he hadn't been summoned back to Washington.

That was about where he was, and it was pretty much nowhere. His first thought was to direct the plane to L.A. and follow Lowry's suggestion. As it was, they were headed for Oakland. Hannan had insisted that Traeger must first consult with Don Ibanez. Because Hannan had liked the report on the old man's behavior in that parking lot? In any case, the insistence had seemed whimsical. But he had put the obvious question. If Grady didn't have the miraculous portrait, had Morgan brought it to the San Francisco airport and then been killed while at the wheel of his car? Whatever had been in the trunk of his car was missing.

"Which is why Grady didn't have it," Ray Whipple said. "If

Morgan could deliver it, that meant Grady no longer had it. He wouldn't have wanted to admit that, so when he saw the charges he might be facing he took back his whole story."

Traeger decided not to correct the assumptions of that declaration.

Hannan had been insistent. "Talk to Don Ibanez."

"Okay."

"Traeger, the stolen image was life-size. How could it fit into the trunk of a car?"

Lots of ways, if you didn't mind making a smaller package of it. Rolling it up maybe. But Traeger remembered Don Ibanez in that parking lot. His reaction to that empty trunk was odd. In fact, every time Traeger had talked with the old man, Don Ibanez had not seemed overly anxious about the missing Virgin of Guadalupe.

More than merely puzzling, that was beginning to look significant.

The San Francisco Giants were at home and Smiley and Steltz were looking forward to a few games while they awaited word from Traeger. Alerted by Hannan, Don Ibanez was waiting for him with a car. So up the Napa Valley they drove, with Don Ibanez narrating a history of the area. Traeger listened, looking at the passing scenery, keeping his eye out for other wild geese he might chase.

Clare opened the door of the hacienda and greeted Traeger warmly. He went inside while Don Ibanez went off to make a visit to the basilica. On a patio in front of the house, George Worth was seated, a glass of wine in his hand. He lifted it in greeting. There was another glass on a glass-top table. Clare's.

"Won't you join us?"

He would. Clare poured Traeger a glass of wine. "I had a long talk with Lowry."

The reminder of the Catholic Worker house in Palo Alto made Worth uncomfortable. Lowry had told Traeger of the star-crossed romance—his phrase—between George Worth and Clare Ibanez. Was Worth wavering in his dedication to the poor devils who showed up at the house? Looking around, at the grounds, at the hacienda, at Clare when she handed him his wine, Traeger couldn't say that he blamed George Worth if he was finding this setting more attractive than the one in Palo Alto.

Later Don Ibanez joined them and soon they were called to the table. The fare seemed modest after the feast Traeger had had at Empedocles. Afterward, they left the young people to themselves and adjourned to Don Ibanez's study. The old man lit a huge cigar after offering one to Traeger, which he refused. He got out his cigarettes, and for a moment they smoked in silence.

"So, have you figured it out, Mr. Traeger?"

"No."

"The portrait of Our Lady of Guadalupe would not have fit into the trunk of that car we saw a week ago in San Francisco."

"It could have been rolled up."

"That would have done irreparable damage."

"Morgan wouldn't have cared about that."

"He would if he expected to receive the money that Mr. Hannan so generously put up."

"If he didn't have it, what did he expect to turn over?"

"A portrait of Our Lady of Guadalupe."

"Which he didn't have."

Don Ibanez was smiling. He was enjoying this.

"Oh, he must have had what was stolen from the shrine in Mexico City."

"I'm not following you."

"Because I am being deliberately mystifying. The original painting had been removed from the basilica earlier, before the theft, when rumors circulated that some such deed was planned. It was replaced by a copy."

"Are you telling me that all this commotion has been over a copy? That all those monks down there in charge of the shrine would have had to do was announce it and everything would have subsided?"

"Traeger, you will think me naive, but I never imagined the effect the theft from the basilica would have. I flew there, as you may remember, creating the false interpretation that I had been kidnapped. I put it to them just as you did."

"They refused."

"Would you have believed such an announcement?"

Traeger thought about it. "Running that risk would be better than letting all this violence continue."

"You must remember that the basilica no longer seemed to them a safe place to keep what was entrusted to them. Finally they have given their permission."

"Permission?"

Don Ibanez rose. "Come, there is something I want to show you."

They went outside through French doors and Don Ibanez led him across the lawn to the basilica. He turned on the lights, some of which illumined the portrait of the Virgin behind the altar. Don Ibanez drifted toward it, went around the altar, and stopped. He looked up at the portrait. Traeger was beside him.

"That is the original, Mr. Traeger. It was brought here for safekeeping."

Where would you hide a book? In a library. Where would you hide the original painting if not in an exact replica of the basilica in Mexico City? Traeger looked up at the Virgin, at her unreadable eyes. He felt more anger than relief.

"Who else knows of this?"

"You." Don Ibanez frowned. "And Miguel Arroyo."

"You have to make this known."

"First we must return it, Vincent. Then an announcement can be made."

❖

When Don Ibanez said that only he himself, Arroyo, and now Traeger knew that the supposedly stolen original was safely stowed in a miniature basilica on an estate in Napa Valley, he was obviously not thinking of the many supernumeraries who had been involved in the secret transfer.

How many of the monks in charge of the basilica had known what was taking place? Don Ibanez had no idea, nor did he seem to think it mattered. Obviously any or all of them were trustworthy. "Their lives are dedicated to Our Lady of Guadalupe." This was clearly a self-evident truth for the pious old man.

Once Don Ibanez had agreed to give a temporary home to

the original, the question had arisen as to how to make the transfer. The monks had suggested Miguel Arroyo, who was a frequent visitor to the shrine. Don Ibanez had overcome his reluctance to rely on the young firebrand. Why not fly it to his estate by private plane? It was Arroyo who had pointed out the risks. Air traffic was far more closely monitored than those who crossed the border in vehicles or on foot. A detailed rationale for the flight would have to be given, and then the secret would be out.

Arroyo's plan was to truck the image from Mexico City to Napa Valley. Just drive it across from Tijuana? Arroyo had calmed Don Ibanez. Arroyo had contacts, men he could trust. His plan had been adopted and it had been successful.

"How many men in the truck?" Traeger asked.

Don Ibanez seemed surprised by the question. "Two. No, three. And Arroyo of course."

"Arroyo was in the truck?"

"At his insistence. He would be armed and if his trustworthy companions proved otherwise . . ." Don Ibanez frowned.

"And who installed the image in your basilica?"

"Carlos, Arroyo, and myself. Not that I was much help. I directed the installation."

"Carlos?"

"My gardener."

"That's an awful lot of people to keep a secret."

"But they have, haven't they?"

"So far."

"That is why we must return it as soon as possible. Once it is back where it belongs, you can tell the press the whole story. And then all this trouble will be over."

"And how will I return it?"

"You have command of one of Mr. Hannan's planes. I have spoken to him in utter confidence." And then, as if anticipating the obvious objection, he added, "Mr. Hannan does business with the Mexican government."

"I was thinking of our own."

"Ah."

It was Smiley who, the following day, came up with the solution. He would file a flight plan to Catalina Island. They would fly there with the original in the plane, land, then file another flight plan to Miami. He would enter Mexico over Baja, touch down at Mexico City, and unload Traeger and his precious cargo. He would be on his way within an hour and report the mechanical difficulty that had necessitated the unscheduled stop in Mexico City. Traeger considered it from every angle he could think of. It looked workable.

"A week from today," Don Ibanez said.

"A week!"

"I will fly to Mexico City and make all the arrangements there."

"What about Arroyo?"

"There is no need to bring him into this. He can rejoice with us when the deed is done."

The delay still bothered Traeger. His only consolation was that this time, there would be fewer people in the know as to what was happening than there had been when the image had been brought to Don Ibanez's basilica. Smiley was used to doing hush-hush things for Hannan and was told that the stop in Mexico City had something to do with Empedocles.

"Getting it down and ready to go will be a problem."

"George Worth can help us."

And so it seemed settled, except for that week's delay. George Worth seemed happy enough with the thought that he could put off his return to Palo Alto with a clear conscience.

It was the following day that Neal Admirari came up the driveway to the hacienda.

❖ IV ❖

"Wait, there's more."

Neal Admirari had had occasions before to think that it is a small world. How often someone who should have been a thousand miles away had come upon him in, if not a compromising position, one that was difficult to explain. Of course things were different now that he had finally married Lulu. Lulu who was a continent away. Lulu who had become the monitor of his habits, regulating the amount he drank, asking if his insurance was paid up whenever he lit a cigarette. Women like to organize men. It was that simple. He liked it, more or less; it was different. Still, he was enjoying this little respite from wedded bliss, pursuing the spoor of Lloyd Kaiser.

Lulu thought he was nuts. She could be right; after all, he had married her. Joke. He didn't mean that. He loved Lulu. He had loved her for years. But he had grown used to having his passion unrequited and the three weeks of marriage provided an animal contentment he had never imagined. Lulu was quite a girl. Well, no longer a girl, but Neal knew what he meant. So it was that, driving up the Napa Valley, he was torn between homesickness and the sense that he had, however fleetingly, regained the freedom he had lost when he married Lulu.

How easily the concierge in the Whitehall might not have dropped the remark that put Lloyd Kaiser in a new light. The simple pilgrim who had been gunned down in the basilica in Mexico City was now revealed as a man who had cavorted with a woman not his wife for three days in a Chicago hotel. Of course Kaiser was a widower, but even so it was difficult to put together the pilgrim and the swinger. Neal would cast him in the role of penitent.

And Catherine Dolan was another surprise. Former academic, holder of several lucrative patents, divorced, she and Lloyd had known each other as teenagers. The Chicago interlude might have been a sentimental reunion that moved on into something else. Neal had not known what to expect when he showed up at Catherine's apartment building overlooking Lake Calhoun in Minneapolis. To learn she was off in California and using Jason Phelps as her forwarding address added more tang to the mixture. Phelps had made a name for himself as the tireless debunker of religious phenomena. The only thing he hadn't taken a shot at was the appearance of the Virgin to Juan Diego. But somehow Neal felt that several more unrelated items were gathering into a unified explanation.

He had been about to turn into Phelps's drive, when he thought of Don Ibanez just up the road. First he would see if Don Ibanez knew what was going on at his neighbor's. So it was into Don Ibanez's drive that he turned and there was Traeger. Neal hopped out of the car and reminded Traeger who he was. "Rome, North American College . . ."

"I remember."

"You can bring me up to date."

"On what?"

"Your investigation."

A member of the press grew used to the equivocal manner in which people were apt to regard what must seem mere curiosity.

"Where've you been?" Traeger asked.

"Walking up and down in the world, like the devil in Job."

"You drove."

Neal let it go. Biblical allusions were seldom grasped in this secularized world.

Clare emerged from the hacienda with George Worth at her side. Traeger introduced him.

"A member of the yellow press."

"I run an ad in the yellow pages," Neal said, striking a light note. He took out his handkerchief and wiped his brow. Portrait of a weary reporter dying to be offered a drink. Clare obliged and they all headed for the patio. Minutes later, Clare emerged with a pitcher of sangria, the tinkle of ice cubes accompanying her return. Don Ibanez, it emerged, was away for several days.

"Do you see much of your neighbor, Jason Phelps?" Neal asked her as she poured.

"Not now. I worked for him but I've been replaced."

"That's difficult to believe."

He had to wait a moment before she realized he was flattering her.

"The new person is far more qualified than I was."

"Catherine Dolan?"

"How did you know that?"

"It's a long story. What is she like?"

"As I said, qualified. Competent."

"Would you happen to know where she's staying? There's something I must tell her."

Clare grew embarrassed. "She's staying at the house."

"Phelps's? Good, that simplifies matters."

"In what way?"

"It's confidential."

Traeger, too, seemed to have lost his edginess. Maybe it was just the wonderful weather in Napa Valley. It wasn't until after dinner that Neal was able to separate Traeger from the others.

❖

"That's quite a tangent, isn't it?" Traeger said after Neal sketched out for him the book he was writing.

"All books are tangents. What do you think of this theory?"

And Neal outlined the complicated plot that had been forming in his mind. The turning point came when he questioned his initial assumption that Lloyd Kaiser had gone to Mexico City as a penitent. At first, his three nights of whoopee in Chicago had seemed to give the basis for repentance. Conscience stricken, hitherto straight arrow is off to a shrine of Our Lady to make amends.

Traeger was getting impatient.

"So who did he spend that time in Chicago with? Previous interpretation: childhood sweetheart, reunion after all these years, they fall into one another's arms and make up for all the lost time."

"What kind of book are you writing?"

"A blockbuster. I thought I was doing a sidebar and it has brought me right back to the central story."

"All books are tangents."

"A diverting remark, that's all. Did you know Kaiser was an author?"

In the past few days, Neal had gone through the whole Kaiser oeuvre (which he pronounced "oover"). It had been a revelation.

"What has happened to books for kids, Traeger? You and I might think kids are reading later versions of *Treasure Island* and *Huckleberry Finn*. Not on your life. The whole genre has become liberal propaganda, slanted, warping young minds. Revisionism. Not true of Kaiser, however; his shtick was rewriting history for kids. You wouldn't recognize it."

"Well, you said this was a tangent."

"Wait, there's more." He had put his hand on Traeger's arm, then thought better of it and took it away.

Traeger took out a cigarette and Neal eagerly lit it for him. "You want one?"

"Yes." Camaraderie, that was what was needed. Traeger was not responding as he had hoped. But now came the coup de grace. He made it sound like mowing the lawn. After the Chicago romp, Kaiser is off to Mexico City. ("I'll come back to that.") So what does his beloved do? She flies out here and volunteers to work for Jason Phelps.

"Jason Phelps, Traeger! The great debunker, particularly of Marian apparitions."

Neal sat back.

"Wow," Traeger said. He was being sarcastic.

"So what was Kaiser's reason for going to Mexico City if he wasn't a penitent? He knew what was going to happen! He was there to take part in the Holy Heist."

"Neal, he was shot dead."

"Of course he was shot dead. He knew too much."

Neal sat back, searching Traeger's face for some glimmer of sympathy.

"Stick to tobacco, Neal."

"Traeger, have a check run on Kaiser. Have a check run on Catherine Dolan."

"You want me to write your book for you, too?"

"You don't like it?"

"It's one helluva story. Have you ever thought of doing a novel?"

❖

When Neal called Lulu to bring her up to date, he summarized his session with Traeger by saying he had put a bug in his ear.

"So what happens now?"

"The ball is in his court."

Of course he didn't mean that. Expressing the complicated theory aloud had not made it seem more plausible to Neal Admirari. If things didn't work out, he would take Traeger's advice and turn it into a novel.

❖ V ❖

"My dear, I am an anthropologist."

Jason Phelps felt like an Old Testament figure with Catherine in the house, and in his bed, too, a bit of a surprise that, but she seemed to regard his attentions as a patriarchal blessing. Of course she did not know the Bible. Bookstores overflowed with Bibles, new translations, new fancy bindings, passages highlighted, notes, companions, concordances. The Vulgate, the Greek Septuagint, and the Hebrew Bible were easily purchased. Online, there were Bible courses galore. On EWTN there was Mother Angelica with a big Bible before her, holding forth like an evangelical preacher. Biblical literacy should have been at an all-time high, but still *the* book was a closed book in most of modern America. Catherine was typical, not an anomaly. It wasn't just that she had been raised a Catholic and was untouched by bibliolatry. She was a scientist. A microbiologist. Who is narrower than a scientist? Whose eyes are more blinkered? When Jason had said to Catherine that evolution had less historical basis than the book of Genesis, she had taken it as a joke. For most of her adult life she had accepted as her faith the silly reductionism that served as explanation in the self-described hard sciences, that meant to distinguish them from such things as anthropology. If Catherine was experiencing a crisis in faith, it was of an unusual kind. It wasn't that she wanted to rid her mind of the conviction that science would eventually explain everything; she was tempted to return to the devotions of her youth.

"Science explains everything away, Catherine."

"You don't mean that."

"Why?"

"You are a scientist yourself."

"My dear, I am an anthropologist."

She was eager to hear him debunk the objects of popular devotion, Lourdes, all the rest. The shroud of Turin. He was suddenly weary of all that. Archeologists in Israel had recently unearthed a shroud as old as that at Turin was said to be and comparative tests were immediately suggested. Ah, the union of science and religion. Phelps had countered all the arguments for the authenticity of the shroud of Turin and it hadn't made a particle of difference. True believers were no more moved than a biologist would be when told of the flaws in evolutionary theory. Science and faith based on revelation were both religions. It was not science versus faith. Soon they would be combined into a single faith. Phelps had become bored with all the so-called hard sciences. They were the last thing criticism was directed on.

His neighbor Don Ibanez fascinated him. Phelps entertained the idea that the two of them, old men, beyond the enthusiasms of youth, were kindred spirits. Any suggestions he had made along those lines had been greeted with amusement by the descendant of the conquistadores.

Before Clare had come home to live with her father, he and Don Ibanez had almost become friends, exchanging visits, sitting over wine in the twilight, feeling no need to talk, let alone to argue. Phelps felt there was some odd parallel between Don Ibanez's incredible miniature basilica and his books and papers. Two monuments to seemingly opposed obsessions. But he himself had become bored with his own obsession with the pious beliefs and practices of others.

Far out behind his house, Phelps had had a patio constructed, a table and chairs under a half dozen palms. The object was to enjoy the valley spread out below, but when seated there, he also had, off to the left, an unimpeded view of Don Ibanez's basilica. Once or twice, he and Don Ibanez had sat out there together sipping their wine, but for the most part it was the locale of Jason Phelps's solitude. Sometimes he nodded off in the cool night air and would come awake with a start. He learned to bring a sweater, lest the arthritis in his shoulders flare up.

One night out there he had awakened to see something going on at Don Ibanez's basilica. The yard lights were on, and a truck had been backed across the lawn, its back doors open to the doors of the basilica. Voices came faintly to Jason on the night air. Listening, Jason smiled. Don Ibanez must be installing some new item. The work, whatever it was, went on for more than an hour, but Phelps sat on, seeing and hearing Don Ibanez directing the activity. Finally it was over. The truck doors were closed and it moved away across the lawn. Don Ibanez, alone, went inside his basilica and closed its doors. The windows of the little church glowed. Perhaps Don Ibanez was at his devotions. Jason lit a cigar and smoked with great pleasure. He might have been keeping a vigil with Don Ibanez.

He awoke with a start, the lighted cigar in his lap. He pushed it away and tamped out the burn in his sweater. The basilica was now dark. Jason Phelps rose slowly, his limbs stiff. He managed to bend over and retrieve his still lighted cigar. Its length could have told him how long he had been asleep. He didn't care. The point now was to get inside and into bed and sink into real sleep.

The following day his neighbor had asked if he might store something with him, a bulky foam package. Jason was surprised at the request, given the size of Don Ibanez's hacienda. But he agreed to the odd request. What else are neighbors for?

Now Jason looked back on that time as one of both solitude and peace. He missed the solitude, and peace was gone, not altogether unpleasantly. Clare had returned and he had induced her to come help him with his papers, curious to learn if she shared the untroubled outlook of her father. Apparently she did. His little jibes had amused rather than disturbed her. And such a lovely young woman, lovely and impervious to his indirect if unmistakable amorous advances. After sixty he had come to see that the usual wariness was no longer there, neither in young nor in older women. There had been a time when his life had been more riotous than a youth's. Students, of course, succumbed; the more independent they considered themselves, the more eager they were to be subservient to his demands. Attracting them was one thing; disencumbering himself of them was another. If only they had all been like dear Myrna.

And then, not long after the nocturnal comings and goings, the truck backing across Don Ibanez's lawn, Miguel Arroyo had stopped by. Jason had listened impatiently to all the young man's drivel about Justicia y Paz. Miguel was clean-shaven save for the mustache and might have been mistaken for an Anglo despite his efforts to appear the savior of illegal immigrants. He seemed to glory in the appellation "illegal."

"It's not their fault."

"That they were born in Mexico?"

"That California was stolen from us."

When Jason had come to Berkeley years earlier, lured across the country from Yale by the enormous salary and promise of limitless research money, he was unprepared for this motley state. His first impression was that half the people were from Iowa. Latinos were a buried population, a subculture of no moment, but all that had changed and people like Miguel Arroyo emerged from under their rocks.

"No violence is necessary to attain your ends. All you need do is go on breeding as you do."

"Centuries of oppression require an outlet."

It was ludicrous that Miguel regarded his life as oppression. But what was the point of making the observation? Doubtless the young man had taken on the oppression of others as his own. The theft of the image of the Virgin of Guadalupe had come as a bonanza.

"Of course you believe all that," Jason had said to Arroyo.

"I will not mock the faith of the simple."

Meaning that he distinguished himself from the simple. Meaning no doubt that he did not share their faith. The man was an opportunist.

❖

And then Catherine had come, sent on to him by Myrna.

"She is in danger of lapsing back into her faith, Jason."

"And I am to forestall that?"

"Wait until you meet her."

When Catherine arrived, Jason thought he understood Myrna's remark. Was his old student acting the role of procuress? And so it had developed. Their lovemaking was remedial, therapeutic, a means of weaning Catherine's soul from the allure of the faith her last lover had retained.

"I should have sensed that, Jason. He wore a medal."

"Not one you conferred on him?"

She ran her hand over his chest.

"Do you know of Pascal's gamble, Catherine?"

"I didn't even know he went to casinos."

He reviewed the argument for her, his tone almost bored. Either there is a God or there isn't. If you live as if He does not exist, then die and find that He does, an unpleasant fate awaits you. Live as if He does exist, and the gates of heaven swing open to you. And if, having lived as if God exists, and He doesn't, you'll die but there won't be any you to be disappointed. Belief is the best gamble, that is the idea.

She tugged gently at the ends of his mustache. "And you have placed your bet?" She sounded disillusioned. Earlier, she had been shocked when he dismissed the whole legend of Our Lady of Guadalupe as unimportant.

"Unimportant! Jason, people are shooting one another over it."

"It is not a religious war. It is not a war at all." He thought of Miguel Arroyo, for whom it was all political, a matter of power. Spokesmen for the people always long to be the people's masters.

George Worth was another matter. Jason had long been stymied by Dorothy Day, who was the inspiration for what Worth was doing in Palo Alto.

"Are there many workers in your soup line, George? I mean on the receiving side."

There was little pleasure to be had from twitting the young idealist. Let him go on ladling out soup. Like Dorothy Day, he was completely devoid of politics.

And then one morning Catherine had answered the door and come back to the study manifestly upset.

"It's a reporter."

"I have no appointment with a reporter."

"He wants to talk to me. About Lloyd Kaiser."

"So talk to him."

"Please send him away."

Her reaction interested him. He urged her to talk with Neal Admirari.

❖ VI ❖

"Would you like a drink?"

"I've already talked to his family."

"So his daughter tells me."

"Is she a friend of yours, too?"

"I only met her once."

"At Lloyd's funeral."

"Yes."

"The daughter, Judith, was very touched by your being there."

"I was not there for her sake."

"His loss must have been hard on you."

"Why are you asking me such questions?"

"I explained. I am writing a book about the theft from the basilica in which Lloyd died."

"Are you interested in all the victims?"

"Lloyd was an American. The only one killed. That is what piqued my interest."

"What has that to do with that missing picture? Isn't that what your book is about?"

"One needs an angle, Catherine. Lloyd is my way into the story."

What an annoying man he was. No, she was annoyed, but he was not particularly annoying. Persistent, yes. Attractive in a way. Staying with Jason made her aware of how much younger Neal Admirari was. Her own age. Well, somewhere in his fifties. And he had led such an interesting life. He had begun the interview in a disarming way, ticking off the things she had done, then alluding casually to the years he had spent in Rome.

"Are you Catholic?" she asked.

"Should I show you the secret handclasp?"

He held out his hand, took it back, extended the other, his right. Was he left-handed? There was no wedding ring. Lloyd had been left-handed, as was she. She took his hand, smiling.

"Is there a secret handclasp?"

"Surely they taught you that at Saint Helena's."

The parish in south Minneapolis where she and Lloyd had grown up, where they had attended the parish school. The girls had worn uniforms, blue skirts and white blouses with "Saint Helena's" embroidered on the pocket. The boys had worn blue slacks and white shirts and ties that were always askew. Somewhere she had a class picture, sixth grade, all of them at their desks, artwork pinned above the blackboard on the back wall.

Some of the class had to stand along the side wall so the photographer could get them all into the picture. Those seated at desks had their hands flat upon it, thumbs and index fingers touching. "Make a Christmas tree," Sister Rose Alma had told them. Catherine had been in a front seat, because she was small. Lloyd was among those standing.

"That was a long time ago."

"Why would a good Catholic girl be staying with the notorious Jason Phelps?"

"Did I say I was good?"

If they were anywhere else, sitting in a bar, say, she could imagine his almost pleased reaction leading on to more. The thought in turn pleased her. She had always known she was attractive to men; she had grown older but that had not stopped. Oh, the age of the men increased, as did hers. She thought again of Jason and realized that she did not want Neal Admirari to guess that she slept with Jason. What a circumlocution, "slept with." Of course, Jason did fall asleep immediately afterward and she would slip away, feeling like a concubine. That was the etymology of concubine, wasn't it? One who sleeps with. Sharer of the bed. She had first read of concubines in Pearl Buck.

"Do you know Pearl Buck?"

"No, but I know a silver dollar."

She laughed. He was fun. Did she ever laugh with Jason? "We were talking about your book. You are writing a book, aren't you?"

"Contract signed and sealed. A decent advance."

"What's an indecent advance?"

"I could show you."

Her laughter brought Jason into the room. Of course he was surprised. She had been so fearful about talking with Neal Admirari and here they were laughing and having the time of their lives.

"You should offer your guest something to drink," Jason said.

"Why don't you join us?"

He sniffled. "Time for my nap."

Neal Admirari had risen to his feet when Jason appeared.

Now he crossed the room, introduced himself, and put out his hand.

"Watch it, Jason," Catherine warned. "He'll give you the Catholic handshake."

Jason looked at her and then at Neal. "I never heard of that."

"It went out with Vatican II," Neal told him.

"Maybe it will come back. Like Latin."

"I've read everything you've written," Neal said.

"Oh, I doubt that."

"I mean the polemical stuff."

"You'll be a better man for it."

Jason gave a little wave then and left them. She could hear him slowly ascending the stairs to his room. If Neal Admirari were not here, she would have been following him up. She felt that Neal had spared her that.

"*Would* you like a drink?" she asked.

"Do you ever get away from here?"

"What do you suggest?"

He suggested the motel in Pinata where he was staying. There was a bar. How long had it been since she had been out of this house? She had come through the town when she first arrived. It hadn't looked like much.

"Can I go as I am?"

He inspected her. "You look wonderful. They may ask for your ID, however."

He helped her to her feet, held her hand for a beat too long, and then they went out to his car. It was like going on a date, with Daddy in bed upstairs.

⁂

The motel was called the El Toro and there was a bullfighting motif in the bar where they ordered margaritas. When she licked the salt on the rim of her glass she watched him watching her. He lifted his glass.

"Olé."

"I knew his sister Teena."

They laughed. After a sip she told him of the statue of Ole Bull in the park above Minnehaha Falls.

"A toreador?"

"A violinist. Norwegian, I think. Minneapolis is a very Scandinavian town." She told him of *svenskarnesdag*. And once she had seen Prince Harald when he came on a visit. "Where did you grow up?"

"Who said I have?"

It *was* a date. All the patter she had used in her sexually active days came back, the zest that meeting someone new always brought, wondering what would happen next and not really wondering, knowing that it was up to her. Of course that was out of the question now, wasn't it? On the third margarita it seemed inevitable. Would she like to see his room? She gave him a long thoughtful look and stood.

"You can show me the Catholic handshake."

After she undressed and slipped into bed, it was of Lloyd Kaiser she thought, not Jason.

❖ VII ❖

"I'm turning in early."

Smiley and Steltz were standing by, flight plan filed, plane fueled, off to a final Giants game before the departure. Traeger had rented a U-Haul and he and George Worth had been several times to the basilica considering the job they had to do. It did not seem that complicated, except for the size of the image and the awe to be felt in bringing it down and packing it in the foam crate. Don Ibanez, for all his devotion—perhaps because of his devotion—was now anxious to have the image returned to Mexico City. The old man was not given to any display of feeling, but Traeger sensed his anxiety. Traeger himself was struck by the fact that, quite by accident, he was about to fulfill the mission he had undertaken for Hannan. There had been frequent calls from Empedocles, monitoring progress.

"You'll get a bonus for this, Traeger."

"How will I know? We never settled on my pay."

"Let's just say you'll be happy."

It seemed an odd suggestion from the zealous Hannan that money would make him happy.

Traeger had decided against telling Dortmund what was planned. There were too many involved already for peace of mind, but it was not a transfer that could be a one-man operation. He could wait for Dortmund's reaction when the deed was done.

The only fly in the ointment was Neal Admirari, who had come to the hacienda to consult with Frater Leone. They went off to the basilica and, half an hour later, Admirari returned with a springy step.

"You're Catholic, aren't you, Traeger?"

"You taking up a collection?"

"You wouldn't have taken a job like this if you weren't."

Admirari did not of course know what was planned. Traeger wished the reporter would hit the road.

"I thought you came out here to talk with Catherine Dolan."

"Wonderful woman."

"If you say so."

"You got something against her?"

"Not that I know of."

Admirari seemed about to say something, then apparently changed his mind.

"Was she of much help?" Traeger asked.

"What do you think of Jason Phelps?"

"I don't know him."

"Has it ever occurred to you how much he looks like Don Ibanez?"

"No."

"Think about it. I wouldn't say twins, but close."

"The mustache?"

"The height, too. And age." He paused. "Phelps is an odd duck."

"Catherine seems to like him."

Admirari looked away. Why didn't he go away? The last thing needed once they got going was a reporter in the vicinity.

Later, talking with the returned Don Ibanez in his study, a thought occurred to Traeger.

"You already had a copy of the image in your basilica, didn't you?"

"Of course."

"Which was replaced by the original?"

"That's right."

"What did you do with it?"

Don Ibanez smiled. "Jason Phelps has it."

"Phelps!"

"Not that he realizes it. When Clare was helping him, I asked her to get Phelps's permission to store something at his place."

"The image."

"A copy," Don Ibanez corrected. "A very exact copy."

"So why wouldn't he know he has it?"

"The foam container we have prepared for the transfer, it is modeled on the one holding my copy. As soon as the original is packed, we will retrieve the copy and put it in place."

"Who will help?"

"Frater Leone, although it will break his heart not to have the original here. And Carlos, if we need him."

"Carlos?"

"The gardener. Carlotta's father." Carlotta worked in the hacienda.

"And Tomas."

"Oh, Tomas would not be of any help. He has a very narrow notion of what a driver may and may not do."

Frater Leone, the monk, was an old friend of Don Ibanez, who described him as "my spiritual director." Traeger hadn't seen much of the priest. He pretty much kept to himself. Of course he said Mass every day in the basilica and sometimes came to meals in the hacienda.

"Like me, he is preparing for death," Don Ibanez said.

Who isn't? Not in the way Don Ibanez meant, perhaps, but who could ever drive completely from his mind the thought that at any moment he might die? In Traeger's case, that thought had usually been accompanied by the violent means that might bring it about. He didn't like to brood, that never helped, but in planning the transfer of the original to Mexico City he was aware of all the ways the plan could go wrong.

❖

The night before the planned transfer, Admirari was still hanging around.

"Where you staying?" Traeger asked, although he already knew Admirari had a room in the El Toro Motel.

"Why don't we go there and have a drink, Traeger? Wine's great, but . . ."

"I'm turning in early."

"I was worried about that. So I brought this."

He opened his briefcase and brought a bottle of scotch into view. "What do you say?"

"Maybe one. I don't want to think of you driving down that road half smashed to your hotel."

Traeger took him away from the others, to a little-used patio.

"All we need is a couple of glasses and water."

"No ice?"

"When did people start diluting good liquor with ice?"

"I think you're going to tell me."

"If I knew I would."

Admirari filled one of the glasses half full and handed it to Traeger. He handed it back. "I just want a sip."

"Then I wish it were single malt."

But he obliged. The glass he now handed Traeger was maybe a quarter full. Admirari put a splash of water in his glass, then raised it in a toast.

"To the ladies."

"I thought we were alone," Traeger said before sipping.

Admirari let out a sigh and put his legs out before him. "Are you married?"

"No."

"Never?"

"Just once."

He was damned if he was going to talk to Admirari about his wife. Sometimes at night he was still awakened by her call. In the dark it was possible to believe that she was still with him, in the next bed.

"How about yourself?"

"Traeger, I'm practically a newlywed."

"I wondered where you and Catherine went yesterday."

"What do you mean?" Admirari nearly spilled his drink.

"I don't tell a joke very well."

"Jeez. We went to town to have a margarita."

"At the El Toro?"

"Some bar." Admirari fell silent. He became morose. "God, I've led a footloose life."

"I don't want to hear about your adventures."

"What adventures?" He looked alarmed.

"Who did you say you married?"

"I didn't. Her professional name is Lulu van Ackeren."

"Is she an actress?"

"A journalist. I've been in love with her for years." There were tears in his eyes.

"Why don't you give her a call?"

"Not yet."

Did he mean the time difference?

He had another sip before calling it a night. He couldn't have gotten Admirari out of there any sooner anyway. On the way to his car, Admirari seemed to be trying to convince himself that he was sober as a judge. He might have been walking on a rope. Traeger waited until the car went down the drive.

Before turning in, he looked out at the basilica. George and Clare were in town, where the U-Haul was being kept until they needed it, which—he looked at his watch—would be six and a half hours from now. He went to bed.

There is a kind of sleep that isn't sleep, the only kind he could expect before a dangerous assignment. Was the transfer dangerous? If it went off as planned, it wouldn't be. He slept and dreamt that he was awake, on the alert.

❖ VIII ❖

"I came to help."

At three o'clock, Traeger awoke before his alarm went off, depressed the button, and rolled off the bed. He was already dressed, having slept in his clothes. He left the hacienda, walked out toward the basilica, then cut across a field to Jason Phelps's property to pick up the container with the copy of the portrait. As arranged by Don Ibanez. Before he came out from the trees he saw, despite the hour, the old man silhouetted against the house. There was someone with him. Traeger stopped, holding his flashlight with which he was to give the signal against his leg. He thought it might be Catherine. No, it was a man. He retraced his steps, loping across Don Ibanez's lawn and up the road. Five minutes later, he came stealthily along the side of the house and stopped. He could hear voices. One was Phelps's. He half expected the other to be Neal Admirari's. No. The other man was Miguel Arroyo!

Traeger came out of the dark and cleared his throat. Arroyo jumped in fright but Jason Phelps turned slowly.

"What's he doing here?" Traeger asked.

Phelps was surprised by Traeger's tone. "He spent the night."

"It's still night."

Arroyo, seeing who had materialized out of the dark, stepped forward. "I came to help."

"Help what?"

Arroyo glanced at Jason Phelps, who chuckled. "I could have carried it over myself."

He meant the white taped container lying on the tiled patio floor. It was identical to the one that Traeger and George Worth had readied for the original and which now lay in the basilica awaiting the execution of the plan.

Traeger was trying to decide what to do. He did not know how Arroyo had learned of the transfer, and he didn't care to know. His instinct was to call the whole thing off. If there was this kind of glitch at the beginning of the carefully worked out plan it would affect the whole chain of events. He was going to have to do something about Arroyo. But not here, not now, not with Jason Phelps looking on.

Traeger went to the container, stooped and picked it up, and started toward the spot from which he had first seen that Phelps had company.

"Let me help," Arroyo said, catching up with him.

Traeger shoved one end of the package at him and kept going. When they were out of earshot of Jason Phelps, Arroyo whispered, "Lowry told me."

Traeger nodded. But Lowry knew nothing of the plan to get the original back to Mexico City. He couldn't have known that it was here in Napa Valley. Then came the only possible explanation. George Worth. Had he talked to Lowry? Had Lowry then talked to Arroyo? From Worth to Lowry to Arroyo. It sounded like a double play.

When they came onto Don Ibanez's lawn the U-Haul was backing toward the basilica. Don Ibanez stood in the open doors of the church. He and Jason Phelps did look alike; Admirari was right.

George Worth was as surprised to see Miguel Arroyo as Traeger had been. Arroyo let go of his end of the package and went to speak to George.

"Miguel Arroyo?" Don Ibanez had stepped out of the basilica doorway so Traeger could enter with the package containing the copy. At the front of the basilica, there was an illumined vacancy behind the altar. Traeger laid the package over the last two rows of pews.

"He was at Jason Phelps's."

"Then he knows. . . ."

"I think I have the explanation."

Miguel and George came around the truck. Arroyo seemed eager to justify his presence and helped George open the truck's doors. Traeger decided that the transfer would go on as planned. But Don Ibanez had one more request.

He led Traeger halfway to the altar, before which Carlos knelt, his arms extended. Don Ibanez got to his knees and indicated that Traeger should kneel beside him. The old man's prayer was short. "Mary, Our Lady of Guadalupe, bless and protect this man and his mission." He bowed his head for a moment, made an elaborate sign of the cross, and began to rise. Traeger helped him to his feet.

Carlos helped carry the precious foam package to the truck and they slid it in. The package Traeger had brought from Jason Phelps had been taken behind the altar, the copy it held to be installed later.

The truck doors were shut; Traeger shook hands with Don Ibanez. Frater Leone, looking as if he had never gone to bed, came out of the basilica, wide-eyed. Don Ibanez said something to him and the priest raised his hand in blessing. Arroyo blessed himself, then brought his thumb to his mouth and kissed it.

"I want to come along."

"No way." Traeger pushed him aside and climbed behind

the wheel. George Worth got into the passenger seat. Traeger made a change of plans. Simplify, simplify.

"George, I'll go alone. There's no need for you to come."

"But we . . ."

"Are you armed?"

"Of course not."

"That's what I mean. Hop out, George."

It was Arroyo who all but pulled George out of the cab, slamming the door shut. If he couldn't go, George couldn't go, was that it?

Traeger put the truck in gear and moved over the lawn toward the driveway, visible enough in the first intimations of a new day. When he went past the hacienda, Clare was standing there, in a robe, looking beautiful.

❖

Traeger had hesitated about renting a U-Haul. A pickup with a cap top would have done, or a traditional station wagon whose seats could be flattened. But the gaudy and obvious was often the best disguise. When precious works of art are moved from museum to museum, there is always a decoy van calling attention to itself to mislead potential thieves. Well, the U-Haul was both decoy and the real thing. There was a governor on the motor, top speed fifty-five, which was okay on the mountain roads but when he got to the interstate the limited speed was annoying. He should have disengaged the governor. He shook his head. A U-Haul was one of the most familiar things on the road, but a U-Haul going seventy or seventy-five would call attention to itself.

He had to be right about the way Miguel Arroyo had heard of the transfer. How else could he have known? But all the way to the airport he picked flaws in the explanation. George Worth lived in another world, but he couldn't be that stupid. Traeger might wonder about the man's preference for a soup kitchen even if it meant estrangement from Clare Ibanez, but there were men like that. Idealists. Dangerous.

It was even more difficult to think of Lowry passing on the information to Arroyo. Or was it? He remembered Lowry urging him to go see Arroyo just before Washington had summoned him back and decommissioned him. The much publicized assassination attempt looked more and more like a staged diversion.

He was in early morning traffic now, by definition madder than that at any other time of day. Cars whizzed by him and even in the slow lane he got the horn, flashes of lights, and then an irate motorist swung out and around him, no doubting cursing the U-Haul as he shot by. It took Traeger's mind off the problem of Arroyo.

They would be mounting the copy now above and behind the altar in Don Ibanez's little basilica. That was probably already done, the doors of the basilica closed. He imagined Clare being joined by the young men and her father. Frater Leone would be keeping his vow. He meant to spend the time until the transfer was complete in prayer and fasting. Traeger took comfort in that. He had no idea how God processed petitions, but he would bet that the prayers of Frater Leone would get through without a hitch.

Signs indicating that the airport was coming up began to appear. Uselessly he pressed down on the accelerator, but the U-Haul was giving him all the speed the governor allowed. Twenty miles, then ten, and finally he was turning in and taking the road to the area where private planes were accommodated. The windows in the tower angled down from top to bottom. A light glowed atop it. Traeger drove across the tarmac to where Ignatius Hannan's plane had already taxied from its berth. He turned his lights off and on as he approached. A door opened and Jack Smiley hopped out.

If everything went as smoothly as getting the package into the plane, the prospect before him looked good. He and Smiley tipped the package, eased it in, and put it on its side in the aisle of the cabin.

"Are we cleared for takeoff?" he asked Smiley.

A thumbs-up. Smiley had on the right sort of sunglasses; his cap was crushed in the appropriate way. He pulled the cabin door shut and started forward, where Brenda Steltz was checking things out.

"Who won?" he asked Smiley.

He hung his glasses on his ear. "I struck out."

Glasses back in place, he went forward and got into his seat. Well, well.

✣ IX ✣

"How long have you been flying?"

Traeger felt the tension drain from him as the plane taxied to the end of the runway. He could hear Smiley on the radio. So the pilot hadn't been lucky last night; let him be lucky now. But it was Frater Leone's prayers that Traeger was counting on.

At the end of the runway, there was a pause of a minute or two and then Smiley gave it the throttle; the plane gathered speed. From the window beside him Traeger saw parked planes and the hulks of buildings flash by, the light on the top of the tower went on and off, and then the plane began to lift. Traeger settled back. Is there any sensation more exhilarating than being in a plane as it first lifts off and then points itself heavenward, rising, rising? This is going to work out, Traeger thought. This is going to work out just fine, as planned, perfectly. For a few minutes at least his doubts and wariness left him.

At about five thousand feet, Smiley began the slow turn that while still rising would take them out over the ocean. City lights were still on below and then they were gone. The Golden Gate Bridge was catching the first rays of the rising sun. Then there was nothing but water beneath. At first, lights from boats came and went below, fishing boats perhaps, but then there was only the water, more and more visible as daylight increased. Steltz unbuckled and came back.

"It went well?" With her cap off and her mane of blonde hair visible, not even her uniform could make her less of a woman.

"So far."

She busied herself in the little galley. The coffee was ready to go, as the plane had been, and soon its aroma filled the cabin.

"Who won the game?" Traeger asked her.

She turned to him, tried haughty, switched to dumb, then grinned. "We did."

Well, well. Perhaps Smiley was just being a gentleman.

Steltz handed him his coffee in a mug bearing the logo of Empedocles.

"How long have you been flying?"

"Since I was a little bird."

"That long ago?"

Her nose wrinkled nicely. She took two coffees up front, but left the door between cabin and flight deck open.

Traeger had developed the theory that at his age he could appreciate the beauty of women without danger to his freedom. There were two things wrong with the theory. One, it was false, and two, what he called his freedom didn't match the ringing promise of the word. For weeks he had been surrounded by attractive women, some young, some not so young, but youth in a woman is an equivocal thing. Laura Whipple, née Burke. Carlotta. Clare Ibanez. Catherine Dolan. And Steltz. He was more rather than less susceptible to such women now. The one thing his theory had going for it was that he enjoyed being a spectator of the great game between the genders.

❖

Catalina Island had long been a favorite destination for sailors, as well as the likes of John Steinbeck, Humphrey Bogart, and other Hollywood types. Once getting there by boat had been the only way, but now there was the airstrip on which they were descending. The only point of the stop was to position themselves for their entry into Mexico over Baja and for Smiley to establish the premise for their unscheduled stop in Mexico City. Something about the instruments, nothing serious, just something to grumble about to the crew topping off the tanks and that would be remembered if any stink was raised about altering their flight plan. Steltz remained in her seat. She looked over her shoulder and lifted her coffee mug.

"Almost there."

"Who won the ball game last night?"

"I already told you."

"Who's we?"

"The Giants! Who else?"

Traeger decided that he needed to have his mind scrubbed out. Maybe he should have a talk with Frater Leone. He remembered Neal Admirari going off with the priest to the basilica, then coming back with a springy step. And he remembered Admirari's reaction to the mention of Catherine Dolan. Good Lord, he did need his mind scrubbed out. It is the curse of the bachelor to imagine that everyone else is making out like crazy. Smiley and Steltz would roar at his suspicion. Wouldn't they?

Traeger ended by apologizing to the lady whose miraculous image was there in the aisle, packaged in foam. Shame on him. For weeks that image had been a problem, the cause of violence. And also of desolation among the simple faithful. Traeger said a prayer or two, one for his wife, may she rest in peace.

❖ X ❖

The band was playing Dvořák.

The airport of the capital was miles from the city but nonetheless as they approached it they could see the bowl in which the city sat, a blurred vision through the noxious air. Smiley was chattering away to the tower in what he referred to as Flenglish, the universal language of aviation, which Shakespeare would not have understood. They were in their descent now, the powerful little Empedocles jet coming in for a landing. The wheels went down with a satisfying thump. Traeger tried not to feel the elation that soon his mission would be accomplished.

Smiley, taking directions from ground control, taxied toward a waiting crowd. Traeger saw a band, banners, vested priests, a bishop in miter with crosier. This hadn't been part of the plan at all. There was to have been a swift and secret passage to the basilica, the installation of the image, and then the great announcement. Traeger almost looked forward to the role he would play then, explaining how the restoration had come about.

Smiley taxied slowly toward the crowd, which seemed to move toward them. He cut one engine and looked around at Traeger.

"Did you expect this?"

"They probably heard the Giants got lucky."

Steltz narrowed her eyes.

Smiley braked the plane; Steltz came back to open the door

and let down the steps. With Smiley's help, Traeger eased the foam package through the door. As they went down the steps, the band went into action. A surpliced priest, swinging a censer, came toward them, stopped, wheeled, and led them toward the bishop. In one movement, the group fell to their knees. The band was playing Dvořák, "Going Home." Traeger felt a catch in his throat.

With help from his crosier and several priests, the bishop got to his feet. He came forward then and kissed the foam container that now Traeger alone held. Smiley and Steltz, as per plan, would take off in minutes and resume their altered flight plan.

Traeger ceded the packaged image to four monks who had black skullcaps on the crowns of their heads, monks from the basilica. A hearselike vehicle would carry the image to the shrine. The bishop gave Traeger a triple blessing, but he traced the cross on himself only once. He was told he could sit beside the driver of the vehicle and he slid in. The driver gave him a hundred-kilowatt smile. He had a crushed cap like Smiley's. The bishop and his party went to their vehicles and the parade began.

For that was what it was. They snaked through Mexico City, whose streets were lined with weeping, cheering people. The bishop without his miter appeared through the roof window of his limousine and cast blessings right and left. It was an event, no doubt of that, and why not? The image whose theft had caused such desolation was on its way to its place behind the high altar of the shrine. Soon pilgrims could pass under it, sending up their prayers to the patroness of Mexico and of all the Americas.

Finally the procession, which grew and grew in length, reached the great plaza before the basilica. The bishop, his miter once more in place, and vested priests, robed monks, thousands of tourists, followed Traeger and the foam package inside. Traeger was holding it high, despite its unwieldy size, as he had seen priests carry the lectionary to the pulpit for the reading of the gospel.

Traeger walked up the main aisle toward the altar. When he stopped, he eased his burden to the floor. Immediately he was surrounded. Television cameramen jostled for position, anxious to capture the great moment. The bishop bowed to Traeger, who got out his knife and knelt. Cutting through the tape that held top and bottom together, he felt he was involved in an ad hoc liturgical ceremony. When all the tape had been cut away, Traeger lifted the top and stepped back. The bishop, again on his knees, took Traeger's place. Two monks came forward to take the image from its container.

One of them wore a pectoral cross, apparently the abbot of the monks to whose care the shrine was entrusted. He, like the bishop, knelt. But only for a moment. The bishop waited as several monks prepared to take hold of the framed image. The monk with the pectoral cross, who obviously was in charge, suddenly fell back and let out a cry. Traeger could not understand what he said. But the bishop did. He actually dropped his crosier and elbowed his way in among the monks.

A moment later he turned to Traeger, horrified anger in his eyes.

"This is a copy!" he cried. "This is only a copy!"

CHAPTER THREE

✣ I ✣

Death to the gringo!

Every means of communication from satellite to word of mouth and everything in between spread word of the attempted hoax at the shrine of Our Lady of Guadalupe.

Those who had crowded into the basilica in the hope of seeing the sacred image lifted once more into its customary place fell back in horror. The bishop in all his glory had collapsed weeping on the floor of the basilica.

A copy! It is all a trick.

The awful truth rippled through the basilica and on to the crowd in the plaza.

Off it went on radio and television.

Within minutes it was known everywhere in the world. And beyond. An orbiting NASA craft, one of whose crew was from Guadalajara, received the news as they were passing over Central America. And there among the dials and switches and winking digital readouts was a picture of Our Lady of Guadalupe. The astronaut crossed himself and kissed his thumb. The rest of the crew bowed their heads. Within the hour the ACLU issued a statement protesting this breach of the wall between church and state in outer space.

Once more people flooded into the streets. The cities of

Latin America had known nothing like it before, not during revolutions, not for the World Cup, not at carnival, not when news of the theft first came.

Insult and sacrilege had been carried to a second degree. This was more than could be borne.

❖

It had been scarcely a month since the theft of the image and the intensity of the reaction had somewhat diminished, although indignant, scandalized anger smoldered on in the breasts of the people. Needless to say, those engaged in battle along and beyond the northern border, crossing themselves as they took aim at another image of God two hundred yards away, had a more direct and satisfying outlet for their rage. It was not for themselves they fought, nor was it for Mexico. Ah no, it was for the Virgin.

Once men had gone off on crusades for similar causes. The protection of the holy places where the great episodes in the life of Our Lord had transpired. The recovery of the true cross, of the nails that had been driven into his sacred body. Was it any less noble to take up arms for the recovery of the sacred image of Our Lady of Guadalupe?

Although there were, of course, mercenaries and adventurers involved in this armed conflict, the majority on both sides were true believers. But how could a passion for secure borders compete with devotion to the Mother of Jesus?

Even in areas where the most blood had been spilled, armed engagements had become less frequent, more defensive than offensive. One could almost imagine a prolonged armed truce. But perhaps that is what secure borders are. Peace has been defined as the tranquillity of order. For those in combat, peace is not getting shot at.

On the diplomatic level, exchanges had continued. The American government was asked to return what it did not have. The Latin American republics demanded that the Yanquis get it. Insults were hurled by politicians without authority. But undeniably, four weeks after the outrage in the basilica in Mexico City, the first fervor had subsided.

And now a crude hoax had been attempted!

When the transfer was planned, there was to be utter

secrecy throughout. Of course the monks knew that the image was being brought back. But given the delicacy of the operation, all announcements were to be made after the fact. Such were the arrangements that Don Ibanez had made for the return of the miraculous image of Our Lady of Guadalupe. But what is a secret except something you are told and asked not to pass on? Word got out. Rumor at first, and there had been many rumors. The pilgrims who wandered dazed across the plaza and into the basilica felt the sense of loss most keenly. Where was the Virgin they had come all this way to venerate? Vendors had developed optimistic scenarios. Soon everything would be as before. Was her return too much of a miracle to expect of the Virgin?

The bishop was informed by the abbot. That seemed an obvious courtesy. From the moment of the theft, he had conducted himself in a way that provided a model for all. The theft was an insult, it was a crime, it was sacrilege. It was all those things. But why had it been allowed to happen? Let others with penetrating hindsight speak of the lax security at the basilica. Let some even grumble about the monks in whose care the basilica was entrusted. The bishop stood in the Plaza Major, beautifully vested, arms extended, tear-stained face raised, and took all the blame upon himself.

It is I who have sinned.

It is I who became too familiar with the presence of your holy image, as if it were owed to us.

This terrible thing had been sent upon them as a sign and a warning. The absence of the Virgin's image called attention to her absence from their hearts.

This sermon, more than anything else, calmed passions in the city and in the country and beyond. It appealed to the penitential spirit latent in every heart pumping with some Indian blood.

Great acts of asceticism were performed. Many fasted. Some moved bare-kneed across the plaza to the basilica. Two men dragged a huge cross for two hundred miles. Sharing the burden, they then had drawn lots to see which of them would be crucified at the shrine. Only quick action on the part of the now extremely alert security forces prevented the execution of this pact.

But it captured the minds and imaginations of millions. The bishop visited the one man in jail and the other in the hospital, where he was recovering from the loss of blood. The one nail that had entered him had found an artery. When the bishop blessed him, he blessed him back. With his unbandaged hand. He was written of as the Good Thief.

※

And now, when the prayers and acts of penance seemed finally to have been answered, when the procession in which the holy image, still wrapped in its foam case, moved ever more slowly to the basilica, collecting people as it went, it was as if a great collective hallelujah had gone up.

She is back! She has returned!

The beads of rosaries moved rapidly over crooked index fingers, counted off by the thumb. *Santa Maria, Madre de Dios, ruega por nosostros pecadores.*

The expectation, the pent-up joy that everyone seemed to have stored up as a final and complete expression of gratitude for the great event, was about to burst—and then, pfffft. The first reaction was deflation. The great crowd in the plaza seemed to collapse as, inside the basilica, the bishop had collapsed on the floor overcome by grief.

And then came anger.

Rage.

Soon, there was a great armed surge northward, through Sonora, across the border, with Phoenix the objective. Within the week, the streets of Phoenix would teem with people indistinguishable from the crowds in the streets of South and Central America. A ragtag band would now claim to be in control of one of the great cities of the American Southwest, control meaning the occupation of several buildings and of a television station.

But that was yet to come.

The following day, in Washington, an explosive device did some damage to what is called the National Cathedral. Only a senator or two expressed dismay. Whoever had thought that bulky imitation of an English cathedral symbolized the religious commitments of the American people was risibly mistaken. Not even the ACLU took seriously the suggestion that the cathedral was analogous to, say, Notre Dame in Paris, where even the most profligate of presidents prayed on state occasions, kneeling on a prie-dieu for all his mistresses to see.

When the Lincoln Memorial was defaced, there was a stronger reaction.

Homeland Security raised the level of danger to the maximum.

In Mexico City the demand that the gringo who had attempted this hoax be brought immediately to justice became a mantra.

Death to the gringo!

String him up!

And, an indication of time spent up north: Get whitey!

✣ II ✣

Only a good plan could have gone so wrong.

The gringo was on the run.

After the bishop cried out in anguished disappointment when the foam case was opened, Traeger was elbowed aside as the crowd surged forward. This had the effect of moving him backward, stumbling, nearly falling. Another man would have begun rehearsing what he might say to the bishop when he recovered. Traeger was not that man. He knew a blown operation when he saw one.

In a minute he was outside, cursing the ruse of sending Smiley winging toward Miami, presumably leaving Traeger to savor the triumph of the restoration of the image. Traeger himself was heading north. His mind was full of the scene at Don Ibanez's little basilica. How had the shift of foam cases been made?

But that could wait. First he had to get the hell out of this country. He had been made a fool of, but he had felt foolish before, not quite like this, but close enough. He shed his suit jacket as he went, handing it to a beggar. He opened his shirt. He grabbed a floppy hat from a stand as he went by it. From another vendor's stand he snatched a serape and a pair of sandals. In a side street, he took off his street shoes and got into the sandals, a change he would regret in the hours ahead. The woman to whom he handed his shoes was surprised, but she quickly covered them with her shawl and clutched them to her bosom. Aswim in the sea of the people, Traeger pressed on.

A mile from the basilica, he saw armed men clambering into a truck. He hopped aboard, sat, pulling his knees to his chest, covering his face with the brim of his hat. He left the truck when it had cleared the city, heading north still, taking a rifle with him, along with a bandolier an eager warrior had removed in order to get more comfortable in the lurching truck.

The distance from Mexico City to Sonora just below the Arizona border seemed to melt away as the determined, now silent, bands moved to the north. Clad as he was, and armed, Traeger was anonymous among so many. When addressed, he grunted or spat, sometimes both. He did not dare attempt to speak. His Spanish was rusty and in any case was a different language than that being spoken around him.

Several times, he clung to trucks filled with grim-faced men. Once he rode a burro so small he helped it along with his dangling feet. He decided the luxury was too costly. He could stroll and make better time.

It was deep night when the mass of which he had become a part eventually reached the border, a flood of thousands, many of whom broke through the hurriedly called-up units of the National Guard. Some would go on and claim to have occupied Phoenix.

In a Red Roof Inn, Traeger managed to commandeer a room and lock himself in. The one thing he had been determined to keep was his cell phone. He turned it on, scrolled through the address book, punched a button, and listened to the phone ring far off in New Hampshire.

He cut off the call before it was answered. Reporting to his employer? Traeger no longer considered himself the agent of Ignatius Hannan. From now on, he would be acting for himself. It was he who had been made an ass of, not Hannan. The thought of calling Dortmund came and went. First he had to think, to reconstruct how he had been duped.

He reviewed every stage in the execution of what had seemed a good plan. It was a good plan. Only a good plan could have gone so wrong. The face that kept looming before him was that of Miguel Arroyo. When he had come upon Miguel standing beside Jason Phelps in the shadow of the covered patio behind the retired professor's house, he should have aborted the plan. His earlier guess as to how Arroyo had learned of the planned transfer was only that, a guess. Worth told Lowry and Lowry told Arroyo. If the first part of that seemed remotely plausible, the second made no sense. Why would Lowry, if he had been informed by Worth, pass it on to Arroyo?

How then?

Arroyo had been the means of getting the original of the image of Our Lady of Guadalupe from Mexico City to the basilica on Don Ibanez's estate. Was it possible that the old man, in a magnanimous gesture, out of a sense of noblesse oblige, had decided to let Arroyo in on the plan? But why not inform Traeger if he had?

All that could wait. Traeger lay back on the bed, reviewing step by step what had happened. The rental of the U-Haul might have caused speculation. And ordering the foam case. Of course he had imagined that those who had been in the Chinook that came banging down at Theophilus Grady's hideaway would still be at work. It was they, or their fellows, who had assassinated Morgan, only to find that what he had attempted to sell was not the original image. Had they tried to take Hannan's million as well, ending up with a suitcase of Ray Whipple's clothes? The descent on Grady would have been a second frustration to them. Eventually, they had to believe the Rough Rider. He had never had the missing portrait. So their search would have gone on.

Most sobering of all, everything that Traeger had done up there in Napa Valley had doubtless been under surveillance.

And then he remembered his surprise when Don Ibanez told him that the copy of the image that had hung in his little basilica had been given shelter by Jason Phelps. Was it with that he had driven to the airport and Smiley had flown to Mexico City?

Where was the original now?

Was it hanging again behind the altar in Don Ibanez's basilica? Surely the old man would know the original as easily

as the bishop had recognized a mere copy. Traeger remembered the calm with which the old man had reacted after the
theft of the image from its shrine. Of course. He had known
what was going on. So, too, in the long-term parking lot at
the San Francisco airport, Don Ibanez had taken part in what
he would have known was a game. Buy back a copy of the
image that was hanging in his little basilica? Whoever else had
bamboozled Traeger, Don Ibanez certainly had. But always it
was of Miguel Arroyo that he thought.

If Traeger had ever doubted, he knew now where he was
going.

❖ III ❖

The preordained results of a sound free trade policy.

Reality is what appears on the television screen, and from the
beginning events in the Southwest had been reduced to the
dimensions of that screen, scenes of undeniable battling soothingly reduced to isolated incidents. But surely now the nature
of the problem would be recognized, patriots would arise in
the House and Senate and demand action rather than more
words. This did not happen, save for Gunther and a few other
marginalized lawmakers. This became understandable when a
thoughtful essay written for *Foreign Affairs* by the presumptive
secretary of state in the presumptive new administration was
released to the blogosphere, the glacial wait for print publication unacceptable in present circumstances.

What was happening, the author explained, was more or
less what both parties had envisaged when NAFTA was passed,
creating the hope of a single great free trade zone reaching
from Alaska and the arctic regions of Canada down through
the States and on into Mexico to the canal. A single economic
unit, but the demands of free enterprise would lead on to political union as well. This had not been clear perhaps in the
original Republican proposal, heatedly opposed at the time by
Democrats, but it had been a Democratic administration that
had gotten the bill through and a subsequent Republican administration that had enlarged it, mapping out the highway that

would enable goods to pass freely north and south, and proposing an immigration bill that would have been a giant step toward political consolidation. Unfortunately, that immigration plan had to be put on a back burner when the radio demagogues went after it. But that had been a delay, not a defeat. Whatever the differences between the parties, and the author acknowledged that they were many and deep, as deep as the chasm between the rich and the poor, on the matter in question the parties stood united. The so-called invasion of Arizona and the encirclement of San Diego were nothing less than the preordained results of a sound free trade policy.

His counterpart, the presumptive secretary of state in the unlikely event that the other party should win the election, signed on to the piece as to something self-evident.

The governors of Arizona and New Mexico, who had flown to Washington—some said fled to Washington—expressed their dismay and disapproval. Of course the invaders had declared that the two governors had been replaced. More than half of the Arizona state patrol, with all their cars and equipment, had defected to the invaders. "Republic of Arizona" had replaced "State of Arizona" on their vehicles. Their representative was currently looking for someone with whom to discuss their jeopardized pensions and medical plans.

Whatever truce had been struck on the matter between the two major political parties, talk radio insured that what its irrepressibly loquacious star called the majority voice was heard. Impeachment proceedings had been launched in hundreds of constituencies. Third parties appeared like mushrooms, plus a toadstool or two. Independent militias were forming from the Dakotas to the Carolinas.

The White House announced that the surge had been a success. Iraq at last was a free and democratic country.

As for the homeland of the patron of this pleasant state of affairs, the picture grew increasingly gloomy. The National Conference of Catholic Bishops was discussing amalgamating with its brother bishops across what had once been the southern border of the United States. When they went into session, the matter was unctuously committed to the patronage of Our Lady of Guadalupe. Many diocesan papers, a majority in the

Southwest, now used Spanish as their principal language, devoting a few columns to English readers as they once had to Latinos.

Thus began, however unwittingly—the farsighted prelates had often gazed on the obscure woods of the future and got lost in the trees around them—the politicization of the outrage that had been committed when the sacred image of Our Lady of Guadalupe had been spirited away by a band of gunmen. That sacred image, wherever it was, was of the patroness of all the Americas. God forbid that she should become a cause of division among her devotees.

A resolution was introduced in the Senate that stated the sense of that body that Our Lady of Guadalupe was not a symbol for Latinos alone but for gringos as well. (The resolution used these designations.) It was, of course, defeated.

The Rough Riders of Theophilus Grady rode again, their number swollen with ardent new recruits. Paul Pulaski spoke from Constitution Hall in Philadelphia, an informative presentation of the role that the original Minutemen had played in the establishment of the United States. They had been menaced by British loyalists, but in the end freedom had prevailed and a new country was born. There are counterparts of such British loyalists among us now, he warned, and they are in high places. They had hijacked the republic. The time for decisive action had arrived.

In Richmond, an assembly hurriedly gathered to declare that the original secession of the southern states was once more effective, given the manifest ineptitude and lack of patriotism on the part of the federal government. An addendum to the declaration was hastily added, stressing that this did not mean the reinstitution of slavery. Gray uniforms began to appear on the island in Charleston Harbor that held Fort Sumter.

⚘

In all this Sturm und Drang, the actual location of the original sacred image of Our Lady of Guadalupe seemed no longer of primary concern.

Miguel Arroyo had moved his headquarters to the Justicia y Paz buildings in San Diego, on the alert for developments.

✣ IV ✣

"Can we take it along?"

"Where is Vincent Traeger?"

Ignatius Hannan put the question to Laura and Ray Whipple, letting them in on the carefully prepared plan that Don Ibanez had confided to the founder of Empedocles. Smiley had signaled Hannan from Catalina and again from the Mexico City airport, from the latter saying, *"Finito,"* and that was enough. Then, after a short stay in Miami, he had headed north with Steltz at the controls, napping in the cabin. But it had been Smiley who brought the plane into the Manchester airport and taxied to the Empedocles hangar. Hannan was not there to meet him. News of a disastrous sort was coming in from Mexico City.

Hannan got in touch with business counterparts there to find out what on earth had happened. He listened in disbelief. Traeger had brought the wrong package! All that careful planning, and flawless execution—he was proud of Smiley and Steltz and he would tell them so once he cooled down—and then, after a triumphal procession to the shrine, alerting everyone what was under way, the bishop had been presented with a copy of the portrait and collapsed on the floor of the basilica. Pandemonium broke out. There had been hours of chaos. They were lucky to get the bishop out of the basilica in one piece. His crosier was in several pieces.

"What about Traeger?" Hannan asked.

None of his informants knew, hence Hannan's question to Laura and Ray, who sat across from his desk. Ray did not look pleased that they had been left out of the loop. But Laura, seeing what was coming, was glad.

"He double-crossed us," Nate said, trying the thought.

"That makes no sense."

"None of it makes sense."

"Why would he go through with the plan you've now just told us of for the first time if he didn't intend to deliver the original?"

"You think he was double-crossed?"

"That makes more sense, Nate." Ray crossed his legs, which in his body language meant that he was ready to be attacked.

What made no sense to Laura was that Don Ibanez had been in possession of the original all along. Riots had taken place, blood had been shed, the whole country seemed to be coming apart at the seams, and he could have stopped all that in a minute. She said all this aloud.

"He must have had his reasons," Hannan said.

"I would love to know what they were."

Nate picked up the phone, thought better of it, put it down. "I'm going out there."

"What in the world for?"

"Just to be there. When I talk to Don Ibanez I want to look him in the eye."

Did Don Ibanez now occupy the role of double-crosser? Who would be next? Thank God she and Ray had just learned of this complicated plan. Once he had delivered the original, Traeger had been scheduled to give a public account of what had happened. The assumption was that the wild joy greeting the return of the original would cover any gaps in the explanation. But after the great hoax, Traeger had simply disappeared.

"Does Don Ibanez still have the original?"

Nate Hannan looked vacantly at Ray. "You two coming with me?"

Laura called Smiley, apparently waking him, and asked if he were up to a return flight to the coast.

"Flying is my job."

"How about Steltz?"

"I'll ask her."

He seemed to have covered the phone with his hand.

"We'll be ready in an hour," he said a moment later.

"You can take turns napping on the way."

"Good idea."

The two pilots seemed to be fooling around as she and Ray had before they married. But Steltz had a husband somewhere, grounded because of incompatibility. They had better be discreet, or Nate would give them the old heave-ho. The founder of Empedocles seemed to be missing a cylinder or two when it came to women. Had he ever even had a girlfriend? He certainly had none now. A eunuch for the kingdom of Empedocles' sake? That had covered it until the big conversion, brought on by watching Mother Angelica on EWTN. Now it was for the kingdom of heaven's sake, at least as Nate understood it.

Boris was abject when Laura told him they would not be eating the dinner he was preparing.

"No! Impossible! Does he want me to throw it out?"

"Ask a few friends in."

"Friends? I have no friends. I'm a chef."

"You and Lise then."

"Bah. She eats like a bird."

"I'm sorry, Boris."

"Sorry!"

"Can we take it along?" Nate asked when Laura told him of Boris's reaction.

A picnic on the plane? Boris would slash his wrists at the idea that he could just pack up the five-course dinner whose preparation had occupied him for much of the afternoon. "Don't suggest that, Nate. Please."

※

Commercial airlines offered bonus miles so that passengers could suffer through more hours like those that had earned the bonus points. The last time Laura had flown commercially had been a revelation. The idiotic security precautions, the interval between the seats that made crossing one's legs impossible—business class and first had been full up when she booked the flight—a little bitty pack of peanuts and a plastic cup of the soft drink of your choice to stave off starvation. There hadn't been an empty seat on the plane. They had been delayed an hour and a half on the runway before the plane was cleared for takeoff. With pretty smiles, the cabin crew ignored the discomfort of their passengers. To think that once all this had been romantic. *Fly the ocean in a silver plane, see the jungle when it's wet with rain. . . .* In an aisle seat, Laura had been lucky to see the clouds. Okay. She was spoiled.

"We'll have to get our own plane, Ray. Eventually." The remark had the suggestion that some far-off day they would retire. Maybe not so far off if she could get pregnant, a condition that so far had eluded their best efforts. Sometimes Laura thought they were being punished for having anticipated the joys of marriage.

Ray put his arm about her waist. "After the baby comes."

He wanted to be a father almost as much as she wanted to be a mother. Was that their ticket out of bondage? Like Boris, they served at the whim of Ignatius Hannan. Like now, off to California on a moment's notice.

❖

It was Nate Hannan, not Smiley, who slept his way across the continent. He never slept while flying. Or being flown. Sometimes he went up front and took the controls, no automatic pilot for him. Laura always knew when Nate was at the controls. The wings would make little dipping motions, the plane would climb out of its assigned altitude, then dive back to recover it. He was like a kid. Well, the planes were his toys. He had three of them and was always on the alert for something better. Maybe she and Ray could buy one secondhand from Nate.

God knew, they would be able to afford it. Once their astronomical packages were pooled they were as rich as Rockefeller. Well, not quite. Not nearly as rich as Ignatius Hannan, of course. But according to the statistics Laura had seen, they were up there in the top three percent. And, oh, the taxes.

"What's the exemption for a baby, Laura?"

"I'll look it up when I'm pregnant."

Had he been fishing? Did he think she could keep a thing like that to herself?

"We can name it Ignatius."

It? "She wouldn't like that."

Laura had started a novena to Our Lady of Guadalupe, Saint Anne not having come through. She had had to vary the original prayer: "Good Saint Anne, get me a man, as quick as you can." Well, after all, Saint Anne had gotten Laura a man, not quickly maybe, but no matter. What saint was the patroness of pregnancy?

❖

When Smiley said they were approaching the Oakland airport, Nate stirred.

"Did you arrange for a car?" he asked Laura.

"Of course."

When had she ever let him down? Smiley brought the plane in, landing gently as always. On that commercial flight Laura had been shocked by the way the huge plane hit the runway, then threw its engines into reverse, so passengers had to put their hands on the seat ahead to avoid pitching forward.

When they left the plane and crossed to the waiting car, they noticed that there were two cars. Don Ibanez stepped out of one. Hannan headed for the old man as if he might tackle him.

"How did you know I was coming?" he demanded.

"A man named Boris told me that you were on your way."

"My chef."

"Is he always so grumpy?"

Nate decided that they would not cancel the car Laura had arranged for.

Nate said, "I'll go with Don Ibanez and you can follow."

Ray saluted, but Nate was impervious to sarcasm.

On the drive, following Don Ibanez and Nate, Ray said, "Well, out of the loop again."

Laura, too, would like to have known what the old man was telling their boss.

❖ V ❖

"Did you ever read *War and Peace*?"

Neal Admirari had not come back nor had he telephoned. Catherine tried to regain the old love 'em and leave 'em attitude that had carried her through some pretty pleasant years. Until Lloyd. And this silence was too painfully reminiscent of Lloyd. Had Neal, too, run off to do penance somewhere? She had caught a glimpse of him in the bathroom mirror, before she closed the door, his head propped on the pillow, a stricken look on his face. What had that meant?

He came on like a seasoned man of the world and even when they had gone up to his room, she had cynically assumed that for him it was instrumental; he would win her heart, or at least her body, and then she would open up and tell him whatever it was he needed for his stupid book. And it was a stupid idea. She didn't care if a publisher had fallen for it and given him a contract and a decent advance. A decent advance.

She smiled. He was fun, she had to give him that. She called the El Toro and asked for him. Would she like to leave a message? So he was still there.

"Try paging him in the bar."

She waited. The bartender came on. She heard him call, "Is Neal Admirari here? Call for Neal Admirari."

He repeated the message against a background of voices, laughter. Half a minute went by. She could hear the name repeated, others taking it up.

"I guess not."

"Thank you."

She felt twice as ignored as she had before. She had used her cell phone to make the call, going out into the backyard for privacy. Jason was at his desk, sniffling. It had been two days since she had taken his nap with him. At her age she could hardly claim the time-honored excuse. Besides, what would it have mattered? A concubine can always find a way to please. It seemed more important than ever that it had not been a fleeting one-afternoon stand with Neal Admirari.

Jason had slept until ten this morning and a young man named Miguel Arroyo joined him for breakfast, coming through the tall doors from outside. She was introduced to the head of Justicia y Paz. Arroyo seemed annoyed that she did not know what that was.

"Ah, my dear. We are living in historic times and you are dozing through them." Jason wagged a finger at her. At his age, he should not try to be cute. Catherine saw that Arroyo was wondering at her presence in the house. She looked at him speculatively, as if he could be a means of revenge on the fickle Admirari.

"You slept through it all?" Arroyo asked.

"All what?"

Now Jason was wagging a finger at Arroyo. Catherine left them, going into the office, looking at her work table, suddenly wanting to be anywhere but here. Like at the El Toro bar. She went up to her room and turned on the television, a sign of how bored she was. There were riots in Mexico City. She watched uncomprehendingly and turned the set off. She became aware of the sound of a television downstairs. Television? Jason? She went down to see the two men huddled in front of the set.

"What's happening?"

Arroyo help up his hand, ignoring her. She could have slapped him.

"The best-laid plans," Jason murmured.

"Oh, I don't know," Arroyo said.

He rose and turned to her, turning on the charm. "I'm so glad to have met you." And to Jason, "I must get back to San Diego."

"San Diego?"

"I've made that my command post. I thought you had heard."

"Sometime you must explain all this to me," Jason said. He rose and went with Arroyo to his station wagon. Arroyo shook hands with Jason and was off.

Her cell phone sounded in her purse, and Catherine felt her heart skip. She pulled it out and answered it, scooting into the front room as she did so.

"You must think me a beast," Neal said.

"Why would I think of you at all?"

"Reciprocal bumblepuppy."

"What on earth is that?"

"Are you free?"

"Of what?"

"I can be there in fifteen minutes."

She hesitated. She did not want him coming here. Going off with him would require some explanation to Jason.

"I'll meet you at the El Toro."

He hesitated. "The El Toro it is."

Margaritas again, why not? But she would not go up to his room again. If he asked. He was as enigmatic as Jason and young Arroyo, chattering about Mexico City.

❖

"Explain it to me."

He couldn't believe how disinterested she had been to the sequel of the theft from the shrine in Mexico City. The Holy Heist. He said the phrase as if it had a bad taste. All that theft had meant for her was the loss of Lloyd, as if she had had him to lose. If he hadn't been caught in that gunfire, would she ever have seen him again? She found herself delighted that Neal Admirari had called, that they were sitting here in the bar of the El Toro sipping margaritas. Maybe she would go upstairs with him again. If he asked.

Neal was talking now about the Holy Hoax. An attempt to palm off a copy of the Virgin of Guadalupe to placate the faithful.

"Did you ever meet Traeger, Catherine?"

"Yes."

"He's the one who tried to pull it off."

"Tell me all about it," Catherine said, trying not to look bored.

He actually reviewed the events of recent weeks, the skirmishes along the border, the formation of vigilante groups.

"That had begun to lose steam, but now." He stopped. "Did you ever read *War and Peace*?"

"*War and Peace!*"

He sat forward, excited. "There they are at Bald Hills, old Prince Bolkonsky, his daughter Marya, and Mademoiselle Bourienne, the saucy French companion. Smolensk has fallen to the French. The invasion of Russia is well under way. But life just goes on as before at Bald Hills until . . ."

"You make me want to read it," she lied.

"I am suggesting an analogy. *We* are being invaded. It's only a matter of time until San Diego is occupied."

"Isn't it already?"

"I mean by Latinos."

"I'll repeat myself. It already is."

He looked at her, relaxed, smiled. "I'm not trying to frighten you."

"Oh, but you do." She looked at him over the rim of her glass. She had licked away the salt without visible effect on him. "Do you know Miguel Arroyo?"

"Of course. Justicia y Paz."

"He was irked that I didn't know of it."

"When was that?"

"This morning. He came to see Jason."

"Miguel Arroyo? I'm surprised Jason Phelps even knows him."

Well, Catherine had been a little surprised herself. She was more surprised when Neal described Arroyo's call to arms.

"He's as bad as Theophilus Grady, capitalizing on that theft."

"So where have you been for two days?"

"Resting up." He smiled.

"Are you all rested now?"

She might have been inviting him to his own room. He was eager and reluctant all at once. Afterward, running her hands through his hair, she said, "I won't tell your wife."

He sat up as if he were doing exercises. "How did you know?"

"A girl knows." A girl! But it had been just a teasing remark. No wonder he felt guilty. Catherine tried to remember how it was to feel guilty about doing what she wanted to do.

❧

It was one in the morning when she left him. He made the usual pro forma protests, but she mussed his hair. "You need the rest."

"Hey, I thought I was pretty good."

"Compared to what?"

"Lloyd Kaiser?"

She slapped him, hard, and immediately wished she hadn't.

"I'm sorry. I shouldn't have done that."

"I'll turn the other cheek."

He rolled over and was mooning her as she went laughing out the door.

❧

Lights were on in the house when she came in the driveway. Was Jason still up? He was. Waiting for her. He rose from his chair with an effort and stood glaring at her.

"I want you to leave. Move out. Go. Now."

"Jason, it's the middle of the night."

"You can get a room at the El Toro Motel."

All right. So he knew.

"I'll leave in the morning."

"Immediately. Now."

He moved toward her as if he would strike her. She wheeled and went up to her room, where she packed a few things helter-skelter, as anxious to go now as he was to have her leave. Not that she could take everything now. Would she come back for the rest? The old goat. Did he think it was a treat for her to cater to his feeble desires?

He was seated again when she came down. She walked past him and out the door without a word. She put her things into the trunk, got behind the wheel, and just sat for a moment. The lights in the house began to dim. She could go to the El Toro Motel. No, for some reason that was out. What then? Feeling like a fool, she called Clare. It took a long while for her to answer.

"Clare, this is Catherine. Jason has thrown me out of the house. I have nowhere to go."

"He threw you out of the house?"

"It's a long story."

Silence while she thought.

"Of course you can come here. I'll be looking for you."

❖ VI ❖

Mistress Quickly, if you will.

Neal Admirari shaved while he showered, not wanting to look himself in the eye. He was filled with self-loathing. Once was bad, but the second time was unforgivable. No, don't say that. God is mercy. Lulu would be another matter. He could not wait until the weekend, of course. So he must go back to Frater Leone, a wonderfully otherworldly man, and with the same story after two, no, three days. God would forgive him, all he had to do was confess, but Lulu? He did not even dare talk to Lulu until Frater Leone lifted his hand and said the formula of absolution over him. He would feel like a newborn babe then. Oh, there was still the temporal punishment due to sin, of course, the object of all those indulgences, but say what you will, they had built Saint Peter's.

When he stepped out of the shower, he heard the room phone ringing. He grabbed a towel and began to rub his head.

Catherine? Dear God. It had to be. Lulu would call his cell phone. He could of course just ignore it, but that would only put off the evil day. He was going to have to make a clean break with Catherine. There was no point in going to confession otherwise. A firm purpose of amendment, that was what he needed. And besides, Catherine now knew he had a wife. Such a sporty antinomian wench she was. He smiled. Mistress Quickly, if you will. His smile faded. But even a wench can misunderstand and what woman can be as antinomian as a man? Just a lapse in his own case, of course. He felt weighed down by the moral law, in the breach, if not in the observance.

He went to the phone, avoiding the sight of himself in the mirrors, naked as a jaybird, overweight, but still irresistible to women apparently. He closed his eyes, threw back his shoulders, and picked up the phone.

"Yes?" he said in a grave voice.

"Neal?"

"Lulu!"

"You must have turned off your cell phone. What time is it there?"

"Aren't you going to say you love me?"

"I've forgotten what you look like."

"Love starved."

With Lulu's voice in his ear, it was impossible to believe that he had succumbed to the blandishments of Catherine, and twice! He liked to think of it as passive, she the aggressor, he the seduced. It seemed to diminish his guilt.

"Good. I'm coming out. Neal, everything is falling apart. It's frightening."

There he stood, still dripping from the shower, hair only half dry, as heavy with guilt as Hamlet's uncle, hearing his wife saying she would join him. He averted his eyes from the bed to whose adulterous sheets with such dexterity he had posted . . . He knew he was rattled when he turned Shakespearian.

"Or I could come there, Lulu. I've done what I came to do."

"Done? Are you mad?" She inhaled, then paused. "Oh, your book."

He drew himself up. The towel was now around his shoulders, the rest of him naked to his enemies. "My book. It is why I am here, my love."

"Neal, everyone is converging on California. Everyone who isn't trying to get to Mexico City. This *is* your book, for God's sake."

"Of course it is."

Just like that, his professional persona was back. Shakespeare, thou art not living at this hour. Ah, Byron. Lulu spoke with excitement.

"And to think you're right there in the eye of the storm."

"Lulu, this is the story of the millennium."

"I wonder if we'll survive."

For a millennium? "How soon can you get here?"

"Getting a flight is hell."

"Keep me posted."

"Keep your cell phone on."

"It needs recharging."

"Who doesn't?"

❖

And so, renewed in body if not yet in spirit, Neal headed up the road to Don Ibanez's. There was more traffic than usual. Several Oakland taxis. A television truck. My God, the brethren were arriving. As he approached Jason Phelps's drive he saw the chaos on the road ahead. Don Ibanez must have closed and locked his gates to the media. Neal managed to pull into Phelps's drive. This was risky, with Catherine on the premises, but faint heart never lost fair lady. He hopped out, went up to the door under the overhang, then thought better of it. He went back down the drive and pulled the gates closed, shutting out the competition. The media had no respect for private property.

He rounded the house, remembering the study whose french doors opened onto a patio and gave the professor an unrivaled view of his domain, and of much more besides. He was in luck. Phelps was at his desk. No sign of Catherine. The doors were open. Neal stepped inside. Phelps looked up.

"You!" He rose as if pulled up by wires.

"I hoped you'd remember me."

"She's gone! I threw her out."

Catherine? The poor girl. "Gone?"

"You will no doubt find her at your place of assignation."

Neal looked puzzled.

"The El Toro Motel!" the old man roared. It was like seeing Don Ibanez drop his patrician manner and have a fit. Phelps was clearly in a rage.

"I don't understand."

Phelps looked at him exophthalmically, his face empurpled. Suddenly he sank into his chair and buried his face in his great, gnarled hands.

"Don't mock me, sir," Phelps croaked.

Neal pulled up a chair. Phelps looked at him through his fingers.

"Don't grow old," he advised.

Neal found all this an annoying distraction. Of course Catherine had hinted at the old man's amorous advances, which, in her telling, she had resisted. Apparently she hadn't. What is more pathetic than a lovesick septuagenarian? The thought of Catherine with this old and feeble, however venerable, man, was almost as effective as absolution.

"You surely don't think that Catherine and I . . . Professor Phelps, I am a married man."

The hands dropped. Something like hope came into the great pouched eyes.

Neal affected a laugh. "Catherine jeopardize her position here? For me?" The laugh became genuine. Take her, she's yours.

"I asked her to go. In the middle of the night. I threw her out. I assumed she had come from you."

"When was this?"

"After midnight."

"My dear fellow, I had been in bed for hours then." True enough. No need to elaborate. Phelps was taking heart. But what truth seeker is not vulnerable to an artful lie?

"But where did she go?"

"Have you checked at the motel you mentioned?"

Phelps snatched up the phone. He didn't know the number. Neal tossed an El Toro matchbook onto the desk. It was a risk, but Phelps was clearly deep in self-deception now. He called the motel. Neal turned and looked out the open doors. Far off was a little area with benches, overhanging palms, and to the left, just visible, a bit of Don Ibanez's basilica. He could hear Phelps on the phone. He heard him slam it down.

"She isn't there!"

"You say you asked her to leave?"

"I threw her out into the night!" Was he going to cry?

"Then I suppose she left. She may be on her way back to Minneapolis."

The old man fell back in his chair. He seemed grateful for Neal's guess. Neal leaned toward him.

"What do you know of the events at Don Ibanez's?"

"Events." Phelps was reluctant to emerge from his cocoon of self-pity.

"The great hoax. It began here. Haven't you been keeping up on the news?"

What was the collapse of the country compared to the loss of a concubine? Catherine had used the word. Strange woman, and alluring. Neal could easily have taken on again the feelings that Jason Phelps was trying to master. The loins are never completely monogamous.

"They picked up the package I'd been keeping for Don Ibanez."

"Tell me about it." Calmness was all. "What package?"

Phelps described it, as if to dismiss it from memory; it was an irrelevancy to him in this time of trial. "A foam package, taped."

"How large?"

"What in God's name difference does that make?"

But Neal was putting two and two together and hoping they were still on a base ten system. Had the missing portrait of Our Lady of Guadalupe found refuge under the roof of a notorious atheist and debunker of such things? But why would Phelps have been told what the contents of that package were?

"There was an exchange?"

Phelps clearly wanted Neal out of there. He had picked up the phone again and punched numbers he read from a notebook. Neal rose. As he went out the door, he heard Phelps say, "Myrna, this is Jason."

❖

Neal went at a good pace to the back of the property and as he did his view of the basilica came and went as the terrain altered and trees were thick or thin. When he reached the little cluster of benches under the palm trees he saw what seemed to be a path leading into Don Ibanez's property. It might have been his reason for turning into Phelps's driveway rather than joining the traffic jam on the road ahead. Thank God he had shut the gates to Phelps's driveway. But they were unlocked. Neal hurried along the seeming path, in the direction of the basilica.

❖ VII ❖

"Three packages?"

Don Ibanez led Nate Hannan into the little basilica, stood facing the altar, and bowed his head. Hannan followed suit, but the founder of Empedocles did not intend to pray for long.

"That is where the original hung?"

A mournful sigh. "That, of course, is a copy."

Don Ibanez told them the story later, over wine in his study, his tone the desolate one of a man who regretted ever taking part in such a deception.

"The monks at the shrine were warned that such a theft was planned," he explained.

One response would have been to turn the basilica and surrounding area into an armed camp, and even then there was no assurance that the outrage could have been prevented. And so Don Ibanez had been approached.

"By the monks?"

"Miguel Arroyo was their intermediary."

"Was he the one who warned them of the planned theft?" Ray asked.

Don Ibanez looked at him with his tragic pouched eyes. "I don't know."

"Go on, go on," Nate urged.

The plan was worthy of the most sensational thriller. Remove the original and replace it with a copy. Spirit the sacred image out of the country and hide it where no one would dream of looking. "Where would you hide a book?" Arroyo had asked. "In a library."

And what better place for the original picture than in a little basilica exactly like the shrine in Mexico City, though of course on a smaller scale? An artful copy of the image had hung behind its altar from the time of its construction. Now the original would be there.

"I did not sleep during the days it took to get it here," the old man said. "But once it was safely here . . ." A beatific expression erased the lines of his face. To have the object of his principal devotion mere footsteps from his house, to be able to visit it at will, untroubled by crowds of pilgrims. "Frater Leone spent hours on his knees in the basilica. And so did I. Those were wonderful weeks."

Ray said, "Except for riots, gunfire, general chaos."

The beatific expression was replaced by that of a lost soul. "Exactly. No one was more shocked than I at the reaction when a theft did take place. I myself flew to Mexico City to beg the monks to say they knew where the original was. Blood was being shed."

"That was when you were supposedly kidnapped," Laura said.

"Yes. Miguel Arroyo tried to dissuade me. But I was determined to go."

The monks, when Don Ibanez spoke with them, were convinced that any such announcement on their part would be dismissed as the excuse of faithless custodians whose precious object had been stolen.

"I could see their point. But I could not agree. They were impervious to argument. The picture was safe. They were convinced that Our Lady would not permit the violence to continue. I returned."

But the violence had continued. Finally the return of the miraculous image was agreed to. The bishop, when consulted, was convinced that people would be so overjoyed by its return that all violence would cease. There would be a triumphant procession to the shrine. . . .

And so the plan for the return was worked out.

"With Arroyo?"

"No, no. With your man Traeger."

Hannan made a face, but said nothing. Ray asked Don Ibanez to describe exactly what had happened here at the little basilica as the plan was put under way. They all leaned toward him as he went through it, the hiring of the U-Haul, the readying of the Empedocles plane.

"Let's stick to what went on here," Nate said.

"It was the way I had packaged my copy that caught Traeger's attention. Two hollow halves that enclosed the picture and then were taped together. Another such case was ordered. When all was in readiness, the copy was brought here from Jason Phelps's."

"Jason Phelps!"

"He was kind enough to let me store it with him."

Laura said, "I am surprised that he would let even a copy of that picture into his house."

"Perhaps he wouldn't have if he knew what the package contained."

"Okay, okay," Nate said. "Then what?"

"The original had been taken down and stored in the same way as the copy by Frater Leone and Carlos and placed behind the altar."

Ray said, "Why didn't you use the same package?"

Don Ibanez looked at him.

"Open the package, take out the copy, replace it with the original, and tape it up again."

"That would have been simpler," Don Ibanez conceded. "I suppose we thought things would go more quickly if the original was already packaged."

"And who did that?"

"Frater Leone and myself. And Carlos. When the top half was put in place, covering that benevolent image, I was reminded of when I buried my wife." His lips trembled and he looked away. Nate waited impatiently. Don Ibanez got control of his emotions. "She is buried in the basilica. As I will be."

"So we have two packages. I suppose they looked identical." Nate clearly wished that he had been here to direct operations. It was difficult not to agree. But as Don Ibanez had said, Nate's man Traeger had been on the scene.

"To the untrained eye they were identical."

"What do you mean?"

"Frater Leone knelt by the package containing the miraculous image and embedded a crucifix in the Stryofoam, fixing it with Scotch tape. It looked even more like a coffin." Thoughts of the late Dona Isabella seemed to assail the old man.

The package containing the copy had been laid across the backs of pews by Traeger when he brought it from Jason Phelps's garage.

"When did Traeger make the switch?" Hannan asked. "That is the question."

"Nate," Ray said, "if a switch had been made, the original would still be here."

"Do you think Traeger left with the original?"

Laura asked, "Where is the copy that you stored with Jason Phelps?"

Don Ibanez looked tragically at her. "In Mexico City. Surely you know . . ."

Hannan was excited now. "Look, my friend. There you are in the back of your basilica. There are two more or less identical packages, one of which, as you can attest, contained the original image stolen from the shrine in Mexico City. The other contained a copy. If Traeger left with a copy, the original remained. If he left with the original, wouldn't you have hung the copy where it had hung before?"

"But I did. You just saw it."

"And a copy was in the package taken to Mexico City. What happened to the package containing the original?"

"Three packages?" Laura suggested.

"There were only two!" Don Ibanez cried.

Hannan smacked a fist into his other hand. "So Traeger made the switch after he left here."

Ray said, "Let's back up. Who brought the copy from Jason Phelps?"

"Traeger. Arroyo helped him although there was no need for that. Despite the frame, it was not that heavy."

"Arroyo was here?"

"I could scarcely exclude him from the return, when he had been responsible for its coming here."

"You called him and he came up from San Diego?" Laura asked.

"No." He paused. "I don't remember. I must have."

"When was the original packaged?"

"Just hours before we began."

"It was in the basilica?"

"Behind the altar."

"Unguarded."

"Oh, Frater Leone insisted on keeping a vigil watch with Carlos throughout the night."

They all fell silent.

⚜

Don Ibanez was exhausted. Nate clearly wanted to discuss all this out of earshot of the desolate old man.

"Traeger," he growled.

Ray just looked at him. "Arroyo. He's all over the place."

Laura went inside to find Clare. "Oh, my poor father," she cried, coming into Laura's arms. Laura was consoling her when they were joined by Catherine. Laura stepped back.

"Did you sleep well?" Clare asked Catherine.

A smile and a sigh.

"Catherine has been helping Jason Phelps with his papers," Clare explained.

Laura said, "Where could I find Frater Leone?"

"He's with someone now." Clare turned to Catherine. "With Neal Admirari. The man who wanted to interview you."

"Is he staying here, too?" Laura asked.

"Oh no. He just arrived."

"How on earth did he get through that crowd?"

"Good question."

"Would Frater Leone be talking to him here, in the house?"

"I think they went over to the basilica. Father prefers to hear confessions there."

Catherine dipped her head, then looked away. Laura went off to the basilica. She might just go to confession herself.

✤ VIII ✤

"I get bit."

The plane circled over the San Diego harbor, and, looking down, Traeger thought there were more naval vessels there than usual. Imagine them shelling the mainland. Well, remember Charleston. But it had been the rebels that did the shelling there.

The landing pattern brought them down alongside the Marine Corps base and Traeger had a good look at the huge parade ground. For years the buildings had retained their World War II camouflage, but that was long gone. Now there were even women recruits. A bad joke. How do you tell a male and female grunt apart? First you have to get them apart.

Traeger had caught this flight out of Flagstaff, which was calm and cool after the chaos of Phoenix. He didn't bother to change his wetback appearance and there had been a little hesitation on the part of the clerk when he slid a credit card across the counter. He followed it with a passport.

"You've grown a beard," said Sally with a smile. "Sally" was written on the badge dangling from her neck.

"It's for a movie."

"Oooh." She studied his ID again, trying to place him.

"Just a bit part."

She nodded and looked as if now she understood.

"I get bit."

Her trilling laughter followed him to the gateways.

At the San Diego airport the crew from Homeland Security was now a division of the California militia. Mostly the same personnel, however. Everything Traeger had with him was in a single shoulder bag so he breezed right through to the rental car counter.

During the days since his escape from Mexico City he had gone over and over the failed plan, wondering just where it had gone wrong. Somehow there had been a switch of the cases and he had gone off with a copy to Mexico City. He was lucky to have escaped with his life. He had contacted no one yet. He was working for himself. He did not like being made an ass of. Who does? But by amateurs?

He drove toward Old Town, where the San Diego branch of Justicia y Paz was located and which Arroyo had grandly announced was now headquarters. Maybe all of California would look like this if Washington kept ceding territory, like Kutuzov retreating from the invading Napoleon. But the Old Town was largely quaintness, a tourist draw. Would there ever be tourists again?

In Phoenix he had called up Justicia y Paz on the web. The San Diego branch. Of course it had a site. It was the buildings Traeger wanted to get familiar with. Spanish and English ran in double columns down the page but they were broken from time to time by photographs. He had skipped over the beaming face of Miguel Arroyo and kept scrolling down to the buildings. When he had a good sense of the layout, he scrolled up to the founder and head of Justicia y Paz. He studied the smiling face of the man who had made an ass out of Vincent Traeger.

"Adios, amigo."

Does anything ever quite match its website? The buildings were as pictured, but they were smaller than they had appeared. The administration building, a hospitality house—soup kitchen, that is—and a building that seemed to have been lifted from an old army base. The homeless found a home there. Traeger pulled into the lot in which Arroyo's car had been bombed.

When he went inside, the receptionist rose and told him he was in the wrong building. She pointed him to the barracks.

"Miguel Arroyo is expecting me."

She seemed surprised when he spoke. But she could not put together his costume and the eastern seaboard voice he had assumed. It was a one-story building, with labels and arrows all over the place.

"I can find my way," he said, and headed down the hall.

"Wait! I have to announce you."

Doors were opening along the corridor but there were no heroes among the curious. A bell started ringing, some kind of alarm. But the door on the far right side of the corridor had opened and Miguel Arroyo came out to see what the hell was going on. He came toward Traeger with his biggest smile.

"Amigo, no ahi."

"I wasn't sure you'd recognize me."

Arroyo stopped and the smile began to fade. Who was this peon?

"We can talk in your office." He took Arroyo's arm and then recognition came.

"Everything's okay," Arroyo called over his shoulder. "Turn off that alarm."

Traeger shut the door behind them. Arroyo regarded him warily.

"I've been worried about you, Traeger."

"I was sure you would be."

"But there's a manhunt on. How did you get here?"

"It took you a moment to recognize me, didn't it? Besides, I'm trained for this sort of thing."

"Amazing."

"How did you do it, Arroyo?"

Arroyo took a chair and so did Traeger. "Just review the whole thing, Miguel. I really do want to know how you managed it."

"You're not seriously suggesting . . ."

"Cut the bullshit. Thanks to you I went on a pointless mission to Mexico City, where I might have been lynched if I hadn't vamoosed."

"What a journey that must have been."

"I thought of you all the way. Now here we are, alone at last. I decided against really blowing you up in your car. I want to know how you did it."

"And then?"

"One thing at a time."

"Traeger, as God is my judge, I did not do whatever you think I did."

"What do I think you did?"

"Tell me. I have no idea."

The phone on the desk rang; Arroyo picked it up. "Not now. Nothing. I'm busy."

Traeger suggested that the way to do this was for Arroyo to describe everything that happened that morning before Traeger drove off in the U-Haul.

"What can I say? I was visiting with Jason Phelps when

you showed up. That was my first inkling that something was afoot. I helped you take the package to Don Ibanez, remember?"

"So we brought the package. There was another ready for delivery to the shrine in Mexico City. Somehow it was the copy I put into the U-Haul and took to Mexico City. You should have been there when it was opened."

"I've seen pictures. Traeger, believe me, you've been news."

"I'm being hunted."

"What have you got to fear? The beard was a good idea, by the way."

"How did you make the switch?"

"I could sit here all day and deny I did that and you wouldn't believe me."

"So quit pretending you didn't do it."

Arroyo dropped into thought. He hummed and looked away. He turned to Traeger, his expression altered. "Maybe I do know what happened that night."

"Of course you do."

"No, no. This is a guess. But a good guess."

Traeger waited. He had been conned once by this guy and he didn't plan to have it repeated.

"Phelps," Arroyo said. "Jason Phelps. That has to be it."

"Arroyo, if that's the best you can do . . ."

"But it has to have been Phelps. Look, I told him everything that was about to happen. How could anything go wrong at that point?"

"You said you hadn't known."

"Don Ibanez had called me. That's why I was up in the valley."

"How can I tell when you're not lying? When you're not talking?"

Arroyo winced. "I suppose if I'd been through what you have I'd suspect everyone else, too. You realize everyone thinks you still have the sacred image. Or know where it is."

"Why else would I take a copy to Mexico City and risk my life?"

"It doesn't makes sense. Just as your thinking I did what you said doesn't make sense."

He sat forward, excited now. He had thought something was funny when he had been talking to Phelps before Traeger showed up.

"He knew all about it, Traeger. He stood there in the dark chuckling over what a surprise was coming."

"He said that?"

"As God is my judge."

Traeger might have been willing to consider this stupid suggestion, but that addendum saved him.

"Look, Traeger. My saying it will never convince you. Why don't we go up there and confront Phelps? You can get the truth out of him."

"I can't seem to get it out of you."

"Traeger, please. I will put myself in your hands. Let's go up there and if I'm deceiving you, you just go ahead and do what you people do to deceivers."

The thought of getting Arroyo out of the headquarters of Justicia y Paz had its appeal. Here he was surrounded by minions.

Arroyo stood. "I'll go tell them to get my car ready."

"Use the phone."

"Right." He picked up the phone and gabbled in Spanish too swift for Traeger to follow. He hung up. "It will be here in minutes. Do we have a deal?"

"Is that a john?"

"Be my guest."

"Lock your door."

"Of course." Arroyo went to the door and locked it.

In the john, before he did his business, Traeger looked out the little window. That was when he saw the cruisers pulling in. The son of a bitch.

He raised the window, got his legs out first, and then levered himself up and out, dropping to the ground. He beat it around to the front of the building where cruisers were disgorging an ugly crew, all of them with weapons at the ready. Traeger strolled to his car, hopped in, and moved slowly out of the lot. Not quite twice, but close. The son of a bitch.

❖ IX ❖

"I was only teasing."

Catherine sensed that Laura wanted to be alone with Clare, so she went off and left them. But her mind was seething with the thought that Neal Admirari had all but rushed from her side to the comforts of the confessional. Her own memories of confession were not unpleasant, until she had reached the age when she had embarrassing things to whisper through the grille, her heart in her throat, expecting the worst. It never came, but that did not make those moments of anticipation less painful. To have to say such things to a man, however anonymous and invisible he was, stirred up in her the first intimations of feminism. She had married in the Church but by then that was for her merely a matter of form. She had been raised Catholic, she was marrying a Catholic, so of course they were married by a priest. When her marriage went sour, it seemed yet another argument against her already wobbly faith. Had she even gone to confession prior to her wedding?

Getting a divorce had seemed the decisive severing of all links to her childhood. In what she would not have called her promiscuous days, her many affairs had seemed so many declarations of independence—and independence from many more things than her one-time religious beliefs. Catholicism was only one of a whole host of outmoded opinions and practices that had to be put down by the kind of liberated woman she had become.

But even pleasure palls and she became, if not chaste, a far more discriminating partner. However infrequent, those liaisons did not remove her fierce aversion to entangling alliances. Whence then her desire to see Lloyd Kaiser again? How sweet the memory of their walks beside Minnehaha Creek, how innocent yet thrilling those evenings when they sat on a bench overlooking Lake Hiawatha. Whenever she thought of them, her head tipped to the left and she lifted her lips to a remembered Lloyd. She felt that she had given him something far more important than her virginity. She had offered him herself, body *and* soul, as she would then have put it.

He had taken neither—they were both too inexperienced, too frightened—but the offer had been made, and that was the essential thing. And so, disappointed with what she had become, she had initiated contact with him. They had corresponded, usually by email, they had talked endlessly on the phone, and then they decided to see each other in person, face to face, always a risky thing after so many years. The same photograph had appeared on the jackets of his books for some years. Doubtless he no longer looked like that. When he asked for her photograph, it took her days to find one to send. In the end, she sent a snapshot. For better or worse, that was how she now looked. But she had been pleased with the looks she had.

And then Chicago, the Whitehall, those glorious orgiastic days and nights. My God, how insatiable they were. That had become her great regret. It had been wrong to make herself so readily and so frequently available to him, but she had been more eager than he. That had been a mistake. What he thought of her, when the pleasures were over, was hinted at in their good-bye. And ever since learning how he had died, it seemed inescapable that she had become an object of remorse for him.

And now Neal Admirari! Neal, the professional Catholic, as she thought of him. It was thus that he earned his bread, or cheese: he was a church mouse, and not as poor as. He was obviously doing very well. Oh, she blamed herself. He could be forgiven if he thought her the aggressor. But she was so ashamed of her conduct with Jason, that going to bed with a younger man seemed . . . She stopped. Almost equivalent to absolution?

"Catherine?"

She turned and there was Neal.

"All shriven?"

He tossed up his hands and rolled his eyes. "How did you know?"

"Because you're all aglow."

"You're thinking of my watch."

In bed, in the dark, he had pressed the stem of his watch, lighting up its face. He was pleased as punch at her reaction. "And it's a Timex."

Now he became serious. "If you want to go, Frater Leone is still in the basilica."

He was serious! "Did you go into detail?"

"My dear, the airiest abstractions suffice. Confessors are seldom prurient."

"I wouldn't know."

"Don't put it off, sweetie. This very night thy soul will be required of thee."

"Just my soul?"

He brought his hands piously together and closed his eyes. They snapped open.

"What's been going on around here?"

"Apart from importunate penitents?"

"That's good. Alliteration is the soul of language. Not to say its body. No, I mean, who's here?"

"Ignatius Hannan, for one. Do you know him?"

"He's here? That must have been one of his planes that flew Traeger to Mexico City. Has Traeger shown up?"

"You should ask Clare. There are two others with Hannan."

"Have you seen that mob down by the gates?"

"Neal, I have no idea what is going on. And frankly, I don't give a damn."

"Come, come, Scarlett. You can't mean that."

"Jason Phelps threw me out of the house in the middle of the night."

He looked solemn. "He told me."

"The bastard. I wanted to hit him with something heavy, railing at me like an Old Testament prophet, his face distorted. But I went meekly to my room, packed a few things, and left."

"And came here?"

"Thank God for Clare."

"Indeed, indeed."

"I still have half a mind to go over and do violence to that old goat."

"Use the other half. It's water over the dam."

"Move on?"

"It's the only way."

"Is that what you intend to do?"

He studied her. "Catherine, you know I'm a married man."

"Oh, stop it. I was only teasing."

"You are good at that."

"I'll tell your confessor."

They had walked outside, in the direction of the basilica, but Catherine made sure they gave it a wide berth. Despite her banter, she was more impressed than angry that Neal had knelt and confessed their sins. And been forgiven. She had believed that once. Whose sins you shall forgive, they are forgiven. Imagine just going in there, finding that priest, and telling him everything, all the sins of her past life. In airiest generalities, as Neal suggested, but acknowledging them to God. To God. All the feelings she had had in Indianapolis at Lloyd's wake and funeral, seeing Judith and the others, all of them good as gold, came rushing back. And she had thought Jason Phelps could cure her of the desire to again be the innocent girl of long ago.

They had reached the point where the path came from Jason Phelps's place and suddenly there was Miguel Arroyo.

"Where is Don Ibanez?" he asked without preamble.

"In the house."

"I have to see him." But before he rushed off, he asked, "Is Traeger here?"

Neal said, "I should think that this is the least likely place he would be."

Arroyo rushed off. They sat on the lawn and shared a cigarette. "My wife is coming out."

"From what?"

"She will arrive in the morning."

"So we have time."

"Stop that."

She put her hand on his arm. "Can't a girl joke?"

"Fool around?"

"Now you stop it. I'm glad your wife's coming. You shouldn't be allowed to run around alone."

"As long as I can run around."

"You are awful. And fresh from the confessional." Catherine turned toward the path. "I have to go over and retrieve my other things." She paused. As if asking him to come along.

"Be careful."

"He's more in danger from me than I am from him."

❖ X ❖

"De nada."

Traeger pulled out of the Justicia y Paz parking lot, having wended his way among the police cruisers, whose doors hung open, their rooftop gumballs flashing. When he reached the street he hesitated. Right or left? Traffic was crawling past, drivers gawking at all the activity, so right seemed the best bet, but then a gap in traffic revealed the unpaved parking area across the street, next to the barrackslike homeless shelter. Traeger eased his car through the gap, got across, and, once in the unpaved lot, did a U-turn and parked. He had a good view of the main building and all the frantic activity.

Cops rushed in and out of the building; others, having gone through it, came running around its sides. They scanned the horizon. Miguel Arroyo appeared on the front steps, shouting, imploring. Traeger could sense the reaction of the cops to all this civilian instruction. The cops did not get into their cruisers, but they began to shut their doors. The gumballs continued to spin, even in daylight emitting piercing little beams. And then the helicopter arrived.

At first Traeger thought it was a television station's aircraft. Its logo was similarly garish, lots of red and yellow and green, its aft rotor silver. The legend became legible beneath the churning blades. "Republic of California." At least it wasn't any of his old comrades in the Company, unless some had changed their allegiance. The helicopter seemed to be searching for an open space but the parking lot was out. It rose above the building, turned, dipped, and then settled gently on the roof.

Traeger saw the window from which he had exited. From time to time, a head appeared, looking left and right, and then was replaced by another. Riflemen appeared up top, looking over the ledge surrounding the roof. Minutes went by, ten, fifteen, more, and it was dawning on them that the man they had come for was not there. Arroyo was now at the side of the building, pointing at the still open washroom window, and then trying to decide which way the fugitive had gone. He spun around. Toward the street? All those cruisers seemed to rule that out. Toward the back? Traeger half expected him to drop to his knees and sniff, trying to pick up a scent. Ah, he had it. He pointed decisively toward the open area to the right of the building. As if to confirm his guess, he marched toward it and a half dozen cops followed reluctantly. It was some consolation to see that Arroyo was running out of credit with the cops. The little group stood there for some minutes, studying the ground like Indian scouts, looking indecisively around, then drifted back toward the building, followed by the badgering Arroyo.

Another hour went by before the search was called off. At the outset, all those who worked in the building had been escorted to the parking lot. The receptionist was at the center of a little group, arms waving, head tossing, her mouth going a mile a minute. She held her audience for a time, but then they drifted away. She went to a cop and took his arm and apparently began the recital again. Traeger could have given the guy a medal for his indifference to the receptionist's excited jabber. Were they beginning to think that the whole thing was a false alarm?

The final act was Arroyo's. He stood on the steps of his building, haranguing the cops who were getting into their cars, nodding at him, ignoring him. The gumballs were turned off, one by one. The riflemen had disappeared from the rooftop. Arroyo did everything but get down on his knees and beg. What was he asking them to do? He kept pointing to the north. The blades of the helicopter, until now turning lazily, revved up and it began to lift. It came out over the front of the building, and Arroyo's clothes began to ripple in the downdraft. Now he was shouting at the helicopter. But then it went up, up, and away. The cruisers left one by one. Traffic sped up. Arroyo slapped his hands down on the sides of his legs, turned, and went inside.

Traeger had long since turned off the engine of his car. It

was not clear to him what he would do next. The afternoon wore on and then employees began to leave, coming out in twos and threes, separating, getting into their cars and driving away. Soon there were only a few cars left. Then one. To the right of the entrance. Traeger would have given anything for a pair of binoculars. Was that the director's parking spot? Was that car Arroyo's?

However ignominious his exit from Justicia y Paz, the whole crazy business made it clear that his hunch that Miguel Arroyo was behind whatever had gone wrong with the great plan to return the sacred painting to Mexico City seemed justified. How had he done it? Until Traeger knew how he had been made a fool of, he could not rest. The car radio, when he turned it on, was full of Spanish chatter about the rogue ex–CIA agent who had been terrorizing Old Town and the headquarters of Justicia y Paz. They were expecting a statement from Miguel Arroyo shortly. It never came.

Traeger was already a fugitive. He had seen the stories, watched TV in Phoenix and Flagstaff. He had hoodwinked the venerable Don Ibanez; he had betrayed Ignatius Hannan, the legendary founder of Empedocles; he had mocked the simple faith of the Mexican people by trying to palm off on them a copy of the sacred image rather than the original he was to have brought. When asked if it was certain that Traeger had left the valley with the original, Don Ibanez had nodded slowly.

"Hey, I'm just a pilot," Smiley had said. "Talk to the boss."

But Hannan wasn't talking to the media. What could he say? Laura Burke Whipple said simply, "We were betrayed."

Up until now, although sought, his whereabouts were unknown. Now, as the result of the excitement at Justicia y Paz, it would be known where he had last been. If Arroyo was believed. The cops might doubt, but employees in the building, particularly the receptionist, could vouch for his claim that Traeger had been there.

Eventually the sun went down on his wrath, but did not extinguish it. Sure of his quarry, having him under surveillance, Traeger was willing to bide his time. The next move was up to Arroyo. Meanwhile he considered the cock-and-bull story Arroyo had fed him earlier. Trying to involve Jason Phelps in his story seemed an indication of how imaginative it was. But where in hell was the original?

For days, ever since the travesty in the shrine of Our Lady of Guadalupe, Traeger had been putting that question to himself. The switch had to have been made at the outset. Again and again, he recalled carrying the foam case from Jason Phelps, with that idiot Arroyo scampering around, helping with his burden. Could it have happened even before he reached the little basilica with the package containing a copy? For the matter of that, Traeger had never seen what was in the package he carried from Jason Phelps's. He remembered as vividly as could be laying it over the backs of the pews in the basilica. The other package was on the floor behind the altar. Already taped. Don Ibanez knelt before the altar, beside Frater Leone.

Traeger pressed his eyes shut. Then what? He wanted to run it off like a film, but people seemed to obscure his vision. Don Ibanez, George Worth, Clare, the priest, and Arroyo. Speed it up or slow it down, all Traeger could see were two foam packages. So how had it been done? He wanted to pound on the steering wheel, he was so frustrated.

Across the street, the administration building seemed deserted, but that one car was still parked near the entrance. Traeger waited. It was after six when the front door opened. A woman came out. The receptionist? It was. She turned and tried the entrance door and then, assured it was locked, tapped down the steps and headed for the car. Its lights flashed as she approached; she pulled open the door and got in. Traeger was hunched forward, sure that now Arroyo would have to appear and hop into the passenger seat. Please let it happen. But the car backed out of the space, turned, and headed for the street. Watching it disappear, Traeger felt that Arroyo had done it to him again. He could have bellowed in frustration.

An old guy in jeans and a ragged T-shirt came out of the barracks and began to check the coffee can ashtray for something long enough to light. He looked at Traeger and Traeger looked at him. The man made a gesture with his fingers. Traeger got out his cigarettes, shook a couple free, and held them out. The man was at the car like a shot. Traeger rolled down the window and handed them out.

"Muchísimas gracias."

"De nada."

He waited for the wino to scamper away, banking one of the cigarettes in the pocket of his T-shirt. He broke the other in half and put one half in the pocket and the other in his mouth. He sat on the steps before lighting up, leaning back, content. Traeger almost envied him his irresponsible life. Happiness is a bummed cigarette.

Across the street a car came around from behind the building, an open convertible. At the wheel was Miguel Arroyo. Traeger got his motor running. Traffic was light now, but Arroyo took his time about entering the street, as if he were trying to make up his mind. Finally he pulled out, crossed into northbound traffic, and entered it. For a wild moment, Traeger had thought Arroyo had spotted him and was going to come into the lot in which he was parked. Crazy, of course. He doubted that Arroyo would want to confront him without a posse at his back.

Traeger shot across the lot and into the northbound lane, keeping the convertible in sight. Where was Arroyo headed?

At Los Angeles, Arroyo got onto 101 and floored it. Obviously the convertible was a soupy little vehicle. But Traeger's rental responded adequately. He just needed to keep the convertible in sight.

This legendary highway created the impression, almost as much as the interstates, that the citizens of California—now the Republic of California, at least below Santa Barbara—lived in their automobiles. A river of cars, lights on now, increasing the sense of flow, moved northward. Another river moved south. Ceaselessly, like other rivers. That Arroyo was in an open car made it easier to keep him in sight, but Traeger was tense, determined not to let the son of a bitch elude him.

He set the cruise control at eighty, but cars continued to whip by him in other lanes. Arroyo had settled into a steady speed. For hours, Traeger followed him along the beautiful highway. To the right, mountains loomed, their tops still catching some of the setting sun; to the left, coming and going out of sight, was the ocean. Traeger decided that Arroyo was headed for Napa Valley. Maybe to square his silly story with Jason Phelps, though how he could enlist the help of the crusty old agnostic Traeger could not see.

✢

It wasn't until San Luis Obispo that Arroyo turned into a filling station. Traeger had been watching his gauge anxiously, belatedly realizing that the car had not had a full tank when he rented it. It seemed a harbinger of a dropping of standards of efficiency in the new regime.

Arroyo ignored the self-serve lane and went inside while his car was fueled. Traeger, with several rows of pumps to screen him, filled up. He moved forward and parked near the exit, so he could follow Arroyo out. Arroyo would have availed himself of the restroom inside. Traeger did not want to think of his own discomfort. He would wet his pants before he took a chance on losing Arroyo. More and more he was convinced that the founder of Justicia y Paz was taking him to the big showdown.

It was going around Oakland that Traeger lost Arroyo.

✢

Arroyo had put up the top after filling up and it was harder to keep him in sight. Traeger drew closer but got into the far left lane to stay out of Arroyo's sight. There was no point in getting careless, even though he was certain Arroyo had no idea he was being tailed. But suddenly he was gone. Traeger looked around. He couldn't have turned off. Had he dropped behind? Traeger slowed and was immediately given the horn by the maniac who was tailgating him. He flicked his signal to ease into the next lane and got another horn. The hell with it. He bulled his way across the lanes to a chorus of horns. But where the hell was Arroyo's convertible?

He had lost him. Anywhere earlier along the road, Traeger would have been baffled. But, having come this far, he was sure that Arroyo was headed up to Napa Valley. Having convinced himself of that, Traeger stopped at a roadside restaurant, got comfortable, then ate. He went into the washroom again before leaving, leaning toward the mirror. The beard could go, but the mustache kept. He went out to the car, got his kit, and came back inside. Patrons of the washroom took little notice of the man shaving himself at this hour of night. The beard was a bear to remove, even using his nail scissors. His face emerged and, running his hand over it, Traeger realized how much he had hated that beard. He got rid of the mustache, too. What good was half a disguise? Outside near the pumps there was a convenience store, where Traeger bought a baseball cap and T-shirt. It was a Dodgers cap and the T-shirt touted the Raiders. Sports fan at large.

Back in the car, he felt more relaxed than he had in days. The visit to Arroyo, however it had ended, made clear that Arroyo was his man. And where else could he be headed than up the valley to . . . Don Ibanez? Jason Phelps? That small uncertainty brought back the tension. This was no time to relax. He made pretty good time going up the valley road.

The El Toro Motel looked full, its lot jammed with vehicles. Traeger went on by and headed toward the hacienda of Don Ibanez. But half a mile short of it, he saw the media crew camped at the gate. He slowed and nosed up to the closed gate of Jason Phelps's place. He got out and tried the gate. It wasn't locked. Lights out, he drove in, got out and shut the gate, and left his car near the garages, remembering how he had carried the foam package over to the basilica.

He pulled down his baseball cap, feeling like Pettitte before his fall, studying the catcher's signals, and started for the back of the property. When he passed the office, he saw that the desk lamp was on. Jason Phelps lay forward, his face on the desk. The eyes were open but didn't seem to be looking anyplace in particular. The French doors were not closed. Traeger stepped inside, crossed to the desk, and looked at Jason Phelps. The back of his head was a battered mess, blood pooled on the desk blotter. Phelps had gone wherever atheists go when they die.

Traeger got out of there, almost running to the path that would take him onto Don Ibanez's property. He heard voices and stopped. He recognized Neal Admirari's voice and that was enough. The last thing he wanted to do was run into a member of the media. He had to get to Don Ibanez. Together he was sure that they could figure out what had happened with the original sacred image, how the packages had been switched, or whatever. The original had to be here still. Maybe even hanging again over the altar in Don Ibanez's basilica. Traeger needed a miracle.

He backtracked and regained Jason Phelps's property.

�֍ PART III ✤

Holy Hermano

CHAPTER ONE

"For God's sake, get a doctor."

Neal had just turned from watching Catherine go off down the path when he noticed Miguel Arroyo near the basilica. Kneeling.

"What's wrong?" he asked, going toward him.

And then he saw the body. "My God, is that Phelps?"

Arroyo gently turned the body over to reveal the face of Don Ibanez. Arroyo rose to his feet.

"I was afraid of this."

"Is he dead?"

"Take his pulse if you want."

Neal danced back. "What were you afraid of?"

Arroyo took Neal's arm and started toward the house. "Traeger is back."

"Traeger!"

"He showed up at my office in Justicia y Paz. He threatened me." Arroyo stopped and looked back. "I hate to just leave him lying there like that."

Was he suggesting that Neal stand watch by the body? "What can happen to him?"

Arroyo sighed. "Who will break the news to Clare?"

"Not me."

Arroyo looked at him, nodding. "I feel the same way. I wish there was another woman around."

"Catherine just went back to Jason Phelps's place. Should I get her?"

"How about the woman who works for Hannan?"

"Oh, they've gone."

It was George Worth that they found when they entered the house. Arroyo asked him to come outside.

"George," Arroyo began. He took a deep breath. "George, Neal and I have just made a terrible discovery."

Neal was thinking of his room in the El Toro Motel and wishing he were there. It wasn't the Plaza, the El Toro, but at least there weren't bodies lying around. Dead bodies. Careful, careful. He reminded himself that Lulu was on her way. Thank God. He wanted to sink into married normalcy, make love to his wife for a change, get the hell out of California before the whole state seceded.

Arroyo had taken George's arm as the three men hurried toward the basilica.

"What is it?"

For answer, Arroyo led him up to the body. George bent over it, then crouched beside the body. He put his hand on Don Ibanez's neck.

"For God's sake, get a doctor."

Glad to be released, Neal started running toward the house.

"And Frater Leone," George cried after him. "Have him come immediately."

"What's going on?" Clare asked when Neal burst into the house.

"Oh, my God. Look, I have to call a doctor. And a priest. Frater Leone."

Clare's eyes widened and her lips parted, but no sound emerged.

"Is it my father?"

"Out by the basilica. George and Arroyo are with him. Where's a phone?"

Clare went outside and he watched her hurry toward the basilica. A phone. Where was a phone? And then he thought of his cell. Jeez. He got it out and punched in 911.

❖

Only an ambulance with its siren screaming could have dispersed the media at the gate, but when the gate was opened to let the ambulance in, members of the press followed, like infantry accompanying a tank. George Worth had left Frater Leone with Don Ibanez and gone to open the gate; now he directed the paramedics to the body. Miguel Arroyo stood in the middle of the drive, waiting for the advancing cameramen and reporters. The television truck had trouble getting past the ambulance, but soon its crew was out and ready to shoot. Arroyo had waited patiently, holding up a hand to still the impatience of others. Neal drew close.

"I am Miguel Arroyo of Justicia y Paz," he began.

"What the hell is the ambulance doing here?" a reporter shouted.

"Something terrible has happened to Don Ibanez, whose hacienda as you know this is. We will soon know whether he will live or die. His attacker was the rogue former CIA agent Vincent Traeger, who had told me he intended to do what he has now done."

No need to tell this gathering about the bungled effort to take the miraculous picture of Our Lady of Guadalupe back to its shrine in Mexico City. That was the story that had brought them here. But the mention of Traeger interested them more than the condition of Don Ibanez. Neal realized how little fellowship he felt with this bunch.

Arroyo began to review what they all knew about events in Mexico City and groans went up. Arroyo ignored them, going on to make his case against Traeger. Speaking directly to the television camera, he told of Traeger's visit to his office, how he had confronted the man and then sounded the alarm. When the forces of law arrived, Traeger had managed to escape.

"And came here," Arroyo said, his voice rising. "Came here to attack one of the most beloved residents of Napa Valley."

"Why?"

"To silence the man who knew what Traeger had done with the sacred painting of Our Lady of Guadalupe."

And then, with the camera on him, Arroyo brought out a cell phone and summoned the forces of law and order.

Neal turned and went to the hacienda. He saw George Worth, who had left the paramedics to their task, comforting Clare. Neal looked out to where the ambulance crew were doing their stuff. Frater Leone was there, too, doing his stuff. The sight of the priest brought uncomfortable memories. Neal made a wide circle around the group and headed for the path down which Catherine had gone.

There was a lamp on in the study. Jason Phelps seemed asleep at his desk. Neal went inside and tiptoed through the study. At the foot of the stairs, he could see lights above. He mounted them, calling softly, "Catherine? Catherine?"

When he got to the head of the stairs, Catherine rushed out of a room and threw herself into his arms.

"I didn't do it, Neal. I swear to God I didn't do it."

The feel of her in his arms brought back memories he had promised to expunge. He held her closer. "Everybody does it," he whispered.

She freed herself and looked at him with horror. "Didn't you see him?"

"The paramedics are with him, Catherine. And the priest."

"With Jason?"

He tried to take her in his arms again. With the professor dozing, they had the house to themselves. "No, no. Don Ibanez."

And then she was looking past him. Neal turned and there was Vincent Traeger, standing as if he had suddenly materialized out of nothing.

"What the hell is going on next door?" Traeger asked.

Neal stepped back toward Catherine. He was thinking of what Arroyo had said. It was not a comfortable feeling, confronting a man who was the object of a two-nation manhunt, even with Catherine there for company.

"Something has happened to Don Ibanez," he said, amazed at how calm he sounded.

"Arroyo, that son of a bitch. So he got both of them."

It was into Traeger's arms now that Catherine rushed.

"I didn't do it! I came into the office and found him. He was already dead."

"You didn't do it," Traeger assured her.

Was he confessing?

"Arroyo. Have you seen him?" he demanded of Neal.

"At the moment he's holding a press conference next door explaining how you attacked Don Ibanez."

As if he had disappeared, Traeger was gone, thundering down the steps.

"What happened to Don Ibanez?" Catherine asked.

Neal opened his arms and she came into them. "It's a long story, my dear. Where can we sit?"

❖ II ❖

"Get some sleep."

Lowry had told Traeger to meet him at the Old Curiosity bookstore in Palo Alto.

The bookstore provided periodic respite from the galley and common room of the Catholic Worker house and, despite the mock proletarian dress of the customers and the bright is-there-anything-I-can-do look of the clerks, Lowry liked it.

There were the books, of course. He particularly liked the radical chic stuff—it gave him shelves of things to ignore. And there was free coffee for those who didn't bring their own from Starbucks, gripping the capped containers as if they were their life support. Coffee and rockers in which to read. Not many students; those who could read were studying the posters that fluttered from kiosks helpfully dotting the campus. Here the customers were middle-aged and fighting it equivocally. Women with gray hair worn long as a girl's, denim skirts made from jeans, the metal-studded pockets emphasizing their rear ends, blouses with scooped necks, beads as big as the jawbreakers of old, the righteous look of the nonsmoker. The men were worse. Sandaled, long-haired, earlobes pierced and wearing discreet rings, half-glasses that lent their eyes a curious look in several senses. Lowry loved them all. They brought back his misspent younger years. Here he could rock and read and observe the customers and forget the lost souls for whom he cooked.

He had Miscamble's *Truman and the Cold War* open on his lap. He had always liked Harry, a foe worthy of one's steel, unaware that he was surrounded by comrades. I'm from Missouri.

So was Lowry, from Joplin, a town he hadn't seen in forty years. Truman's decision to drop the second bomb, on Hiroshima *mon amour*, was sympathetically discussed by the author. It brought back memories of V-J Day when everyone thought that all wars had ended.

When he came in, he had stopped at the counter and asked if they had *Mein Kampf.* The owner was at the register, short and wide and wild haired.

"What is it?"

"A German cookbook."

She drew her top chin into the rest of them. "We don't carry cookbooks."

The question had established his right to browse.

Lowry rocked himself to his feet, returned the book to a shelf, and went outside for a smoke, enjoying it less than the shocked and angry looks of passersby. Human sacrifice would not raise an eyebrow, but cigarettes! There was a bench, a mandatory thirty feet from the bookstore's entrance, in the shade, large dying leaves yellowing on the walk.

The call from Traeger had come as the former agent was fleeing Napa Valley, on the run again as he had been for a week. He had to talk with Lowry, why he didn't say. Lowry gave him directions to the bookstore when Traeger nixed the Catholic Worker house. Maybe Traeger would know when the hell George Worth was coming back. If he was coming back.

Coeds sauntered by, showing their bellies in front and tattoos on their caboose. The mandatory backpacks made them walk with a forward tilt. Lowry tried unsuccessfully to remember what concupiscence had felt like. He would leave that to George. Would George finally succumb to the lure of Clare Ibanez and set aside the dreams of his youth? The poor devil reacted to the primal desire as if it were a temptation of the most sordid sort. George was not cut out for poverty if only because he had chosen it. The vow of poverty was another thing. Did you ever see a thin Franciscan? Poverty weighed no more heavily on most friars' shoulders than the two other vows had on some. Ah, how the media had lapped up all those clerical scandals. Imagine those hypocritical degenerates doing what everyone else was urged to do! Or presumed to be doing already. Someone sat beside him.

"I was just about to go inside when I saw you here," Traeger said.

"How goes the battle?"

"You got another of those?"

Lowry handed him the pack of Basics. "You look like hell."

"Tell me about Arroyo."

"I saw him do his Zola on television. *J'accuse!* Pretty impressive."

"The son of a bitch."

"Does he have a mother?"

"I have to get some sleep. Then we can talk."

"You can use George's office. There's a cot there."

"I could sleep on the floor."

"To do penance?"

"I haven't eaten since yesterday."

"How about some soup?"

When they rose from the bench, Lowry asked, "Where are you parked?"

"It doesn't matter. It's a stolen car."

So they walked back to the Catholic Worker house, where Lowry scrambled some eggs and fried some sausage. The smell coming from the kitchen roused several guests who were dozing in the common room. Lowry turned on both vents over the stove.

"Better have this in George's office," he said, carrying the platter under his apron. Traeger opened the door and they went into the office. Seated at the desk, Traeger finished the eggs and sausage in minutes.

"You were hungry."

"I didn't dare stop. Except to change cars."

"Grow a beard."

"I just shaved it off."

"The sunglasses are a little obvious."

Traeger seemed to have forgotten he was wearing them. He pushed them to the top of his head. His eyes were bloodshot, his face drawn.

"Get some sleep."

❖

It was many hours and two meals later when Traeger came out of the office. He was hungry again. This time it was bacon and eggs.

"We have a limited menu."

"It's delicious."

"It would be even if it weren't."

Traeger just looked at him. "Arroyo tried to kill Don Ibanez. Why?"

It wasn't that Traeger thought Lowry had the answer to the question; he needed to talk about the mess he was in. He had been accused on television of attacking the venerable Don Ibanez, who was still in a coma. The killing of Jason Phelps had been added to the accusation. But it was the attempt to palm off a copy of the picture of Our Lady of Guadalupe that had galvanized the California constabulary, state and local.

"My old buddies are after me, too."

"So what's your plan?"

"I prefer improvisation."

A sound came from Traeger's shirt pocket. His cell phone. He answered it.

"Crosby! Where are you?"

✤ III ✤

"It makes no sense."

Some of Nate Hannan's nutty ideas had their attractions and Laura stifled her critical sense.

"Good idea," she said when Nate suggested she go to Rome and consult with her brother John. Ray looked at her with surprise.

"In what way?"

It didn't matter. The creator and head honcho of Empedocles had made up his mind and that was that.

"You want me to go along?"

"Ray," Nate cried. "I can't have you both gone at once."

"Call it a trial separation," Laura said sweetly.

Not smart that. Nate looked as if he might have second thoughts. What did he think married life was like? "Absence makes the heart grow fonder," she added and Nate nodded. When do clichés fail to click?

Twelve hours after that conversation, Laura was looking across an outside table at John, one of many just plunked down in the street opposite the Vatican's Saint Anne's Gate by the trattorie and ristoranti that flanked the narrow thoroughfare in the Borgo Pio. It made more sense for tourists to just take a chair and order than try to maneuver through the tables.

"Is Traeger working for Hannan?" John asked.

"He was. It's hard firing someone you can't find."

Even so, Nate had hired Crosby again. Memories of the pay packet he had received the first time did not make Crosby reluctant to sign on again.

"You want me to find Traeger? Then what?"

"If you find him you'll find that missing picture."

"Everybody's looking for him now," Crosby had said.

"Not everybody knows him as well as you do."

Once Crosby was on his way, Nate had come up with the idea that Laura should consult John. "And here I am," she had said brightly as they started across Saint Peter's Square. He was in cassock and collar and thin as a rail.

"Laura, what help can I be?"

"Well, you can help me order."

She had the cannelloni and a salad. She wrinkled her nose when she tasted the wine.

"It's just the house wine, Laura."

The back house?

"It's not much worse than what we drink at the Domus." The Domus Sanctae Marthae, the residence inside the Vatican walls where John had his rooms. As director of the Vatican Library he had a penthouse on its roof, but that had been the scene of so much violence he still preferred the Domus. He refilled her water glass.

It was over dessert that John hit on a way to help. Maybe. Hector Padilla, native of Mexico, now a member of the Congregation for Bishops. "He's a Benedictine. He was a member of the community that looks after the shrine of Our Lady of Guadalupe before he became a bishop."

"When can we see him?"

John looked at his watch. "Later. It's siesta time."

"Do you take a nap?"

"Is the pope German?"

That made it easier to admit that she herself was sleepy. John walked with her to the entrance of her hotel, the Columbus on the Via della Conciliazione, and didn't kiss her good-bye. Who would know they were brother and sister? The elevator held one passenger comfortably; with two, it was intimate. She remembered being in it with Ray. Already she missed him.

❖

Bishop Padilla looked like stout Cortés when he extended his hand. Laura took it and he lifted it. Kiss his ring? Well, why not? They were in a parlor in the Domus Sanctae Marthae, where the furniture was baronial, with high uncomfortable chairs and a table on which two vases of roses flanked a dramatic crucifix. It looked like an altar. Above it hung a reproduction of Our Lady of Guadalupe, eyes cast modestly down. Was that why John had chosen this parlor?

They sat and John told the bishop why his sister was here. A pained look came upon the episcopal face.

"My poor community," he said. "They all feel to blame, particularly the abbot."

It was from his fellow monks at the shrine of Our Lady of Guadalupe that he had heard the story, supplementing the media reports.

"And all this rioting and shooting and God knows what else. I suppose that was the motive for the theft. If it was, it worked all too well. And they thought that replacing the image with a copy was shrewd. I would have opposed sending the painting off to Napa Valley if I were there."

Spiriting the image off to a replica of the shrine in California did seem stupid, if only because it had led to a real theft.

"Do you know Don Ibanez, Bishop?"

"He was a regular visitor to the shrine. A very devout man. How is he?"

"Still in a coma."

"Poor man. I'll say a Mass for him. He is a great benefactor of ours. And he provided a refuge for Leone."

"Frater Leone?"

Padilla smiled. "Not everyone is meant to live in a community. For a monk that is a great defect." He stopped. "I should talk, but I miss monastic life. Leone would be happier as a hermit."

Of course Bishop Padilla had heard all about the reaction in Mexico City when the package had been opened and proved to contain only another copy. His eyes drifted to the picture on the wall.

"What I don't understand is what happened at the other end, in California."

"No one does," Laura said.

She told him what they had pieced together when she and Ray and Nate had flown out to learn how the great plan had gone wrong. Don Ibanez had assured them that the original had been put into the foam box. Frater Leone had done that himself, taping it shut after he did so. Of course it was the second foam package that interested him. The one that contained the copy that had previously hung in Don Ibanez's little basilica.

"The man who had kept it for him was murdered."

"Dear God."

And Traeger, who had been hired by Nate Hannan, was accused of the murder, and of the attack on Don Ibanez.

"He is the man who recovered the third secret of Fatima," John reminded the bishop.

"Why would he do these things?"

Laura shrugged.

"It makes no sense. He was accused of trying to deceive us with a copy of the image. Surely he must have known—anyone would have known—that such a deception was impossible. And he is being sought because he had somehow retained the original? Why would he take a trip to Mexico City and attempt such a hoax if he did have the original?"

"You can see why we're anxious to ask him such questions."

But Padilla was not finished. "And then return to California and murder one man and nearly murder another. What possible motivation would he have?" Padilla might have been talking to himself as he posed these questions. He shook his head. "No, someone else is responsible. Someone for whom Don Ibanez and his neighbor represented a danger."

"Do you know Miguel Arroyo, Bishop?"

Padilla frowned and rubbed his face. "I cannot believe the community entrusted the sacred image to that man. But they did."

"And he brought it safely to Don Ibanez."

Bishop Padilla nodded. "I suppose that was why he was there when the painting was readied for its return."

❖

Later Laura said to John, "Well, he wasn't much help."

"I wonder."

"Wonder what?"

"He didn't quite say it, of course, but it's clear he suspects that Miguel Arroyo is the explanation of all these mysteries."

❖ IV ❖

"No more questions?"

Even though his way had been smoothed by Laura, Crosby was not welcomed with open arms when he arrived at Don Ibanez's hacienda. Clare reminded him of one of his own daughters, the one who was most like her mother. She had a sweet dignity that was more effective than a bum's rush. You would have thought she was already in mourning.

"How is your father?"

"Thank you."

For asking, apparently, but what was the answer? "Is he still in a coma?"

The man behind her made a face and gestured with his head. Ah. "Perhaps I should talk with your brother."

Her laughter came as such a surprise that Crosby took a step back. She was still laughing when she introduced George Worth. Well, at least the ice was broken. Worth led him through a huge living room with beamed ceilings and what looked like a walk-in fireplace. The motif was Spanish, though Crosby could not have said what he meant by that. They were no sooner settled than a girl came out with olives and wine and glasses.

"Thank you, Carlotta. *Vino de la casa*," Worth said to Crosby, pouring. The label on the bottle read "Juan Diego."

"Is that his name?"

Worth looked up at him as if now he was going to break out laughing. "House wine?"

"I meant the label."

"Juan Diego is the name of the saint to whom Mary appeared. Our Lady of Guadalupe."

"Of course." Well, he knew it now.

"What does Mr. Hannan expect you to do?" Worth sipped his wine and Crosby did, too.

"Good wine," Crosby said, and it was. "He wants me to find Traeger."

Worth's eyebrows lifted. "A lot of people are trying to do that."

"I know."

"What will you do if you find him?"

"Traeger and I are old friends, from agency days."

"CIA?"

"That was a long time ago. Hannan hired me before he hired Traeger."

"Were you fired?"

"I have a business to run."

"But you have time for this?"

"As I said, Traeger and I are old friends. I don't think he did these things."

"You'll have to come up with a substitute."

"First things first."

"How will you find him?"

"That's a trade secret. What I want to do first is just look around here, get the lay of the land. Who all lives here?"

"Clare is all alone now. Her father is in the hospital, of course. He is out of intensive care, though. Frater Leone never leaves his bedside."

"Frater Leone?"

"A priest. A Benedictine. He received permission from his community to live here."

"Is he the chaplain?"

Worth liked that. "That's a good description. He says his Mass in the basilica. Lately he's been saying it at the hospital."

"And the girl?"

He had to think. "Oh, that's Carlotta."

"What do you call her?"

"She takes care of the house. Her father is the gardener. Carlos."

"Is that everyone?"

"Tomas, the driver, lives over the garages. And I'm staying here, too, of course. To be with Clare."

"Pleasant duty."

Worth seemed actually embarrassed. "Clare and I were students together at Stanford. I run the Catholic Worker house in Palo Alto."

"What's that?"

He thought a bit. "Call it a homeless center."

Clare didn't join them and, after they'd had their wine, Worth took him out to see the basilica. The scene of the crime, as he did not call it. As they walked toward the church, Worth explained that it was an exact replica of the shrine in Mexico City, only on a smaller scale. Crosby knew that, but wanted Worth to tell him even things he already knew. Worth had stopped.

"This is where we found Don Ibanez," he said.

They stood there as if they were commemorating the event. "What's that over there?"

"That's where Jason Phelps lives. Lived. Don Ibanez sold him the property for his retirement home."

"Were they friends?"

Worth smiled. "They were as opposite as you can imagine."

"Enemies?"

"Hardly that. Jason Phelps was a notorious atheist. I thought you knew."

Crosby had known. There seemed to be a little path connecting the two properties. They went into the basilica then. Worth blessed himself and genuflected. Crosby followed suit.

"The Blessed Sacrament is reserved here." There was a red lamp glowing in the dark basilica. Then Crosby noticed the man. He was kneeling on the floor, arms extended, immobile. Worth said, "Carlos."

"Ah."

When they were outside again, Crosby said he would just look around, if that was okay.

"Of course."

"Do Carlos and his daughter live in the house?"

"Carlotta does. Her father has a little house out back."

"I'll just go when I'm through. Thanks."

"No more questions?"

"Do you have more answers?"

"I'd have to hear the questions."

"I just want to see where it all happened."

They shook hands and Worth went off to the house. Crosby circled the circular basilica and saw a little cottage fifty yards off. Adobe brick, tile roof, flower beds, trimmed bushes. It looked like a house in a fairy tale. He thought of the old man kneeling on the floor of the basilica, his arms flung out as if he were on a cross.

Down by the garages, where Crosby had parked, there was a shedlike addition to the far side of the building. It was where trash was kept before it was picked up. He ducked his head and went in. Flies, the odor of garbage. In the far barrel a huge white piece of plastic was visible. No, foam. He ran his hand over the pebbled material and his fingers touched something. He pulled the plastic half out of the barrel. There was a small crucifix embedded in the material, with Scotch tape over it.

⚜

He was about to get into his car but didn't. He passed the hacienda and went out toward the basilica again. Carlos came blinking into the light. He looked at Crosby but kept on going around the basilica. Crosby wanted to take a look at the path that connected these beautifully kept grounds with the place next door.

When he emerged from the tree-lined path, he saw two women standing on the lawn. One was holding a spade. They were silent. He thought of himself and Worth standing at the spot where Don Ibanez had been found. He cleared his throat as he neared the women. They turned their heads; one looked at him angrily, the other with an expression he would not have told his wife about.

"My name is Crosby."

He told them why he was here. The flirty one said her name was Catherine.

"Find him!" the angry one, Myrna, said.

❖ V ❖

"Jason never called me that."

When Catherine called to tell her what had happened to Jason Phelps, Myrna must already have been on her way. Of course the death of the famous anthropologist would have been in the news across the now divided nation, but less because he was a scientist than because of his notorious criticisms of the Catholic religion and all its works and pomps. The phrase had sounded familiar and Catherine had asked Jason why.

"Because you were raised Catholic, my love. You renounced Satan and all his works and pomps."

So she had. Why was disbelieving in Satan harder than disbelieving in all the rest?

Of course Catherine hadn't known Myrna was on her way until she showed up. After the body was taken away, Catherine once more took possession of her room. It was either that or go to the El Toro Motel.

"That's where I'm staying," Myrna said.

"That's silly. Stay here."

"You act like the chatelaine."

"That's what I've been, more or less." No need to tell Myrna that Jason had thrown her out of the house.

"Catherine, when I told you about Jason I had no idea you had designs on him."

"How could I have? I didn't know him then. Actually, it went the other way. And then became mutual, of course."

"Of course."

It was amusing to watch Myrna react. Well, after all, Jason Phelps had been the great love of her life. Only the difficulties of academic employment had made her leave him. Later, well, it was too late. "They couldn't afford me and I can't afford California," she had once explained to Catherine. At the time it would never have occurred to Catherine to say that Myrna could have lived with Jason. Now she realized why Myrna had sounded so funny when Catherine had telephoned her weeks earlier, after getting settled in. She had left little doubt as to what "settled in" meant.

Now, Myrna asked, "Did he drive all the nonsense out of your mind?"

"Oh, the sessions we had. Sessions of sweet, silent talk. That isn't right, is it? I don't know what I would have done without him."

Myrna simply could not control her expression when she was annoyed. Annoyed? The woman was jealous.

"I *will* stay here, Catherine. I'm going to check out of that motel."

"I'll come with you."

"There's no need for that."

"Myrna, I've been so lonely."

❧

What memories the motel brought back. While Myrna went to pack, Catherine wandered into the bar, to find Neal Admirari sitting at a table with a beautiful, if slightly plump, woman across from him. It was the panic on his face that drew Catherine to the table. Neal scrambled to his feet.

"This is Lulu. My wife. This is Catherine, Lulu." He acted as if his wife had come upon them in bed together.

"I thought all the media people had decamped."

"Neal is writing a book," Lulu said. "Will you join us?"

"A book!" cried Catherine, sitting down. This was more fun than teasing Myrna.

Neal was nervously explaining to Lulu who Catherine was. "She was Jason Phelps's companion. Is that the right term?"

"Jason never called me that." The devil. Lulu smiled complacently. Well, a good look at Neal without the fog of desire explained why. Catherine found it hard to believe that she'd been smitten by this unprepossessing man.

Myrna had come to the entrance and was peering into the bar. Catherine waved, and Myrna wheeled her suitcase bumpily over the flagged floor to the table. To Catherine's surprise, Neal greeted Myrna.

"Don't tell me you're checking out."

Myrna gave him a look. Lulu was regarding Myrna with interest. What would she have seen but an almost anorexic woman with short hair and a sour puss? If Lulu had to suspect someone, Catherine wanted it to be her. No, she didn't want that, not really. Had she ever found Neal Admirari attractive?

"You and I are practically permanent residents here," Neal said. "I will feel deserted."

"Well, now you have me," Lulu purred. Poor Neal was going to catch hell if Catherine was any judge. But because of Myrna?

"Catherine, can we go?"

"Oh, do have a drink with us," Lulu trilled.

"I don't drink," Myrna said, a statement in several senses.

A shocked silence fell. Catherine got up. "It's so nice to meet you at last, Lulu. Neal is like a new bridegroom."

"That's what he is."

"Really!"

Myrna had begun to wheel her suitcase toward the exit of the bar. Catherine shrugged to the newlyweds and went after her.

❖

"What a loathsome man," Myrna said in the car.

"He's writing a book."

"He doesn't look as if he can read."

"You made quite an impression on him."

"What do you mean?"

"Myrna, it's not your fault if men find you attractive."

Whew. Myrna smiled smugly. What a temper the woman had.

They got Myrna settled into her room. When Catherine told her it had been Jason's, Myrna hesitated. "I am not superstitious."

"His ghost only walks at night."

"Stop that. Can you imagine what Jason would think if he heard you?"

"I think he does."

"Catherine, please! What arrangements shall we make?"

She meant Jason's body. "That's what I wanted to talk with you about, Myrna."

"No funeral. No public ceremony. He'll be cremated. We'll bury him here."

And that was why they were standing in the yard, having buried the urn containing Jason's ashes some fifteen yards from the doors of his study. When Crosby came up the path, they were observing a minute of silence.

Crosby wanted to see where Jason's body had been found. As he said this, he glanced down at the freshly covered grave. Myrna gave the mound a final pat with the shovel.

"We'll plant flowers later."

"Oh, he'll love that."

Myrna glared at her. Inside, when Catherine described how Jason had been found, fallen forward on his desk, Myrna shuddered.

"I'll leave you two alone."

After Myrna was gone, Catherine said, "She's an incorrigible matchmaker."

Crosby didn't understand, or pretended he didn't, which was just as bad.

❖ VI ❖

"Is that paint dry?"

Traeger was almost surprised when Crosby called, not because he knew the number—think of all the calls they had exchanged during that wild-goose chase to Pocatello; all he'd have to do was review his calls—but because he was back on the job.

"Has he fired me?"

"How can he fire you if he can't find you?"

"So we're working together again."

"Right. Now where can we get together?"

Will Crosby was a straight shooter, no doubt of that, but Traeger was wary nonetheless. It was one thing for Crosby to have his cell phone number; it would be something else to know his whereabouts.

"How did Hannan describe your job?"

"To find you."

"And then?"

"Vic, I know you didn't do any of those things."

"So do I, but a fat lot of good it's doing me."

"Do you know George Worth?"

Traeger's wariness came back. He was sitting in Worth's office as they talked. But Crosby couldn't possibly know that, could he? Or was he fishing?

"I know him."

"He gave me good advice. All we have to do is find the one who's guilty and you're off the hook."

"You needed Worth to tell you that?"

"Sometimes it's good to have the obvious stated."

"Where are you calling from?"

"I just left Don Ibanez's hacienda and am driving down the valley."

"Do you know where Palo Alto is?"

"I can find it."

"Route 101 will bring you there."

"Where in Palo Alto?"

"There's a bookstore called the Old Curiosity Shop. Just ask for it."

"I'll get there as soon as I can."

"You should be there before I am." No need to tell Crosby he was already in the neighborhood.

"The Old Curiosity Shop. Who runs it, Little Nell?"

"Wait until you see her."

After hanging up, Traeger had second thoughts, but then he had third thoughts. If he couldn't trust Crosby, he was in very deep doo-doo indeed.

"Were you talking to yourself in there?"

"A call from my partner."

"I thought you were single."

"An old colleague. He was working for Hannan before I was, but we were on the same job. Now that I'm missing, Hannan has brought him back."

"To find you."

"That's right."

"You trust him?"

"I'll be careful."

He thought of going as a jogger and checking out the bookstore to make sure Crosby had come alone. Any associates he might have would get in place early. But if Traeger jogged back and forth past that store, they would get more curious about him than the bookstore. Besides, he would be taking his backpack and joggers don't wear backpacks.

"Would you like me to ride shotgun?" Lowry asked.

Traeger thought about. He liked it. "You can go as you are." He walked to where secondhand men's clothing was piled or hanging from rods. He picked an old gray sweatshirt and a tattered pair of jeans.

"Tennies will go nice with those."

Anything but sandals. His feet were still sore from that trek to the border from Mexico City. Without a couple of truck rides, he would have been crippled. He found a pair of running shoes, huge, maybe a size fourteen. They felt nice and loose when he got them on. The bookstore was five blocks away, but they walked.

❖

Lowry took up vigil on the bench near the Old Curiosity Shop and opened the book he had brought. He meant to read, of course, but in the circumstances the book seemed a prop. There were benches on the opposite side of the street, at intervals of twenty-five yards, shaded. The bench Traeger wanted was already occupied by a hawk-faced woman with orange hair and a malevolent expression. She watched Traeger watching her. He whispered to her.

"What?"

"Is that paint dry?"

She sprang to her feet, nearly losing her balance, and tried to get a look at her bottom. She appealed to Traeger. He shook his head.

"Why didn't they put up a sign?"

Her purse, on a long strap, almost touched the sidewalk.

"When did they paint it?" she demanded.

"God only knows." Traeger sat down and brought out his cigarettes. She gasped as if he were a flasher. With his arm on the back of the bench, Traeger watched her stomp away, her purse swinging rhythmically. He lit his cigarette, got out his laptop, and put his backpack on the bench to discourage company. He found that he was in a Wi-Fi area and checked the news of the day. The *Drudge Report* featured his photograph under which, in caps, was written FUGITIVE. That picture was at least ten years old, but Traeger hadn't changed that much. He switched screens, checked his email, and found a message from Dortmund. "Watch your back." Just that. He felt like the lady who thought she had sat on wet paint. He put the computer away.

Across the street, Lowry was supine on his bench, head on its armrest, hat pulled over his eyes. His open book lay on his chest. Some shotgun.

It was nearly two hours later that the car came slowly up the street, the driver leaning forward, scanning the storefronts. He went past the bookstore, parked, and sat in the car for several minutes before getting out. It was Crosby, in a suit and carrying a briefcase. He walked slowly past the bookstore to the bench where Lowry lay. At the sound of his voice, Lowry sat up and Crosby stepped back, all apologies. Traeger swung his backpack over a shoulder and crossed the street.

"Is this man bothering you?" he asked Lowry.

"Hello, Traeger. Now what?"

"We'll use your car."

⚜

Lowry had a meal to prepare, so Traeger and Crosby went to George Worth's office to decide on a plan of action.

"You left by the window?" Crosby asked when Traeger told him about the encounter with Arroyo in Justicia y Paz. He seemed to be enjoying the narrative too much.

"Luckily I saw the parking lot filling up with police cruisers."

Crosby liked it when Traeger told him of parking in the lot across the street and waiting for Arroyo.

"The hunted becomes the hunter."

Traeger scowled. "But he got away."

"Where is he now?"

"It's where we want him to be. That's where you come in."

Traeger listened while Crosby made the call to Justicia y Paz and told them he had been hired by Ignatius Hannan to track down the rogue agent. He was told to hold. He took the phone away from his ear and held it out so Traeger could listen. Not Muzak to soothe the savage breast but "The Battle Hymn of the Republic." The door opened and Lowry came in, still wearing his apron. The guests were being fed.

"Will Crosby." Crosby was addressing the phone, which was back at his ear. "Miguel Arroyo?"

Ah. Crosby again explained the mission he was on, insisting that he needed to talk to Arroyo.

"Where?" Crosby looked at Traeger, but Lowry took the phone from him.

"Miguel? Lowry. Here's my suggestion. Why don't we meet in Santa Ana, at Bishop Sapienza's? Of course I'll be there."

He listened for a moment. "Right. Good. *Más tarde.*"

Lowry hung up the phone. "Neutral territory. I don't think he'd have agreed to come here. Besides, Santa Ana splits the distance."

"Is he in San Diego?"

Lowry looked dumb. "I didn't ask."

But he recouped by explaining the attractions of a Santa Ana meeting. "Arroyo thinks Sapienza is a fan of his." The bishop, when Lowry reached him, said that he would be happy to host the great confrontation.

It was a half hour later when the three men set off for the rendezvous in Santa Ana.

When Traeger asked Lowry if the Catholic Worker house could get along without him, he said, "George Worth is coming back."

❖ VII ❖

"Have you been naughty, Neal?"

Lulu found an item on Zenit announcing that the resignation of Emilio Sapienza, bishop of Santa Ana, California, had been accepted by the Holy Father. The bishop was quoted as saying that he planned to spend his remaining years serving the poor more directly than he had been able to do as bishop. She read it aloud to Neal, who was lying on the bed in their room in the El Toro, and he just grunted in reply.

But Lulu was so excited that she forgot all about their first real argument. What in the hell had Neal been up to out here? Every floozy in the bar acted as if she knew something Lulu didn't. Neal's indignant reaction when she mentioned this made it clear that something had been going on.

"Catherine seems pretty chummy, Neal."

"So was the wife of Bath."

"Is that a confession?"

"Lulu, sweetheart, you're not wearing your stole."

"What did she wear? If anything?"

"The wife of Bath? A terry-cloth robe."

"Have you been naughty, Neal?"

If he hadn't been, why did he get so angry? He wasn't going to be quizzed in this way, God damn it. If she didn't trust him, what kind of a marriage was this anyway?

"That's what I'm trying to find out."

"Why didn't you just ask her when you had the chance?"

"Because I already knew the answer."

He stormed out of the room and Lulu went into the bathroom and cried. But it didn't come easily; she had to force the tears, putting her face up close to the mirror and trying to see herself as a betrayed wife. Rosita, who did the rooms, probably knew everything that went on in this crummy motel, but Lulu could not bring herself to question the woman. Instead, she called the desk and asked if Myrna had checked out, knowing that she had.

"Myrna."

"I don't know her last name."

There was humming on the line and then, "Myrna Bittle? She's no longer staying with us."

"Darn. When did she check in?"

"She checked out." The clerk became audibly less cooperative. "Is there something wrong?"

"Good heavens, no. How many days was she here?"

After a pause, the clerk said, "Five days."

"That's what I thought. Thank you."

Myrna, thin as a rail, who seemed never to have learned how to smile? She tried to imagine it. She couldn't. Catherine, now, well, Lulu knew the type. But Catherine was staying in

Jason Phelps's house. Lulu went back to the bathroom, rinsed her face, put on some lipstick, and went down to the bar. Neal was in a booth, glowering.

"Can I buy you a drink, handsome?"

"Ask my wife."

"She says it's okay."

She sat next to him and bumped him over with her bottom. "I have a confession to make."

He looked warily at her.

"While you were away? I don't know what came over me, Neal. It was a regular orgy. There were three or four of them."

"Let's go back to the room."

Afterward, exhausted, he napped, but Lulu couldn't get to sleep so she got up and logged on and found the item on Zenit. She was still researching when he awoke.

"I am going to do an article on that man, Neal."

"Definite or indefinite?"

"Sapienza, Neal. Think of it."

Neal thought of it. Of course he knew how Sapienza had distinguished himself from the other bishops as soon as he was installed in Santa Ana. He had sided with the migrant workers in every dispute; he had marched; he had spoken out. But every time he was written up there was mention of Disneyland and Busch Gardens and that diminished the impact of the story, as if Sapienza were engaging in California radical chic. Neal began to respond to her enthusiasm. He sat up. He got dressed.

"You're right. What in the hell are we doing here?"

"Messing around."

"We can do that anywhere."

⚜

Sapienza looked ten years younger, slapping around the house in huaraches, a big billowy shirt of a half dozen colors, and khaki pants. He even looked slimmer, but that was probably the shirt. He greeted them as if he had been expecting them. He showed them the letter, his face aglow. It read like a form letter, of course, and was signed + Hector Padilla, OSB. Congregation for Bishops. But at the bottom of the page, in the same ink as the signature, was a little addendum. "You have been an example to us all. God bless you. We must get together soon."

"OSB? Are those letters in the right order?"

"They are if you're a Benedictine. He's a good man."

Lulu told Sapienza of her intention to do a piece on him. He held up a hand. He wasn't wearing his episcopal ring. Did he think he had been reduced to the ranks?

"Absolutely not. I will fold my tent like the Arabs and as silently steal away."

"Emilio, you owe it to people . . ."

He lowered his chin and looked at her. Lulu felt deflated.

"Of course I don't need your permission."

"You wouldn't act against my wishes."

What kind of a piece would it be if she couldn't interview him? Of course, she could take his self-effacement as the theme, make a virtue out of necessity. The bishop who avoids publicity.

Neal said, "What's this about working more directly with the poor?"

"What do you know about the Catholic Worker?"

"I was a volunteer as a boy."

"A volunteer boy?" Lulu was trying to make the best of her disappointment.

The doorbell rang and Sapienza acted as if he wanted to ignore it.

"Should I see who it is?" Lulu asked.

He was still thinking when she got up and went to the door. Traeger looked at her through the mesh of the screen. Traeger!

✤ VIII ✤

Unintelligent design.

Catherine figured if Myrna could bronze the house and turn the whole thing into a monument to Jason Phelps, she would do it. Why bother about the future if you didn't think there was a future? When you're dead, you're dead. Wasn't that the theory? Let the underclass mumble their prayers and hope for heaven, living on and on forever in unimaginable bliss, but Jason and Myrna and others like them thought they knew better. People were just accidental combinations of matter and, however intricate the circuitry, it wasn't made to any plan. It just happened. Unintelligent design. Calling that science didn't make it any less ridiculous. Catherine remembered Jason's heretical remarks about the hard sciences. The sure way to get Myrna's goat was to refer to Jason as if he were somehow still there with them. Not in their memories, but *there*. And yet, from time to time she would look out and see Myrna standing over the little mound under which were the ashes of Jason Phelps. What was the point of mourning if he were only ashes?

The trouble with such thoughts was that they rebounded on her. It wasn't some big theory that had caused her to bid adieu to the beliefs of her youth—it was a bad marriage and then a string of affairs that had the look of desperation when she allowed herself to remember them. What a swinger she had thought herself to be. Gather ye rosebuds while ye may and while ye may be merry. How sad. Sometimes Catherine thought that the big cure that Jason Phelps, recommended by Myrna, was supposed to effect in her had boomeranged. But she didn't want to think about that either.

The business with Neal Admirari had turned her life into farce. Stolen moments with an overweight, middle-aged man in love with himself. Poor Lulu. Only she envied Lulu, not because she had Neal, for heaven's sake, but because she was, well, together in a way that Catherine knew that she herself was not. So she went over to the hacienda to talk to Clare.

When she came up along the path to the lawn of the hacienda, she looked toward the basilica and saw Frater Leone. He reminded her of something, she didn't know what. Maybe her lost innocence. She walked slowly toward the priest. He turned at her approach.

"He can't receive visitors yet." His hands were hidden under his scapular. He bowed. "Forgive my abruptness. Don Ibanez has just come home from the hospital."

"Wonderful." Wonderful for Clare, too.

As they walked toward the house, Frater Leone described Don Ibanez's condition in great detail. The blow on the head had not been as damaging as was thought. He had also suffered a slight stroke.

The priest said he would relieve Clare, who was keeping vigil by her father's side. Before leaving the room, he turned. "Did you wish to see him?"

"Later," Catherine said. Ye gods.

"He will need speech therapy," Clare said when she came down. "But thank God he is out of danger. From now on he can only improve."

"Where's George?"

Clare fell silent, looking into Catherine's eyes. "Come."

They went out on a patio. George had gone back to Palo Alto.

"For good?"

"Catherine, he can't make up his mind."

"About you?"

"He wants me to decide the question. If I say so, he will abandon the Catholic Worker."

It sounded like blackmail to Catherine. Either way, Clare would bear the responsibility. George could console himself with the thought that, left to himself, he would have continued the noble work. Catherine didn't know what she thought about such good-hearted efforts. It certainly seemed to give an emotional charge to those engaged in the work. Was that fair? She didn't know. She just didn't see what the problem was. Marry Clare and live happily ever after or spend his life ladling out soup to derelicts. Of course, he wanted Clare to join him on the soup line.

"Doesn't he have anyone to talk sense to him?"

Clare didn't like that. "He has consulted Frater Leone."

"What did he advise?"

Clare smiled. "The poor you will always have with you."

That was Delphic enough to cover either choice. George had wanted to ponder it in Palo Alto.

"He feels guilty about being away for so long."

"Well, after all. Your father . . ."

Clare knew that Myrna was staying in Jason's house, but had yet to meet her. "Why don't you bring her over for a drink later?"

"Myrna doesn't drink."

"I would like to welcome her to the neighborhood."

"She's out jogging."

Clare was glad to hear it. Of course she was a jogger, too. If what propelled Myrna through her daily miles was the thought that in the end she would be transformed into someone like Clare, she could hang up her running shoes.

❖ IX ❖

"Cui bono?"

Traeger was as surprised as Lulu van Ackeren when she came to the door. Lulu looked terrified and when Crosby and Lowry joined Traeger on the doorstep, she was even more so.

"Bishop Sapienza is expecting us," Lowry said soothingly.

And then Sapienza was at Lulu's side. "Ah, come in, come in."

Once the door was open, Traeger brushed past the bishop, wanting to check out the house. Had Arroyo already arrived? But all he found was Neal Admirari. The columnist was working at his computer at a table near a window that admitted the delightful aroma of oranges from the grove behind the house.

"Long time no see," Admirari said.

"When did you get here?"

Sapienza and the others appeared. Traeger didn't like it. Coming to Santa Ana made sense if that could lure Arroyo, but a house full of reporters? Crosby, on the other hand, seemed delighted.

"Perfect. Church, state, and press."

"What's going on?" Lulu wanted to know.

Sapienza took her aside to explain and Neal followed them into the kitchen. Traeger was about to move to the window Admirari had abandoned as providing the best vantage point when he heard Arroyo's voice. In the kitchen, chattering away to the bishop and the reporters. Lowry put a hand on Traeger's arm. Crosby sauntered into the kitchen.

"Arroyo? Thanks for taking the trouble."

"I want him caught as much as you do. He's a madman. I'm lucky to be alive."

Arroyo and Crosby came in side by side. At the sight of Traeger, Arroyo stopped talking and moving, stunned. He looked behind him. Sapienza smiled reassuringly.

"Miguel, we are going to clear up the mystery and confusion of these past weeks."

"Emilio, this man is a fugitive. There is a price on his head."

"Perhaps you can collect it."

Arroyo thought he understood the situation now. Crosby had snookered Traeger into this meeting and arranged for unimpeachable witnesses. He ignored Traeger as he went past him.

"I would feel a lot better if that man were handcuffed."

Traeger went to Arroyo, put a splayed hand on his chest, and pushed. Arroyo staggered backward, made a grab for a lamp, and brought it down on top of him as he hit the floor. As soon as he did, he rolled to the side, drew a gun, and lifted it toward Traeger. He got agilely to his feet. His eyes remained on Traeger, but it was Crosby he addressed.

"How stupid do you think I am? I suspected that you two were working together. The house is surrounded. Bishop, you surprise me."

"Not as much as you surprise me, Miguel. Put away that weapon."

"I don't think so."

Sapienza paused. "Very well. If it makes you feel safer. In any case, I want to know what part you have played in all these events."

"Why did you kill Jason Phelps?" Traeger asked.

He was trying to quell the impulse to rush at the cocky little Arroyo, weapon or no weapon. By God, he would not be flummoxed by him again. But his question had a curious effect. Arroyo lowered the weapon.

"Nice try, Traeger. I suppose I also attacked Don Ibanez."

"These are recent matters, Miguel. No need to go into them now." Sapienza picked up the fallen lamp and took the chair Admirari had vacated. "Let's all get comfortable while you exonerate yourself."

"Exonerate myself?"

"The miraculous image, Miguel. Where is it?"

Arroyo seemed genuinely astonished by the question. He looked reproachfully at the bishop. "If I knew I would tell you."

Crosby had followed the bishop's example and gotten seated. Neal and Lulu were clinging to one another in the doorway that led to the kitchen. Traeger remained standing, his eye on the no longer menacing weapon, eager to get his hands on Arroyo.

"From the beginning, Miguel," the bishop said.

Arroyo looked at him, at Neal and Lulu, at Crosby and Lowry. "I'll sit down when he does."

"Traeger," Crosby said. "Please."

All the days since he had fled Mexico City after the fiasco of opening the foam case and finding that the whole elaborate plan, so smoothly executed, had resulted only in the delivery of a copy of the missing painting, the long and exhausting trek to the border, making it to Phoenix and then Flagstaff, flying to San Diego to confront Arroyo and then having to leave by the washroom window with troopers swarming through the building, losing Arroyo when he followed him up 101—all that and now this roomful of people, filled Traeger with doubt and suspicion. Whose side was Crosby on? Who in his right mind would want to be on Traeger's side? Crosby's mission was to get Traeger. Was this meeting a trap?

Sapienza reached out a hand and took the weapon from Arroyo and Arroyo sat. Warily, Traeger moved to the side of the room, wanting a way out if it came to that. The aroma of orange blossoms wafted in the open window and filled the room. The image of himself exiting the washroom through that little window came and went. Had Arroyo been bluffing when he said the house was surrounded?

Arroyo got comfortable. The chair he was sitting in had wooden arms, green leather cushions, a colorful blanket thrown over its back. He smiled at his audience.

"Very well. This is what happened."

It was Arroyo who had alerted the community in charge of the shrine of Our Lady of Guadalupe that the theft of the sacred image was planned.

"How did you know that?"

"Actually, Bishop, I invented it. Something dramatic had to occur in order to bring things to a head in the Southwest, in California particularly. Our people were being treated as invaders of a country that is rightfully theirs. What would arouse them more surely than the desecration of the most revered image in the Americas? I sought and received Don Ibanez's cooperation. The monks knew and trusted him. Transferring the image to the replica of the shrine that Don Ibanez had built on his property appealed to them. The image was taken down, a copy replaced it, and I brought the original to Don Ibanez's little basilica, where it hung safely during all the turmoil."

"If the theft was a ruse, there would not have been the sacrilege of armed men storming around the shrine. People were killed, Miguel."

Arroyo seemed torn between adopting the bishop's mournful air and a smile of triumph. The smile won. "All things work together for the good, as someone must have said. Even monks can be indiscreet. Only the abbot and the prior knew of the transfer. The others in the community did not, but they had heard of the impending theft. Word got out, and the Mexican authorities contacted Washington, doubtless because I had suggested that the Rough Riders were the thieves."

"And were they?"

"Crosby and Traeger wll be able to verify my guess. I think a team of their old companions in arms shot up the shrine and stole the copy. Of course they must have thought they were engaged in a preemptive strike. Do you know a man named Morgan?"

Crosby looked at Traeger.

"Morgan is dead."

"Hoisted on his own petard, to coin a phrase. A double agent. He contacted me, having learned that it was I who alerted the monks at the shrine. His fellow agents contrived to get the copy they had stolen into the hands of the Rough Riders. Then Morgan made his fatal proposal. He would sell the copy, get the reward Ignatius Hannan had offered, and disappear to wherever such people go."

Traeger thought of that scene in the long-term parking lot at the San Francisco airport. He thought of Gladys Stone. Was she another mole assigned to keep an eye on Morgan?

"Okay, Arroyo. So you got the picture to Don Ibanez's basilica. Let's talk about the plan to get it back where it belongs."

"Traeger, I confess that I am as confused by that as you are."

"I'm not confused, damn it. How did you make the switch?"

Arroyo looked at Sapienza. "I suppose I could be flattered by this suggestion of my shrewdness. I cannot tell you how I felt when I learned what had happened when Traeger delivered that package to the shrine."

His eyes went to Traeger. "How did you do it? You left with the original painting. Everyone trusted you, Don Ibanez trusted you, and you betrayed them."

"Cui bono?" Sapienza murmured.

"I don't understand," Arroyo said.

"Miguel, you can't seriously expect us to believe that Traeger would insure the failure of his own plan. What could he possibly gain from that?"

"I never had the original," Traeger said. "The package I delivered and which held only a copy was put into my hands by Don Ibanez himself. It never left my sight. I had no idea that I was taking such precautions over a copy. So where is the original, Arroyo?"

"I repeat. I do not know."

"As God is your judge?"

"It had to be you, Traeger. Why? Only you can tell us. But I can guess. You could arrange to deliver it to Ignatius Hannan, who would doubtless have enriched you for your troubles. For that matter, you could have done the same with Don Ibanez. Did you attack him when he reacted in shock to your proposal?"

"Miguel, Miguel, please stop. Let me summarize." Sapienza brought his hands together as if in prayer. "Consider the point we have arrived at. Traeger accuses Arroyo of knowing where the original is."

Traeger exploded. "Is that why I've been chasing all over creation trying to find it?"

Sapienza parted his hands and showed a palm to Traeger. "Arroyo in turn accuses you. Of course both of you protest your innocence. The question is, how do we resolve the matter?"

"Excellent," Neal Admirari cried. "How do we?"

It was then that Traeger saw a file of cruisers approaching the house. By God, it was a trap. All this palaver had been meant merely to hold him until the police arrived. In a trice he was at the window. He leapt through and headed for the orange grove, the soft soil gripping his feet in their size fourteen tennis shoes and making speed difficult. He became aware of figures ahead. The grove seemed full of cops. He changed direction; he felt cornered. He stumbled, trying to draw his weapon, when a shot rang out and he felt a piercing pain in his upper leg. Then they were upon him, bringing him to the ground, pinning him. He was flipped on his back and his weapon taken. The face of Crosby appeared, looking down at him with a sad expression.

"Nice going, Traeger."

CHAPTER TWO

❖ I ❖

"Sapienza thinks I'm lying."

Neal watched Traeger being hustled away, handcuffed now as Arroyo had wished him to be earlier. Crosby walked at Traeger's side, talking away. What was he doing, gloating? He had done what he was being paid to do, find Traeger. But what had finding him solved? The miraculous image of Our Lady of Guadalupe was still missing. Traeger was put into an unmarked vehicle by two huge men in civilian clothes. The uniformed troopers in their cruisers led the procession as they drove away.

Lulu had decided that the meeting in Sapienza's living room and the capture of Traeger in the orange grove behind the house overrode any reluctance on the part of the now retired and inclined to be retiring bishop.

"Emilio, you'll be on every website. You might just as well get in a few words yourself."

He had said neither yes nor no, taking Miguel Arroyo off to his study and closing its door. Lulu asked Neal to spell "cui bono" for her. But it was her mention of websites that had caught Neal's attention. He had just learned that a half dozen papers had dropped his column, and that made a baker's dozen in the current year. All the talk about the demise of the print media seemed suddenly credible. He had resisted the claim as hyperbole. In every airport terminal he passed through there were stacks of newspapers—local, national—and magazines! There seemed to be a magazine for every conceivable hobby or interest. The covers were almost as hilarious as those in the supermarket checkout line. "Build your summer home with pine cones." "Lose fifty pounds in minutes!" "Double your computer's speed." It was the number of magazines devoted to electronics and computers that struck him. Without telling Lulu, he had sent an e-mail to Nick Pendant at Mercury. Just hello and how are you? If Pendant didn't connect the message to his earlier efforts to sign up Neal, he was not the new employer Neal was looking for. And of course there was the book.

What a stroke of luck to have been here, an eyewitness to the exchange between Arroyo and Traeger. It had looked like a standoff—not to say a Mexican standoff—to Neal until Traeger had suddenly dived through the window and headed for the orange grove. His flight seemed to answer the question that had just been put: which one, Traeger or Arroyo, was telling the truth?

Crosby came in, looked vaguely at Neal, and asked where the bishop was.

"In his study with a penitent."

Crosby shook his head. "Traeger thinks I double-crossed him. He thinks I lured him here so he could be picked up."

"Why did he run?"

"Because Arroyo had pulled a similar stunt on Traeger in San Diego. Once he saw the cruisers arriving, he took off."

"Well, he didn't get far."

"Did you ever try running through an orange grove?"

"Not recently."

Crosby looked at him in disgust. "It doesn't mean he's guilty of anything!"

"Of course not. Can I have your full name for the story I'll be writing?"

"How would you like a knuckle sandwich?"

"I never eat while I'm working."

The study door opened and a pensive Arroyo came out. Then, seeing Neal, he put on the charm. "You saw it all, Admirari. You heard it all. I'm counting on you to get the story out." He leaned toward Neal. "Sapienza thinks I'm lying," he whispered, inviting Neal's disbelief.

"He's been around sinners too long."

"You are writing this up, aren't you? My God, what a scoop."

"I never thought of that."

Arroyo stepped back, then smiled. "I'm not telling you how to do your job."

"Keep it that way."

Sapienza had come to the door of his study. He beckoned Crosby inside. Neal was curious to know how the session between the bishop and Arroyo had gone. He went over to Lulu, who was plinking away at her computer.

"What are you writing?"

"Are you kidding?" She tossed her head, getting the hair out of her eyes. He leaned over and kissed her.

"For *Commonweal*?"

She turned to him. "Neal, this is a web job."

That sounded like something from *The Joy of Sex*.

"Did I tell you about the offer Pendant made me?"

"Take it, Neal! You're on the *Titanic*."

"This life saver?" He patted his belly. "One week on a diet and it's gone. Maybe sooner." Lose fifty pounds in minutes!

Neal went out the front door to a porch shaded by a wooden trellis from which pots of flowers hung. He tried to get comfortable on a metal chair and brought out his cell phone. At the moment, even email seemed too slow.

Pendant was delighted to hear from him.

"You asked me to call you before I accepted any offer."

"I'll match it, Neal." A pause. "I'll more than match it. Who is it?"

"Would that be ethical?"

"Ethical? We're the media."

"I keep forgetting."

Pendant wanted a fax number where he could ship his offer. "You read it over and then we'll talk some more. I want you, Neal. I'll get you more readers in a day than your column gets you in a year."

"Give me your fax. I'll send you one and then you'll know where to send yours."

He snapped his phone shut and Lulu came out. "What are you grinning about?"

"I'm being seduced."

He told her about the call. To his surprise, she was delighted. "I thought you'd dither until it was too late."

"You think it's a good idea?"

"Do you know how many readers you'll have? What is he asking, twice a week, three times a week?"

"He's not that demanding a seducer. What's wrong with weekly?"

She shrugged. "They'll archive it. It'll be there all week anyway. Neal, you have to hold out for top billing. We'll get a flattering photograph taken. We'll demand a lead-up to your debut. Fanfare, razzmatazz."

"I thought I'd start off with the big showdown here today."

"Then you'd better get at it. I'll send Pendant Sapienza's fax number. Can I be your agent?"

"Be patient."

She took a metal chair and sat. She squirmed. "This chair makes me feel like I'm being branded. I wonder where they took Traeger."

❖ II ❖

"I never got the knack of that."

Ignatius Hannan was elated when Crosby called to report about Traeger—until he realized that the miraculous image of Our Lady of Guadalupe was still missing.

"What did he do with it?" Nate demanded. Laura, listening in on another phone, thought that her boss was entitled to one stupid question.

"He doesn't have it, Hannan. For God's sake, ever since Mexico City he been trying to find it."

"Then why did he run?"

"Have you ever been surrounded by half a dozen police cruisers?" Crosby reminded Nate of Traeger's experience in San Diego. "It was dumb, I grant that, but I understand it. I wouldn't want to be Arroyo when Traeger gets his hands on him. That guy is lying."

"He's committed enough violence," Nate said. He meant Traeger. "Laura, you on?"

"Of course."

"Look, you talk with Crosby. I've got calls to make."

"Tell me about the meeting at Bishop Sapienza's," Laura said when she had Crosby all to herself.

Crosby was quick but thorough. Laura felt that she had been in the room during the confrontation between Arroyo and Traeger.

"Why do you think Arroyo is lying?"

"Because I know Traeger is telling the truth."

"Where did you flunk logic?"

"What the hell does that mean?"

"What if neither of them is lying?"

There was a long pause. "Then I'm right back where I started."

"It's a possibility. What charge did they arrest Traeger on?"

"Suspicion of robbery for now."

"Where did they take him?"

"They were state troopers. In uniform." A pause. "Most of them."

"Go see him. We'll arrange for a lawyer. You're going to need his help."

"I'll need all the help I can get."

"Call back after you've talked with Traeger."

❖

In the kitchen, Boris was busy about many things. On the stove, in a large pan, a corruptingly aromatic sauce simmered. On one of the tables lay the roast that would become a London broil, a favorite of Nate's, right after Big Macs. Boris, whistling tunelessly, was breaking eggs one-handed into a stainless steel bowl.

"I never got the knack of that," Laura said, picking up an egg. She gave it a whack and then, still one-handed, tried getting the shell open so she could add its yolk to the bowl. The shell collapsed in her hand and she had to dance back not to get yolk all over her. Boris smiled a tolerant smile. He broke another egg. One-handed. Effortlessly.

"My hands are too small," Laura said, going to the sink and washing her hands and arms.

"Or the eggs are too big."

She heard voices, male and female, from the room in back where Boris and his wife Lise ate. Wiping her hands, she peeked in. Smiley and Steltz, all lovey-dovey over their coffee, standing by. Nate thought that maybe later he would have to go to Atlanta.

"Did you hear what happened to Traeger?"

Smiley looked with exaggerated innocence at Laura. "What happened to him?"

"He's been arrested."

"What for?"

Did Smiley even care what the point of the flight to Mexico City had been? Ah well, he had the distraction of his copilot. A beautiful woman, if you liked wide-spaced eyes and a slight lisp.

"When did you meet Ray?" Brenda asked Laura, the question coming out of nowhere.

"When we were both single."

Take that, you wench.

"Brenda's husband was just granted a divorce," Smiley said.

"From Brenda?"

"Who else?"

"Now all you have to do is kill him and you'll be free."

Smiley looked concerned. Until death do us part. "Would he fire us?"

"Jack, half the time he doesn't remember that Ray and I are married. Work it out with God."

She had a choice on how to think of herself as she went back through the kitchen. A vocal upholder of the moral law on which the fate of nations rests, or a prissy spoilsport who had forgotten the sins of her girlhood. Boris asked if she would like to take another crack at it. He meant eggs.

"One's my limit, Boris."

❖

An hour later, Ray returned from Boston, where he had been on business. "I wanted to stay for the game," he complained.

"Crosby found Traeger, but they arrested him."

"Crosby?"

"Traeger. I'm waiting for Crosby to call back after he's seen Traeger. Nate will want to provide legal help, don't you think?"

"He will if you suggest it."

But Crosby did not call back. Well, who knew the difficulties of visiting prisoners, particularly so soon after the arrest? She put through a call to Crosby.

"The reason I haven't called, Laura: I haven't found him yet."

"Did he get away?"

"He was never brought in."

❖ III ❖

"I was arrested."

Traeger was shoved into the backseat, followed by one of his captors, who tossed in Traeger's backpack before getting in. The other suit got behind the wheel. Around them, the cruisers began to pull away. The driver let them lead but as he followed, the distance between the car and the last cruiser grew. Suddenly the driver turned onto a side road, and the car shot forward. Traeger looked at the man beside him. Old stone face, and he was wearing sunglasses. A similar pair of sunglasses had regarded Traeger from the rearview mirror until the right turn was taken.

"What's going on?" Traeger asked.

His companion lifted a hand. There was something about the man that struck Traeger as familiar. "Take off your glasses."

"Welcome back, Traeger," he said, removing the glasses.

"Craig!"

"I was in Albania with Theo Grady."

Traeger was flooded with relief. He had been rescued, snatched from the idiots Arroyo had twice set upon him. The driver was Wilberforce, but he must have been after Traeger's time in the Company. Without sunglasses, Wilberforce looked like a college boy. A dressed-up college boy. At the moment, he was busy getting as far from all those cruisers as he could.

"How's the wound?" Craig asked Traeger.

"It seems to have stopped bleeding."

"We'll have it looked at as soon as possible."

"What did you tell the troopers?"

"That it was a federal case."

"But they've seceded. They've set up their own republic."

"I promised to discuss that with them when you were being booked." A small smile, not smug, but definitely satisfied. "We'll switch cars soon."

Traeger held out his wrists. "How about taking these off?"

Craig examined the cuffs. "They're not ours, you know." Traeger remembered the cop who had managed to get them on him, helped by the other one who had a knee in Traeger's back. Craig was trying a key and not having much luck.

"We'll have to take care of those later, too."

❖

Five miles away, in a Latino neighborhood, all the store signs in Spanish, Wilberforce turned into a car wash shed and pulled into line. He pushed open the door and got out.

"Fold your arms," Craig suggested.

They strolled through the shed and out again to a car that seemed to have just been washed and polished. The keys were in it. Wilberforce got behind the wheel and Craig, Traeger, and his backpack got in behind. The car moved away from the shed and again they were on their way.

"Where are we going?"

Once more the little smile. "To the scene of the crime."

Within minutes, Wilberforce found a drugstore and bought bandages for Traeger's wound. The next stop was a hardware store; Wilberforce hopped out and went inside. When he came back, he handed a sack to Craig. A hacksaw. Minutes later, Traeger really felt free again. He put the cuffs in his backpack.

"Souvenir," he said, giving a little smile of his own.

His leg wound was more of a burn than anything. The bullet

had only grazed him. An angry red crease, but it was more painful than a typical flesh wound. He spread the disinfectant salve Wilberforce had bought over it, and then slapped on a bandage.

As they sped along, the feeling of relief lifted and thought began. As with Crosby, he was wondering why he should trust these former comrades. Remember what had happened on the roof of the North American College just last year. Supposed allies were suddenly revealed as enemies. He put his head back and closed his eyes, remembering Pocatello. He let the figures that had emerged from the Chinook form. One of them had been Craig or a reasonable clone thereof.

"Call Dortmund," Craig said, as if he were reading Traeger's thoughts.

"Good idea." He got out his cell phone, scrolled through the numbers, and punched Dortmund's. It was answered on the fourth ring.

"Traeger."

"Did it all go off well?"

"All?"

"Your rescue. I assume that you are now in the custody of Craig and Wilberforce."

"Everything is fine." He tried to make it a question.

"Once I gave them your cell phone number, they were able to pick up your trail. How did things go at Bishop Sapienza's?"

"I was arrested."

"Oh my."

"I was rescued from the clutches of law and order."

An elderly chuckle came bounding off a satellite into Traeger's ear. The car was now making good progress on 101. He said as much to Dortmund.

"And your destination?"

"The scene of the crime."

Craig gave him the small smile.

"Good. Good. Well, remember the password."

"Remind me."

"Watch your back."

❖ IV ❖

"I've got to make a call."

After Crosby had reported to Ignatius Hannan and been passed on to Laura, he told Lowry and Bishop Sapienza of the offer of legal help for Traeger.

"Not quite the upshot we were looking for," Lowry said. "We were outfoxed."

Sapienza frowned. "Of course, Miguel is a scoundrel of the worst kind, the kind that is certain he's fighting for a great cause."

"What did you two talk about?"

Sapienza dipped his head. "He said he wanted to go to confession."

"Did he?"

"My lips are sealed."

Any help the bishop might have been seemed neutralized by Arroyo's pious ploy. "That doesn't mean I can't accompany you, however. Where would they have taken him?"

It took a while to find out. The state police were reluctant to admit that they didn't know where Traeger was. The feds had him. The feds! And feeling like a fool, Crosby remembered the two suits who had handed Traeger into the car. He turned to Lowry.

"Outfoxed again."

Fifteen minutes later he got an excited call from the state police. They had found the car, abandoned in a car wash.

"Where could they have taken him?"

Crosby fought the grim possibilities that suggested themselves. For weeks, Traeger had been known as the rogue CIA agent. For everyone concerned, that designation was as good as a target on Traeger's back.

"I've got to make a call."

"Ah, Crosby," Dortmund drawled. "I've been waiting to hear from you."

"You know what's been going on?"

"My dear boy, I've been out of the loop for years."

Crosby began to give the swift resume he had given

Laura. "Yes, yes," Dortmund interrupted. "So he has been abducted?"

"Could they have been ours?"

"One might very well think so. I have heard from Traeger."

"Where is he? Where is he being taken?"

"They must assume that Traeger knows where it is. What everyone has been seeking."

"Did he give any indication where . . ."

"The scene of the crime." Dortmund chuckled. Crosby hoped to get as old as Dortmund so he could find this funny. "The scene of the crime," the old man repeated.

That had to mean the estate of Don Ibanez in Napa Valley.

⚜

After the call, Crosby announced where he was going. Somewhat to his embarrassment, Bishop Sapienza gave him a blessing before he left. Crosby hurriedly crossed himself. It was as if he were going into battle. On the way north, he dropped Lowry in Palo Alto.

"The bookstore, Crosby. The Old Curiosity Shop. I have an hour or so before I have to prepare the evening meal."

⚜

A road once traveled can seem longer or shorter, depending, and 101, traveled as often as Crosby had done, seemed twice as long. The late afternoon traffic was fierce; road rage seemed just around any gentle bend of the concrete ribbon. As one will, he tried to review the events of the day in the hope of feeling less silly. If Traeger had contacted Dortmund, Traeger must know that Crosby had not set him up in Santa Ana. But Dortmund had an oblique sense of humor. What fun it must be for him to be monitoring these events from the safe haven of retirement.

Before heading up the valley, Crosby realized he was hungry, and once he had admitted the thought, his stomach began a conversation with itself. Even so, he begrudged the time it took him to enter the drive-through of a McDonald's and pick up a sack full of cholesterol-rich goodies. He nibbled french fries as he pulled back into traffic.

He did not know the make of the car that had been picked

up in the car wash, but it was possible his own was known. Not just possible. His own edge had proved to be dull, and he was dealing with active agents. How long had they been following his movements? Long enough for him to lead them to Bishop Sapienza's apparently. He hoped that parting blessing had taken.

Dortmund had not been all that forthcoming when Crosby asked if Traeger had been rescued by two of their own. If rescue was the word. He liked Traeger. It had felt good to be working with him again. He remembered the long drive to Pocatello, which had been the result of his being on the ball and pursuing the vehicle that left long-term parking. Traeger had obviously thought highly of that move. It seemed to have made up for the time he had tapped with his keys on Traeger's window outside St. Louis all those weeks ago.

Nice going, Traeger.

Crosby winced. When he had said that to the fallen and wounded Traeger, the cuffs being wrestled onto his wrists, it had been a cheap shot. Would Traeger recognize the repetition?

❖

Coming through the town of Pinata, approaching the El Toro Motel, Crosby considered pulling in and getting a room. What he would really have liked was twelve hours of sleep. Start fresh in the morning. But he couldn't leave Traeger to his fate, whatever it was.

How peaceful the road looked. Crosby drove slowly now. As he neared Jason Phelps's place he saw the gate standing open. Impulsively, he turned in, cutting his lights and ignition as he did so, gliding to a stop by the garages.

He eased himself out of the car, then stood behind it. If he shut its door slowly enough maybe it wouldn't make any sound at all. Silence seemed to envelope him as he stood there and then slowly it gave way to the twitter of bugs, the rustle of leaves as the palms swayed, other unidentifiable noises. There were lights on in the house. No one seemed to have heard him. Crosby went along the side of the house, toward the path that connected this property with the vaster holdings of Don Ibanez from which it had been cut out. Maybe now, with Phelps dead, it would be reincorporated into the estate.

Light from the study windows lay upon the lawn. The doors were open. But no one was visible in the study, so Crosby continued toward the lawn. He stopped in midstep when he saw a figure standing motionless not ten feet away. Arms folded, head bowed, the light from the study cast her prolonged shadow into a deeper darkness. A woman. Not Catherine Dolan.

As if she sensed his presence, the woman turned. A strangled gasp and then she was running for the house. As soon as she was inside, she let out a piercing scream that followed her through the rooms.

Get the hell out of here, Crosby told himself. Get on that path and get out of here. But his car was in front of the house. He had to find out if Traeger had been brought here. If the woman gave him a chance, he could explain. Where was Catherine?

He was standing now in the still open doors of the study. He heard a sound.

"Catherine?"

"Who is it?"

She came into the study slowly but, recognizing him, adopted a fetching expression.

"Myrna," she called. "Myrna, it's all right."

❖ V ❖

What had happened?

It pained Miguel Arroyo that people like Emilio Sapienza and Don Ibanez disapproved of him, people whose approval he desperately wanted. It was one thing to rally the troops and act the role of heroic savior of his people with unquestioning followers. But the bishop and Don Ibanez, and Lowry, too, regarded him as something between a clown and a menace. And now there was Traeger. The protest march in Los Angeles, miles of immigrants swarming through the streets, bearing taunting signs and banners, had been bad enough, but his dramatic call to arms had taken him across a line, one that separated him from Don Ibanez.

The old man's theory made sense if patience was your virtue. Time would solve the problem; after the passage of a few years Latinos could take over democratically, since they would outnumber Anglos. That made sense, but it did not call for a leader. What would merely happen inevitably provided no role for a hero. But what had the alternative led to? Arroyo did not like to think of people dying out in the desert, because it was difficult not to feel responsible. The rush of adrenaline as his rhetoric rose before a sea of adoring faces made him cry out things that surprised even himself. The call to arms had seemed inspired when he made it, as if the call were the thing. But, my God, people had responded.

Traeger's appearance at the San Diego headquarters of Justicia y Paz, to which Arroyo had moved in the hope that he could control events, had been a shock. Traeger was a desperate and determined man; he had been on the run for days and looked it. What a fool Traeger had made of him. Arroyo did not like to remember leading the troopers through the building to his office and pointing at the washroom door, whispering that Traeger was in there. But when they burst through the door the open window was eloquent of what had happened. But how far could Traeger have gone? The search of the area around the building began with eagerness but that soon faded. They all went away. Those who worked in the building left for the day. Only Magdalena, the receptionist, remained.

"Who was he?"

"A fugitive."

"I tried to stop him, Miguel. If you hadn't said it was okay . . ."

"You did well." On his office phone, he had instructed her to call the state police, certain that Traeger could not understand his rapid Spanish.

"He got away." She pouted. She was a pretty girl, in the full flower of her midtwenties. But she would age and bear children and gain weight. Why was that a sad thought? At the time, it had been a protective thought. Even in defeat, especially in defeat, he wanted to recoup his lost face, and how better than a little fling with Magdalena? Remembering, Arroyo felt virtuous for not taking advantage of the adoring receptionist. He had sent her home.

✤

When Traeger had gone out Bishop Sapienza's window, having seen, as Arroyo had, the approach of the state police, Arroyo could have cheered. It was his word against Traeger's and of course vice versa. If it had come to that, the only way to resolve the issue would be for all of them to pack off for Don Ibanez's estate and reenact the crime. What would the result of that have been?

Arroyo had been the key man in getting the image of Our Lady of Guadalupe to that little basilica behind the hacienda of Don Ibanez, but not even the venerable old hidalgo had given him much credit for that. Don Ibanez had been too awed at housing, in the replica he had built of the shrine in Mexico City, the very image that was venerated there. Arroyo had been of two minds about returning the image. Its theft had galvanized Justicia y Paz. Once it was returned, there would only be the slow, if inevitable, demographic takeover of the Southwest. But he had agreed. Not that his agreement had been sought. But his presence there when preparations were made for the return of the image signaled his agreement. What had happened?

Arroyo could admit to himself that it made no sense to think Traeger had somehow switched the original for a copy. If he had, he would never have gone through the charade of spiriting it back to Mexico City and risking the reaction of the bishop, and everyone else, with the great revelation in the basilica when the package was opened. No, Traeger must have thought he had brought the original. These were thoughts that he had resisted until Traeger had shown up in San Diego, convinced that Miguel Arroyo had somehow switched cases. Oh, he had felt a little tremor of pleasure at the flattering thought that he had done that under the eyes of so many witnesses. But someone had done it. If not Traeger, if not himself, who?

The answer seemed to lie in yet one more visit to Napa Valley. Clare must be made to see how much he sympathized with her father. Was the old man still alive? Someone had assaulted him. And someone had killed his neighbor Jason Phelps. When Miguel started north he wished that he had not alerted the state police that Traeger was at Bishop Sapienza's, making the whispered call from the porch. It would have been far better for all of them to be going to Don Ibanez's together, where they could collectively figure out what in hell had happened before that package had been taken away by Traeger.

As he drove, he imagined Traeger in that U-Haul going to where the exchange was made. Some arrangement he had made with his old comrades? But that ran into the difficulty that then Traeger would not have taken a copy to Mexico City. Had Traeger been duped? They had all been duped. But by whom?

❖ VI ❖

"He was an old man, Will."

When Catherine Dolan led Crosby into the house, through the study and into the living room, the woman Crosby had frightened out back was there, huddled with a little old lady.

"Myrna, it's all right," Catherine soothed. "We know him."

"He crept up on me!"

The little old lady lifted her eyebrows and pursed her lips, obviously finding the suggestion that Myrna was the target of sex-starved men amusing. Her name was Gladys Stone. Crosby got the story from Catherine after she had prepared their drinks and led him outside.

"She just showed up, one of Jason's great admirers. All she wanted was to see where her hero had spent his last days. When she heard about our working on Jason's papers, she insisted we let her help."

"Is she any help?"

"Not really. She wanders around outside a lot as if every inch of the property were sacred. She sits by his grave as if she were his widow. And she will sit in the desk chair for hours even though she knows that it was the chair in which Jason was murdered." Catherine made a face. "But tell me what you've been doing."

She had put her arm through his and led him out into the yard, toward the area where chairs were grouped beneath the swaying palms. The drinks she had made were potent, the gin scarcely taking on the taste of dry vermouth.

"And the screamer?"

"Myrna?" Catherine purred beside him. "Now she *could* be called Jason's widow. Common law widow."

Crosby sipped his martini. No need to pursue that remark. It would take them down paths he sensed Catherine would not be reluctant to go. From where they sat, he could see the lights of the hacienda.

"How is Don Ibanez?"

"He's home from the hospital." Catherine seemed to regard the question as a distraction. "I feel so isolated here. Myrna and now Gladys act like vestal virgins, sad to go on living themselves now that Jason is gone."

"The poor devil."

"How do you mean?" She leaned toward him. Crosby's eyes were getting used to the dark.

"What a way to go."

"He was an old man, Will."

"Even so."

There was someone in the study, the old woman, Gladys. She came to the open doors and was about to pull them shut but before she did so, she leaned into the night.

"Catherine?"

"Shhh," Catherine said to Crosby. "She can't see us."

Crosby was becoming uncomfortable. Catherine made their being out here seem, well, what it wasn't. He rose and started toward the house, emptying his glass as he went. He called back, "I don't want to frighten another woman."

"You don't frighten me."

But Catherine got to her feet and came after him. The old woman in the open doors of the study saw them coming. She did not scream.

❖

Some minutes later, in the bathroom, he put through a call to Dortmund after calculating the time in the east.

"Ah, Crosby. How goes the battle?"

"I'm at Don Ibanez's."

"Has Traeger arrived?"

"He's coming here?"

"I should imagine. How is the old man?"

Don Ibanez. The question suggested that Dortmund himself

was in the flush of youth. Crosby told him what Catherine had told him.

"Catherine?"

Crosby explained that he was actually in the house adjacent to the estate of Don Ibanez.

"With two ladies?" Dortmund seemed to be chuckling.

"Actually three." He explained about Gladys Stone.

"Gladys Stone," Dortmund repeated after a pause.

"Have you spoken to Traeger?"

"He calls in from time to time."

"Recently?"

"Crosby, I would suggest that you go next door."

"Good idea." He hadn't liked Dortmund's suggestive tone when he mentioned the women staying at Jason Phelps's home.

"And Crosby . . ."

"I know. Watch my back."

When Crosby emerged, he announced where he was going.

"I'll come with you," Catherine said. "I want to see Clare."

❖ VII ❖

"You know the layout there."

They stopped above Oakland, to stretch their legs and because Wilberforce needed to use the men's room. The area into which they had driven was brightly lit, a convenience store, the service station, several cars at the pumps. When Wilberforce returned, bouncy with relief, Craig asked Traeger if he would mind sitting up front.

"I want to catch forty winks."

"Do you count them?"

"My dad always called a nap that."

"A nap in Napa Valley," Wilberforce said brightly.

When Wilberforce got them back on the road, Craig was already settled down in back. Traeger wondered if he were acting wisely with these two. The ride had begun with his apparent arrest, but as the miles rolled away, they might have been three agents on a mission.

"What exactly is your mission?" he asked Wilberforce.

"To get hold of that stolen picture and return it."

"The agency seemed less than zealous about that."

"Not since Grady made fools of us."

When they got to Pinata, Craig had had his forty winks. He suggested that they pull into the motel and get organized. Some minutes later, they were seated at a corner table in the El Toro bar.

"The stolen picture has to be up there, Traeger. At the estate of Don Ibanez."

Traeger said nothing. It was the simplest assumption. Besides, it was his own.

"You know the layout there."

Traeger nodded.

"Who all is there?"

"Don Ibanez and his daughter, the gardener and his daughter, and Tomas the driver."

"He wasn't at the San Francisco airport when Morgan tried to pull a double cross."

Suggesting that Craig and Wilberforce had been. That long-term parking lot had been a crowded place on that occasion. Craig must have called in a helicopter when things went wrong and some hours later descended on Grady's hideout near Pocatello.

"You two working alone?"

Craig thought about it. "As far as we know."

"Watch your back."

Wilberforce laughed. "That's what Boswell always says."

Boswell? What an original. Traeger was going to mention that Crosby could be at Don Ibanez's, too, but he let it go. After the conference at Bishop Sapienza's, where the decision had seemingly been reached that they must all head for Napa Valley to decide whether he or Arroyo was telling the truth, Crosby would very likely have headed here once he found out that Traeger had been spirited away. Surely he must know that by now. And Arroyo? This occasion, too, threatened to become a crowded one, and Traeger didn't like it.

"Here's the plan," he said, hunching over the table.

"What'll it be, gentlemen?" The waitress.

They ordered beer and waited until it was served and the waitress was gone.

"Okay, what's the plan?"

"Jason Phelps's property was carved out of Don Ibanez's estate. From the back, there is a path leading toward the replica of the Mexico City basilica. Okay. We drive up there, pull into Phelps's driveway, go around the house and back to that path. In that way, we can find out who all is there before announcing our presence."

Wilberforce said, "I want to see that little basilica."

"Are you Catholic?"

"On my mother's side."

When they had finished their beer and gone out to the car, night was falling. Before getting in, Traeger looked around. Someday he would like to come to Napa Valley just to enjoy the scenery.

For the first part of the drive, Wilberforce used just driving lights, but there was need of more light before they got to Phelps's driveway. There was a car parked by the garage. It looked like the one Crosby had showed up at the Old Curiosity Shop in.

"Let me go in first," Traeger suggested. "We don't want to startle Crosby."

"Crosby?"

"We were agents together. Ignatius Hannan hired him." No need to go into all the details. "He was the big guy who came along when you took me to your car in Santa Ana."

"What did Hannan hire him to do?"

"To get that stolen image."

"Jeez."

"And to find me."

"He lost you."

"That's why I don't want to startle him."

"You want us to just wait here?" Craig didn't like it, and who could blame him?

"I think it's best."

"We're not working for you, Traeger."

"We're all after the same thing."

Wilberforce said, "Why don't Craig and I go out back to the path you mentioned?"

Traeger thought. "Good. Take the path and go over to Don Ibanez's. Now that it's dark, the house will be lit, and you can see what if anything is going on there."

Craig liked that even less.

"Okay. You two go around to the back. There is a study with french doors that open onto the lawn. I'll go in the front. Let's hope that Crosby remembers you two from Santa Ana."

Craig said, "We'll go in the front; you go around back."

Traeger would have given anything to be on his own, but if it hadn't been for Craig and Wilberforce he'd be in the pokey in Santa Ana.

"Good enough."

They got out of the car and eased its doors shut as quietly as they could. Traeger had his backpack, which held his weapon. He watched the two others go under the overhang to the front door and then moved swiftly around the house, getting out his pistol as he went.

In the back, he went out from the house, staying clear of the light from the study which illumined the lawn. Someone was sitting at the desk in Jason Phelps's study. A little old lady. A familiar lady. Good God, it was Gladys Stone, the flirty sexagenarian from the Rough Riders headquarters. What was she doing here?

Craig and Wilberforce came into the study with another woman, not Catherine Dolan. And then Craig and Wilberforce were shaking hands with Gladys, whom they clearly knew. Traeger backed further away from the house, trying to figure out the meaning of that group in Phelps's study. His earlier hunch that Gladys had had something to do with Morgan's bloody end came back to him. During the long ride from Santa Ana, he and Craig and Wilberforce had grown too chummy.

Wilberforce opened the french doors and called into the night, "Traeger?"

He hesitated. But curiosity about Gladys got the better of him and he walked into the lighted area of the lawn. That was when Gladys pushed past Wilberforce, gripping a weapon with both hands. Before it went off, Traeger had turned and dashed for the connecting path. Gladys got off three rounds before he got to the path.

✤ VIII ✤

Crosby fired a warning shot.

Clare's anxiety about her father had diminished considerably since his release from the hospital, but the idea had been that he would recover more quickly in the familiar setting of the hacienda. That afternoon, when she had relieved Frater Leone and sat by her father's bed, holding his hand, he had tried to talk but, as before, the sounds that emerged were not language. She patted his hand.

"I understand, I understand."

His eyes glittered as he shook his head. He must be worried about the miraculous image of Our Lady of Guadalupe. How insignificant that seemed compared to her father's illness. To distract him, she began to talk.

"Daddy, who attacked you?"

The question seemed to relax him. He turned his hand over and squeezed hers. The jumble of sounds coming from his mouth might have been an answer to her question. From the doorway, Frater Leone beckoned to her and Clare rose and went to him. He took her into the hallway.

"There are people downstairs."

"People?"

"Catherine Dolan and the man Crosby."

Good Lord. She considered letting George, who had actually delayed his return to Palo Alto, entertain them, but Frater Leone was clearly eager to take up his vigil by the bedside again. Clare nodded and headed for the staircase, passing the room that was Frater Leone's as she went.

Catherine seemed to be enjoying having two men to dazzle when Clare came into the living room.

"Laura called," George told her. "She and her husband are on their way here from the airport."

"What on earth for?"

Crosby said, "Traeger escaped. I thought he was being arrested by the state police but he was spirited away. I think he's coming here."

"Here! My father is supposed to have absolute rest and quiet."

It was a silly remark; Clare saw that as soon as she had made it. George came and took her arm in his. "How is he?"

"Oh, George." She pressed against him and his arm went around her. Why oh why couldn't they be just another couple?

"Laura, the image that wasn't taken to Mexico City has to be here. Naturally, Traeger won't rest until he has it. He's bound to come here."

Crosby stopped. There was the distant sound of gunfire. He drew a pistol from under his arm and dashed for the door.

Two men brandishing weapons came running toward him from the pathway that linked the estate with Jason Phelps's place. Crosby fired a warning shot and immediately the two disappeared, falling to the ground. Belatedly, Crosby recognized them as the men who had put Traeger into the car in Santa Ana. By that time, he, too, was on the lawn, trying to make out what the other two were doing. He had the great disadvantage of the lighted house behind him.

"Crosby?"

"Who are you?" He rolled away as he answered, not wanting to tell them where he was.

"Craig. Wilberforce and I are agents. We rescued Traeger."

"Where is he?"

"Why don't you stand up?" said a voice behind him. Crosby looked up at a young man whose weapon hung at his side.

"Wilberforce," he said, giving Crosby a hand and pulling him to his feet. Craig materialized out of the night. That was when Crosby saw another figure move swiftly behind the basilica.

"Are you two alone?"

"Until we find Traeger. Gladys took a shot at him."

"Gladys?"

"She must have been active when you were."

❖

When Traeger burst onto Don Ibanez's lawn, he slowed and moved away from the hacienda. And the pathway. In a minute, Craig and Wilberforce came crashing along the path.

After their big reunion with Gladys and the shots that had been taken at him—three shots—he no longer felt part of the team. As soon as the two agents appeared, Will Crosby came out of the hacienda. The idiot sent up a warning shot and Craig and Wilberforce went to ground. Crosby was lucky they hadn't taken him out, but then Crosby, too, disappeared. Their voices came to Traeger; Crosby was definitely rusty. Did he think this was No Man's Land in World War I, with enemies chatting with one another from opposing trenches? A figure flitted past the lighted windows of the hacienda. Wilberforce. When he helped Crosby to his feet, Traeger took cover behind the basilica. When he looked out again, the trio had gone into the hacienda.

At sounds behind him, Traeger, too, fell to the lawn. There was a small house back there, several windows alight. The man coming toward him was Carlos.

The little man seemed to be groaning as he approached. *Santa Madre, Santa Madre.* Traeger lay as still as still, but Carlos's mind was clearly occupied. He walked within ten feet of Traeger lying on the grass and disappeared around the basilica. After a minute, Traeger followed and saw him enter the basilica. He eased the doors open after they had closed behind the gardener and went inside.

Carlos was on his knees in the aisle, groaning as he moved toward the altar. He stopped short of it and held out his arms. *Santa Madre, Santa Madre.* Traeger left the gardener to his devotions. Outside, he could see and hear Crosby talking with Craig and Wilberforce. All three had their weapons on display. They came onto the lawn and stopped. A great whirring sound was approaching, and then the lawn lit up like noonday as the chopper trained its lights on the ground below. Craig stepped forward, waving his arms. There was the sound of an automatic weapon from the chopper and Craig went down.

Traeger went around the basilica, keeping out of the glare of the overhead lights. The area illuminated diminished as the chopper settled down. That was when Wilberforce opened fire on the men emerging from the chopper.

Traeger had reached the far end of the hacienda and he went around it to a patio and let himself into the house. There was the sound of terrified talking in the living room. Traeger took the staircase and went up it two at a time. He came into a hallway with an open lighted door at the end. Traeger opened a door and let himself into a darkened room, pulling the door shut behind him.

Standing in the dark, breathing heavily, listening to the thumping beat of his heart, he tried to figure out what was happening. The helicopter had not been of the kind that had descended on Grady's hideout near Pocatello. Were the Rough Riders riding again? Like everybody else, they would be certain that the missing image of Our Lady of Guadalupe had to be here, where the pointless trip to return it had begun. Grady's men had taken care of Morgan, but why would they open fire on Craig? Traeger decided to get into the action. Why was he cowering in a dark room when things might be coming to a head?

He opened the door to find Frater Leone about to open it. The priest was astounded to find Traeger in what, it emerged, was Frater Leone's room. Traeger turned on the light. His eyes seemed to be directed by Frater Leone's to the huge image of Our Lady of Guadalupe propped against the wall. Suppressing a delighted whoop, Traeger reached out to touch it. The search was ended!

Only it wasn't. "It is a copy," Frater Leone said. "As you can see."

The image was on canvas. Traeger could have cried out in disappointment. He pushed past the priest to go downstairs.

By the time he came into the living room, the chopper had gathered up its wounded and was lifting off, no lights on now. Wilberforce emptied his weapon at the chopper but without effect. In a minute it was gone, and silence descended. Craig was being carried inside when a car came up the driveway. It stopped and Laura and Ray Whipple got out, all smiles. Clare was on the phone, summoning medical aid for Craig.

"Where have you been?" Wilberforce asked Traeger.

"Reconnoitering."

That exchange made Traeger's presence known. In every eye that looked at him he could see distrust and accusation. He put his pistol away. There was the sound of another car arriving and Arroyo joined the group.

"Okay, Traeger, where is it?" he asked as he entered the room.

Traeger was about to make a profane remark when there was a voice behind him.

Frater Leone had come down the stairs, his hands beneath the scapular of his Benedictine habit.

"I will tell you," he said.

❖

Neal Admirari felt that he was living the last chapter of his book. What had begun in Mexico City was finally to be explained. The ascetic-looking priest looked sadly around at his audience.

"The image is hanging behind the altar in the basilica." He pointed. "It never left here and I am responsible for that. What a blessing it was to have her here in our midst. You can imagine the emotions stirred up by her departure. And so her departure was prevented."

"But how?" Arroyo demanded.

"She had been put into a foam case, which was put behind the altar until the departure began. The image was removed, and a copy substituted. Come, you can see for yourself."

And so the group left the hacienda and walked to the basilica. Inside, Frater Leone turned on the lights. A kneeling figure with outspread arms did not move. Frater Leone led the group around him. He stared up at the illumined image. It was Clare Ibanez who spoke. "It is," she cried. "That is the original."

Frater Leone turned away from the image with reluctance. "Now I am ready to pay the price for what has been done."

"No!"

The anguished cry came from Carlos, who staggered to his feet and came to Frater Leone, where again he fell to his knees.

"Father, you must not say that. I was the one. You had no idea what I had done."

Frater Leone was trying to help Carlos to his feet, but the

old gardener shook him away. "I confessed my crime to you. You know that I am the guilty one."

Traeger had gone forward and stood looking up at the illumined image. Where would you hide a book?

Beside him, Wilberforce said, "I wish my mother could see that."

Lulu took Neal's hand and led him away. "We're all going inside to celebrate."

❖

Inside, Frater Leone went upstairs to be with Don Ibanez. Carlotta was with her desolate father, so Lulu volunteered to make the drinks. Clare went to help her. When Traeger came in, thinking a guard should be posted at the basilica, Laura brought him his drink.

"Mission accomplished," she said.

But Traeger's eye was on two newcomers, A short-haired, sour-faced woman he didn't know, and Gladys Stone. Gladys was shaking her head at what the other woman was saying to her. And then those old eyes saw Traeger. She reached into her purse and pulled out a pistol and was trying to get a bead on Traeger despite the crowded room. Traeger had not yet got out his own gun when the woman beside Gladys picked up a pottery vase and brought it down on the old woman's head. Gladys slid to the floor. Traeger crossed the room and picked up Gladys's fallen weapon.

"Thanks," he said to Sourpuss.

No one else seemed to have seen what had happened.

EPILOGUE

✧ I ✧

"Te Deum laudamus."

The milk white Alitalia plane approached the field from the east, gliding with dreamy slowness to its assigned runway at the Mexico City airport. When it landed, a cry went up from the some fifty thousand who had managed to get an invitation to this first event of the papal visit. The plane taxied toward the waiting crowd, which only with difficulty was held back by the police. A great stairway moved toward the now opened door of the aircraft. All was in readiness, but a long minute passed, and then, there he was, the now familiar figure in his white cassock, white zucchetto, and ruddy Bavarian countenance. His arms lifted in response to the hysterical welcome and then he came slowly down to the reception committee gathered at the foot of the stairway.

This was not an ordinary visit, he told them. His scheduled visit to Mexico would take place later in the year as planned. He had come on this occasion as a pilgrim like each of them, to witness the reinstallation in her shrine of the miraculous image of Our Lady of Guadalupe.

"Your Mother has come home!" cried the Holy Father. "*Our* Mother has come home!"

Saint Peter, like the other apostles, had been granted the gift of tongues in order to announce the good news in every human language. Popes have always been polyglot, some more than others, and if Benedict XVI spoke Spanish as a learned language, his words were celestial music to the delirious crowd. The dignitaries were shepherded away.

Awaiting them were the cars of the motorcade that would take the pope, along with dozens of cardinals, archbishops, and bishops from all over Latin America, through the streets of Mexico City, thronged with men, women, and children, many of them holding high above their heads copies of the famous image. But these were slowly lowered when the lead vehicle, specially built for the occasion, approached. In it, through bulletproof glass for all to see, was the centuries-old image of Our Lady that had appeared on the tilma of Juan Diego and whose adventures in recent weeks had been the news of the day throughout the world. The crowd was on its knees as the pope, the whiteness of whose clothing seemed whiter in contrast to the black limousine from whose windowed roof his upper body emerged, scattered blessings over the ecstatic devotees of the Mother of God.

The crowds grew thicker as the procession approached the shrine; the motorcade slowed to a mere crawl as the passage through the clogged streets became ever narrower. Behind the motorcade, most of those who had watched it pass fell in to follow it to the shrine. There an enormous gathering awaited in the plaza before the great circular basilica. Many men wore the costume Juan Diego had worn all those years ago when the Lady appeared to him. Women of every class had donned the clothing of simple peons. The modern dress of the other girls and women, however stylish, was of unusual modesty, the beauty of the senoras and senoritas concealed for the occasion, their heads veiled in black lace mantillas. When the vehicle bearing the sacred image entered the plaza the vast crowd seemed to exhibit the systole and diastole of the human heart, pulsing forward and then back again to let the motorcade through. The shouts, the cheers, the weeping suddenly ceased and a vast silence fell.

The silence deepened as the image was taken from its special vehicle. The monks of the abbey in their Benedictine habits were given pride of place. Several cardinals, trying to

remain at the pope's elbow, were kept at bay by sharp Benedictine elbows. Six men of massive height and strength now
took possession of the image. The doors of the basilica were
open, but inside there was as yet no one. The pope followed the
sacred image inside and up the main aisle to the prie-dieu that
had been prepared for him before the altar. All those who could
fit inside the basilica, and more, followed. The image disappeared behind the altar. An unbearable minute went by and
then she rose slowly into view and was returned to her place.
A collective sigh filled the basilica. Weeping was the order of
the day. The pope, sunk in prayer, from time to time lifted his
eyes to the image of the Mother of God and his Bavarian eyes
were moist with tears.

Your mother has come home.

His private prayers finished, the pope rose to his feet, bringing the vast throng to theirs, and intoned the *Te Deum*.

Throughout the country, throughout Latin America, in
churches and cathedrals all over the world, that great hymn of
thanksgiving went up to heaven. "*Te Deum laudamus, te Domi-
num confitemur . . .*"

✣ II ✣

Other probes were made.

On land he had purchased a few miles out of Guadalajara, a
retired American who styled himself Geraldo Bradley grum-
bled through the delay as the well-digging crew watched the
events in the capital on a television set placed on the tailgate
of one of their trucks. Amanda, his wife, who had not been an
enthusiastic supporter of her Geraldo's plan for their twilight
years, wore an I-told-you-so expression.

"You're lucky they didn't decide to put it off until mañana."

Long years of married life had taught Geraldo when to
speak and when to remain silent. He lit a cigarillo, and Amanda,
who was downwind, disappeared into the house.

Finally the television was turned off and the great rig, which
had been put in place the previous day, began the task of
drilling for water. Surveys of the property had been ambigu-

ous. Only God knew how deep they would have to go for water. "China," Amanda had muttered. "They'll bring in tea if anything."

But it was not tea that came gushing forth after an hour's drilling. A great black fountain arose from the earth, washing away the drilling equipment and showering the area with ebony drops. Oil! Geraldo's initial disappointment gave way to elation at the realization of what was happening. Spattered like Spencer Tracy and Clark Gable in the movie sometimes seen as a golden oldie on late night television, Geraldo danced around the gusher. Even Amanda did a sedate two-step in celebration of this incredible outcome.

In subsequent days, government officials descended on the site. Against all previous surveys, there proved to be a veritable ocean of oil beneath Geraldo's property and the surrounding area. Geraldo's property was swiftly nationalized with a handsome recompense that would send Amanda and Geraldo north to a more appropriate retirement in Phoenix. Other probes were made. Oil seemed to be everywhere. Within weeks, the oil deposits of Mexico increased by a factor of fifty.

Stewardship of Mexican oil had not been a model of prudence in the past. But with these amazing discoveries, something happened. A new and populist political party was formed, many of its members already elected under other labels, and the decision was made that this time everyone would benefit from the wells that sprang up like cactus around Guadalajara, and beyond. Elsewhere, similar discoveries were made. The population of Mexico would soon be as prosperous as the citizens of Saudi Arabia.

When Benedict XVI was driven along the border in the Popemobile the day after the reinstallation of the image of Our Lady of Guadalupe, the scene had already been transformed. Gunfire had ceased. The border, like many borders, had become a mere being of reason. One had to know it was there in order to know it was there. No longer did emigrants approach it stealthily; no longer were border patrols necessary to prevent illegal entries.

Within a month, the traffic would be in the opposite direction as immigrants, legal and illegal, flowed back to their now prosperous native land. There was talk of a miracle.

❖ III ❖

"I won't if you don't."

Lulu found Neal Admirari's reason for abandoning his book on recent events unconvincing. A hurried, sensational, and inaccurate book by a writer who had four hundred titles to his credit, if that was the word, had appeared soon after Our Lady of Guadalupe was returned to her shrine.

"It's a pile of junk, Neal. Yours will eclipse it."

"Lulu, it's not my kind of thing."

"But the advance!"

Hacker, Neal's agent, had assured him that there would be no demand that he return the advance. Both parties had entered into the agreement with goodwill. Circumstances had changed. The agreement had been made under the implicit understanding of *ceteris paribus*. Of course Hacker's fifteen percent was also a consideration in the agent's interpretation of the contract Neal had signed.

What Neal couldn't tell Lulu was that Catherine Dolan had forced him to abandon the project. He had been interviewing her, wanting more details on the days she had spent with Lloyd Kaiser at the Whitehall Hotel in Chicago.

"How would you like it if someone wrote of the times we spent together in the El Toro Motel?"

"Who would be interested? Present company excluded, of course."

They were in Catherine's Minneapolis apartment and she seemed changed with the setting. Where was the sensuous woman with whom he had frolicked in California?

"Lulu would be interested," Catherine said softly.

"You wouldn't!"

She smiled her new Mona Lisa smile. "I won't if you don't."

After that he couldn't risk going on with the book. Hell hath no fury like a woman unscorned. Trying to think of another way of doing the book made it sound too much like the quickie account that Lulu had disdained.

"Pendant and Mercury have doubled my income, sweetie."

"And will no doubt double it again. I was thinking of prestige."

Lulu's own reflective pieces on the theft of the image of Our Lady of Guadalupe had drawn high praise and there was talk of collecting them into a book. That had provided a more convincing reason for dropping his own project. A man and wife writing rival books on the same subject?

Before he left Catherine after that final interview, they talked of Jason Phelps.

"Do you know, I thought you had killed him, Catherine."

"Myrna did."

Myrna? The cropped-haired, dour academic? Catherine told him that long ago when Myrna had been a graduate student at Berkeley she had fallen in love with Jason. At least her admiration for him had seemed like love. They had an affair, which at the time and in retrospect was the high point of Myrna's life.

"She didn't take it very well when she learned of Jason and me."

"But he threw you out of his house."

"She didn't know that. I did enjoy teasing her. What an awful friend I was."

"You aren't serious that she killed him, are you?"

"Oh yes. She told me so herself. I didn't realize she was staying in Pinata."

"She was there all the time I was."

"I must have been out when she came to the house, trembling with remembered ardor. She slipped into the study and came up behind Jason sitting at his desk. She covered his eyes with her hands and kissed him on the head and blew in his ear. It was when he sighed and said, 'Catherine?' that, enraged, she picked up a bogus Polynesian war club and hit him. Again and again."

"Good God. Why would she tell you?"

Catherine looked at the windows and at Lake Calhoun beyond. "It was proof that her feelings for him were stronger than mine. I think she expected me to accuse her to the police."

"Why didn't you?"

"Perhaps I didn't want to give her the satisfaction."

"Do you see her still?"

"We're having lunch at the Minneapolis Club tomorrow. Would you care to join us?"

"Maybe some other time."

Like never.

✢ IV ✢

The priest felt guilty, too.

It was after a conference with Bishop Sapienza that George Worth turned over the Palo Alto Catholic Worker house to Lowry. The bishop had convinced George that he ran the risk of ruining Clare's life as well as his own.

"You have done much good, George. But you are not a monk."

George resisted, of course; the prospect before him seemed all too easy if he accepted the bishop's advice. In the event, it was more difficult to convince Lowry than himself.

"George, I'm a second banana. I couldn't run this place."

"You're running it now."

"Pro tem."

George reported Lowry's resistance to Sapienza.

"I'll talk to him."

The upshot was that Emilio Sapienza became George's successor. The bishop's own misgivings about the locale had been overcome, although from time to time he would still murmur, "Palo Alto, Palo Alto."

"But now you're out of the shadow of Disneyland," Lowry soothed.

In reply, Bishop Sapienza gave a passable imitation of Donald Duck.

✢

Don Ibanez bought Jason Phelps's place and Clare and George were installed there after their marriage in the little basilica, with Our Lady of Guadalupe, albeit only a copy, smiling her benediction on them. George began the engrossing task of learning to become his father-in-law's successor as the manager of the vast holdings in Napa Valley.

Don Ibanez had recovered his speech, but was showing his age. He walked less erectly than before and spent much time working with Carlos on the grounds around the hacienda. He held no grudge against the gardener for having struck him with a shovel. Having discovered that Carlos had sequestered the original image behind the altar and allowed Traeger to go off with a copy, Don Ibanez hurried from the basilica intending to announce it to the world. Carlos had followed him and, outside the basilica, unable to accept the prospect that the object of his devotion would be removed, picked up a shovel and struck his venerable employer. He had confessed what he had done to Frater Leone, which was why the priest could not, even if he would have, accuse the gardener. Taking the blame on himself seemed the Christian thing to do, even apart from the restrictions of the seal of the confessional.

The priest felt guilty, too. He had helped Carlos hoist the original into place behind the altar of the little basilica and put the copy in his room. While Don Ibanez was in a coma, Frater Leone had poured out the tale, more or less his own confession. After all, he had been as pleased as Carlos that the true image of Our Lady of Guadalupe was once more in the little basilica.

❖

Miguel Arroyo watched with dismay as the Latino population of California was halved, and still the hemorrage continued. Sometimes he thought that he, too, would move to Mexico. He settled for the post of honorary consul in San Diego, which did not entail a change of citizenship. He was clean-shaven now and reportedly drank more than was good for him.

❖ V ❖

"Do you say the rosary, Vincent?"

Nate Hannan was not at Empedocles when Traeger stopped by, having gone off on retreat with the Trappists in Kentucky.

"Is there an airport near there?"

Laura lifted her hands. "He took Amtrak!"

"Did he buy it first?"

"It never even occurred to him." She sounded surprised, or perhaps relieved.

Laura wanted him to sign some papers, which he did, and then she slid a check across her desk to him. Traeger was astounded at the amount.

"You did what you set out to do. And Nate wanted to take account of the difficulties you experienced in the process."

"How about Will Crosby?"

"Don't worry about Crosby."

Traeger promised he wouldn't worry about Crosby. Good old Crosby. Traeger would never forgive Crosby for firing that warning shot, but all's well that ends well. He got in his car and headed south.

Dortmund was being rigged up with a new supply of oxygen when he got there, and Traeger waited until his old mentor was again snuffling satisfactorily through the plastic device in his nostrils.

"Don't feel sorry for me," Dortmund said as Traeger pushed the old man's chair out onto the patio.

"I don't."

"Good. I can handle that myself."

After they were settled, Traeger went inside and brought out a couple of beers.

"I never liked beer before, Vincent. Now I do. Do you suppose it is deterioration of the taste buds?"

"Buds lite?"

They talked of recent events, and Dortmund did not agree with Traeger on the matter of Crosby's warning shot. Traeger let it go. Craig had recovered. No need to tell Dortmund of the king's ransom he himself had received from Hannan.

"So Boswell has retired."

"He was let go," Dortmund corrected. "Sometimes even this administration recognizes when they have a skunk in their midst."

A minute's silence. "How few good apples there were, Traeger. You, Crosby, one or two others."

"Poor Morgan."

"He wanted to be rich Morgan."

They talked of Theophilus Grady. With the cessation of

hostilities and the disappearance of illegal immigration, the Rough Riders had melted away. Grady had been hired by the Albanian government to train their special forces.

"Tell me about Gladys Stone."

Dortmund sighed. "You can take the girl out of the agency, but can you take the agency out of the girl?"

"Girl?"

"She was a girl when I met her."

"She thought she still was." He told Dortmund of the old girl's flirtiness when he was in pursuit of Morgan.

"She always idealized Mata Hari."

"Who was she working for anyway?"

"Gladys."

"She might have killed me."

"But she didn't. I'm told she plans to marry a man who is a driver for Don Ibanez."

"Tomas?"

"Is that his name?"

"She's too old to get a license."

"Now, now."

They sat in silence as the afternoon shadows lengthened.

"Do you say the rosary, Vincent?"

"At wakes."

"I've taken it up again. It is soothingly repetitive."

When Traeger rose to go, Dortmund said he would stay there on the patio. Telling his beads? Traeger shook the old man's hand and started for his car. Dortmund called after him.

"Watch your back."

ALSO FROM RALPH McINERNY

THE THIRD REVELATION

*

An astounding miracle.

Two vicious murders.

A secret that could change the world.

The Rosary Chronicles begin.

*

Retired CIA operative Vincent Traeger spent years working undercover in Rome. But when the Vatican's secretary of state is brutally murdered along with a prefect of the Vatican Library, Traeger must not only solve the murders, but fight an unseen enemy and navigate a treacherous maze through history, faith, and his own past if he is to discover the astonishing truth.

penguin.com

M498T0609